ENLIGHTENED BY THE ECLIPSE

ANNA ELLE

Cover designed by: Pandora_Arts

Editing, proofreading and formatting: Emberlust Press

Publisher: Anna Elle, New Zealand.

Print ISBN: 978-0-473-69873-7

Ebook ISBN: 978-0-473-69874-4

To my friend C.J., thank you for encouraging me to write this book. Without your push, I never would have done it. And thank you to the readers who encouraged me to publish it!

CHAPTER 1

CLEMENTINE

I was in a very wet forest. I smelled the moss and lichen growing on the trees and heard the creek at the bottom of the leaf-littered slope. My body itched and burned as I jogged. I heard a guttural growl that shook every cell in my body. My running shoes pivoted as I looked back to where the sound came from.

What the hell was that?

The crunching sound of my shoes resulted in the forest turning deathly quiet. Dad promised me that this track was safe to run, but as the light glittering through the trees dimmed, I began to think that maybe he had been wrong.

I heard the growl again, picked up my pace. The loop I was on went up toward the river, turned, then circled past some old hunter's cabin and then back toward home. As I passed a tree with an old broken ladder that went up to a dilapidated tree stand, I heard it again—that growl. Then, out of nowhere, an ethereal howl echoed and bounced off the trees.

Shit, run!

I sprinted as a large tawny wolf came out of the treeline and started to chase me. There was no way I could outrun a wolf. I was dead! The tawny wolf snapped at my heels as I sprinted down the path. I felt his body slam into mine as I crashed into the rotting bark of a tree. I felt it crumble against my body, then suddenly, I was flying—no—*falling*. I fell hard and fast, over the cliff's edge that led to the river below.

I WOKE UP WITH A START. It was always the same dream—one that has continuously haunted my sleep for the past five years —of a wolf chasing me and me falling to my death. When I first started having the dream, it had been a pitch-black wolf giving me chase through the city of Vancouver. Recently, it had changed into a tawny-brown one with a forest as my new surroundings. I still didn't know what was scarier; the fact that wolves were chasing me in my dreams or that I was out jogging in the first place. I hated exercise.

"Vincent!" I heard my father yell as I rolled over in bed, sticky with sweat. "Vincent, hurry up! You are going to be late!" *Bang. Crash.* "Clementine, you should get up too."

My mother named me Clementine. Yup, like the orange—a pretentious and unforgiving name, really. I reached out my hand and picked up my glasses from the bedside table, placing them onto my pug nose. My eyes were turquoise in colour and too large for my round face. The glasses made them bug out even further, so they looked like two large turquoise pools. My hair was long and a rich shade of black. I tried to keep it around my shoulders, but I was forever cutting it as it tended to grow super-fast. The same could be said of my fingernails and body hair.

"You get it from your father," my mother had once told me when I complained about the girls making fun of me in the locker room.

"It's disgusting, Mom. I'm disgusting."

"You, my baby girl, are beautiful."

"I don't feel beautiful."

"What would make you feel beautiful?" I smiled shyly at her and pointed to the paper-thin models in a magazine. She shook her head at me. "They aren't real. You are real! And you are much prettier than they are," my mom had said sincerely.

Mom had been the best. She really was. She always tried to find a way to boost my self-esteem. And that was how our regular mother-daughter beauty appointments started. My mother would take me to get waxed and groomed, and we got mani-pedis if only to stop the locker-room bullying.

My mom was my best friend—my only friend. When Mom got sick near the end of my second year of university, I stopped going to our beauty appointments. It didn't feel right doing it without her. My hair grew rapidly, both over my body and on my head. I shaved now and again, but mostly I just wore pants. The growth was never-ending, and my hair had grown down to the top of my ass-crack, an onyx colouring, dead-straight, and thick. Regardless of this, I still hadn't returned to the hairdresser. Instead, I chose to sit next to my mom's hospital bed, as the chemo turned her green in colour. And my textbooks sat forgotten on the table as I supported my mother while she hurled.

I GOT out of bed and stretched. It was an impressive stretch, or as impressive as the whole five-foot-fuck-all of me could muster. I went to the bathroom and removed my coke-bottle glasses to wash my face. Without my glasses, I could barely see four inches in front of me. I placed my thick frames back on before I dry-shaved my legs. I combed through my hair and braided it to the side—the hairband ending about two inches above my ass when I threw it to land at my back.

I returned to my bedroom and put on a pair of shorts and a simple blue t-shirt. Unhooking my mother's necklace from the edge of my bedroom mirror, I placed it around my neck before I Dad hollered out once more.

"Clem!"

"I'm coming!" I shouted. "Keep your wig on, old man," I mumbled.

"I heard that," he growled.

My father had this uncanny ability to hear me even when I was mumbling out of typical earshot. I knew that he was not actually hearing me. He knew me so well he simply figured I would be muttering something under my breath, so he often called me out on it. And he was always right.

We had moved back to my dad's hometown after my mom died, and I hated it. We had been here less than a week, but I knew I didn't want to give it a chance to grow on me. And it probably literally would grow on me. There seemed to be wet flora everywhere. Blackfern Valley was a small town in the middle of British Columbia—a small town nestled far into the forest where it was super damp, both physically and on my mood.

When my dad met my mom twenty-five years ago, he moved out of this pokey little town and settled in Vancouver to live their happily-ever-after. My parents suffered three miscarriages before I was born. And another five years after that, my annoying little brother Vinny arrived.

We had a lot of love and laughter in our little family before Vinny started acting out. Dad watched Vinny like a hawk, and the "Dad Law" had come down hard lately. Then, my mother died six months ago, and Vinny got worse. Before we knew it,

Dad had packed us up and shipped us off to the middle of butt-fuck nowhere.

Don't get me wrong, Vinny wasn't a bad kid; he just started acting out as every pubescent teenager did. On top of the standard hormones and testosterone that ran rampant through his system, he had also lost his mother to cancer, and the grief made him lash out. It was hard being fifteen.

At twenty years old and being an adult, I didn't have to move with my family to Blackfern Valley, but I couldn't leave them. Not now. Dad told us that this town had once been good to him growing up. In Blackfern Valley, he would have support with Vinny now that Mom was gone. He tried to convince me to re-enrol at the University of British Columbia—UBC—move into a rental property, and kickstart my life again. It sounded good in theory, but...

Once upon a time, I studied medicine. When my mother got sick, it all hit too close to home, so I dropped out. Being a doctor didn't interest me anymore.

I ENTERED the poxy little canary-yellow kitchen and looked at all the boxes that had yet to be unpacked. Vinny sat at the small round dining table and scowled into his cereal.

"What's up, jerk?" I asked.

"Dad is riding my ass."

"What about this time?"

"I got into a fight at school." We've been here three days. How the hell had he gotten into a fight already?

"Again? Vinny, this is a new school! You're supposed to try and make friends."

Vinny made a scoffing noise at the back of his throat. "You're lecturing me on making friends? You haven't had a friend in your life. You're the biggest loner I have ever met." His green eyes were red-rimmed and glassy. He looked like shit.

"What have you been smoking?" I growled under my breath so as not to alert our father.

"Nothing!" His eyes shifted away from me.

"So, drugs and fighting, huh? Wow, kid, you are going places!"

"Back the fuck off," he snarled.

"Grow the fuck up," I countered. "You realize Dad moved us here for you, you little punk. You were getting into too much trouble back in Vancouver that he uprooted our lives to bring you here, give you a fresh start, and you're throwing it in his face."

"I didn't ask him to bring me here!" he shouted angrily.

"Well, tough shit." My dad entered the kitchen from the mudroom. He looked at both of us with an exasperated expression. Tucking his hair behind his ear, he closed his eyes before opening them again.

I looked at Dad and noticed how old he appeared—his grief hadn't helped any. His pitch-black shoulder-length hair was covered in grey. His emerald eyes looked tired and were ringed with a subtle silver. I noticed it more when he got upset; the silver seemed to sparkle then. He had a scruffy stubble and deep wrinkles by his eyes. He looked his son directly in the eyes and gave a deep sigh, pressing his forefinger and thumb onto the bridge of his nose.

"Vincent, we can talk about this later. Hurry up. You are going to be late for school."

"You expect me to go back there? There are only a few weeks left, Dad! I'm not missing out on anything!" Vinny questioned.

"Yes, I expect you to go back to school regardless of how many weeks are left. And Clem is going to take you."

"I am going to what now?" I looked at him incredulously. I

wasn't walking my toad of a brother to school. He was fifteen, not five.

"I am too old for a babysitter," Vinny snarled.

"If you started acting more your age, I wouldn't need to assign one," Dad levelled with him. He turned to me. "Please, Clemmy. I don't trust he isn't going to ditch."

"Me walking him won't stop him from ditching school, Dad. He'll just wait for me to leave, and then he'll walk straight out the front gate."

"Oh no, he won't." Dad's tone held a warning that made Vinny shrink in his seat. "Josiah has informed me his son Sean will hang out with him from now on. And trust me, Vinny won't be able to shake him."

"Who's Josiah?"

"You may meet him one day. He's an old friend of mine," he said evasively. I sighed. Dad had been acting weird ever since Mom's passing.

"Come on, you little asshole, let's take you to school."

Vinny stood up and called me a name under his breath before he picked up his schoolbag and headed for the front door.

"Oh, Clem." Dad stopped me. "Um, please be careful. You are allowed to be here, and if anyone tells you otherwise, I want you to let me know, okay?"

"What the hell are you talking about?"

"Nothing," he rushed out a little too quickly. "Just... I know how hard it is for you to make friends and how you tend to be bullied. I'm just reminding you that you're allowed to be here."

I steeled my emotions. I was an adult now. There was no way anyone was going to bully me.

CHAPTER 2
LIAM

Buzz. Buzz. Buzz. I awoke to an annoying buzzing noise. I opened my eyes and looked around the room. Where the hell was I? I tried to move and found a very naked female body partially draped over me. I tried to turn to the other side and noticed another exquisitely nude woman leaving me pinned to contemplate my escape.

Gently, I climbed over the one on the left and looked back, grinning. The brunette with milky white skin stirred and shifted onto her stomach before letting out a little sigh, fading in to sleep once more. The bottle-blonde had her hands tucked under her cheek and was drooling slightly from her plump pink lips.

I wracked my mind, trying to remember their names. *Pfft, what does it matter?* They only slept with me for one reason, and I wasn't going to complain when I got the two of them at once... *more* than once. I grinned to myself again. Perks of being the alpha's son, I guess.

Buzz! Buzz! Buzz! It started up again. *Oh right!* I looked around the room and found my black t-shirt and jeans. No underwear, too restrictive. I pulled my jeans off the floor and shoved each leg into the holes in a rush, carefully tucking my dick back before pulling up the zipper. *Buzz! Buzz! Buzz!* My phone was still going, but thankfully the girls remained asleep so there wouldn't be any awkward goodbyes. I put my t-shirt on quickly as the phone vibrated against my ass cheek.

I shoved my bare feet into my boots and walked out the door, answering my cell as I did.

"Hi, Dad," I said.

"Where are you?"

I looked around. "Um, a university hall of residence, by the looks of it."

"Do I want to know, Liam?"

"Probably not," I confirmed as I walked down the hallway— my footsteps echoing off the walls.

"What are you doing, Liam?" he grumbled.

"Well, I was sleeping. Now I'm talking to you," I quipped, redirecting the obvious lecture coming my way. "What do you need?"

"Your brother needs a lift to school."

"So why are you telling me?" I grumped.

"I thought you could use this time to get some brotherly bonding in."

"What has the little turd done now?" Ever since my brother turned fifteen, he had become the biggest jackass. All pups went through the same thing when they turned fifteen. Their bodies became rampant with hormones, and until they got their wolf, they were a nightmare to be around. My brother had turned sixteen five months ago and got his wolf, but he still acted like a jackass.

"His buddies got into a fight with Patrick's boy."

"Patrick's boy?" I thought for a second. "Oh, the half-breed."

"Yeah, some pups decided to make fun of him on his first

day of school. Sean didn't even attempt to stop it. So now he has to show Vincent the ropes of pack life."

"What's that got to do with me?"

"There's some resistance on Sean's part. I was hoping you could talk to him and make sure he actually attends school."

Sure, because I'm the best influence on a sixteen-year-old boy. "And no one else could take the idiot to school?"

"No one that he looks up and listens to," my father responded.

I finally arrived at my rust bucket of a car. "Alright, Dad. I am forty-five minutes out. Tell Sean to be at the end of the driveway. And let him know I expect breakfast."

My car door whinnied on its hinges as I opened it. You would think being the alpha's son would give me the perks of a flashy sports car or something, but my dad believed in more of a humble upbringing, so a tiny little Honda Civic is what I drove. And let's be honest, I would only be driving around in an ostentatious car to pick up the ladies, and if last night was a testament, I didn't need any help in that department.

Dad wasn't always alpha of the Blackfern Pack, though. Ten years ago, there was an uprising, an internal coup, to overthrow the malicious alpha that once was our leader. He was a grade-A asshole who refused to take a mate and bear any children, killing any she-wolf that got pregnant with his kin.

My father originally wanted no part in the coup. He was a humble carpenter, raising his two boys in a small house on the outskirts of town. This was where Alpha Jed had put him, as my father was the only one who possibly had the strength to overthrow him. Alpha Jed couldn't outright exile him, but he did distance him as far away from the pack as he could. Out of sight, out of mind I suppose had been his approach.

Eventually, the insane dictatorship of Alpha Jed grew astronomically, and Dad had no choice but to join the secret militia.

When I asked him about it years later, he said he just wanted to set a good example for his kids. Humble and soft-hearted was my dad, but that demeanour shouldn't fool anyone; after all, the man had managed to usurp and kill his brother.

Dad could have used his alpha tone on my brother to make him stay in school, but he rarely used it. He tried to stay away from anything that reminded him of how his brother Jed had run the pack. In his mind, using his alpha tone was just the start.

I honked my horn at the end of the driveway that led up to the pack house. We had moved in here ten years ago, and my mom and dad had spent time fixing it up because it had suffered some damage in the fight between the alphas. The pack house was basically in the middle of Blackfern Valley, but the high school was ten kilometres away from us on the Northern end.

A dirty-blond teenager came running down the driveway with his backpack slung over one shoulder. He opened the passenger door and slumped inside.

"Where's my breakfast?" I grumbled.

"I ate it." I smacked him over the head. "Hey, I was kidding, you stupid mutt!" He opened his bag and pulled out a piping-hot breakfast sandwich.

I placed the sandwich in my mouth and shifted the car into drive, spinning the steering wheel and stomping on the gas.

"So, where were you last night?"

"Uni."

"Yeah, right," he scoffed.

"Where do you think I was?"

"I'm not stupid, you know. I know the she-wolves lift their tail for you."

"Do they now?" I mused, smirking at my kid brother.

"So, how was it?"

"How was what?"

"The boning?"

I laughed. "Did you seriously just call it that?"

"What else would you call it?"

"Studying?" He made a scoffing sound again. "So, tell me about this Vincent kid?"

Sean shrugged. "He's a little awkward, I guess. He doesn't know about pack hierarchy, and he pissed off Murdoch."

"Murdoch Evans?"

"Yeah."

"That kid is a little punk."

"He's the Beta's kid."

"He's still a punk. What did Dad say?"

"That I should be leading by example and not beating on half-breeds. Especially a half-breed who has not only grown up without a pack but doesn't know he has a wolf manifesting."

"How can the kid function at school if he hasn't been told about his heritage yet?"

"I dunno. Not my problem. I have to babysit the half-breed and ensure Murdoch doesn't go for round two."

"Are you going to tell the kid?"

"Who?"

"Vincent."

"Am I going to tell him what?"

"About what we are?"

"No, Dad compelled the whole school not to say a word."

"Dad did what now?" I stopped at a stop sign and looked at Sean to make sure I had heard him correctly. His hazel-brown eyes displayed gentle rings of light gold, indicating that his wolf was making an appearance.

"Dad said it's not our place to tell Vincent, so he used his alpha tone and compelled everyone not to let it slip. It's Vinny's stupid dad who will have to tell him."

I started driving again. "I'm surprised Dad did that."

"You and me both. And trust me, his dad will have to tell him soon. Vinny is about to meet his wolf."

"What makes you think that?"

"When he was fighting, his eyes rimmed with silver."

"Shit."

"Silas told me that his wolf will be powerful too." Silas was Sean's wolf's name.

"How does Silas know that?"

"How does Silas know anything? These wolves are fucking weird with their ethereal-cosmos shit."

I laughed.

We pulled up to the school gate.

"Thanks for the ride." Sean opened the door.

"Yeah, bro, all good." I watched for a moment as my brother went to stand by the school gate. I smiled as I saw him attempt to hit on the young she-wolves heading toward the school. I was about to turn away when I spotted Cassie and smiled. I forgot she had just started a job teaching at the local high school. I watched her firm ass straining against her red mini skirt and felt Lucian start to stir. *Shit, Cass, you really shouldn't wear a skirt like that around these teenage boys.* My eyes creeped on her for a bit longer, and then I found myself opening the car door.

Maybe I'll just give Sean some pointers on how it's done.

CHAPTER 3

CLEMENTINE

"DAD, I'M NOT A TEENAGER ANYMORE," I grumbled, looking away from the pity bound to be displayed in his eyes.

"I know, Clem. It's just, people in this town can be cruel."

I raised an eyebrow. "I thought we moved here because this town would be good for Vinny?"

"It will be."

"But you just said it can be cruel."

"Yeah, to outsiders, it can be."

"And I'm an outsider?" I watched as the tops of my father's ears turned pink. He was getting stressed.

"No, that's not what I'm saying."

"Then what are you saying, Dad?"

"I was just trying to be supportive," he rushed out. "Your mom just died, you dropped out of med school, you moved to a new town where you don't know anyone. I just want you to know I'm here."

"If people are cruel?" I added.

"Something like that." God, my dad could be weird at times. He was avoiding eye contact, and his ears were still flushed. He closed his eyes and appeared to be trying to calm himself down, before setting his gaze upon me once more. "There is a small university about an hour out of town, you know."

"That's nice."

"If you wanted to go and have a look—"

"I don't."

"What are you going to do, Clem? You need to get your life back on track." His voice was soft.

"So, you think throwing myself into studies will do that?" I bristled.

"You love to study."

"Loved. Past tense. Textbooks just smell like chemo and vomit now."

He looked pained. "Clem."

"There's a bar and grill place hiring in the middle of town. Maybe I can get a job there."

"You want to wait tables?"

"What's wrong with waiting tables?"

"Nothing is wrong with it. But Clem—"

"Hey, Penis Breath, are you coming or what? Hurry your ass up!" Vinny shouted, breaking through Dad's passive-aggressive lecture.

I looked toward the front door and sighed. "Dad, you didn't want a second born, right?" I asked innocently before I turned and left the house.

BLACKFERN VALLEY LOOKED like something out of a movie. I had no idea small towns like this even existed in the real world until we'd moved here. I grew up in an apartment in central Vancouver, so having cute little houses popping out of the forest as we walked up a black-paved road was surreal. We turned onto the next street and walked in silence. I should have said something to my brother; given him words of encouragement, or even an earful about doing drugs. Instead, I stayed quiet. We've never been close, and I didn't think it would change now that we lived in the sticks.

"Dad said he needed to talk to both of us," Vinny broke the silence.

I looked over at my brother and took him in. His hair was the colour of wheat, and his face was covered in pale freckles of the same shade. He was the male replica of my mom but with my dad's emerald eye colour. My eyes were emerald at one point too, but sometime around my fifteenth birthday, they turned a weird turquoise colour and shortly after that, my eyesight started to deteriorate severely.

Vinny had grown much taller over the last few months. He was gaining a little muscle on his arms, and his baby face had sharpened. Maybe he would be built like my dad, not short and curvy like me.

I adjusted my glasses and flicked my braid off my shoulder. I really needed to cut my hair. "Sounds ominous."

"He said he's been meaning to talk to me for a while, but Mom was sick and..." his voice trailed off.

"Did Dad say what it was about?"

"No, just that it was important."

"Did he say when this lecture was going to happen?" Vinny shook his head. I rolled my eyes at his lack of knowledge. *What a pointless conversation.*

My brother scuffed his feet as he walked. He was trying to find something to talk about. Maybe he wanted to discuss what was actually going on with him?

"Do you want to talk about it?" I offered.

"No."

"I'm here, you know."

"I don't want to talk." He closed up, and I swore his emerald eyes were ringed with silver before he looked away.

When he looked back, they were fully green and looking at me with disgust. It must have been a trick of the light. Eye conditions ran in the family. Each one was unique, though. Mine was deterioration. Dad had an eye condition that ringed his eyes with silver, almost like an early onset of cataracts, but it never appeared to get any worse. I really didn't wish eye conditions on anyone. For now, I would just have to keep an eye on my brother and maybe talk to my father about getting him to an ophthalmologist. God knows losing your eyesight as a teenager sucked.

After twenty painfully silent minutes, we walked up to the front gates of the local high school. Waiting against the gate with his arms crossed was the most ridiculous teenage boy I had ever seen. He was insanely bulky, as if full-on steroid usage was the culprit.

"That's Sean," Vinny mumbled. I looked confused. "The guy Dad was talking about. The one who is going to babysit me."

"Holy shit. That kid does not look fifteen."

"I think he's sixteen."

"Not my point. He's far too jacked to be in high school," I mumbled, eying up the juiced-up-looking teenager with disgust.

"Ew, are you checking him out?"

I gagged. *What?*

"I think I vomited in my mouth a little bit." Sean hadn't noticed Vinny yet. He seemed self-righteous as he checked out some young girls heading toward the school.

"At least Murdoch isn't around," Vinny mumbled, and I looked at him. My brother looked angry.

I sighed. Murdoch must have been the kid giving him a hard time. I wanted to offer him support, but I didn't know how. I wasn't exactly popular, and I've never stood up to my bullies before.

I continued to watch Sean's pathetic peacock display. He flashed the girls a smile, and the sound of giggling made me shudder. Sean ran his hand through his short blond hair and flexed his muscles toward the group. Great, all I needed now, on top of everything else, was my stupid little brother getting onto the steroids and turning into more of a jackass. Reticent memories were threatening to burst forward.

I need to get out of here.

"Ok, well um… be good, I guess."

My brother flipped me the middle finger and stomped over to where Sean was. I turned to walk away and smacked directly into something hard.

What the actual fuck?

My hand went to my nose, which took most of the hit. A numbing pain shot up my nasal bridge, making my eyes water. It hurt to touch, and I gave myself a few seconds to pull myself together.

I opened my eyes to see what I had hit, and my gaze scaled up to find the warmest brown eyes staring down at me. My gaze watered behind my glasses, but I could have sworn I'd seen the guy smile, which made my heart flip.

CHAPTER 4
LIAM

"Shit, are you okay?" I asked the short little she-wolf that crashed into me, her gentle honeysuckle and pear scent invading my nose. She looked up, her hand covering the tiny upturned pink tip protruding from her face. She was shorter and curvier than the other she-wolves around the place. It made her stand out.

I was surprised to see she wore glasses. Photochromic lenses obscured her eyes, but they seemed to be the most interesting shade of bluey green. Said glasses didn't appear to be a prop or some fashion statement either. They seemed to be corrective lenses. *What the fuck?* Wolves didn't suffer declines in vision.

I breathed in her scent again. As the intoxicating honeysuckle and pear notes swirled around, I managed to take in the undertones of her canine heritage—definitely a wolf. *Wait, what's that smell?* I sniffed again; her wolf seemed tainted. As if it was mixed with something else. Human?

Oh, shit. This girl must be the other half-breed—the older sister.

A subtle pink stained her cherub face, and she looked away from me.

"Sorry, I didn't see you there," she mumbled. Her voice was soft and sweet.

My wolf came forward, curious at the anomaly in front of us. She took half a step back and apologized again before side-stepping me and started to walk away. Her tiny little legs scurried as her perfectly round bottom popped in her shorts. My wolf urged me forward, intrigued. I caught up to her in four long strides.

"I didn't catch your name," I said casually.

She spun in a fright. Surely, she should have heard me or smelled me? It's very hard to sneak up on a wolf.

"C-Clem." She looked around shyly as if making sure I was talking to her. Her cute button nose was red from where she smacked into me.

"Clem?" I asked unsure if that was what I heard. Even with my wolf hearing I still couldn't make out what she had mumbled. She nodded and continued to anxiously look around. When she noticed I was watching her, she blushed pink again. My wolf was pushing forward again, his interest piqued further with her reaction.

"My name is Clementine." She anxiously wrung her hands together. "Like the orange," she added unnecessarily.

I laughed, and her blush went full red across her cheekbones. "Nice to meet you, Clem. I'm Liam." I extended my hand, and she once again looked around nervously. She reluctantly took my hand, and I was surprised when I felt a low buzzing at our contact.

She snapped her hand away and looked at it curiously before she started to stumble backward. "Um, I should go." And with that, she hurried down the street before I could say anything more.

So that was the half-breed," I murmured to Lucian.

"She's cute." He sat, swished his tail, and cocked his head as he watched her ass bounce away.

I scoffed. *"You think most she-wolves are cute."*

"Okay, fair call. But this one is interesting. She didn't have a wolf."

"What do you mean? I smelled it."

"I did too. Yet, she doesn't have one. I couldn't sense her wolf spirit."

"Weird."

"Like I said, interesting."

I got in my car and drove toward the pack house with Clementine on my mind.

DAD WAS PLANING SOME WOOD, the tiny curls of wood scrapings falling to the workshop floor, when I got there.

"Hi, son. Did Sean get off to school okay?"

"Yeah, he was flashing his pathetic muscles to some she-wolves at the gate. It will be good when he finally shifts; he won't have to try so hard. The girls will flock to him."

Dad shook his head in response.

Traditionally we meet our wolves on or around our sixteenth birthday, but that didn't mean we shifted straight away. It took me three months into my sixteenth year before Lucian finally wanted to run. He had burst out of me so fast I had felt like my entire body had been ripped apart. Lucian learned his lesson, though; his behaviour had knocked us out for a good thirty minutes. As my dad ran with the pack that night, my mom had stood over us on four paws. Sean was laughing hard when I had come around. He was lucky that Lucian didn't kill him too. Lucian, like most pups, was a wee bit of a hot head.

"And Patrick's boy? Did you see him?"

"Yeah, scrawny little runt of a half-breed."

"Liam," he scolded.

"I'm joking, Dad. We were all scrawny at fifteen."

He smiled softly. "I am glad Patrick brought Vincent back after the boy's mother died."

"So, you think Vincent will be able to turn?"

"Well, that's why Patrick brought him here. He said it looks like his wolf is manifesting. It's a fifty-fifty chance, and it looks like Vincent won the genetic lottery and got the gene. His elder sister, not so much."

"I met her too."

"Clementine? Really?" He stopped planing for a moment, a surprised expression strewn across his features.

"She smells like a wolf, Dad."

He shook his head. "No, you must be mistaken. She would only smell like a wolf if she got her wolf at sixteen. But it never appeared."

"I'm telling you, Dad, she smelled like a wolf."

He raised an eyebrow, then shook his head. "I have never heard of a half-breed smelling like a wolf if they don't have one."

I sat on the builder's horse and watched my father work. "Half-breeds are rare. How would you know?"

"It's just one of those facts that are passed down from one generation to the next. Made the elitist wolves able to get rid of half-breeds if they didn't turn at sixteen," he grumbled angrily, then looked in my direction, his brown eyes softening. "When Patrick turned to Alpha Jed and said that he had found his mate and she was human, he was basically run out of town. The alpha was clear that if he stayed with her and they bore children, and the children didn't manifest wolves, they would be strung up and murdered in the square, along with Lacey for it would be her fault the kids had no wolf."

"That's disgusting."

"Yeah, but to be fair, he could have just killed her on the spot. He thought he was being merciful by giving Patrick a choice. His mate or his pack."

"And he chose his mate."

"Yeah, and he got the fuck out of Dodge while he still could."

"But Alpha Jed died ten years ago."

"I know, and I offered for Patrick and his family to return, but he said no."

"Really?"

"Yeah. I wanted Patrick to be my beta. He refused."

"Why would he turn down that honour?" Lucian bristled at the thought.

"He said he needed to protect his mate and children from the people who were still in league with Alpha Jed. When Vincent started showing the aggressive signs of his wolf, he decided he had to bring him back. He was going to leave Clementine and Lacey behind, but Lacey was diagnosed with cancer. It was an impossible decision.

"Then, roughly eight months later, he buried her," Dad said sadly. "He was in such a state. Suddenly, he had one shifter-child and one human one. He couldn't leave. He tried to convince her to go off to university to protect her from the pack, but she was grieving, and he couldn't let her do that alone."

Lucian pined and started to push images of a shy and awkward Clementine in my frontal lobe. He felt terrible for her.

"So, I promised him she would be safe in the pack." I smiled softly at my dad's gentle nature. "Liam, she has no idea we are werewolves."

"Sean told me the Vincent kid doesn't know, and now you're telling me she doesn't either? How the fuck doesn't she know?"

"It was Lacey's wish that the kids grew up not knowing. It

was a need-to-know basis, and with the fifty per cent chance, Patrick agreed to wait and see if his kids manifested wolves before he told them what he was."

Dad said fifty per cent, but we both knew it was closer to a twenty-five per cent chance that a human mate could produce a wolf heir. There was very little knowledge on half-breeds, partially due to the fact that most of them were usually miscarried early on in their gestation.

"She's going to figure it out. It's a town full of werewolves, for fuck's sake," I growled.

"Patrick knows this, but he's trying to find the right time to tell his kids about it."

"Should have told them from the beginning," I murmured to Lucian, and he nodded in agreement. He had been pacing in my head since Dad started explaining Patrick and his family's history.

"I still don't understand how he found a human mate. I mean, that is rare in itself and there aren't any humans in this town."

"There is one now," Lucian smirked, flashing an image of Clementine back into my mind again. I ignored him.

"Patrick and I had gone backcountry camping in the Rockies. We stumbled across these human girls who were also camping. One thing led to another, and..." He looked at me and shook his head. "You don't need to hear about a couple of horny twenty-year-olds. Especially when one of them was your dad. Anyway, when the full moon came, we shifted. We moved as far away from the girls as we could, but when Patrick turned, Perseus, his wolf, led him straight to Lacey." He smiled at the memory. "She was shocked to wake up and find a wolf looming over her. I got there just as he shifted back and announced that she was his mate."

I laughed, and Lucian joined in. We imagined a poor human

girl resembling Clementine, being shocked at a wolf shifting back into a very naked male, draped on top of her.

"Yeah, then a month or two later, I found your mother, but by then, Patrick was already living in Vancouver."

"Still should have come back to the pack ten years ago when you called."

"He's here now," Dad said firmly. There was no alpha tone to his voice, but it was obvious that this conversation was over and not to be further debated.

I OPENED up my economics textbook. I had a big test coming up for one of the summer courses I was taking, and Lucian wasn't helping me any.

"*What is it?*" I grumbled.

"*I hate economics.*"

"*Shut up. I actually need to pass this test.*"

"*When we are alpha, what good is your degree going to do?*"

"*Earn us a living?*" I quipped.

He flattened his ears. "Still, did you have to pick economics? Snore." Ten minutes later, Lucian was still pacing.

"*Enough, Lucian.*"

"*Can't help it. I'm antsy.*" Of course, I get the werewolf with ADHD. "*I need to run.*"

I looked down and noticed my hand was reddening where I had been absentmindedly scratching it. My hair started to stand on end as I continued to scratch, the fibers slowly becoming thicker and patchier. My skin tingled—no—it burned. I breathed and tried to stop the change from happening. Even after six years with Lucian, I still had issues controlling him. He came from alpha blood, and he was testy at the best of times.

"Seriously, Lucian?" I kept pushing him back. He growled his defiance. *"Fine, you stupid mutt. Let's go for a run. But then I have to study."*

I stripped off my clothes and walked straight into the pack house kitchen before running out the French doors and leaping off the back deck. I landed on four tawny paws and sprinted into the forest behind my house, picking up speed as I went, letting out a couple of excited yips. Okay, Lucian had been right. We definitely needed a run.

CHAPTER 5
CLEMENTINE

OKAY, maybe Blackfern Valley was a lot bigger than I thought it was. I swear I was lost. I really had no sense of direction.

Where the hell am I?

I kept walking aimlessly for another twenty minutes. Houses had started to thin out—not that they were very close and abundant to begin with. I could feel the sweat start to pool around the base of my neck and in the canyon of my breasts.

God, this humidity is going to kill me. But I kept walking.

The black tar seal had ended; now, it was mostly dirt and gravel. Okay, I was certain I had gone in the wrong direction.

I turned around and smacked into something.

Ouch, my poor nose! It was getting a hell of a beating today.

I looked up and saw another large body obstructing my view of anything else, then took a step back. "Sorry about that," I murmured, rubbing my nose.

"You know, glasses are supposed to help you see, yet you're walking into me." His voice was smooth, but there was something cold about it. My defensive walls instinctively went up.

"Yeah, well, they don't work if you creep up on people as they are turning around."

I looked up and met the icy cold blue eyes that matched the voice so well. My heart flipped. He was beautiful. He had dark hair that sat around his shoulders, tanned skin, and muscles bulging out of his black tank top. His eyes were framed with thick dark lashes, which made his eyes pop. As I checked him out, he was doing the same, but instead of admiring me, he had that all-too-familiar look of disgust on his face.

"Is it her?" a nasal voice asked.

"It has to be," another said.

I stepped back again and adjusted my glasses.

"Wow, she wears glasses. Like what the actual fuck?"

"And she's fat."

I bristled at the last comment, and turned to face the girls who were chatting quietly with each other. I was surprised I'd heard them at all. Both were tall and had an athletic build, so yeah, in comparison to them, I was a little chubby. They had blonde hair that billowed gently behind them in the slight breeze. Their eyes were crystal blue and held utter hatred as they looked at me. What had I ever done to them?

The male of the group I had walked into regained my attention.

"You need to learn your place," he growled. "And I'm going to have fun teaching you." My hackles rose at his predatory gaze. There was something off about him.

"Cool, sure, well maybe you can start by teaching me the way out of here. I'm super lost." *Wait. Did I just say that?*

His eyebrows rose, and the girls sniggered.

"You sure are," Barbie One said.

"You know your kind aren't welcome around here, right?" Barbie Two added.

"My kind? And what does that mean? Someone who hasn't bleached the brain cells out of their head?" It was like I had no control over my mouth.

"Oh, my God! Lincoln, did you hear what she said to me?"

"Well, I'm assuming he knows how to listen, but that might be a stretch, so who knows." I shrugged. *Holy shit, where the hell is this hostility coming from?* I was usually the type that does everything to avoid confrontation.

"Put the stupid bitch in her place, Lincoln. Show her who we really are."

His eyes raked over Barbie One and flashed her a toothy grin before he looked at me.

"What is your name?" he asked.

"Clementine," I said with much more confidence than I felt. It was almost as if my name alone would protect me, would instill fear into him. It was a stupid notion. The guy was obviously unhinged. *Stop making this worse. Just back up and apologize. Keep your head down and leave.*

The look in his eyes was primal, and I instinctively took a step back. "You know, if I squint, you could almost be pretty." I took another step back as he stalked forward. "Maybe if I take you from behind... That way, I don't have to look at your ugly face," he growled. Another step forward. My heart raced, and my entire body tensed.

Surely, he isn't about to attack me?

"Tell me, Clementine, do you like it rough?"

"Look at her. She's probably still a virgin."

My eyes snapped to the Barbie girls for a moment, but they were obviously whispering to each other.

Did I imagine that?

Lincoln took advantage of my split-second distraction and closed the gap between us.

I let out a little shriek as I stumbled backward. "K-keep away from me." This time my voice held no confidence; it was high-pitched and full of fear. His eyes seemed to flash at the sound of my terror, and his nostrils flared slightly. "Come near me and I will scream."

He grinned, and his eyes flashed again. "Good, I like it when they scream."

A loud growl came from nowhere, and a massive wolf jumped out of the treeline. If I was afraid before, I was petrified now. I froze where I stood, my heart hammering in my chest. The wolf was beautiful with thick tawny fur and big brown eyes. He was gorgeous but incredibly terrifying. It was eerily similar to the wolf that had been haunting my dreams.

Shit! Maybe I'm still dreaming?

The wolf bared its teeth, but this time not at me. It bared them at Lincoln, who arched his eyebrows at the wolf, and smirked.

A low guttural noise came from the wolf's throat, and his ears were flat against his head. The wolf's brown eyes were unblinking as they stared Lincoln down.

When I could finally move, I took a step back and reversed right into a tree.

Shit!

The girls started backing away, but a masochistic Lincoln stared down the wolf contemptuously.

Oh, this dude is a Grade-A idiot. Does he really think he can take on a wolf?

Something clicked in me, a lesson from long ago. There was never just one wolf. The breed was known to run in packs. Panic set in as I started to look around the treeline, waiting for his mates to come and eat us for lunch. And let's face it, if the wolves did come out, they would probably go for me first. I was the only one with decent fat stores. I kept an eye on the treeline as the gentle breeze rustled the lower leaves.

The wolf's loud growl brought me back to the situation

unfolding in front of me. His teeth dripped with saliva, and I could see the pink gums above his canines under his furled lip.

Fuck me, those are some big teeth!

One of the girls gently grabbed Lincoln's arm and tugged him backward. She wasn't looking at the wolf, and seemed to be naturally submissive. Finally, the guy started moving away. He looked at me with contempt.

"This isn't over, Clementine." The wolf snarled loudly at his words, and the guy glared at the animal before he turned and bolted with his girlfriends.

The wolf finally turned and looked at me.

Oh, crap!

It was my turn. Why hadn't I taken the opportunity to run? He cocked his head like he was examining me before giving a little huff, then darted back into the forest.

Suddenly, I could breathe again. I hadn't realized I had stopped, but the oxygen burned as it re-entered my heaving lungs. I took a few deep breaths, but my body didn't calm. Looking around, I realized I was alone again.

With my newfound breath, I did something I really hated doing. I ran, and I ran fast.

CHAPTER 6

LIAM

THE MUD under my paws felt amazing as I whipped past the trees. The forest smelled fresh and wet with slight hints of honeysuckle. I splashed into a stream playfully and bounded against the gentle current, spooking the tiny fish back under their rocks. I lapped up some water as I trotted through the stream. It was icy cold and refreshing as it zinged around my tongue.

A gentle breeze swirled past, making some leaves fall into the stream from the canopy encroaching it.

"Wait," Lucian said softly.

"What is it?"

"I smell something."

Suddenly, Lucian fought me for control. His ears started to twitch, and he sniffed at the air. He growled low. I gave up on fighting Lucian for control and let him follow his instincts. He started cantering north with impressive speed. He must have gone at least five kilometres before slowing down and lowering his underbelly to the forest floor. He began to shuffle and creep forward in an army-like crawl, hiding under a bush that faced the street.

The honeysuckle smell was more potent here. I sniffed, enjoying the perfume and noticed the delicate tones of pear, canine and human.

Wait, what's she doing all the way out here? "Fuck, Lucian! You are such a stalker," I growled at my wolf.

He shook his head and indicated that I should be watching.

I took control back and stuck my nose toward the road. Everything was hidden, but my black, wet snout was sticking out of the shrubs. I sniffed the air again, secretly enjoying her scent.

I peered through the leaves of the low bush and watched as the scene unfolded in front of me. Clementine was just as flustered as she was this morning, and she appeared to be nervous. Or maybe that was just her regular persona?

I scented Tammy and Nola Lawson before I saw them. Their overly sweet scents collided with each other and irritated my nostrils. Lucian snorted and scratched his nose with his paw in response. The smell was so invasive that I could taste its sour aroma in the back of my throat, and it took everything in me not to gag and give myself away.

"That was a huge mistake," Lucian muttered, shaking his head, indicating a time when I used to have 'fun' with the twins.

"Yeah, well, now they're Lincoln's problem," I grumbled. *"Speaking of Lincoln, if the twins are here, then so is—"*

I looked around. Yeah, there he was. Lincoln James. God, I hated him. To be honest, hate was too soft of a word, really. I absolutely loathed Lincoln with every fibre of my being.

He was next in line to be beta before Dad overthrew Alpha Jed, and when that happened, he became the world's biggest asshole. Even now, ten years later, he was still trying to best me. He started pursuing the twins shortly after I had, and those two loved it. I, on the other hand, was disgusted. I don't mind sharing she-wolves and doing the whole casual thing, but when the twins tried to play Lincoln and me off each other, I shut that down real quick. I wasn't sharing with him. Lincoln, of course, thought he won. I let him believe that. The truth was, I couldn't stand the twins. Sure, they were phenomenal in bed, but no amount of good sex could make up for their personalities.

I glared as Lincoln crept up behind Clementine. Lucian started to fight me for control again. He had a sudden primal need to protect her.

"Let's just see how she handles herself," I said to Lucian as his ears flattened and he growled at me.

Clementine turned and smashed right into Lincoln's chest. Her hand went to her nose, which was now even redder than it had been this morning. I listened intently as the conversation unfolded. The Lawson twins were being vicious behind their hands, knowing that Clem was human and wouldn't be able to hear them.

"Fucking bitches!" Lucian growled.

I ignored him and felt him start to pace around my mind, anxiously watching Clem.

My heart stopped, then started hammering loudly.

Wait, what did Lincoln just say?

Without realising what I was doing, I jumped out of my hiding spot and stood between Lincoln and Clementine. The honeysuckle scent was being masked with unclothed fear. The smell of her terror made Lucian's hackles stand on end.

I opened the mind-link to all three of them and growled. *"All of you, back the fuck off!"*

Lincoln looked at me and smirked. *"Nah, I think I will take her for a trophy. See how far I can make a half-breed scream before her weak heart gives out,"* his voice carried through my mind. Lucian snarled menacingly.

"All of you are going to leave her alone!" I said, looking at the

twins who were instantly submitting to me. I could smell the arousal forming between Nola's legs and the fear coming from Tammy. If I could smell it, so could Lincoln. Sure enough, his nostrils flared, and his eyes narrowed on me with pure hatred. *"Take your skanky twins and get the fuck out of here before I rip you apart."*

He smirked, regaining what little of the composure he had lost. *"Didn't peg you for a half-breed lover."* He peered over in her direction and sneered. *"She's a little chubby, don't you think? And blind too."*

"Back off, Lincoln," I growled. *"I'm not going to warn you again."*

"Who do you think you are? You're not my alpha."

"No, the alpha is a lot kinder and more lenient than I will ever be. If you touch her, he may just banish you. But if you touch her, I will fucking kill you. Do not cross me, Lincoln. This is your only warning."

Tammy's eyes widened as she felt the alpha strength come off of me.

She grabbed Lincoln's arm. *"Let it go, Lincoln. Come on. She's not worth it."* Her voice shook as it came across the mind-link.

"This isn't over, Clementine," Lincoln said aloud.

I almost lost complete control of Lucian, who was triangulating on his jugular; what would be a kill shot if I allowed it. Instead, I let out the largest warning snarl I could muster and pushed Lucian back with all my might.

I waited for them to move ten feet before I turned around to look at Clementine. Her blue-green eyes were wide with panic behind her thick lenses, and her full pink mouth was open in fear. I cocked my head at her and saw her take a little step to the side.

"She's afraid of us," Lucian whimpered.

I gave a half-amused huff and decided to leave her to it.

My fur itched with rage, and I knew I needed to run so as not to track down Lincoln and finish what he had started. Lucian was all for taking him out, once and for all. But as he looked at Clementine, his anger was replaced with a protective instinct.

FROM UNDER THE canopy of the bushes, we watched her. Clementine stood for a few moments, trying to pull herself together before she put one foot in front of the other and started to run. I followed through the treeline to ensure Lincoln didn't come back, and winced as I watched her almost fall a couple of times as she ran, but I didn't assist her. I didn't want to scare her again.

"We could shift, and then you could go help her?"

"Sure, Lucian, let's just walk out there buck-naked and ask the shy girl if we can walk her home," I scoffed. *"We should stash shorts over the forest so that if we need to talk to her, we can just shift. It sucks she doesn't know about us, and it's not like we can mind-link with her."*

"That only would work if she had a wolf and was a member of this pack," Lucian grumbled as he watched her perfect apple bottom bounce down the street.

"If she had a wolf, we wouldn't feel the intense need to protect her," I replied honestly.

CLEMENTINE WHEEZED after the first two kilometres and rested her head against a tree to catch her breath. Her plump pink lips panted hard as she licked them. She took her glasses off and used the hem of her t-shirt to wipe her face. The soft creamy skin of her torso got my attention before she covered it again.

I didn't notice I had crept forward from my hiding spot. Or

rather, Lucian had crept forward. She looked directly at me, and I froze under her gaze. The biggest, most stunning eyes were staring right at me. Turquoise. I felt she was staring right through me, and my heart started to pound in my throat. I was mesmerized by her aquamarine eyes and struggled to stop myself from creeping even closer. She scrunched her eyes before perching her glasses back onto her nose. I scurried back under the bushes as she squinted in my direction. She shrugged and turned to walk down the street. She hadn't seen me. I felt relief and disappointment. Had I wanted her to see me?

Lucian grunted and pushed us forward. I was still in a daze, thinking about her beautiful eyes and the flash of creamy skin, so I let him take the lead. I shook my head and tried to concentrate as he followed her toward the centre of town. She stopped at a crossroads and appeared to be trying to get her bearings. After a few moments, she picked the road that led her west.

Thank God she didn't go east.

Lucian would have needed to duck out of the forest and follow her like a lost puppy through suburbia if she had turned that way.

After another kilometre, I saw her smile. It was a small one, but that subtle expression radiated on her cherub face. She walked straight up to a small bungalow and bounced up the front steps, crashing through the front door.

Lucian waited for a few more moments. Then a few more.

"Okay, she's safe now," I commented. Lucian didn't move. I tried to take back the reins, and Lucian snarled. *"Don't snarl at me!"*

Lucian and I were not in sync. We still had issues to work through, which was the only reason we weren't alpha yet. I needed to be one with my wolf before Dad would hand down the pack. When our souls finally merged, it would be visible in my eyes. There would be a permanent ring around my iris that indicated that the two halves of our one soul had combined. And currently, Lucian and I were far from making that happen. In fact, I don't think it will ever happen. No matter what I did, he'd still remain a hothead.

"I am not a hothead."

"No, maybe not. But you are a Peeping Tom right now. Clem is safe. She's home. Let's go home and study," I said.

Lucian grumbled and reluctantly allowed me to retake the lead.

"There is something different about her. I just can't put my paw on it," he mumbled before retreating to the back of my mind.

"Yeah, buddy, she's a half-breed," I said, rolling my eyes.

CHAPTER 7

CLEMENTINE

WHEN I ENTERED THE HOUSE, I went straight down the hallway and into the tiny bathroom for a shower. I needed to wash the sweat off me and the disgusting, skin-crawling sensation of what almost happened.

What kind of person threatens sexual violence against another? And what kind of person just stands by and watches? No, not only watches, but eggs it on. What the hell was wrong with those people?

Then there was the wolf. I had never seen a wolf before. I grew up in central Vancouver, and wolves didn't tend to come into the city. In fact, I was probably one of the only Canadians who could say that the largest and scariest animal they had ever seen had been a deer. The only other animals I had interacted with had been squirrels and chipmunks. I even avoided my friend's cats and dogs thanks to allergies. And one time, when there was a bear on campus, I walked the opposite way than the crowd. I had an adverse fear reaction to anything that could eat me.

Seeing that wolf had thrilled me as much as it had terrified me. It was a huge culture shock, and a reality check. I wasn't in the city anymore. I'd seen a wolf! A real-life wolf who jumped out of the thicket to save me.

No! Don't be stupid, Clem. Wolves don't act like that. We probably stumbled onto its territory, and it was giving us a warning or something.

It had all been very bizarre.

I scrubbed myself with fragrance-free hypoallergenic soap and rinsed myself off before stepping out of the shower, wrapping myself in a towel. I picked up my dirty clothes and walked into my bedroom, quickly moisturised, then dressed in a fresh pair of denim shorts, a white camisole, and a cream-coloured lace cardigan. I studied myself in the mirror. My hair was still in its perfect braid, and my eyes seemed to pop vividly behind my glasses. I took my mother's medallion necklace from the dirty clothes pile and returned it to my neck.

After disposing of my dirty laundry in the hamper, I went in search for something to drink.

"Vinny get off to school, okay?" Dad asked as I entered the clean kitchen.

Surprisingly, all the boxes had been unpacked, dismantled, and stacked neatly by the mudroom door. Dad was up on a ladder repairing the kitchen light fixture.

I gently moved around his ladder and toolbox, making my way toward the fridge to get a cold glass of much-needed water.

"School? I thought you told me to drop him off at a biker bar. When I left, he was getting a skull and crossbones tattoo on his back. Those bikers seemed like such nice guys! They weren't even going to charge him." I smirked.

Dad shook his head and threw me a grin that twinkled in his eyes.

"Speaking of bars. How did you get on at the bar and grill place?" he asked.

I placed the cold glass against my cheek, trying to get some relief from the blistering heat.

"I never got there. I got lost."

"You got lost," my father repeated slowly. "In Blackfern Valley?"

"Dad, there are barely any street signs, house numbers, or navigational tools around here. It's like they want people to get lost." I gave him a small smile and watched him as he fiddled with an exposed wire.

"But you obviously found your way back, okay."

I nodded, then reluctantly told him the next part. "Yeah. I ran into a little bit of trouble though."

"What kind of trouble?" His voice sounded deeper than usual.

I looked into his green eyes encased with silver and instantly regretted saying anything. He didn't need the added stress. "Nothing really. Some guy gave me a hard time."

"What guy?"

"I don't know, Dad, some idiot and his Barbie girlfriends," I said exasperatedly.

Not only did I not want to give my dad the added stress of knowing someone had bullied me, but I also didn't want to tell my dad what had almost happened. My mom was the one I could talk to about personal stuff. My dad was a little more challenging to have those conversations with. It's not that he didn't try. He just wasn't Mom.

"What happened, Clemmy?" he asked again, climbing down from the ladder.

"Nothing, Dad." He stared at me and waited. "Honestly." I started to twitch under his scrutiny. "Okay, fine! I think the guy was about to attack me, and his two bimbo friends were egging him on. I think they were going to let him..." I shivered at the thought. "Anyway, this big fucking wolf scared him off. It was enormous. I didn't know wolves could get that big. I thought it was going to eat me, Dad. But it disappeared back into the bush straight after it scared off this Lincoln guy."

My father was furious.

I thought he would start asking questions about the wolf. Surely the fact that his daughter was next to a dangerous wild animal would bring out a red-riding-hood style lecture, but he didn't seem to give it another thought. Instead, he seemed more worried about the guy who had almost attacked me.

"Lincoln. As in Lincoln James?"

"How would I know?"

"That guy is trouble. Stay away from him." His voice reverberated against the kitchen walls, and I could feel the anger rolling off him in waves.

"Trust me, Dad, I don't plan on going anywhere near him."

Dad closed his eyes and started to take deep breaths through his mouth. My father wasn't a violent man, but he appeared to be trying hard to keep his anger in check.

I knew he didn't need this extra stress.

When he opened his eyes, he suddenly pulled me into a fierce hug. If he squeezed any tighter, bones would start snapping. I felt him sniff at my hair. He pulled back, gave me a bizarre look, and then sniffed again.

"What? Do I need to wash my hair?" I took the braid and brought it up to my nose to take a whiff. It smelt fine to me, with subtle tones of shampoo which indicated that it had been a day or two since it had last been washed.

"No, not at all." He shook his head and looked like he wanted to say more, then changed his mind. "It's nothing. Don't worry, Clem." He avoided looking at me and started digging around in his toolkit, deep in thought.

"Okay. I'm going to head back out and explore and maybe find that bar."

Dad dropped his tools again. "I can finish this later. You and I can go out and explore together. Maybe head down to the university. It's about an hour's drive from here."

"Dad!" I put as much warning into my voice as I could.

"Look, we can pop by the bar and get you a job application too." He placed his palms up in a peace-keeping gesture.

"I'm pretty sure I can do that myself," I scoffed.

"If you can find it," he retorted.

I responded by flipping him the bird, but I knew this wasn't about my lack of coordination here. This was still about Lincoln.

"Dad, I'll be fine. If I start going out with my father as a chaperone, that Lincoln guy wins."

I walked into Lupus' Bar and Grill and flicked my braid over my shoulder.

"Can I help you?" I spotted a tall and willowy brunette. Her hair was in romantic curls, and her makeup was immaculately shaded and highlighted. She was wearing a black top with an outline of a wolf on her left breast and a name badge on her right breast. *April.* A bottle green apron was pinned around her tiny waist, which made her look almost naked from the waist down, but I could make out the outline of denim cut-offs poking out from underneath the hem of the apron. She had the longest brown legs I had ever seen.

I put on my best customer-service smile and tried to ignore the inferiority complex threatening to make an appearance. "Hi, April! I'm here for a job application. Is the manager in?"

She gave me a once over, and I felt dread solidify in my stomach. Her perfect little nostrils twitched, and she wrinkled her nose. "You...want to work...here?"

"Um. Yes?"

"There are no jobs available," she snipped.

"Oh, but I saw a sign in the window—"

"Yeah, okay, so there is a job opening." She rolled her eyes. "I'm just trying to save you the rejection."

I bristled. "How do you know I will be rejected?"

"People like you always are."

"People like me?" Something inside me shifted. "You know what, April, you're probably right. But unless you're the manager, I don't actually give a fuck about your ideals or opinions. So how about you stop being rude to your clientele and fetch the manager." *Please, please don't let her be the manager.*

April glared at me and then spun on the heel of her sneakers, and I watched as she pressed her French tips into her palms. I scanned the room's tasteful decor and wasn't surprised that there were very few patrons. It was two o'clock, so the lunch rush was likely done, and the after-work drinks and dinner rush would not start until at least five.

A middle-aged woman with short, cropped blonde hair and hazel eyes approached me. "Hi, my name is Tina. April said that you were looking for a job?"

"Hi. I'm Clementine. And yes, I just moved here and am looking to find work."

Tina took a deep breath through her nose and looked at me curiously. "I see. Do you have experience?"

"I used to bartend at the university bar back in Vancouver."

"Oh, yeah? Well, this job will be both bartending and serving food from our kitchen."

"Yes. There was a little bit of waitressing at the university bar too."

"I see." She looked me over again. "The truth is, Clementine, I don't want any trouble. And with you here, I know it's going to cause just that."

"Why would she cause you trouble?" a smooth voice asked.

I spun around slowly and found the guy I had bumped into outside Vinny's school.

What's his name again?

"Liam!" Tina said, taking half a step back and lowering her eyes slightly.

"Tina." He nodded. "Why would hiring Clementine cause you trouble?"

The woman looked at me, then back at him, then back at me again. Her eyes flashed to him, and a vacant expression washed over her face. After a few strange but quiet moments, she looked at me and sighed. "What size are you, honey?"

My brows furrowed in confusion. "Usually an eight or a ten," I offered quietly, "why?"

"Well, I don't have any female uniforms in that size." She gave me a look over again. "All of my girls are a lot smaller." I felt my hackles rise. I had no idea how to respond to that. "Maybe you will fit one of our men's shirts?" She looked at me and nodded. "Wait here. I'll go grab you a few samples."

Tina disappeared, and I got my first decent look at Liam. I was so embarrassed this morning that I rushed away as fast as possible, hoping I would never see him again. But now that he stood before me, I was glad hope hadn't come to fruition.

He was at least six feet tall, with a sculpted body that could have been made from marble. His eyes were a warm mocha, and his hair was cropped short at the back and sides. The hair on top of his head was longer and a caramel brown in colour. It looked like it had natural tones of dark blond mixed in, but it could have been a trick of the light. His jaw was strong, chiselled, and covered in a well-groomed scruff, which emphasized his elegantly straight nose, full lips, and perfect cupid's bow.

Wow!

"If you're going to keep staring at me like that, you could at least buy me a drink," Liam commented.

I felt my face grow hot. He smiled at me, flashing his perfect white teeth. This man didn't have one flaw. He was beautiful. He was perfect. And he was still waiting for an answer. My mouth went dry.

Crap!

CHAPTER 8

LIAM

I COULD HEAR her heart pounding in her chest as she opened and closed those soft-looking plump lips, trying to figure out something to say.

"Come on," I said with a flick of my head.

I led her toward a booth and threw two fingers up to Ryan, my best friend, and the bartender on duty. He nodded at me and started pulling a beer from the tap. Clementine shuffled her feet as she sat down.

"Nervous?" I asked her.

Her shuffling instantly stopped, and she glared at me. "No," she lied. It would have been flawless if I couldn't hear her heartbeat giving her away.

Ryan came over with the drinks himself. *"I wasn't going to trust April not to spit in it."* he mind-linked me. I nodded my gratitude and slid a beer across to Clementine. She stared at it like it was an alien entity.

"Not a beer drinker?" I asked.

She picked up the glass and took a sip. A small amount of head lingered on her upper lip. "I was just curious as to what the catch was," she said as she licked the remaining foam away. My eyes followed the movement.

"*Catch*, why would there be a catch?" Her turquoise eyes bored into mine, but she refused to answer the question. "There is no catch, Clem," I told her earnestly. I took a gentle sniff of her honeysuckle scent and smiled.

Tina chose that moment to arrive with a pile of different t-shirts for Clementine. Clementine's fingers lightly traced the outline of the wolf before she shook the t-shirt out and looked at it, obstructing her from view. All I could see was Lupus' Bar and Grill written across the back of the t-shirt. The shirt would disappear for a second, only to be replaced with another. Then another.

Lucian huffed and swished his tail, waiting. Finally, after what seemed like forever, she gently folded the t-shirts and placed them on the side of the booth. She separated two and put them in her bag before giving me a small smile. Her cheeks were tinted with pink, but I had no idea what had made her so bashful. She looked away again and seemed mesmerized by the uniform t-shirt sitting on the side of the table.

"Penny for your thoughts," I prompted, trying to get the shy girl to speak.

"Just admiring the wolf on the shirt," she said, then added, "I saw a wolf today."

Lucian's ears perked up.

"Oh?" I asked, taking a sip of my beer.

"Yeah. He was massive." Her pink tint darkened. "I'm not used to seeing wolves."

"There are a lot of them around here. It probably won't be the last one you see."

"Really?"

I shrugged. "Yeah. Blackfern Valley is sort of famous for its wolves. You have probably noticed a lot of wolf-themed stuff in town."

"Oh, that makes sense, I guess," she said. "I'm actually afraid of wolves," she added quietly, drawing her fingers down the misty droplets on the outside of her beer glass.

Lucian scoffed.

"What about the one today?"

"It was strange. I got a little lost and some..." She shook her head and redirected her speech. "One moment he was there, and the next he was gone. He didn't seem interested in me at all." She took another sip of her beer. "He was stunning, though." I couldn't help but smile as Lucian puffed out his chest proudly. "Really beautiful," she murmured, deep in thought. She said it so softly that I would have missed it if I didn't have superhuman hearing.

Lucian was pleased.

I looked at the menu, purposely avoiding eye contact as I could feel Lucian pushing forward. After a few moments of battling my wolf, I looked at her again. "So, tell me about yourself, Clem." I tried to ignore Lucian's pacing in my mind.

"Not much to tell, really." She shook her head. "I grew up in Vancouver, and now I'm here."

"What did you do in Vancouver?"

"Nothing interesting," she said, blatantly trying to end the conversation.

Lucian grumbled.

"You like a little mystery, eh?"

"What?" She readjusted her glasses on her face and stared me down, those turquoise eyes twinkling behind her frames. "No. It's just really not that interesting."

"Well, what brought you here?" I prompted, knowing the answer but trying to encourage the shy girl to open up.

"I moved here with my dad and my brother," she offered but said nothing more. I had never met a woman who was as closed off as she was.

Tina came back at that moment to talk Clementine through the schedule she would be working on. It seemed like she would be doing Monday, Tuesday, and Friday nights. She slid across a contract to Clementine and told her to sign it and bring it back on her first shift.

Lucian grinned at me. *"We now know when she'll be here."* I rolled my eyes at him.

"Thanks, Tina." She smiled sweetly at her.

As Tina went to take the extra t-shirts away, I asked her to bring me a large poutine. Maybe food will get Clementine to open up.

"Thank you for helping me with that, by the way," she murmured.

"With what?" I asked, happy that she had initiated conversation.

"Getting me the job."

"I didn't do anything."

"Yeah, you did. I'm not sure what you did, but Tina was about to show me the door, and suddenly she's giving me a job," Clementine said softly, then added, "My dad said that people could be a little cruel to outsiders here."

"Your dad said that?" I asked, hopeful that she would talk more. She took a sip of her beer and just nodded. Lucian grumbled loudly when it seemed like she was finished with that conversation. "There are some right assholes in town, that's for sure. But hey, I'm a nice guy!"

She graced me with a small smile, and I felt Lucian fluff himself. He liked that smile. I took a drink and watched her over my beer glass. She was like no other woman I had met before. Where most she-wolves would be gushing and flirting by now, she sat back quiet and reserved, so any small gesture would start to make Lucian act like a puppy starved for attention. And he wasn't exactly starved for attention. All the unmated she-wolves in the bar right now were checking him out.

"So, what do you do, Mister Nice Guy?" she asked.

"I study business and economics," I offered without delay.

"Oh, wow. Dad said there's a university nearby."

"Do you study anything?"

"Not anymore."

A waitress arrived with the food, then placed her hand on my arm. I looked up to see Nola. Strange that I hadn't smelled her as she approached. However, my nose was already zoned in and enjoying the scent coming from Clementine. Every other scent had weakened in comparison. Lucian growled lowly and huffed out his nostrils.

"Thanks, Nola," I grunted and moved my arm away. She stiffened ever so slightly at my rejection but kept her reaction masked to the untrained eye.

"Any time, Liam." She smiled seductively, and I felt Lucian recoil. She walked away, sashaying her ass in her little shorts, and I felt Lucian shudder violently. Now there was a puppy always looking for attention and approval.

Nola had completely ignored Clementine when she'd made her approach, and knowing what she had done earlier, I couldn't say I was disappointed by it. I felt her eyes on me and gracefully flicked my eyes over to where she was. She was staring longingly at me from across the room, leaning against the bar. My rebuttal was already forgotten. I glared at her before returning my attention to Clementine. Nola had completely ignored her, so I would teach her a lesson and ignore her completely.

"What did you study?" I asked Clementine as I dug into the poutine in front of me.

I pushed it gently toward her, indicating that she could help herself. The portions were already made large as we were in a town full of werewolves, but the large size I had ordered could easily sustain one werewolf and one human.

She ignored the food and looked at me curiously. Finally, she opened her mouth to speak after what felt like a lifetime. "I was studying medicine." I looked over at her, surprised. Of all the things she told me, she could have studied, I wasn't expecting that. "But I dropped out."

"Why would you do that?"

"My mom got sick," she explained sadly. Lucian whimpered in my mind. I could smell the tears manifesting in her eyes, and it took all of my willpower not to reach out and give her comfort. "It brought it too close to home, so I dropped out and moved here with my dad and brother. End of my life story." She finished with a soft snarl in her tone. Her eyes had stopped watering and were now hard, clear, and emotionless.

I just nodded, clearly hearing the warning in her tone to drop it. But I needed to keep her engaged and talking to me about anything; I didn't care what. "You should try this poutine. Gary makes the best one in all thirteen provinces and territories." She raised one singular eyebrow.

"Hard claim."

"It's true." I laughed. She gave me a small smile at the sound of my laughter, and Lucian wagged his tail softly.

"And how do you know this is the best poutine in Canada?" She played along.

"Gary told me," I said deadpan.

Her tinkly little laugh echoed around her, and Lucian gave a big cheesy, wolfy grin in response to it. Her laughter lit up her face and gave the turquoise of her eyes vivacity.

She took a small forkful of poutine and gracefully placed it in her mouth, a cheesy string sticking to her bottom lip. "Okay, not bad. A solid seven out of ten."

"Gary is going to be crushed," I joked, holding my hand to my heart like she had just stabbed it.

"We won't tell him then."

Lupus' started filling up, and soon most of the tables were bursting with patrons.

Clem studied our surroundings with a surprised expression on her face.

"I didn't expect it to be this busy."

I shrugged. "It's the best bar in town."

"How big is Blackfern Valley?"

"About two thousand," I estimated.

"One of the largest packs in British Columbia," Lucian said proudly.

"Two thousand?" She shook her head. "I didn't realize it was that big. My dad told me we were moving to his home-town, and I was expecting maybe five-hundred, tops by the way he spoke about it."

"It's well spread out, so it feels smaller than it is. There is one elementary school and one high school. There are a few other bars, a hardware store, a small doctor's office, a grocery store, and even a small cinema. But most of the people around here hang out in nature. And there's a lot of nature to be had around here."

"I've noticed." She flashed some teeth with her smile. "I think the lichen may actually grow on me."

"Only if you don't move fast enough." I winked. Her cheek-bones tinted with a dusting of pink, and pride glowed in my chest.

Her eyes quickly averted themselves from mine as her shy-bashful nature took over. I was surprised to see her smile turn downward into a grimace. I followed her gaze and noticed the looks some of the she-wolves were giving her. Not only the she-wolves, but some of my pack brothers too.

Lucian fluffed his fur out, and I felt him come forward in warning. I was so focused on Lucian staring them all down that I hadn't noticed her standing up. She put a twenty-dollar bill on the table, and I placed my hand over hers. Her skin was soft and warm.

"What are you doing?" I all but growled.

"Paying for the drinks," she said flatly.

"My shout," I said. She smirked. However, the humour that had sparked in her eyes earlier had gone.

"But didn't you tell me if I kept looking at you in a certain way, I needed to buy you a drink?"

I gaped at her. "So, you admit you were looking at me in such a way?" I joked, trying to bring her playful side out again.

"No, not at all." She shook her head. "But I owe you for helping me get this job." She smiled softly at me again. "And you might be my only friend in this stupid town, so let me buy you a drink." She nodded over at Cassie, who was beelining for me. "Have fun with your date." There was no jealousy or callous tone to her voice, just pure sincerity. And for some reason, that made me feel like shit.

I watched as she walked out of the room, gracefully dodging all the werewolves and going straight out the entrance door without glancing back. I turned to Cassie as she pulled me in for an embrace, her plump boobs pressing against my hard chest, her red hair cascading down her shoulders, and her cerulean eyes fucking me as they raked over every inch of me. I gave her a small smile and showed her to the seat that Clementine had only just abandoned. Her honeysuckle and pear scent lingered on the leather. I put my hand up in the air and mind-linked

Ryan for him to bring over a glass of wine and another beer, and then I tried to turn my focus toward Cassie. But all I could do was think about the last words that had come out of Clementine's mouth.

How did Clementine know I had asked Cassie on a date? And how the hell had I forgotten about it until this second?

CHAPTER 9
CLEMENTINE

I RACED out of that bar as fast as my feet could carry me. My hand was still tingling with a strange sensation, like hundreds of little water droplets were running over its surface. Liam must have some weird static electricity thing going on. It was the only thing that made sense.

I had lost myself in the warm brown hue of his eyes and the gentle caress of his voice, but most of all, I had lost myself in his kindness. Guys who had god-like features like Liam were rarely nice. I was beginning to find myself laughing at his dry humour and wit. I felt comfortable. And then I looked around the bar and noticed three things:

The first was that there was not one ounce of fat on any of the people in the bar. Every single person was slim and gorgeous. The women all looked athletically fit and like they should be on the runway for Victoria's Secret. The men all had bulging muscles, their arms corded and their abs hard. There must have been a gym around here that everyone went to because everyone seemed to be runway or photoshoot ready. That was probably one of the things that Liam left off the list: to live in this town, you must, at the bare minimum, run on a treadmill and do deadlifts.

The second thing I noticed was how beautiful everyone was. The women were well groomed and had immaculate makeup on. Or, if they weren't wearing makeup, they were naturally radiant. And all the men seemed to look like Hollywood super-stars and CFL line-backers. I would have said that the genetics in this place had seriously tipped the scale in favour of your Hemsworth brothers or your Mila Kunis, Jennifer Lawrence, and Kardashian mixes, but then I remembered I came from this DNA stockpile, and I lucked out.

Then, the third thing I noticed was the expression on the faces of these model-like creatures—contempt was what I read on the faces of Blackfern Valley.

In a town of two thousand, it was more than likely that everyone knew Liam. That hypothesis was supported by the fact that the town only had one elementary school and one high school, meaning that the vast majority of the patrons had gone to school with him or his parents at some point. So, when I looked around and saw the disapproval on everyone's faces, I suddenly realized that I was with the town's golden boy.

As I peered around, I realized they disapproved of Liam and me sitting together. I would go as far as to say they disapproved of the friendship starting to form between us, but that was crazy; they didn't even know me. So, I concluded they disap-proved of him sitting with the pug-nosed, chubby chick with glasses.

What made me stand up, however, was when I saw a stun-ning redhead enter the room. She had long legs and was dressed to kill. As her eyes circled the room, a little voice told me that she was looking for Liam, or that she was with Liam. I got up and made my hasty exit to make sure he didn't have an awkward encounter with his date. The only thing that satisfied me was seeing Barbie One's grin turn sour when she spotted the redhead beeline straight for Liam as I made my exit. It appeared Mister Nice Guy had a gaggle of girls after him. I didn't want to be around when he broke someone's heart. It was inevitable it was going to happen. Thankfully, I knew it would never happen to me.

As soon as I left the airconditioned bar, I felt the sticky heat of the summer sun. It felt like I had stepped into a hair dryer on full blast. I adjusted the straps of my bag and stepped off the small decked-out area and onto the dusty road.

I FOUND myself smiling as I walked home. I had a slight bounce in my step as I strolled down the empty streets. It appeared everyone had flocked to the bar straight after work, and I now had the streets to myself to muse and contemplate. All around me were the sounds of nature. I could hear the birds flittering in the trees, the sound of trickling water, a frog croaking, and the sound of a squirrel scurrying.

Wait. I stopped in my tracks, then turned slowly and listened again. My hearing felt amplified.

"No, don't be crazy, Clem! Your hearing has not gotten better," I murmured to myself. This is no different from living in the city. The city was loud, too; the only difference is that I had twenty years to drown out the noise. The sounds of nature only seemed louder than average because I was not used to them. It was just a different kind of noise.

Logic brain for the win! I nodded to myself.

I skipped up the steps to my house and heard my father talking on the phone. I stopped and braced my hand against the door.

"He did what? When? Fuck me! Yeah, I know I need to tell him. Fuck. Okay. Leave it to me. I'm really sorry, Alpha."

What the hell did Vinny do now?

I opened the door and walked into the front room, expecting Dad to be on the couch with his head in his hands. It's a position I've seen him in multiple times. Except he wasn't there. I walked through the house, but he was nowhere to be seen.

"Dad?" I called.

"Out back!" he responded.

Proceeding through the canary-yellow kitchen and into the mudroom, I opened the screen door and let it slam shut behind me as I walked down the porch steps. I found my dad in front of the woodshed, splitting firewood. He had a troubled look on his face as he lined up each block to chop into smaller chunks.

"I thought I heard you in the house," I muttered as I walked toward him.

He looked up at me before slamming the axe down on the next block of wood. The smell of pine infiltrated my nose. "No, I've been out here for the last hour."

I shook my head, confused. "What did Vinny do now?"

"What do you mean?"

"I heard you on the phone. Vinny is in trouble again." My father tilted his head and looked at me bizarrely, but I rambled on. "Is it drugs? I saw his eyes this morning and–"

"Your brother isn't doing drugs, Clemmy." I frowned. "I promise," he added softly. "If he were, he would be out here chopping firewood instead of me."

"Then what?"

"It turns out he skipped school and stole a car," Dad growled.

"Wait, what?"

"Yeah. Sean and Vincent got picked up and are at the police station in Kempthorne."

"What the hell!"

"I think Alph– Uh, Josiah managed to smooth it over with the cops so that no charges will be pressed, but I need to sit down and talk to him."

"No shit! Grand theft auto, Dad!"

"He's going through a lot right now, Clemmy."

"We all are!" I snarled.

"I know, Clemmy. And I'm doing the best I can."

Guilt washed over me in waves, and I chastised myself. "Okay, Dad. So what's the plan? How can I help?"

"You and I will drive to Kempthorne and pick them up." He turned and gave me a small smile. "And it just so happens that the police station is very close to that university I told you about."

I looked at my dad. Was he for real? My brother got done for grand theft auto, and my father was still passive-aggressively trying to get me to enrol in university. I rolled my eyes at him and decided to ignore his comment. I started to move toward the driveway where my dad's work truck sat. Dad hadn't made a move.

"Are we going?"

"Yeah, we are," Dad said, lining up another piece of wood. "I just think we should make them sweat for a little while."

AN HOUR LATER, I was riding shotgun in my dad's slate-coloured Chevy truck on the way out to pick my brother up from the police station.

Like seriously, how the hell does Vinny get himself into these messes?

My dad was in no hurry to get there either. Where I would have driven the truck like a bat out of hell, Dad calmly kept the needle five under the speed limit the entire way.

"I got the job at the bar."

"Oh, good work."

"It's only twenty hours a week, but at least we can now afford groceries or whatever."

"Clementine, that's your money."

"I'm twenty years old, Dad. I can pay my own way." He shook his head.

Proud was the word I would use to best describe my father—proud *and* stupid. He ignored my comment, and I knew I would have to find a way to sneak my money into the house funds.

Dad showed me the small university on the way to the police station. It was cute, and I imagined I could smell the books right from where I was sitting. Books and coffee. I shook my head and steeled my resolve. This wasn't my life anymore.

Dad parked, and I waited in the truck. Sean and Vinny came out of the police station. They looked ashamed when my father was watching, but as soon as his back was turned, they grinned at each other. Their expressions returned to a sombre look as they slid into the back of the cab.

"We are not going to talk about this yet, Vincent, but we will talk about it," Dad said, turning back and looking his son directly in the eye.

"Fine."

Dad's eyes dashed over to Sean. "Your Dad is going to talk to you when you get home."

Sean just grunted.

Dad took that as a response and started the truck.

The ride home was silent. Not one word was spoken. It was a relief when we came across the sign that said we were approaching Blackfern Valley. I smiled when I noticed that what I thought were two mountain peaks were actually two wolves howling. It was artistically designed so that it wasn't noticeable straight away, but there they were, as clear as day.

We pulled up to a driveway that seemed to curve as far back into the woods as possible. I couldn't even see the house from the road.

"Do I need to drive you up, or do you remember the way to your front door?" Dad growled at Sean.

"I remember the way," Sean mumbled.

"Good. Make sure you don't get lost. I'm sure your father is waiting eagerly for you." Sean got out of the truck and slammed the door. "So, what happened?" Dad asked as soon as the truck's tires squealed off the side of the road.

Vinny sighed. "We all went to town for lunch, and Murdoch was showing off his new car to some chicks. He went with some girl into the bathroom, and the idiot left his keys in the ignition. What was I supposed to do, Dad?"

"Um, not steal his car?" I offered.

He pulled the finger at me and kicked the back of my seat. "He totally deserved someone to steal his car. He was flashing it around like, 'Look what my parents bought me for turning sixteen! *Wank. Wank. Wank.*' So as soon as his back was turned, and I noticed the keys were in the ignition, I came up with a payback plan."

"A payback plan?" Dad enquired, eerily calm.

"Well, you said I wasn't allowed to fight him. So, I did the next best thing. I stole his new toy." Dad's lips twitched. I was unsure whether he was fighting a smile or a frown.

"I thought Sean was supposed to keep you out of trouble," he grumbled. "How did you rope Sean into this?"

"Well, he saw me jump in the driver's seat, told me to get out. I said no, and started to back the car up. Next thing I know, Sean is climbing through the passenger window." Vinny chuckled. "So, I pressed the accelerator down a little harder just to scare him. Instead of getting out, he clambered into the seat and joined me in my joyride."

"He joined you?" Dad said, still eerily calm, but his jawbone ticked.

"Yeah. He even taught me how to drive it, and before I knew it, *boom*! We were on the highway heading to Kempthorne."

"Well, I'm glad you enjoyed your little joyride," Dad said, nodding, "because that's the last piece of freedom you'll be getting for a while." His voice was firm and cold, and for the first time since Vinny started telling his story, I saw him retreat into himself, his eyes becoming glassy and rimming with flecks of silver.

CHAPTER 10

LIAM

I WOKE IN MY BED. The sun was glittering through the crack in the curtains and streaming right into my face. I groaned and tried to cover it with my pillow.

"Good morning." The voice startled me out of my sleep delirium.

I sat up and saw a mane of red hair, long bronzed legs and a black t-shirt barely covering her ass—*my* black t-shirt.

"Morning, Cassie," I murmured. She bounced back from the ensuite doorway and rejoined me on the bed. Leaning in slowly, she brushed her lips against mine. Her cinnamon and vanilla scent wafted around me, and I felt Lucian rumble happily. I smiled as she pulled away from the kiss.

After Clementine left the bar and grill last night, Cassie managed to be a beautiful distraction, and I soon was laughing and partying with her. After a few rounds of pool and plenty of alcohol, we managed to tumble back into my bed in the early morning hours.

"What are your plans for today, Alpha?" she asked. Lucian puffed himself up proudly.

"I am not alpha," I gently reminded her.

"No, not yet. But soon." She smiled and gave me an odd expression that I could only describe as longing.

"Not until Lucian and I become one," I muttered, trying to ignore the odd feeling coming over my body. It had started sometime last night but went away as quickly as it had come, making me think I had imagined it. But now, it was back. And it was odd. It started as a light pressure in the back of my neck and shoulders and made me want to shudder or break out in goosebumps. But neither happened, and the light pressure remained.

"Calla says it's not long now."

"How does Calla know that?" I looked into Cassie's big blue eyes, rimmed with an icy purple. Cassie and Calla had become one shortly after we turned eighteen. Most of my friends had already merged with their wolves.

Cassie shrugged. "She just said that you and Lucian will merge when you realize your truth."

Ethereal wolf crap. "And what is my truth?"

"She says you've already found it; you just have to realize it."

"Right." I nodded. "Cryptic."

Cassie's honeyed laughter bellowed out. "I think she's just excited to be close to her alpha." Cassie shrugged.

"Once again. I am not alpha," I growled. "I wouldn't disrespect the alpha by saying so."

"He's your dad. He wouldn't feel disrespected. He'd be proud. He should have passed down the title when you turned twenty-one."

Twenty-one was the youngest age a wolf could become alpha under pack law in Canada. Other than that mandate, each pack had their own nuances. In the Blackfern Pack, it wasn't just turning twenty-one that allowed the inauguration of a new alpha. The alpha-elect also needed to have merged with their wolf. Unmerged alphas were often volatile and untameable. But in saying that, even if an alpha and a wolf had merged and become one, they could still be assholes. Look at Alpha Jed.

Another way to become alpha was to challenge the current one. Once they hit the age of twenty-one, any wolf could challenge the alpha to his pack. However, most don't have a death wish, so it rarely happens.

It almost sounded like Cassie was about to imply that I should challenge my father for the seat.

She wouldn't do that, would she? "He didn't give me the title because I'm not ready." I put as much force into my voice as I could. The small amount of alpha energy I did have rolled off me. She bowed her head and gazed at me through her auburn lashes. I smelled her arousal, and Lucian grinned his stupid wolfy grin. It was a sweet smell, and her ordinary cinnamon and vanilla scent was amplified and projected with something extra sweet, almost fruity in nature. I could practically taste it on my tongue.

And just like that, the pressure over my neck and shoulders returned, and I forcibly made myself stretch and shudder to try and alleviate the feeling. Cassie pressed her heat into my dick, and I felt it spasm in response, the strange new feeling being overridden by my sudden need to be between her legs.

My nostrils flared as I took in her arousal, and my body reacted accordingly. She moved in and took my mouth with hers, rubbing herself against me seductively. My hands found her plump ass and ran over the smooth skin.

"Liam. Where the hell are you?" I froze.

"Way to cockblock, Dad!"

"You're supposed to be at training." His voice carried over.

Oh shit! *"Crap. I'm on my way."*

Cassie had stopped kissing me once my eyes went vacant, a

sign that I was mind-linking with someone. She raised her eyebrows when I refocused on her.

"Sorry, Cassie, duty calls." I rolled out of bed, my dick still at attention as I shoved my legs into my athletic shorts.

"Really?" she huffed. "You're going to leave me like this?"

I turned back to find she was now naked and touching herself on my bed. Her eyes were bright, and the purple ring was sparkling under the intensity of her pleasure. Lucian started to wag his tail and drool. He urged me forward; to take what she was offering so freely. I shook my head, trying to fight for control.

"Sorry, Cassie. I thought you wanted me to be alpha? And being an alpha means responsibilities." Lucian huffed in amusement.

"Being an alpha means dominating and fucking the hot chick on your bed when she's wanton for you." Her voice came out as a sexy growl.

I closed my eyes for a moment, trying to clear my thoughts. "You know the way out."

I shrugged as I exited my bedroom door. I didn't want to be a jerk, but the uneasy feeling between my shoulders was growing steadily, and I was already running late.

I wanted to say it was hard to leave Cassie, naked and willing, on my bed. But it wasn't. My arousal was gone, and even Lucian was starting to agree that maybe going for another round wouldn't have been a good idea.

What I noticed, however, is that as I walked away further from her, that discomfort in my neck had started to ease. I stretched it out as I walked over to the training grounds at the back of the pack house.

"Calla wants to mate," Lucian muttered.

"You mean she wants to have sex."

"No, I mean she wants you to mark her."

"What? That's crazy!"

"Cassie is all for it too. She was practically fluffing at the idea of being luna."

"Why the hell are you only telling me this now!" I growled.

"Because we can only mark each other at midnight on the night of a full moon, and I thought you would like the opportunity to get your dick wet." He smirked.

"I don't want a mate, Lucian."

"Well, you do, but you don't want to choose one. You want your true mate. You secretly are a hopeless romantic, you know," he teased.

I rolled my eyes, even though he wasn't wrong. If I was going to have a mate, I wanted her to be the one made for me as much as I was for her.

"There's a meagre chance of us finding our true mate, Lucian. Look at Dad. He met Mom only because she was visiting from New Brunswick. Most of the mated wolves around here are chosen mates. Very few are true mates."

"She's out there," Lucian said confidently.

"Where?" I grumbled.

He just shrugged and looked at me with a relaxed expression that told me he was being all vague and mystical again. My brother was right. Wolves were weird with their ethereal-cosmos shit.

The training grounds were an ample open space. It once was grassy, but now, over many years of warrior training, the grounds were mostly dusty with small patches of grass and dandelions here and there. From the age of fifteen, pups came here for an hour every second day to do some training with the pack's warriors.

When their wolf manifested, their training was then

increased until the moment the wolf sprung forward and they ran for the first time. They don't have to do intensive training until they have finished high school, and then it's a three-hour stint every second day at the bare minimum. Once they know how to defend themselves in both wolf and human forms, they can continue training as often or as little as they wish.

First, we trained in human form, and once we managed to master that, we went up a level and trained in our wolf form. If we mastered our wolf form, we moved to the final level, which was learning how to manipulate both forms at the same time. That tier was only for merged wolves. Usually, the only ones who did it were those who wanted to become warriors for the pack.

The class I was heading to was training in human form. It wouldn't have any pups in it as it was a school day, and their training was set in the afternoon to prevent them from missing out on their education. I was thankful not to have to deal with the angsty drama that came with the younger wolves.

I strolled up to the grid and gave Ryan a grin. He was the warrior undertaking the training today, and I was meant to be showing leadership skills and helping him. As he was in instruction mode, I waited before I approached him. Once the wolves started to pair off, I went up to him.

"Look who decided to show up!" He threw out an arm and encased my forearm with his large hand in a roman handshake.

"I just left a very pissed-off redhead in my bed for this. You better make this good." I laughed with him. His grey eyes were encased in a ring of brown, and his muscles were bulging out of the arms of his muscle shirt.

"Nola was pissed when you and Cassie disappeared last night."

"I don't care."

"You know she has the hots for you."

"She has the hots for power."

"So does Cassie," he said bluntly.

"Yeah, but Cassie is hot."

"So is Nola."

I shook my head. "Nola is vapid."

"What about the half-breed?"

That surprised me, and Lucian perked his ears up curiously. "Clem? What about her?" I asked, my voice gravelly.

"She's sweet." He shrugged as I raised my eyebrows at him. "She's also a looker under those glasses. I know she is way different than the girls I usually go for, but she looks like she would bounce up and down on my dick with uncontrollable passion." He grinned. "The quiet ones always do."

"Stay away from Clem!" I warned, Lucian coming forward protectively.

"Hey, man, I'm just calling it how I see it."

"She is off limits," I growled.

"How come?" He scoffed. "Don't tell me you fancy her?"

"It's not that." I shook my head, trying to keep Lucian in check. He was eying up Ryan's jugular with interest. "She's new to town. Give her the space to settle in."

"Sure. She can have all the space she likes." He nodded, his eyes full of humour. "I have a huge bed after all."

Snap! My minute control on my wolf slipped, and Lucian attacked even though I was still in human form.

CHAPTER 11

CLEMENTINE

CRASH. *Bang. Slam.* The sound of a loud, angry voice rang out. More crashing, more banging. I rolled over in bed and looked up at the ceiling. I knew I had to get up and deal with this—go play referee. I hated playing the arbitrator.

I rolled out of bed with a groan, shoved my glasses on my face, and padded out of the room.

I walked down the hallway to find my brother in the kitchen, slamming cupboards. My father was nowhere in sight.

"What the hell is going on?" I snarled.

"What do you mean?" Vinny asked.

"I heard you yelling at Dad."

"I wasn't yelling." He looked at me curiously. The silver flecks had gone from his eyes, but his green eyes were red and glassy once again.

"Yeah, you were. You woke me up."

"I didn't mean to wake you, Clem."

"So you weren't just calling him an asshole and still ranting about the fact that Murdoch deserved it?" I asked.

Vinny looked at me curiously. "Well, yeah, I did. But I was talking to myself, Clem. Dad isn't even here."

"What?" I looked at him with the same confused expression he was looking at me with.

He went to say something else, but Dad chose that moment to enter the mudroom, and he must have changed his mind.

"Good morning," he said as Dad came into the kitchen, slightly damp from running through the forest.

"Have you been out this whole time?" I asked, genuinely confused.

"I went for a run. Why? What's going on?" I looked between my dad and brother.

What the hell is going on with me? "N-nothing," I murmured. "I'm going to shower."

I raced out of the kitchen and into the bathroom, slamming the door behind me. I turned the shower on full blast and started to undress. What the hell was going on with my hearing? I tilted my head and listened. Other than the low mumbling noises that told me my dad was talking to Vinny, I heard nothing.

It was evident that Vinny was just louder than he thought he was. I shook my head and jumped under the spray. After adjusting the scolding hot water to a more suitable temperature, I started to scrub my fingers through my hair. It was so freaking long. Too long. After I ran shampoo through it twice, I massaged the conditioner through the ends and up the length of my tresses. I then clipped it back with a claw clip before I started scrubbing my skin with a loofa and my hypoallergenic soap. I took my razor out and shaved my legs and underarms properly. Once I was satisfied I had gotten all the bits I missed yesterday, I released my hair and rinsed myself off.

I WRAPPED MYSELF IN A TOWEL, shoved my glasses on my nose and walked into my bedroom, where I moisturized and dressed in a pair of light grey cargo capris and a dark grey camisole. I put my lacey white cardigan on and threw some roman sandals on my feet. I ran a comb through my hair and left it to air dry. Grabbing my mother's medallion off the corner of the mirror, I sling it around my neck, before walking out to join my family for breakfast.

"I'll walk you to school this morning," I said to Vinny as I sat down and nibbled on the corner of a strawberry-flavoured Pop-Tart.

"Why?"

"Because you're grounded."

"You're not my keeper."

"It's either me or Dad."

"Dad. I'll always pick Dad," he grunted.

I rolled my eyes. "You are such a little–"

"I just don't want you walking me. Okay?"

"Why?" I stared at his green eyes, which seemed full of untamed emotion.

"Because I get enough of a hard time as it is. I don't want people connecting that we're related."

"They're going to know anyway, Vinny. This is a small town."

"Yeah, and so far, all I hear is how the big, ugly, fat chick and her dweeb of a brother are the worst thing that have happened to this hellhole. I don't want any more shit. Okay?"

"People are stupid. Ignore them," I said softly, internally licking the wounds he was creating.

"Ignore them? What planet are you on? It's a small town; you can't ignore them."

"So, you're just going to turn your sister into a pariah?" Dad growled as he came from his bedroom, fully dressed and ready to start his workday.

"She already is one," Vinny snarled.

I glared at him.

"Vincent, talk like that about your sister again, and I swear I won't just make you walk with her to school, I will make you hold her hand." Vinny looked aghast. Dad always came out with interesting punishments, and somehow, he made them stick. "Apologize to your sister."

"Sorry," he grunted angrily, slamming his breakfast dishes into the sink, camouflaging his voice as he added, "Sorry you're a fat loser" under his breath. If Dad heard it, he didn't acknowledge it.

"Vinny, you should be sticking up for your sister."

"You told me I wasn't allowed to get into fights," he said sardonically.

"There's a huge difference between standing up for someone and getting into a fight, Vincent. And you know that." Dad sighed, then turned to me. "Thank you for offering to walk him to school, but I need to go in and speak to the principal anyway."

"Oh. Okay." I shrugged.

Dad turned to my brother. "Vincent, get your schoolbag."

Vinny muttered something under his breath, and Dad glared at the back of his head.

"Are you okay?" Dad asked me.

"Yeah, I'm fine."

Dad's eyes scrutinized mine. "Are you sure?"

"Yeah, Dad. Sticks and stones."

"Are you home for dinner tonight?"

"Actually, I was planning on going on a hot date, then getting busy in the backseat of his car. I even thought I would forgo the rubber this time. It'll make it more exciting." I rolled my eyes at him. "Yes, Dad, I'll be home for dinner. Where else would I be?"

"Well, if you do decide to go on a hot date, make sure you bring him to the house first. I want to at least make sure his car is roadworthy before you take off in it to make my future grand-babies." I snorted a laugh. He smiled at me and downed the last of his coffee. "We need to talk about some stuff."

"What stuff?" I asked.

Vinny showed up with his schoolbag, and Dad placed his coffee cup in the sink. "Later. Come on, Vincent. Get in the truck."

Dad and Vinny went out through the mudroom toward the truck, and I stood there shaking my head.

I quickly hand-washed the dishes in the sink and sighed to myself. I hated being alone in a place I didn't know. I knew I had boxes to unpack, but I decided it could wait. I just wanted to get out of the house. After retrieving my bag from the back of my bedroom door, I decided to go for a walk. Besides, the more I walked, the less likely I would get lost in this stupid town.

I managed to make my way into the town centre and observed as everyone was racing around to get to work or school. I found a small café with a small outside seating area to sit at and ordered a coffee. The waitress came out with one a few moments later.

"Thanks. Hey, do you know if there's a salon around here?" I asked.

She looked at me and plastered a customer-service smile on her face that didn't meet her eyes. "Next block over." She walked away without another word, and I was left to my solitude.

I took a sip of the coffee and instantly spat it out, spraying it all over the gun-metal grey table in front of me. It was terrible. I took another tentative sip and almost gagged.

What on Earth? It tasted like vinegar or something.

I took a sniff. It definitely didn't smell like any regular coffee to me. What the hell had this person made me? I sniffed again. I could smell the roasted coffee and the milk. And underneath, I detected something else. Sniffing again, I knew what it was. Ammonia.

"What the fuck?" I pushed the coffee away. Maybe they'd just finished descaling the coffee machine?

I stood up and walked into the café with my cup.

"Excuse me. I think something is wrong with my coffee," I told the barista.

She looked at me curiously. "Oh, and what's that?" she challenged.

"Did you just clean your machines? It seems it's affected the taste of the coffee." I could smell the ammonia again, stronger this time. Like someone had left the cap off the bottle.

"Well, that's just too bad." She stared me down.

"Could you make me another?"

She looked at me incredulously. "You want another coffee?"

"Yeah. I am unhappy with the one I have."

"Well, I'm unhappy you're here," she said.

"I'm sorry?" My heart thumped in my chest.

"In fact, I don't want you in my coffee shop. Please leave."

"You're kicking me out because I asked you to replace a coffee that isn't up to quality?" The thumping moved from my chest into my ears. I felt my face begin to warm.

"I'm telling you to leave because I don't want you in my shop, or my town, for that matter. I can't control the town, but I can control my shop. Get the fuck out," she snarled.

My face grew red-hot with rage. Instead of telling the lady what I thought, I pivoted on my heel and stormed out of the café.

How fucking rude can a person get! The voice in my head was snarling and vehemently angry. Angry enough to go in and rip her apart. I shook my head, trying to blink back the tears, and once I felt them recede, I steeled my emotions. Maybe I should just see if the salon could cut my hair. A haircut always made me feel better.

CHAPTER 12
CLEMENTINE

I walked into the salon feeling a little nervous. A kind woman with blue-grey eyes smiled at me.

"Hi, I was wondering if I could book an appointment to cut my hair," I rushed out. I felt the tears in the back of my eyes, and my lip started to wobble.

"Hi, honey! Of course, you can. I have time now if you want?"

"Oh yes! Please!"

"My name is Steph." She offered her hand for me to shake.

I reached out and shook her hand. "Clementine. Clem."

I studied Steph, who was middle-aged and reminded me so much of my mother. She had the same wheat-coloured hair and a short stature with a petite figure.

Steph led me to a chair and wrapped a black smock around my neck before running her fingers through my hair.

"What would you like done?"

"Just shorten it. It usually sits around my shoulders, but my mom got sick, and I got distracted."

"Oh, honey! I'm so sorry." She reached around and gave me a quick hug, her eyes tearing up ever so slightly before she continued to run her fingers through my hair.

"I think we'll definitely take the length back, remove some thickness, add a few layers, and get it to sit up and around your shoulders again. It'll make it really bounce." She nodded. "It's so long, but in beautiful condition."

"My hair grows really fast." I met her gaze in the mirror. "We might have to make a regular appointment."

"Absolutely. The girls around here all have fast-growing hair too. Most come back every six to eight weeks for a cut."

"Really?"

She looked at me curiously. "Yeah, must be something in the water." She winked conspiratorially and tinkled out a laugh.

"I did notice all the girls seem to be beautiful," I murmured under my breath. However, she heard me.

"Are they?"

"Yeah." I felt my face warm. "You can't say you haven't noticed."

"There are definitely some beautiful people in this town." She nodded, smiling. "And another beautiful person just joined it. We're very blessed."

I looked at her and blinked. Her face was full of sincerity, and her eyes were full of compassion. She seemed to know what negative thoughts plagued me. She was so much like my mom. I gave her a sad smile of gratitude as she proceeded to clip my hair on top of my head and comb and cut the length that was left down.

STEPH WAS super chatty as she snipped away at my dark locks. Once she got talking, there was no stopping her.

So much like Mom, I thought again.

I discovered she had four kids: one boy and three girls. Her eldest child was named Briar, and she was twenty-five and had just obtained a degree in interior design. She was currently touring Canada and, by the sounds of it, trying to find a boyfriend. Her second daughter, and second youngest was Sophie, who was my age, and studying journalism at Kempthorne University. Her youngest girl, Laurel, was seventeen and in her final year of high school but had aspirations of moving to Hollywood and being a movie star (Steph shook her head and laughed when she said that). Her son was twenty-two and working at Lupus' Bar and Grill. She was super excited when I told her I had just gotten a job there too.

"Oh, you're going to love Ryan." I committed his name to memory. "He works the bar when he isn't working in the squad."

"Squad?" I asked.

She nodded proudly. "Yeah, my boy is part of the warrior squad."

"Is that some kind of sports team?"

She tilted her head and looked at me, then gave me a small smile before nodding. "Something like that."

AN HOUR LATER, I was looking at a whole new me. A river of my hair was at my feet, littering the floor. Steph had styled and shaped my new do, so it sat below my shoulders. It looked amazing, and felt much lighter. I finally felt closer to the me that had disappeared over the last year. I took a sad breath and smiled into the mirror once more.

I LEFT the salon with a bounce in my step. I was happy that I met someone else in this town who was lovely, smiling when I thought about the only other nice person in this town. His warm eyes and smile made me feel at ease. I thought about going to find him to show him my new haircut, but I didn't know anything about him, let alone where to find him. I suppose I could go back and ask Steph if she knew how I could get hold of Liam, but it seemed a bit stalkerish. Blackfern Valley was a small town, and I was bound to run into him eventually.

WITH THE LAST box of my bedroom unpacked, I sighed heavily and looked around the cozy room. Even with all the boxes unpacked and dismantled, it was still tiny. My double bed took up most of the space, leaving little room for anything else. My only other furniture was the single trestle side table shoved hard against my bed and the dresser, which was pushed far into the corner between the window and the floor-length wall mirror.

This house was the same size as our apartment in Vancouver, but somehow it felt smaller. Instead of an open plan living area that branched off into three decent-sized bedrooms, this house was cut up into odd rooms and sections with funny walls that seemed pointless, making the place seem minuscule and crowded. I wanted to tear down the awkwardly placed walls and open things up a bit, but Dad said they were load bearing and would take a little more planning than a random PMS-day and a sledgehammer.

I sighed as I moved the dismantled boxes out of my bedroom, through the kitchen and into the mudroom, where I dropped most of them as I tried to manoeuvre out the back door, toward the garage. I wobbled backward out the door, trying to pick up the boxes as I used my ass to hold the screen door open.

I heard a snicker and stopped. The wind whooshed through the trees, and there was a light crunching noise. I turned and looked behind me, examining the backyard. Empty. It consisted of a rotary clothesline, a woodshed with a large chopping block in front of it and an old giant tree with a rope that had once held a tire swing. The tire rested against the tree trunk, looking old and worn. The backyard had no fence and rolled into the forest behind the house. I scanned the treeline and saw nothing out of the ordinary.

I shook my head and turned back to my task. I must have imagined it. Every few steps, I would stop and look around the yard, convinced that I heard something in the trees. Every time I looked up, there was nothing.

I took a deep breath and smelled the earthy tones of the wet forest behind me; the aroma of pine shavings and oddly, a scent of something deep and rich that I could not quite place were all I could detect. I looked around again. Nothing. I listened harder. Everything was tranquil and still.

"Alright, Clem, you're officially going crazy."

I finally got the boxes out of the house and went down the porch steps to the garage side door. As I placed my hand on the handle, I heard a crunching noise. Spinning around, scanning my surroundings. Again, nothing.

I shook my head and proceeded to open the door. It creaked on its hinges, and I palmed the wall for the light switch, finding it, but no light came on. I tried to hit the switch again, toggling it up and down. No florescent. I knew it wasn't the bulb. Dad had just replaced all of them when we first moved in.

"Stupid old house with its stupid old wiring." I threw the boxes haphazardly forward, hoping they would land in some kind of order.

I hurried out of the garage and slammed the door shut behind me. As I spun around, I scanned the backyard again. I couldn't shake the feeling I was being watched. My heart was thumping in my chest as I stepped toward the forest, readjusting my glasses, then grabbed hold of my mom's medallion with my right hand for moral support.

Is there someone in there watching me?

I took another few more tentative steps toward the low-hanging branches that framed the forest's edge.

Using my left hand, I pushed myself into the trees, slowly turning, trying to hear anything else that wasn't the blood pumping in my ears.

Ring. Ring. Ring. A soft shriek escaped just as my back pocket started to vibrate. I laughed at my stupidity and pulled the phone out of my shorts.

"Hello?" I asked the unknown caller.

"Hi, Clem, it's Tina. I know you officially don't start until tomorrow night, but I was wondering if you could come in and cover tonight. Unfortunately, one of the girls hasn't shown up, and we were pretty swamped over lunch. I am expecting a busy night."

"Ah, sure. No problem. Let me get changed, and I will walk over now."

"Thank you. You're a lifesaver." And with that, she hung up the phone.

I scanned the forest one last time before stepping back toward the house, stopping short when I noticed footprints in the leaf litter. There were at least three different human-sized prints near a tree close to the edge of our property.

And a little further away, in a makeshift clearing, there were obvious signs of recent animal activity. Twigs were broken, and the ground was disturbed by large footprints. Those weren't of the human variety.

If I had to guess, I'd be willing to bet they were canine footprints. Large ones.

When I arrived at Lupus', Tina asked me a little more about my experience. I had told her that I was a pretty decent cocktail maker.

"Most people tend to be beer or wine drinkers around here," she stated.

"I can still pour beer and wine, but my speciality is cocktails," I said. "You have cocktail ingredients behind the bar."

She nodded. "Yes, I suppose we do."

"How about I show you what I can do?" I suggested bravely.

"Okay, make me a cocktail. If I enjoy it, I'll put you behind the bar tonight instead of waitressing."

Enthusiastically, I jumped behind the bar, taking a hairband off my wrist, and sweeping my hair up into a ponytail. I adjusted my glasses before looking around for the items I needed to make my invention.

She sat at the bar and watched with rapt attention as I measured, poured, squeezed, and then threw the lid on and gave the shaker a good shake before producing a cocktail glass and pouring out the highlighter green liquid. I pushed it toward her anxiously. She reached forward and sniffed it before taking a tentative sip. Her brows rose, and she took another sip.

She smiled. "You're a professional mixologist, aren't you?"

I smiled back, my cheeks warming at her compliment. "No, I'm not. I'm just good at it."

She took another sip, and her smile turned into a grin. "Okay, a deal is a deal. You can bartend tonight." She took another sip. "What's this called?"

I looked her dead in the eye and shrugged. "Honestly, I have no idea. I just made it up."

Her mouth gaped. She picked up her drink and made her way over to some patrons who had just entered.

I sighed and placed the apron around my waist, looking around the bar to learn where everything was kept. There were about twelve people in the bar, including Tina and a waitress whom I hadn't met, but knew her name was Kimmie. Kimmie was busy chatting to the chef through the server's window, and I wondered if that was the infamous Gary with his poutine that was the best in all the Canadian provinces and territories. I smiled to myself.

A man approached the bar and looked at me with curiosity. I threw on my best customer-service grin that hurt my cheeks. "Hi, what can I get you?"

"Beer," he grunted, tapping his fingers at the beer tap. "And a cocktail for the missus."

I looked over to where he was indicating and saw Tina chatting with a woman I assumed to be his wife. "What kind of cocktail?"

He grunted. "I dunno, something fruity? Whatever you made, Tina."

He walked away with his drinks a few minutes later, and I was wiping down the bar. I looked up toward where the restrooms were located, and my heart stopped for a moment, then started pounding loudly and uncomfortably in my chest.

CHAPTER 13
LIAM

R YAN MOVED JUST before my fist connected with his face. Dirt and dust kicked up where his feet bounced off the ground.

"What the hell, dude?" he growled as he dodged. Lucian didn't care. He was out for blood.

"Lucian, stop!" I commanded.

He wasn't going to. I had no control: left punch, right punch, front kick. Ryan was blocking as Lucian charged forward in my body. *"Lucian!"* I shouted, wrestling to regain control. *"What the fuck is wrong with you?"*

"Liam! Get control of your wolf," Ryan snarled as he defended himself.

I pushed Lucian back with all my might, just long enough to grit out three words. "Knock. Me. Out."

"You can't be serious?" Ryan's arms tried to encase mine, but getting a good hold was proving impossible.

Lucian was frothing at the mouth, trying to come forward. "Now," was the last word I managed to grit out before Lucian took over again.

Ryan looked perplexed as he kept defending Lucian's advances. Suddenly, Ryan's eyes blazed, and his fingernails changed from short square cut nailbeds into thick dark claws. His teeth elongated as he let out a throaty snarl. He wasn't allowing his wolf all the way through, but he was using both his human and wolf forms simultaneously, utilising the strength and agility of his wolf, but maintaining the advantages of his human form.

Lucian perceived the threat and snarled loudly. His alpha tone vibrated through and around all the wolves in the training grid. Each person dropped to their knees and bowed their head in submission. Ryan's wolf receded, sweat dripping over his brow as he fought the command.

"Lucian, Ryan is our friend!" I reasoned with him.

Lucian shook his head deliberately from side to side like he was trying to clear water out of his ears, then snarled at me again. He was like a rabid animal, wild and demonic.

"LIAM, ENOUGH!" A tone rang out at the same time Lucian sprang forward, ripping my shorts and landing on all fours. His fur ruffled as he shook himself out, then snarled at the firm descending pressure that made him dizzy and bow. It was making him submit. The wave of alpha power had me crumbling to the floor, and Lucian started to whimper. The world was moving, dipping, and swaying. The crushing weight of the power was too much, and I felt the air shudder around me as I shifted back. Lucian had retreated into the far reaches of my mind, and I lay naked and exposed in the middle of the training grid with Ryan and my father looking down at me with concern. That was the last thing I saw before I blacked out.

"WHAT DO you mean he lost control of his wolf?" my dad asked. I felt smooth, cold leather against my naked ass and a light cotton throw landed on top of me.

"I don't know, Alpha. One minute we were joking around,

and the next, Lucian was in full control with Liam asking me to knock him out."

"Thank you, Ryan. Go back to your lessons."

There was the sound of padded footsteps and then a door closing. I felt the couch dip down and a gentle stroke on my face. My eyes were still heavy, and I remained in the back of my mind with Lucian, stroking his fur gently. Lucian was unconscious.

"That wolf is getting more volatile," my mom said, her voice full of concern.

"He just needs to merge with him. He's only unstable because they haven't merged yet."

"No other unmerged wolf seems to have this severe an issue," Mom countered.

"No other wolf is Lucian. Lucian is an alpha. He was always going to be harder to tame."

"How did you tame Jocky?"

"Truthfully?" I heard his voice soften. "I met you."

"So, you're telling me the only way Liam and Lucian will merge is if he mates?"

"No. I'm not saying that. Jocky says we were close to merging anyway. But finding you allowed it to happen faster. You calmed him down and gave him a purpose." Dad sighed. "Trust me. If I thought that Liam's mating would help him tame his wolf, I would have told him to mate with a pack member years ago."

I opened my eyes and looked at my father. He hadn't noticed I was awake. His brown and gold ringed eyes were creased in concern. "He just needs to keep training. Eventually, his mind will become one with Lucian's, and in the meantime, I need to keep a closer eye on him."

"What about the pack?" Mom asked.

"What do you mean?"

"How will they follow him if he's unstable?" Mom whimpered.

"They won't follow him while he's unstable," Dad said bluntly. "But as he works on himself, he will earn their trust, and I'm confident they will follow him when the time comes."

"If not, there's always Sean," I suggested through a groan. I felt like a tanker had hit me as I lifted myself up and slowly moved my muscles. That alpha command packed a hell of a punch.

"Sean will have to go through this with Silas too, who's also of alpha blood," Dad commented. "How are you feeling?"

"Lucian is still out for the count. You packed a real whammy with that command."

"I shouldn't have had to use a command, Liam. What the hell happened?"

"I couldn't tell you." I shook my head. "Ryan and I were chatting, and then he made a comment about Clem and Lucian lost it." I felt terrible. "Lucian has taken it upon himself to be her protector."

"What do you mean?" Mom asked.

"I mean, he gets very protective over her. She's a human living in a werewolf world with no idea what that means or how much danger she could be in. He's decided that she needs his protection."

Mom tilted her head in my direction, then gave Dad a side glance. He returned it with curiosity.

"Well, that's noble, but he needs to learn restraint. People will say things. It doesn't mean they'll act on it," Mom said quietly.

"I know."

"And you need to learn control," Dad instructed.

"I know. I'm sorry."

"Don't apologize to us. Apologize to Ryan," Dad said gently.

"I will."

"Has Lucian indicated to you that he wants to run on the full moon?" Mom asked.

My brows rose. "No, but we aren't merged, so we have to."

"You know mates are found on the full moon–"

"And the mate bond is completed on the full moon. What is this, Mom? The birds and the bees talk again?"

She rolled her cobalt blue eyes at me. "Just before I met your father, Scarlet told me she was itching for the full moon; to run. The itching was because we were close to your father, and she could sense it."

"Sorry, Mom. I hate to break it to you, but I've run every full moon since I was sixteen with this pack. My mate isn't here," I grumbled, then added, "so I guess there's no chance of me merging."

"What if your mate isn't a wolf?" she asked softly.

I looked at her and burst out laughing as I absorbed what she was saying.

"Clem isn't my mate." I laughed some more.

"Why not?"

"Humans cannot be luna."

"Who said?"

"Pack Law," Dad cut across, his brown eyes twinkling with amusement.

"Then why is Lucian all gung-ho about protecting her?" she asked.

"Because he's a stupid mutt with a knight-in-shining-armour complex," I grumbled.

"You've heard the story that Patrick found Lacey on the night of a full moon, right? Maybe you'll find Clem."

"Clem isn't his mate, Sierra," Dad said.

"How can you be so sure?" Dad didn't answer. "Twenty bucks says she is."

Dad's eyes twinkled. "You're on!"

"Are you two honestly betting on my love life?" They turned and smiled at me, love and amusement written over their faces. "I feel for you two if the only entertainment in your pathetic lives is betting on the outcome of mine." I stretched and found that my body was feeling a lot better. Even if Lucian was unconscious, he somehow was healing me. "Alright, I'm out. I'm going to find Ryan. At least he has better conversations."

I removed the blanket draped over me for modesty, rolled off the couch, left Dad's office, and darted down the hall to find some clothes. After throwing on a blue button-down that smelled semi-fresh and a pair of dark denim shorts, I went in search of my friend. I stumbled into him almost instantly. He had already packed his gear from training and was heading toward the pack house.

"Hey, bro." He jerked his chin in that universal male greeting. I rapt my knuckles against his when he put out his fist to bump mine.

"Hey!" I shuffled my feet sheepishly. "Sorry about Lucian. He's a right mutt at times."

Ryan gave a short sharp nod. "You know you aren't ready to do that, right?"

"Do what?"

"The combined fighting."

"What are you talking about?"

"You and Lucian were fighting through your body. You can only do that when you're merged. It's super dangerous to do that without control. Your canines were extended, and you were literally a horror movie's version of the wolfman, dude."

"I didn't even realize. I was too busy trying to push Lucian back."

"Yeah, you fully started your warrior level without any training. If your dad hadn't come out–"

"You would have stopped me."

"I don't think I could have. It goes against Rigby's nature to fight his alpha."

"I'm not alpha," I mumbled.

"I know, bro, but you should feel honoured. The wolves are already starting to treat you as such."

"I'm not ready to be alpha. Lucian isn't ready for it either."

"How is Lucian?" he asked cautiously.

"Down for the count."

"What on Earth happened?"

I looked up to judge his reaction. "He's ridiculously protective over Clem." His eyebrows shot right up, and his eyes went wide. "And before you start on the true mate bandwagon, it's not that. He feels a need to protect her because she's human. That's all. He's always been a hot head with an explosive temper."

"Okay, bro, if you say so. No more mentioning what I want to do to Clem when Lucian is around." He winked. I laughed. It was a hollow one that left a strange feeling bubbling in the pit of my stomach.

"Beer?" I asked with a cheeky smile, covering the anxious feeling that had manifested.

"Yeah. Let's go down to Lupus'."

CHAPTER 14

LIAM

RYAN and I nabbed a booth around lunchtime and ordered a couple of burgers with a side of Gary's infamous poutine. As soon as the beers flowed, we laughed and joked, and it was as if the fight at the training grounds never happened. Ryan's sister Sophie came in with a bunch of textbooks and one of her friends, Stacey. It was apparent they had come in to study together, but when Sophie noticed us sitting there, that plan hit a roadblock, and Sophie and Stacey joined us. The textbooks were pushed to the side and forgotten as the beer flowed.

Sophie was cute. She had light brown hair that waved into the middle of her back, blue eyes, and the warmest smile you'd ever seen. The light smattering of cinnamon-coloured freckles on her nose and over her shoulders popped against her suntanned skin under her white shoe-string camisole. She looked me over with those big blue doe-like eyes, but even I wasn't enough of a jerk to break the bro-code, no matter how hot Sophie was. Stacey on the other hand...

Stacey was a she-wolf I had noticed a few times in passing at university. She lived on campus and wasn't a member of my pack, so I didn't know much about her. She had short blonde ringlets that bounced around her shoulders and hazel eyes that were the colour of maple syrup with flecks of green and gold. Her mouth was thin, and her nose was narrow. She was petite and looked like I could break her just by hugging her too hard. She also possessed a wicked sense of humour and knew her sports. Especially hockey.

A COUPLE OF HOURS LATER, we were still at Lupus', laughing, drinking, and cheering as the lunch rush ended. My arm was casually resting on the booth seats behind Stacey, and I gently played with her blonde curls. Her hazel eyes would meet mine, and she would smile at me flirtatiously. I was listening as she and Ryan argued over hockey. His eyes never left her face, and his lip had curled upwards into a smile each time she got frustrated. The conversation was getting quite heated, and now and again, her eyes would flash with brown rings indicating her wolf was getting agitated. But she never once lost control, and her voice was full of humour the entire time.

"Don't argue with her, Ryan. She's going to be doing sports journalism when she graduates. Trust the woman's knowledge in statistics." Sophie laughed, then added, "which also means that she will probably go and interview players from all your favourite sports teams."

"Mate with me?" Ryan declared.

Stacey threw her head back and laughed. "Is that a proposal?"

"I'll give you all the pups you want. Just get me in to meet Markstrom."

"Wow, with an offer like that, how can I resist?" she said sarcastically, and her cheeks tinted with a gentle pink. Sophie was laughing and joined in on ribbing her brother's undying love for Markstrom and anything Calgary Flames, but Ryan wasn't perturbed.

"Seriously. Ditch the alpha-elect. He's a Canucks fan anyway," he begged Stacey.

I chuckled, throwing a toothpick at him.

———

I LEFT the men's room and returned to the bar area. Lucian was still passed out, and it made me a little nervous. I thought he would have woken up by now, especially since I was sitting next to two she-wolves that smelled damn edible, but he appeared to be enjoying his sleep.

Maybe Dad's command was too much? Maybe he's seriously hurt?

I reached back into my mind, trying to rouse him. It was like I was hitting a wall. I could only access him when we were both awake or asleep without being merged. I managed to stroke him earlier, but that was only because the survival instinct overrode everything else. He needed me, and I needed him at that moment. It was a nice glimpse of what it would be like if we merged. Now, it was as if a seventy-foot impenetrable wall had been erected around him.

I made my way over to the bar, deep in thought, worrying about my wolf, when a sweet voice from behind the bar revved my engines back to reality.

"What can I get you, Mister Nice Guy?" My eyes snapped up to spot Clem.

Her hair was tied roughly off her face in a ponytail, exposing her long creamy neck. Her turquoise eyes gleamed with happiness behind her frames, and her smile was radiant. She must have come in while I was in the restroom.

"You're working today?"

"Apparently." She nodded, looking around the bar. She flashed me another smile, her pearly whites gleaming. "What can I get ya?"

Lucian stretched and stirred in the back of my mind, but I was too busy focusing on the happy smile that Clementine was giving me.

"Four beers?" I said, tapping the beer tap. I seemed to have forgotten how to engage in conversation.

"Sure. I'll bring them over in a few."

I retreated to the booth and watched her for a few moments. She seemed to be brimming with confidence as she took clean glasses and began filling them. The girls were busy chatting with each other when I sat down.

"What's up?" Ryan mind-linked me.

I snapped my eyes to his. *"Really, for a guy who claims he's interested in Clem, you haven't notice her behind the bar?"* His eyes snapped over to the bar, and he grinned at me.

Clementine made her way across the room, balancing the beer on a tray expertly. Her t-shirt was ill-fitted, the fact emphasized by how she had tied the bottle-green apron.

"Hi. I have your beers."

Her eyes darted to Ryan before they found mine, and a small pink stain dusted her cheeks. Lucian started to wake, rumbling and stretching as he came forward.

"You're Clem, right?" Ryan asked.

Sophie's blue eyes were wide, and observing Clem like she was a zoo animal. Stacey took a beer and smiled softly at Clem.

"Uh, yeah. Hello," she said shyly as she put the other beers on the table.

I made the introductions. "This is Ryan, Sophie and Stacey."

"Hi," she repeated, looking at everyone in turn.

"I thought your first shift was tomorrow?" I asked, inhaling her intoxicating scent that seemed to overpower all others in the room. But at least I had finally managed to string together a sentence.

"It is officially, but Tina asked me to help out, and it's not like I have a life," she joked.

"Not yet, but you've just moved here," Ryan winked. "I'm sure your calendar will be full before you know it."

Lucian growled.

She shrugged. "I didn't really have a life before I moved here."

"Why not?" Ryan asked.

"I'm not exactly a social butterfly." She shrugged again. "Well, enjoy your drinks."

She walked back toward the bar, her cute ponytail swaying behind her and her perfect round ass distracting me further.

"Did you smell her?" Sophie whispered to Stacey.

Stacey nodded. "Yeah, she's a half-breed."

"Why aren't you freaking out?" she asked Stacey.

"I've met one before."

"You have?"

"Yeah. My mom."

My eyes snapped toward her with curiosity, and so did Sophie's. Ryan already appeared to be watching her attentively.

"Your mom is a half-breed?" he asked.

"She sure is. Grandpop was a wolf, and Grandma was a human. My mom was their only child. Mom turned when she was sixteen, and Grandpop was thrilled."

"It's so rare!" Sophie gushed. "How did your grandparents find out they were mates?" Her eyes went all large with a whimsical expression as if she was expecting a Hallmark story.

She shrugged. "They chose to be mates."

We all looked at her with the same shocked expression. A wolf chose to mate with a human? It was unheard of.

She sighed. "Grandpop found his true mate the moment

he turned twenty. She was a warrior in his pack. He never got a chance to complete the mate bond before their pack went to war with another. His true mate died in battle. He left the pack to grieve and find himself when he stumbled across my grandmother. She fell in love with him straight away. It was at least five years before he returned her affections and another five before they completed the mate bond." She smiled softly.

I looked back toward Clem, who was wiping down the bar with a cloth.

"It's amazing the bond took hold!" Sophie gushed romantically.

We all knew how incredibly rare it was to have a human mate, let alone the ability to complete the mate bond with one that was chosen over one that was destined. I didn't even know it was possible.

I looked over at Clem, now using a silver scoop to put ice into a small jug. She added two shots of liquor before pouring in a large serving of red wine, adding some citrus fruit, before filling it with pop from the tap.

"Yeah. They were lucky. Grandpop thinks it's because he never completed the mate bond the first time around."

We all sat in stunned silence for a few moments. I looked at Stacey, but before I could say anything, Ryan broke the silence. "That is incredible."

"Yeah, it is. So, that's why I'm used to being around a half-breed."

"Do you know any others?"

"No. Just my mom. And now I know Clem, I guess."

"Clem is human. Her brother has the wolf gene," I mumbled before taking a deep gulp of my beer.

"Are you sure? I thought I smelled wolf on her." Her eyes met mine, and I nodded.

"Me too, but Lucian says she has no wolf. It never manifested at sixteen. She's human."

Stacey's face went vacant for a few seconds as she talked to her wolf. "Wow. Sadie says the same thing. She has no wolf." She tilted her head curiously toward Clem, who was now shaking a silver cocktail shaker with such vigour that it made her boobs bounce in her shirt. Lucian grinned wolfishly as he watched on.

"Another round?" I asked. Or was that Lucian coming through again? It was hard to tell right then.

Before anyone could answer, I slid out of the booth and walked back up to the bar.

"Whatcha making?" I asked, smiling at her.

"Sex on the beach." She blushed and poured the peach-coloured cocktail into a tall glass.

Lucian wagged his tail happily. She walked to the end of the bar and handed the drink to a she-wolf before she returned to where I stood.

"Another round?" she asked.

"Actually, I would like your sex on the beach." Her turquoise eyes snapped to mine. I felt my face warm. *Did I just say that?* "Um, or any other cocktail you like to make," I recovered quickly. Lucian smirked.

"I make a really good Harvey Wallbanger."

"Sure, let's take four Wallbangers."

"Okay. I'll bring them over."

I nodded and walked away, feeling dismissed. "I got us cocktails," I announced to the table.

"Really?" Ryan asked.

"Yeah. Have you not noticed how many cocktails she's been making?"

"Can't say I have been watching her that *closely,"* he mind-linked. I scowled at him, and he grinned.

"You guys are game, right?" Sophie asked us.

"Sorry, what?" I asked half-distracted.

"Jason is having a party on Saturday to celebrate his twenti-eth. You guys have to come."

Twenty was a significant age for werewolves. It was the age you could find your mate, so we liked to celebrate it.

"We'll be there," Ryan answered as I resumed studying Clem.

She had loaded the cocktails and was making her way over. She placed the yellow cocktails on the table, sliding them to each of us.

"Hey, Clem. What are you doing Saturday night?" Ryan asked.

Lucian emitted a low growl. The man flicked his eyes over to me and grinned mischievously.

"Um, nothing. Why?"

"We're all going to a party. You should come." I rushed forward before Ryan could ask her to be his date.

Her turquoise eyes found mine, and the light pink tinge was back on her face. I held my breath and waited. And waited.

And waited.

"Okay. Sure. Sounds fun."

CHAPTER 15

CLEMENTINE

"Okay. Sure. Sounds fun." My heart thumped in my chest. *Did I just agree to go to a party?* I had never really been to a party before. *Shit. Why did I say this sounded like fun?* It sounded like the complete opposite to be honest.

I looked at the four different sets of eyes staring back at me. Grey, blue, hazel and finally, the warmest shade of brown I had ever encountered. Liam flashed me an excited smile, and I felt my lips form a grin and my face warmed. His smile was contagious. *He* was contagious.

"Okay, give me your number," Liam said, pulling out his phone. I shook myself out of my daze, and my already warm cheeks now felt like a furnace.

"S-sorry?" I stammered.

"Your phone number, so I can contact you. About the party."

"Oh, right." I nodded and wiped my hands on my apron before I picked up his phone and entered my digits.

I fumbled the number twice before I entered it correctly, saved it, then handed the device back to him. Our fingers touched briefly, and that weird electric sensation started again.

My eyes flashed to his. Had he felt it too? The gold flecks in his eyes seemed brighter for a moment.

Ring. Ring. I jumped at the sound of a phone ringing, only to realize it was mine. I pulled it out of my apron pocket and frowned as 'Dad' was displayed on the screen.

"Sorry, I have to take this," I murmured as I walked away. "Hi, Dad."

"Hi, sweetie. Just checking in. I should be finishing work around 3:30, and then I thought I would pick up Vinny and some take-out for dinner."

Crap! Dinner. Crap! The talk. "Uh, Dad, there's been a change of plans," I said, walking into the ladies' restroom for additional privacy.

"You have a hot date, eh?" he joked, not missing a beat.

I snorted. "No. Um, I've been called into work tonight."

"Oh, I thought you started tomorrow?"

"I do, but Tina needed me tonight."

"Okay, so the chat will have to wait until Saturday night, then. I won't see you Friday before you head to work, and I have a big job in Kempthorne on Saturday."

My face warmed, and I closed my eyes, resting my head against the wall of a cubicle.

"Uh, Dad, Saturday night doesn't work for me either."

"What do you mean?"

"Um, I've sort of been invited to a party." He went quiet, obviously waiting for the punchline. "Seriously."

"What party? Whose party?"

"I'm not sure," I said honestly.

"Who invited you?"

"Um, this guy Liam–"

"So, it's a date?"

"–and a bunch of his friends are going... What? No!" I blushed harder, mortified at my dad's comment.

There was a pause.

"Okay." He cleared his throat. "I'm glad to hear you are making friends, Clemmy."

Friends.

What a strange concept.

"I better get back to work. Are you sure it's okay that I go to this party on Saturday?"

"Clemmy, you're twenty years old. You can make that decision yourself."

"I know. I just mean that if you need me home–"

"Clemmy, go to the party. The talk can wait."

"Okay, I love you."

"I love you too. Now get back to work before they fire your ass." He hung up the phone with a chuckle.

I walked out of the bathroom and smashed into a hard body. My fingers went up to my nose as large hands attached themselves to my hipbones to steady me.

"Shit! Sorry, Clem." I looked up to find Liam.

Rubbing my nose, I scowled at him. "Liam, what are you doing skulking around the women's restroom?"

"I wasn't– I'm not–" he shook his head and started again. "I came to check on you to see if you're okay."

"Why wouldn't I be?"

"You seemed concerned. Your phone call."

"It was just my dad. Everything is fine." I shook my head and noticed Liam's hands were still on my hips. I blushed. "Um, Liam?" He looked at where my eyes were focused and quickly removed his hands. He cleared his throat and looked away. "Well, I better get back to work." I shuffled past him, and he followed me. Where I turned toward the bar, he returned to the booth and his friends.

I smiled at Kimmie, who was pouring a glass of wine behind the bar, then took my position, and started cutting some citrus fruit for more cocktails.

My phone pinged, and when I pulled it out of my apron pocket, to look, I saw:

UNKNOWN:

> I forgot to mention that these drinks are disgusting in our awkward hallway encounter. I think I'm going to stick to beer.

I looked up to see Liam grinning at me and shook my head. He winked, then returned to his conversation. Butterflies returned in my belly, and I felt myself grinning like an idiot.

"Stay away from Liam," Kimmie snarled as she put her glass on the round server's tray next to me.

"What?" I asked, shocked.

"He has a long line of girls after him, all who are much more worthy than you'll ever be." She smiled as she said this, but it oozed disingenuity. This girl was used to putting on pretences.

"I'm not after Liam." The words tasted bitter. "I promise."

She snorted and walked away to deliver the wine she'd just poured.

I stared after her, nonplussed.

As it hit happy hour, another waitress started her shift. She leaned over the top of the bar and stretched her arm out to me. "Hi, I'm Roman!" She smiled. "You must be the new girl in town."

"I'm Clem," I introduced myself, shaking her hand.

"I'm so excited to meet you!" She was bubbly and radiant with a glowing light brown complexion, dark eyes, and hair. "I met your brother too. Wow, he's an interesting character, eh?" When had she met my brother? How?

"How old are you?" I asked, and she chuckled, crinkles appearing around her dark almond-shaped eyes as she flashed me her white teeth.

"Seventeen. He's in my kid sister's class. Anywho! It's just hit four o'clock, so..." she flicked out her wrists and dramatically continued, "stations everyone!"

As if by magic, more people flooded into Lupus' and she grinned at me, then went to assist them. An hour later, I saw a beautiful redhead walk into the bar.

'Oh shit, she is pissed,' said the quiet voice in my head. I looked over at the booth where Liam and his friends sat. She hadn't seen him yet.

I pulled out my phone and quickly found the message he had sent me. I had to warn him.

CHAPTER 16

LIAM

MY PHONE BUZZED against the table. And I looked down at it.

CLEM:

911. ANGRY REDHEAD.

And it buzzed again a few seconds later.

CLEM:

Let me know if I need to create a diversion so
you can escape.

I looked up and over at Clem curiously, then saw who she was referring to. Cassie walked up to the bar and had just started conversing with Clem.

Lucian frowned and tuned our hearing over to listen in.

"Hi, what can I get you?" Clem asked politely.

"A glass of Sav Blanc and you out of my way."

"I'm sorry?"

"You're Clementine, right?"

Clementine picked up the bottle of white with poise as she gracefully poured the woman a glass of wine. "I am."

"Good." Cassie picked up the glass, took a small sip, and then threw the wine all over Clementine.

I snarled and jumped out of my seat, then was next to Cassie in a flash. "What the hell is going on?"

Clementine removed her glasses which were covered in wine. Her hair and face were soaked. Ryan was behind the bar before I could blink, getting Clementine a towel for her face and helping her wipe the mess off herself. I looked back to see the girls looking shocked. In fact, the whole bar looked dismayed.

"Cassandra?" I grabbed her arm and held it in a vice-like grip. "What the fuck is going on?"

"You left me in your bed this morning for this half-breed of a whore, that's what's going on!"

"I'm sorry... What?"

"You left me, and then I get a phone call saying you've been hanging out here all day with Clementine. That you invited her to go to a party with you."

"What the fuck, Cassie? What's it to you?"

The purple rings in her eyes flashed violently, and Ryan took the opportunity to step forward, tucking Clementine protectively behind him as he witnessed the insanity unfolding.

Clementine was beet-red, and I could smell her tears manifesting behind her eyes. Lucian snarled his protective anger.

"Excuse me," she murmured, feeling her way along the bar, and making her way out from the middle of chaos. Her glasses sat on the counter next to the bottle of wine she had just poured the drink from.

Lucian wanted to go after Clem, but I wasn't going to move. We needed to hear whatever bullshit Cassie was about to spew. Sophie made her way over to us. Her eyes flashed with green rings as she sized Cassie up and down. That was before she noticed Clem's glasses and picked them up. She indicated for Stacey to follow, and they both trailed Clem into the restroom.

"Cassie, Liam has been hanging out with me, Sophie and her friend Stacey all day." Ryan's voice was low and calm.

"Bullshit! Then why is he taking her to a party?"

"What are you? My keeper?" I snapped, crossing my arms angrily. "You're a good lay, Cassie. But that doesn't make you luna."

"Oh, what qualities does the half-breed have that make her a luna?"

"Well, for one, she doesn't lose her shit and throw glasses of wine on people for no reason. From what I do know about her, she'd do everything in her power to avoid conflict," I said, my tone dangerous and low.

"So, you admit it?"

"What?" I asked, genuinely confused.

"You're looking to mate with her."

"You're fucking delusional. I don't want to mate with anyone, Cassie. Not her, but certainly not you!" My growl rolled off my tongue with toxic precision.

Cassie made a whimpering sound. "You don't mean that." She placed a perfectly manicured finger on my folded forearm.

I glared at her. "The fuck I don't." Lucian pawed at the ground in my mind, agitated. "Get the fuck out." My wolf's ears were flat, and my eyes flashed with gold. I wasn't messing around. She needed to leave. Now.

Cassie's mouth opened and shut a few times before she turned on her heel and stalked out.

The deadly quiet bar started humming again, excitedly over what had just happened. I shook my head and watched the redhead storm away, Lucian growling at her with his head low and his hackles raised.

"This was the trouble I didn't want in my bar, Liam. She's going to have to go," Tina growled.

I hadn't noticed she'd come up behind me. Lucian snapped his head around at her.

"You can't be serious, Tina!" Ryan exclaimed. "Clem is innocent in all this. She was just minding her business and got a glass of wine thrown all over her."

"Because she's a half-breed. She's different. People will always treat her differently, Ryan. And I don't want my bar turning into the breeding zone for blood-hate." She looked at Ryan, who was still behind the bar, with a levelling look.

"You're going to punish Clem for being a half-breed?" I growled angrily.

She turned back to me. "What am I meant to do, Liam? This is my livelihood."

"Please, Tina. It was one delusional she-wolf. It won't happen again," I reasoned.

Lucian kept an ear for Clementine and grumbled at my diplomatic approach. Tina placed her fingers on the bridge of her nose between her eyes and huffed out in frustration. "The thing is, Liam, it *will* happen again. I know Clementine is your friend, but if you choose to stay friends with her, the hate will keep coming. You're the most eligible bachelor in town, and until you pick a mate, the she-wolves will get territorial over you. They'll continue to perceive her as a threat."

Ryan's eyes flashed with rage. "It's not her fault the she-wolves are nuts."

"It's not just the she-wolves, Ryan. It's every wolf. She's different. People are going to react."

"Fine, put Clem and me on the same shifts," he rumbled.

Tina's brows furrowed. "Excuse me?"

"Put Clem and me on the same shifts, and I'll watch out for her...and your livelihood," he sneered the last word.

Tina scoffed. "You want to be her bodyguard?"

"Sure, why not? She's kind of cute. Have you seen her eyes?"

he paused. "Have you seen that ass?" Lucian snarled in warning, and started to push himself forward, but Ryan just shook his head at me.

"Chill, dude! I'm just trying to help." Ryan mind-linked me. Lucian huffed and paced in my head, listening for a sign that Clementine was coming back.

"Fine! I'm not happy about it, but fine!" Tina stormed away. She wasn't the only one angry. Ryan was, so was I, and Lucian was barely holding it together.

Ryan sighed. "Well, that was an interesting turn of events."

I nodded, afraid to speak. My hands had started to burn and itch. I looked down and saw my hair thickening. Ryan noticed too.

"Dude, calm."

"I'm trying, man, but Lucian needs to–"

"Lucian needs to chill the fuck out. You're in control here."

I shook my hands, trying to stop Lucian from charging forward. I couldn't see my eyes right now, but I bet they were looking feral and animalistic.

"How about you go check on Clem? I'm pretty sure she needs you right now."

Lucian stopped forcing me to change and tilted his head at Ryan, then toward the restroom doors. He whimpered, and I gave Ryan a grateful smile before heading that way.

I stood outside the ladies' room door and knocked quietly. "Clem? Clementine, are you okay?"

The door opened, and Sophie and Stacey nodded before walking past me, heading into the main area. Clementine came out of the restroom next, her face bright and fresh, and her turquoise eyes were back behind their frames. I could smell the traces of tears that she had washed away.

"You know, when I said, 'create a diversion,' that isn't what I meant." She coughed a laugh.

Lucian huffed at her dry humour.

"I'm sorry that happened to you."

"It's fine. It's just a bit of wine," she lied.

I reached out without realising it and placed my arm around her. She folded herself into my chest, and Lucian rumbled happily. Her honeysuckle and pear scent mixed with the wine's sweet aroma, but it wasn't unpleasant. It seemed to sedate Lucian; he was finally calm.

After a breath, she pulled away, more tears threatening to fall. "Honestly, I'm fine. And I better go talk to Tina."

She took another deep breath and made her way around me.

"Clementine," I said. She stopped and looked back at me expectantly. I had no idea what I wanted to say to her. "I…am sorry about Cassie. That was unfair for her to do that to you. I'm allowed to have friends," I struggled out. She gave me a single nod. "She won't hassle you again." She gave me another. "We're still on for Saturday night, right?"

Her turquoise eyes snapped to mine. "I don't think that's a good idea," she mumbled, looking down at her fidgeting fingers. A nervous habit it seemed.

My heart fell to the pit of my stomach, but I pushed. "Of course, it's a good idea." I smirked, covering my disappointment. "How else are you going to meet people in town?"

"Well, if I manage to keep this job, they will all eventually come to me."

"Please don't back out." The words tumbled out of my mouth before I could rein them in.

Her eyes found mine, her mouth opening and shutting as she struggled to find a way to respond to my plea.

"Make it seem like she's doing you a favour," Lucian suggested.

"Come on. I don't want to go to this party either. Ryan wants to, and he's dragging me along. But once we're there, he'll hit on anything with a pulse and a nice ass. I need someone to keep me company while he makes an idiot of himself. Please don't make me go alone."

She looked directly at me, her eyes intense and curious. Finally, after what felt like an eternity, she nodded. "Okay."

I followed as she walked back down the corridor, giving her little comfort by touching her elbow with my fingers. She sighed when she saw Tina standing at the office door expectantly.

"You'll be fine. It wasn't your fault," I murmured.

She gave me a slight nod and made her way to the office, shutting the door behind her. I turned and walked up to the bar.

"How's our girl?" Ryan asked, pouring me a beer as I sat on a barstool. Sophie, Stacey and their textbooks were gone, as were many patrons. Lupus' seemed almost empty.

"Holding it together," I mumbled.

"How's Lucian?" he asked.

I felt back toward my wolf. He was now calm and content, his tongue lolling out the side of his mouth happily.

"Drugged up like a looney," I muttered.

"Huh?" Ryan furrowed his eyebrows at me.

"He's okay," I clarified, not wanting to get into a conversation with Ryan about my wolf's apparent obsessive issues. I didn't need him to start psychoanalysing my neurotic wolf or me.

"Thank you for taking over behind the bar," Clementine said as she returned to work, her honeysuckle and pear scent wafting over me.

"No problem." He made no effort to move and smiled at her as he started making a rum and coke for someone.

"You shouldn't be serving alcohol, considering you've been drinking all afternoon."

Ryan cracked a grin. "Don't worry about it. I do it all the time." He winked, and I felt uneasy as I noticed a pink tinge highlight her cheeks.

She gave him a confused expression. Werewolves didn't tend to get drunk at the same rate humans did. It was something to do with the super-fast metabolism and healing properties that came with being a wolf.

"Honestly, it takes a lot of alcohol to get me to the stage where I'm a danger to myself or others."

I laughed and shook my head. "Yeah. You can witness that on Saturday night. He'll be dangerous to anyone with a double-x chromosome and a nice ass."

Ryan grabbed a piece of ice and threw it at me, laughing.

"I'm still not sure it's a good idea," she murmured.

Ryan and I heard her, though.

"Of course, it's a good idea. It's the best idea," he exclaimed. "But–"

"No buts! You're coming!" he said forcefully, and she gave him a small but genuine smile that made my heart fall into my stomach for the second time today.

CHAPTER 17

CLEMENTINE

My Friday shift went surprisingly well. And by well, I meant that not one angry patron threw a glass of wine on me. I took that as a win!

Ryan happened to be working as well and joined me behind the bar. I could appreciate Ryan's good looks now that I had no distractions. His eyes were a crystal grey that was ringed in a soft brown. His nose was sharp and angular, and his lips were thin. He had a strong jawline that was cleanly shaven and very straight white teeth. His smooth brown hair had just been cut by his mother, who was complaining it was getting too long— or so he had told me—and was now sitting under his earlobes at the base of his neck rather than at the tops of his shoulders. I never noticed how large he was until I had to stand next to him. He had to be well over six feet tall, and, as my father would say, built like a brick shithouse. I remember his mother saying he was a part of a sports team, and it made me wonder what the game was, because honestly, no average men were this size.

He may have been big, but he made me smile and laugh. He was like a big kid and super fun to work with. I didn't make friends easily, but like Liam, Ryan was easy to get along with.

But I wasn't stupid enough to let my guard down. I could never let my guard down. Not again.

Ryan's sister Sophie was also really lovely. Especially when she and Stacey returned my glasses and found me bawling my eyes out in the bathroom after Liam's girlfriend threw a drink at me. They helped me wash my face and chatted with me nonstop about random stuff to take my mind off what had just happened.

They had called her a bitch and told me she was unhinged. But that's all they said about Cassie. When they asked me if I was okay, I lied, telling them I was fine when, deep down, I was battling with reticent memories of being bullied my entire life by girls who looked just like Cassie.

They were curious about me, trying to get me to open up, but I remained mostly quiet, protecting myself. They continued to chat, gossip, and laugh as though I had been one of their girlfriends, not the bartender who just got wine in her eyes. That's what they were curious about the most—my eyesight.

"Have you ever thought of wearing contacts?"

"No, the thought of putting my finger in my eye grosses me out," I said, forcing a laugh.

"You're so pretty, though. Your eyes are such a beautiful colour, and you hide them behind those thick frames."

"I don't hide behind my glasses. I need them."

"Don't get me wrong. You're pretty either way. But damn girl, I wish I had an eye colour like yours." I smiled crookedly at Sophie's compliment, and the conversation soon moved on.

While we were in the washroom, I could hear heated discussions around the bar and frowned. This argument couldn't be good for business. I was going to lose my job. I was going to lose the first thing that had made me feel normal since Mom's death.

Then I heard a knock at the door and smelled a woodsy

smell that seemed to calm me. When the door opened, I noticed Liam standing there, looking embarrassed and worried and what could be perceived as relief.

When Liam had pulled me into his arms for a hug, I felt a whoosh of warmth run over me as I basked in his scent. I had never noticed it before, but he smelled of cedar and something spicy, similar to all-spice or cloves. Right then, I decided I liked his cologne. But remembering Cassie's reaction and the promise to myself to never let my guard down, I slowly and reluctantly took a step away.

Tina was surprisingly calm about what had happened. After asking me if I was alright, she told me to return to work. There was no mention of firing me, no warnings or anything. She quietly returned to her schedules, and I returned to the bar.

***

SATURDAY ROLLED AROUND, and I woke around ten in the morning, and started my chores around the house. After putting on a load of laundry, I straightened my cramped little bedroom, then made my way to the bathroom, which didn't need a clean. It required a deep burial or an exorcism. Maybe both.

I started to clean the shower, singing along to a random Spotify playlist that was playing out of my Airpods. It didn't matter how often I scrubbed the shower grout; the stale yellow colour would never sparkle or return to its pristine white. Nor would the spots of mould disappear. God, this place was a dump. Dad had sold our beautiful apartment and bought this shithole. I closed my eyes as the ammonia, and pine-scented cleaner invaded my nostrils. The sound of the washing machine dinging on my second load of laundry brought me out of my depressing reverie. After removing the salmon-pink rubber gloves I wore, I stomped out of the bathroom and proceeded to hang my clothes on the clothesline outside.

I walked into the kitchen and found Vinny having breakfast at—I peered down at my watch—*One in the afternoon?*

He'd been taking his grounding seriously and was barely leaving his room. He stunk to high heaven too, and he looked frayed around the edges. I didn't even want to know what he'd been doing in his bedroom all morning.

"If you're going to shower today, you want to rinse off the bottom first. I was attacking it with bleach, and it could do with another rinsing."

He grunted in response.

"Fine. Burn your feet."

"It's already burning my nostrils," he complained.

I rolled my eyes. "It's not that bad."

He wiped his nose as if it was irritated and glared at me.

"Do you want to shower in a place that's growing its own ecosystem?" I asked. I looked at his greasy wheat-coloured hair and grimaced. "In fact, are you going to shower at all? Ever again?"

He responded by flashing me both middle fingers before retreating to his room.

I MUST HAVE TRIED on every item of clothing I owned. Nothing worked. My clothes piled high on my bed as I tried on a black wrap dress next.

Way too much cleavage.

I tried in vain to shove my boobs further into my dress, collapsing on my bed and throwing an arm over my eyes in despair.

During my project-runway rendition, I almost texted Liam half a million times to tell him I was sick and had to cancel. My symptoms ranged from strep throat to the bubonic plague. My thumbs hovered over his text window, but I couldn't bring myself to write anything.

I heard a knock at my door.

"Come in," I groaned exasperatedly.

Dad entered. "I thought you might have had a boy in here with all the groaning that was going on."

"Firstly, gross. Secondly, I can't find anything to wear."

"What's wrong with what you have on?"

"Really?" I glared at him.

He looked genuinely confused.

I sighed in frustration. Where was my mom when I needed her? "You know, we could still have that chat. That way, I can ring Liam and tell him that a family emergency has come up."

"You're using your dad to get out of going to a party?" he mused.

"Dad, you're *supposed* to stop your daughter from going to a party, getting drunk and making appalling decisions. It's written in the dad-manual."

"Hmm." He scratched his chin in a fake ponder. "Must have lost my copy. Thankfully I have a copy of 'How to Trust Your Daughter's Decisions' in my back pocket."

He started pawing at the back of his jeans, pulled out an imaginary book, pretended to turn a few pages, and said, "Ah! Here it is." He cleared his throat. "Make sure you tell your daughter that it's okay to be nervous and that she looks good in everything she wears. See? Stop stressing. It also says to tell your daughter to take a deep breath and have fun. Then there's a gooey bit that instructs me to tell you how much I love you, but I think we can bypass that." I rolled my eyes at him as he smirked. "It also says to take a jacket to cover yourself up." He winked. I threw a pillow at him, and he chuckled as he dodged it gracefully.

"Seriously, though. You said you wanted to chat. The suspense is killing me."

"Nope. I won't be the reason you don't go to this party." He snapped his mouth shut. "However, I will use this time to chat with your brother."

I frowned. "Then I need to be here to referee."

"Nope. I'll be chatting with him about all sorts of stuff you probably don't want to hear." Dad smiled suggestively.

Gross. "I think I would rather go to a party than listen to conversations about socks and dirty magazines."

As he left, Dad laughed and told me to have fun.

I got off my bed and dug around in a cane basket on top of my dresser that held the minuscule amount of makeup I owned. If I was going to a party, I might as well look like I was making an effort. I shook the bottle of foundation before I pumped it onto my fingertips. It sputtered a small amount, and I blended it in as best I could. I frowned at the liquid eyeliner as I gave it a shake too. Carefully, I swiped my upper lid with the felt tip. I blinked and frowned as the liner repeated itself onto the arch of my eye socket. Attempting to rub it off with my finger, the black smeared.

Crap!

Fetching a Q-tip, I wet it with my mouth, then ran over my smeared liner with it to clean it up.

Right, that kind of looks better, I suppose.

I repeated this process with my other eye, learning my lesson about blinking too quickly. After a minute, I blinked, and thankfully, no liner smudged. I took out a very old mascara and frowned at the clumps on the brush. Flicking it over my lashes, the mascara barely stuck, and what had was clumpy and awful. I managed to smooth it out as much as possible with the mascara brush, then put my glasses back on and dug into my cane basket once more. I pulled out a strawberry-flavoured lip balm known to give my lips a dusting of pink. After I combed my hair, it had me smiling happily as it bounced nicely around my shoulders.

Sighing to myself, I picked up my lacey white cardigan and threw it over my shoulders, then put sandals on my feet as I heard a knock at the front door. I put my phone in my bag, and walked to the front door, where my dad was chatting with Liam on the front step.

"Hi, Liam," I said shyly. This was so embarrassing.

"Hi, Clem." He flashed me an award-winning smile. His cedar and all-spice cologne was super strong, making me think he must have only just spritzed himself before leaving to pick me up. It was more intoxicating than overpowering, and I felt myself blush as I remembered I had enjoyed his cologne a little too much the last time I'd seen him.

Biding my father goodbye, we made our way to Liam's Honda Civic, and he opened my door for me like a gentleman. I smiled shyly at him as he closed the door and ran around the front of the car before hopping into the driver's seat.

"Are we picking up Ryan, Sophie and Stacey?" I asked, trying to fill the awkward silence.

"Nope. There's not enough room in my car, so they are meeting us there."

I looked at the three seats in the back and frowned. Even with Ryan being massive, he could have taken the front seat, and I could have squeezed in the back with the other girls.

We drove in the opposite direction of town. Weaving in and out of streets and going to an area I had never been to. I could hear the music from a few streets away and wondered if the police would shut this down before it even started.

All too soon, Liam pulled over and grinned. "Are you ready?"

Oh shit!

Was I?

CHAPTER 18

LIAM

I OPENED Clem's door and held out my hand for her.

"No backing out now, Clementine," I growled playfully.

She gingerly took my hand and frowned before letting go and stared at the house as if it was a murder location in a horror movie. I smiled and shrugged my shoulder in the direction of the house, making her reluctantly take a step toward the party.

It didn't take us long to find Ryan, who was cracking a beer and chatting with another warrior in the squad. He did a double-take when he saw Clementine.

"Wow." He wolf-whistled. "Look how well she scrubs up! Damn, girl!"

A splash of pink coloured her cheeks, and she looked mortified. Her dress was amazing; there was no doubt about that. It was a crisp black number that wrapped and hugged her curves, and sat just above her knees, showing off her stunning legs. She looked fantastic, and Lucian had been yipping and panting in my head since the moment I saw her when I arrived to pick her up. However, I didn't think she wanted to draw attention to herself quite like she was.

"Tone it down a smidge," I mind-linked Ryan.

He looked at me, confused, then back to Clementine, who was looking at her feet and counting slowly under her breath.

"You look very nice tonight, Clemmy," he amended and smiled softly. His words were almost a whispering caress meant only for her.

She eventually brought her eyes up and gave a small, shy smile and a nod of appreciation.

Lucian grumbled unhappily.

THE PARTY WAS PUMPING, and Clem soon loosened up a little as she mostly chatted with Sophie. I kept an eye on her from afar as she participated in a few games of Flip-cup and beer pong. A genuinely large smile radiated on her face.

Lucian wanted to be attached to her hip the entire night, but I convinced him that she needed to spread her wings and socialize. He only conceded when I told him that we wouldn't be far, and not only would we be keeping an eye on her, but so would Sophie, Ryan, and Stacey—if those two could get past their blatant flirting. He grunted in response and paced my head anxiously.

"Are you having fun?" I asked Clem when I walked over to the keg.

She was pumping beer into her cup and dancing to the beat of the music, glowing with happiness and potentially a little drunk. Lucian commented to me about humans being unable to hold their liquor and that we'd have to keep an even closer eye on her as the night wore on. I rolled my eyes at him.

"Loads," she beamed. "I didn't think I would fit in at this party, but everyone is being so nice. And it turns out I'm surprisingly good at beer pong."

"Is that a challenge?" I asked, grinning at her happiness. It was cute and contagious.

"I don't think you want to take me on. I'm dominating the leader board." She pointed to a blackboard, where I noticed her name was indeed at the top. The dot above the 'I' of her name was shaped as a small heart, but I highly doubted she had written her name like that herself.

My smile grew wider. She was making friends and turning herself into a legend. Tina was so wrong about how the pack would react to her. Lucian wagged his tail at her happiness.

"Oh, I love this song!" Stacey exclaimed, and before I could say anything, she was dragging Clementine by the hand to the makeshift dancefloor.

I observed Clementine for a few moments, surprised at her rhythm. Her hips swayed in an erotically-hypnotic way, and I felt my mouth go dry. I needed another drink.

For someone as shy and awkward as Clementine, she was bursting with the power of a phoenix at this party. She had a hidden fire and passion that made me think of how Ryan had once made an unsolicited comment about shy girls having an inner freaky side.

"Did you have to remind me of that?" Lucian growled.

"You know he was kidding. You were out of order attacking my best friend like that," I growled back.

"I already said I was sorry. But there is something about her–"

"Yeah, I know." I rolled my eyes at him.

I made my way to the hard-liquor table to get something stronger than beer. I smiled as I passed Ryan; he was leaning with one shoulder against a wall and hitting on another she-wolf. I turned to give him shit about x-chromosomes and a pulse when I noticed that he was hitting on Stacey, and she was lapping it up, putting her hand on his shoulder and laughing hard.

Wait! Wasn't Stacey with Clementine on the dance floor?

I turned back to the dancefloor, and I couldn't see her. I

peered at the beer pong table, and she wasn't there either. The Flip-cup table was empty.

Where the fuck is she? Lucian growled my exact thought.

I made a point of sniffing the air. Her scent was strong and helped me pinpoint the direction she had headed in, so I followed it. Lucian pawed anxiously. I felt my hands start to burn as the hair began to thicken.

"We'll find her, Lucian. She's still here. She's in the house," I growled.

I followed her scent to the hallway. She had probably just gone to the bathroom. Yeah, her aroma was more intense here. I knocked on the bathroom door. No answer.

"Clementine?" I called through the wooden surface.

"Bust it down!" Lucian commanded.

Before I could stop him, my shoulder rammed the door as my fingers pushed the door handle down hard, breaking the lock. I almost fell into the room but stopped short when I saw Clementine passed out, head against the bathtub.

"Clementine!" I grabbed her face to make her look at me, and she groaned and hit my arm lethargically. "Clem, open your eyes," I commanded, giving her a gentle shake.

She made a mewling noise and fell forward into my chest. I sniffed her honeysuckle and pear scent swirling around me, but this time it didn't calm Lucian. This time it made him angrier. He was vibrating with rage. I'd missed something the first time around, so I sniffed again. There was something bitter coiling in her aroma. I saw the empty cup crumpled underneath her and gave it a sniff. The smell of beer was there, but so was a trace of the bitter coiling fragrance that assaulted my nostrils. I sniffed again.

Fuck me! She's been drugged. Oh shit!

I stood up and lifted her into a bridal carry. She weighed almost nothing in my arms. A warmth spread through me as I carried her through the party. Lucian was of two minds: he wanted to go around sniffing out the culprit who supplied the roofies, but he also wanted to get Clem out of there.

"What happened to Clem?" people asked as I proceeded toward the front door, and my car. I ignored them all and opened the passenger seat, sliding her in and snapping her seatbelt into place.

Shit, where's her bag? She had a purse, right?

"Sophie." I mind-linked.

"What's up, Liam?"

"Did Clem have a purse?"

"Yeah. I have it with my stuff."

"Can you bring it to my car?"

"Um...sure?"

"Quickly," I barked.

Within minutes, Sophie came down the driveway with Clem's handbag. I looked inside and found that her wallet, phone and keys were all there.

At least the fuckers didn't steal from her.

I opened the passenger door and placed the handbag on her lap.

Sophie spotted Clem passed out, and her eyes went wide. "What on Earth happened?"

"Not a word to anyone!" I growled.

"She doesn't look okay, Liam." She was extremely concerned.

"She isn't. Someone slipped something in her drink."

"What the hell? When?"

"No idea."

"Do you want me to find out who?"

I couldn't decide. On one hand, I wanted to know who had

done this, but I also didn't want rumours flying around about Clem more than they already were. There was merit to have all the evidence, however. That way, I could decide what to do with it later. I would need to tell her, of course, and I would need to find some way to convince her not to press charges but to let Pack Law deal with it without telling her what we were.

"Be discreet."

She nodded solemnly. "I will."

"Tell Ryan I will text him."

She nodded again. "Sure."

"Thanks, Sophie." I gave her a brotherly kiss on the forehead before I slid into the driver's seat and planted my foot against the accelerator.

I PULLED up to the pack house and parked my car. There was no way I was taking Clem home like this. Firstly, her dad would kill me. Secondly, Lucian wouldn't let her out of his sight. And thirdly, her dad would kill me. It bore being numbered twice, trust me.

I pulled her into my arms, tucking her bag onto her lap as I lifted her out of my car. I enjoyed her scent, even if it was contaminated with Rohypnol. I kicked open my bedroom door and placed her gently onto the sheets. I put her bag on the floor next to the bedside table, then removed her glasses and admired how her long dark eyelashes fluttered over the tops of her cheeks. Her pouty mouth was pressed into a severe line. The flush of pink from the alcohol she'd been drinking—and maybe the drug—marred her complexion. I touched her face gingerly, testing for a temperature. Slight tingles ran up my fingertips. Was that a sign of a fever or the drug?

I took off her sandals and smiled at her elegantly painted toenails. I hadn't noticed before, but they were a bright lime green. She was like the shy, quiet girl-next-door with an alter ego who was fun and spontaneous and maybe a little rebellious. Perhaps this was her way of letting her alter ego out, even if it was just for a little bit.

Lucian pressed forward, watching her, anxiously whimpering.

"She's going to be okay," I murmured aloud.

"Someone could have hurt her."

"But they didn't."

He whimpered again.

I took off my shoes and shirt and placed them on the side chair in my room, then watched her for a few more moments. Her breathing was slow and steady. Her heart was beating normally.

She's okay.

I left briefly, racing to the laundry to grab a bucket, then to the kitchen to grab a glass of water, digging around in the drawers until I found a very old and unused bottle of Advil. I returned to the bedroom to find Clem hadn't moved. Not even an inch. No, I lied; her lips were now relaxed and pouty again in an almost smile.

I placed the glass of water and Advil on the bedside table next to her glasses, and the bucket on the floor in case she needed to vomit. Then, I gingerly lay down on the bed next to her.

Lucian rumbled contently as her scent enveloped us again.

I watched the rise and fall of her chest with every breath she took. A round medallion was around her neck and sat awkwardly on her creamy cleavage. I looked at her necklace closely. It wasn't just a medallion. It was a moon. She was wearing a full moon around her neck.

How strange.

I didn't want it to choke her, so I carefully took it off and realized the back had an inscription.

Love conquers all.

I leaned over, put it next to her glasses, and then snuggled back down next to her. She sighed in her sleep and rolled into me. My heart stopped briefly, and Lucian got his dopamine fix as he looked at her in amazement. After a minute, I put my arm around her and smiled.

We'd kept her safe.

CHAPTER 19

CLEMENTINE

THAT DAMN WOLF dream woke me again, but I didn't open my eyes. I felt like a fire-poker had been shoved through my frontal lobe. Trying to put my hand to my head, I noticed it was trapped by something heavy. I tried again. Then I became aware of the heat and the comforting smell of cedar and all-spice. My eyes snapped open, and even though the light hurt them, I turned my head and looked directly at Liam, who was fast asleep and snoring softly. His legs and arms had me encased. I gazed at him for a few minutes. His face was soft and relaxed, and his long eyelashes fluttered as he dreamed.

My logical brain suddenly interrupted my thoughts.

What the hell am I doing in bed with Liam?

The pain in my head intensified as I shoved him off me and sat up.

What in the actual fuck? I put my hand to my forehead as the gentle snoring stopped.

"You're awake," a groggy voice said. I looked down at Liam, and his mocha eyes were intense.

"Liam," I said. "Why am I in your bed?" I assumed it was his bed as I looked around the room, not having recognized it. It was simplistic with a white Ikea dresser and a matching desk that had textbooks stacked on top of it. I could see the fine print down the spines that read, *Economical Distribution, Principles of Economics* and *Calculus – Third Edition*.

"Um…" he seemed to struggle with words.

Nervousness ran through my body as I turned back to look at him. "Liam, did you–? I mean, did we–?" I pointed to myself, then gestured to his naked torso, trying not to admire his washboard abs and the smattering of dark-blond chest hair.

His eyes went wide. "God, no! I would never take advantage of you like that!" He looked appalled. "You're fully clothed. And look…" He threw back the covers to where he wore the same black jeans he had on last night. "I'm dressed too."

I blushed at seeing his Adonis belt disappearing into the top of his jeans, then groaned into my hands.

"Oh, my head!" I had a killer hangover.

I thought back to how much alcohol I had drunk. I know I was feeling the tiddly first stages of drinking, but I was nowhere near drunk.

Or had I been?

I tried to figure out the last thing I remembered: dancing, but then everything after that became fuzzy.

"What the hell happened?"

"There's water and Advil on the bedside table for you," he said.

I looked over and took the glass, removing the cap and gulping a couple of the pills down. I hadn't noticed how dry my mouth was until I started drinking. I downed the entire contents and returned the cup to the table.

"So, um, what do you remember?" he asked.

"Not much. I remember dancing and laughing. Beer pong. People were being nice."

"Do you remember anyone slipping anything into your drink? Or giving you a drink that you didn't ask for?"

"No– wait, what?" My head was foggy as I tried to decipher his words. "Wait, what are you saying?"

"I found you on the bathroom floor," he growled. "Someone slipped you something."

An icy chill went down my spine. "What? Who?"

"I don't know, but I swear I'll find out." Panic raced through my body. No way someone had drugged me. There was just... no way. "And when I do, that person is dead."

"No." I shook my head slowly, trying to slow down my heart rate. "Just leave it."

"What do you mean?" His brows furrowed in confusion.

"I don't want to know."

"You don't want to know who drugged you?" He scowled.

Panic was stampeding through my blood. He would never understand. "No. I want to forget it. Just, don't go digging around. It'll make it worse. Trust me."

"Clementine–"

"I said no, Liam!" my tone brokered no argument.

He shut his mouth and slowly nodded his head. I looked away from his heated gaze, knowing he wanted to say more.

"So," I said, trying to break the sudden tension. "Great party, huh? Let me guess; this is the first time you've ever slept with a girl. And by sleep, I mean sleep."

He rolled his eyes and scoffed. "Excuse me. I'm Mister Nice Guy. Remember?"

I smiled at his feigned hurt expression. "Do you make a habit of taking home comatose girls?"

He shrugged at me and gave me a playful wink. "Only ones with beautiful eyes."

I rolled my eyes, and said, "Smooth," even as my heart gave a slight tug.

"Are you okay? I know waking up in my bed must be a little disorienting."

"I'll have you know; I've woken up in a guy's bed before," I said unnecessarily. Internally, I groaned. *Why do I feel so defensive?* He was just looking out for me. He'd been a decent guy, taking me home when he found me unconscious, then putting me to bed and getting me Advil and water. *And look, there's even a bucket!*

"Have you now?" His eyebrows furrowed. "Which guy has had the pleasure of waking up next to you?" There was a dangerous edge to his voice, and my eyes snapped to his. The gold flecks around his irises were prominent, and I swear they moved.

Naturally, I reached out to put my glasses on, and I froze with my hands on the plastic frames. My hungover brain seemed to connect the dots much slower than usual. I could *see* his room! I could see his room *without* my glasses on! I slowly put the glasses up to my eyes, and all the colours and shapes blurred.

"What the fuck?" I swore, jumping out of bed as quick as lightning.

"Clem, what's the matter?" Liam asked, his eyes wide.

"No. I must be dreaming. There's no way! It's not possible!" I started to rationalize out loud, "Yeah, dreaming. That's the reason I've woken in Liam's bed. That's the reason I can see his sexy-as-sin body. That's the only logical explanation, and when I wake up, I'll be in bed in my own bed," I rambled as I paced his bedroom floor.

I never noticed Liam getting out of bed and was now calling my name repeatedly. He placed two giant hands on my upper arms and looked directly into my eyes. "Clementine!" he snarled.

I felt all the colour drain from my face as I took in the rough facial hair, the strong jaw, and the very straight nose before me.

"What the hell is going on?" I asked Liam quietly.

"You tell me. You're the one acting like a crazy person!"

I shook my head in a panic. Liam reached out to pull me into a hug, and I rejected his comfort. That's not what I needed. What I needed was to escape.

"I've got to go," I said, picking up my purse where I hastily deposited my now-useless glasses before slipping my sandals onto my feet.

"What do you mean?" he asked. "What's happened? Clem!"

I threw open the bedroom door and ran straight out, down the hallway, to the kitchen.

Where the hell is the front door?

Quickly locating it, I spun and gave Liam one last look, which I hoped expressed my apology rather than my fear, and I dashed out of the house.

I hastened down the gravel driveway and pulled my phone out, jabbing at Dad's name before placing it to my ear.

"Pick up! Pick Up! Pick Up!" I commanded at the ringing, rushing toward the road. I had no idea where I was. "Pick up!" I shrieked.

"Well, that's a nice way to greet your father." His tone was amused.

"Dad!" I cried.

"Clementine. What's wrong?" Ah, the protective father he became.

"I need you to come get me, but I don't know where I am."

"Are you safe?"

"I think so, but I need– I need–"

"It's okay, Clemmy, you need to stop–"

"I can't stop, Dad."

"Okay, don't stop. Just keep moving. I'll find you. I promise."

I finally made it to the road and turned left. I don't know why that direction seemed like a good idea, but that's the way my feet and instincts took me. It was like an unheard voice was telling me to do so. I kept walking fast, and I swear I smelled my dad's truck within ten minutes. The soothing scent of gasoline, tools and leather mixed with fresh pine that I've associated with him. It's been that way since we moved here, and he had started chopping firewood. I spotted Dad's slate truck coming toward me and waved. He was about a kilometre and a half away.

"Are you okay?" he asked as soon as he'd come to a stop.

I couldn't speak. I just nodded.

He spun the truck around and drove back toward the house.

"You need to talk to me, Clem," Dad said as he pulled into the driveway.

"Something is happening to me," I murmured.

"What?"

"Dad, I think you need to take me to the doctor," I whispered super quietly, but sure enough, Dad heard me.

"Why do you need to go to the doctor, Clem?" He took my hand, and I looked up into his eyes which were full of concern. "Did something...did somebody assault you last night?"

My eyes went wide, and I shook my head hard. "No, Dad! No!" I cried aghast.

Relief washed over his face as he pulled me into his arms. He closed his eyes in silent prayer of thanks before opening them and looking at me again. Then he released me from the hug. He waited for me to speak.

I tried to find the words to tell him. I didn't know where to start.

"Dad, my eyes... I can see," I whispered. He tilted his head, studying me. "I think my JMD is gone," I spoke about my juvenile macular degeneration condition.

He cupped my jaw and looked at my eyes closely. I could see the silvers of his brighten. "Y-you can see? No more blurry lines or dark shadows?"

"No more Stargardt disease," I confirmed. "But that's impossible, isn't it?"

He seemed to be trying to choose his next words carefully. "Not impossible, honey. Have you noticed anything else?"

"Anything else? You mean that's not enough?"

"Have you noticed a voice in your head, a finer sense of smell, or a really good sense of hearing?"

"I don't have schizophrenia, Dad. It's just unexplained good eyesight!" I shook my head in confusion and was surprised that my dad wasn't racing me off to the doctor. I thought about his question again. "I think my hearing has been wonky. I swear, I keep hearing things I shouldn't be able to hear," I mumbled, and he nodded, giving me a coy smile. "What's wrong with me, Dad?"

"Nothing is wrong. I promise you." He opened the truck door and stepped out onto the driveway. I followed him out of the vehicle. "You remember how I said I wanted to have a chat with you?" I nodded. "Well, this is what I wanted to talk to you about. Sort of..." he trailed off and seemed to get stuck in his head, his expression vacant.

"Dad?"

"Yes. Right. Um. Come sit down, eh." He entered the house through the mudroom door, removed his boots, and indicated for me to have a seat at the kitchen table. He pulled out a jar of instant coffee and made us two cups before joining me.

"There's something you don't know about me. Something that I've been keeping from you and your brother. Your mother and I decided it would be for the best, but then your brother started to show signs, and I needed to get him here and teach him, but your mom was sick and–" my father rambled.

"Dad! Just tell me!"

He nodded and took a deep breath. "This town isn't just the town I grew up in. This town is filled with a pack of werewolves."

I snorted into a fit of giggles. "Wait. What?"

"Your brother and I are werewolves," he stated calmly. "As is everyone else in this town."

I stared at him and tried to decipher what he was saying. He couldn't be serious.

Is Dad having a mental breakdown? "What do you mean?" I asked. My hands gripped the warm mug, trying to use the heat as an anchor.

"I mean, I have a wolf spirit that allows me to shape-shift into a wolf. Your brother will get one when he turns sixteen. He's already showing signs of it manifesting–"

I interrupted jokingly. "You turn into a wolf on the full moon? Like something out of a TV show?" This had to be a ploy to cheer me up.

"I don't need to turn on a full moon. I've merged with Perseus, but any unmerged wolf will have to turn on a full moon."

My hangover was pounding at my head again. I was exhausted, and Dad wasn't making any sense. I couldn't tell if he was joking or being serious. But if he was being serious–

"What the fuck are you talking about? Dad, werewolves don't exist!"

He frowned. "That's what I'm talking about, though. I'm saying that werewolves *do* exist. I'm saying that you come from a long line of powerful werewolves. I'm saying that I met your mother, my moon-given mate, and I abandoned my pack because I loved her so fucking much." He was losing it; I was sure of it.

"Dad—"

"It was a death sentence to have a human as a mate and any pups that either carried the werewolf gene or didn't. At fifteen, you didn't show any signs of manifesting a wolf, Clem. You don't carry the gene. But your brother does."

"Dad!"

He continued as if I hadn't tried to stop him. "And I'm sorry I didn't tell either of you sooner, but we thought it was best to give you a normal childhood, especially because of the blood-hate that is rampant with the pure-blooded wolf population. We did what we thought was best," he growled. His eyes were swimming with unshed tears.

I shook my head, wondering how best to approach his mental health, which was obviously deteriorating. "Dad—"

"Watch." He put his hand on top of mine, and his fingernails were no longer there. In their place were long, thick, black claws. He wiggled his long bony fingers, and the claws gently scraped my skin.

I opened and closed my mouth, too frightened to speak. I'd all but stopped breathing. It was even more alarming when I watched his claws retract. The smooth, short-cut nails that were always slightly dirty from his work were now reaching for his coffee cup.

"I thought you said you turned into a wolf, not the wolf-man!" I said, my voice choking around my panic. My brain was still unsure about how to react to what he'd just shown me. *Do I run? Do I pinch myself? Is Dad going to eat me?*

He chuckled softly. "I do. But I didn't think shifting into a 250-pound wolf would make this any easier." He took a sip of his coffee and gave me another look. "I don't know why you're suddenly getting these symptoms, Clem. You have no wolf, but maybe it's because you're in a town of werewolves, and some dormant gene is being awakened, if only partially. You're still my daughter after all."

I was still his daughter.

I was the daughter of a werewolf.

What. The. Fuck.

CHAPTER 20
LIAM

Clem was in a panic. I could smell her stress. It was making Lucian mad, and he wanted to shift to protect her. The burning sensation had started across my skin.

"Clementine!" I growled as I grabbed onto her arms and made her stop pacing long enough to look at me. Her eyes were wide in fear, and her face was paler than usual.

"What the hell is going on?" she whimpered.

"You tell me. You're the one acting like a crazy person." Lucian grumbled at my approach, but I needed to get the girl to speak, and not just to herself. I needed her to talk to me.

Even though I had no idea what she was stressing about, I naturally wanted to calm her down. I wanted to fix whatever was causing her stress. I wanted to hold her and tell her everything would be okay. I reached out for her, and she took a minuscule step back, but that one step felt like a chasm.

She raced forward, picked up her bag, and slid her sandals onto her feet, her lime-green toenails winking at me as she did up the buckles.

"What do you mean? What happened? Clem!" I just wanted

her to stop and talk to me. It was evident that wasn't going to happen. She was spooked. Something had frightened her.

"Did she see you?" I asked Lucian.

"No. I don't think so."

"Then what? Where is she going? What happened?"

"I don't know. She seems freaked out. She was muttering something about being asleep and dreaming."

"And my sexy body." I grinned stupidly at him.

Lucian growled his annoyance.

Clementine reached the front door and gave me one last reproachful look before she dashed out of the house.

Lucian made a motion to shift, and before I could say anything, I heard the ripping of jeans and felt the pain of my bones snapping and rearranging. Lucian cantered out of the house after her.

"Fuck, Lucian! They were my favourite jeans."

"You care about your fucking jeans? What about her? We are not letting her leave like that alone!" he snarled.

"No shit, Lucian! Of course, we can't leave her like that. But you could have let me strip first. What's your plan?"

"To protect her."

"From what?" I asked, sniffing the air as he stalked her down to the edge of the driveway through the trees.

"I don't know! Everything."

I listened as Clementine spoke desperately into her phone, tuning into the conversation for a minute.

"Look, her dad is on his way to pick her up. Once she's safe with her father, we can leave. I don't think a wolf surprising her will help matters right now."

"I wasn't going to let her see me," he grunted in response and hung further back into the treeline, following her at a larger distance as she raced down the road.

A slate-coloured truck pulled over, and she jumped into the cab so fast that if I had blinked, I would have missed it.

"Okay, let's go back, and we can meet up with her at her house."

"We can go like this," he growled, pushing on.

"No. We can't, Lucian. What if I need to talk to her? I can't go up to her naked."

That stopped him dead in his tracks. *"Damn it! We really need to stash shorts around this bush."*

I laughed in agreement as Lucian turned and made a beeline back toward the pack house, shifting into human form as we made it to the front door. I walked naked through the hallway to my bedroom. I frowned at the unmade bed, trying to make sense of what had just happened. I sniffed the air deeply; my room was now marinated in Clem's intoxicating scent. It didn't seem to calm Lucian one bit. He was pacing my head impatiently as I pulled out a drawer and put on a pair of athletic shorts.

Something caught my eye, a glistening metal on top of the black carpet—silver and round. I walked over and picked it up. *"Lucian. Her necklace."*

"What?" In her haste to leave, it had fallen off the bedside table, and she hadn't noticed. I flipped it over and reread the engraving.

"See! And now we have an excuse to go to her. We take the necklace back and see if she's okay."

"Sure, let's just take her boyfriend's necklace back to her," Lucian growled with jealousy. Lucian's comment stopped me dead in my tracks, my hand inside another drawer, reaching for a t-shirt.

"What?"

"The necklace. 'Love conquers all'. You know that some boyfriend got that for her as well as I do. The same guy that she admitted to sleeping with most likely." He swished his tail angrily. *"You're just*

going to return a love token from some guy who isn't even worthy of her?"

I finished getting dressed in silence, but now my head was hammering with unanswered questions.

Her boyfriend. I had never thought to ask. Now it was all I could think about. Had she left someone back in Vancouver? She didn't seem like the girl to do casual, which means it was probably a serious relationship. The whole situation made me feel uneasy.

The uneasy feeling didn't subside as I drove to her house, her necklace burning a hole in my pocket. When I got near her home, I spotted the familiar truck in her driveway, then drove another five hundred metres down the road before I parked.

She's home.

I went through a neighbouring property and snuck into the bush to walk back. I told myself I wasn't spying and wanted to listen in without her seeing me. I had to make sure she was okay before I announced myself.

I reached the edge of her property and looked across the yard. A massive window at the back of her house looked straight into her kitchen. There was a dining table pressed right up against the window, and Clementine and her dad sat at it. My heart pounded as I took in Clem's anxious face. Lucian growled and paced uncomfortably as I focused my hearing.

"I told your brother last night. I wanted to tell you together, but he had another attack of the rage, and I needed to tell him."

"How did he take it?"

"He was relieved. He thought he was going crazy. He thought if he told me, I would lock him up. I'm sorry I kept this from you two for so long."

"So, he's going to turn into a w-wolf?" her voice quivered around the words, frightened.

"Yes, eventually."

"Where is he?"

"I sent him to the pack training grounds to get rid of some of his pent-up energy."

"Pack. Training–" She trailed off and shook her head.

"There's something else."

"What?"

"I need you to be gone by the next full moon."

"Why?"

"I just want to keep you safe. I haven't run with this pack in twenty-five years. I need to make sure the pack is sound before I trust them around you on a full moon."

"Are they dangerous? Are *you* dangerous?" Her voice seemed so small and uncertain.

"No. If there are any blood-haters in the pack, they may try to scare you. Or hurt you. It'll be easier if you're away somewhere safe."

"Do you want me to move away?"

Lucian growled lowly.

"No, Clemmy. I want you to be safe. The alpha has promised me you would be, but I'm erring on the side of caution." He sighed. "This is a lot to take in, I know. And you're putting on a brave face. I know learning about this is scary. Hell, the fact your eyesight is healing has to be scary for you. But this is a good thing! Werewolves heal. Werewolves don't get sick."

"But you said I don't have a wolf."

"Well, your scent has definitely changed since we moved here. I can smell a wolf. But Perseus says that you don't have an active wolf spirit. I'm sorry, Clemmy. I don't know what this all means. Half-breeds are rare, and there's little to no information on them. I wish I could tell you for certain, but we can only guess what it all means."

"So, you think I have some of these werewolf traits, like healing and not getting sick?"

"Something like that."

"Are you immortal?"

"No. We can still die. We get injured, sometimes severely. And a plant called aconite—sometimes called wolfsbane—will weaken us so we can't access our wolves, ultimately killing us. But we don't get colds, or flus, or–"

"Cancer," Clem finished for him. Patrick hung his head sadly. "I think I need some time to process this."

She stood up abruptly.

"Clemmy." She looked at her father. "You know this doesn't change anything, eh? You're still you. And I'm still me. I'm still the man who loves you and raised you."

She gave a single nod and walked away from the kitchen table.

She came out of the house and sat on the back doorstep, hugging her knees. I could smell the tears behind her eyes even from where I was. Without registering what I was doing, I stepped out of my hiding place in the trees and made my way through the yard. She watched me but said nothing.

"Hi," I offered.

"Hi," she croaked.

"Are you okay?" She nodded.

I gestured to the step next to her, and she moved slightly, allowing me to sit next to her. Her honeysuckle scent was finally calming Lucian's anxiety. I didn't say anything for a few moments. I let her absorb the huge news her father had recently unleashed on her.

"What were you doing in the bushes?" she mumbled.

I felt my face warm. "Um..." I coughed. "Listening."

"Listening," she repeated the word slowly as if it were foreign.

"Yeah. I was worried about you after the way you ran out of my house. I came to check up on you."

"Came here…in wolf form?" she asked quietly as if her brain was struggling to accept the truth.

I smiled sheepishly at her. "No. Well, yes. I followed you in wolf form until your dad picked you up. Then, I turned back and came here as me."

"As you." She gulped. "So, you're a-a w-werewolf?"

"Yes. I am."

The silence stretched on. She'd retreated into the shy and quiet girl, and although I loved the sound of her voice and I had the ingrained instinct to get her to open up and talk, I resisted as this news had just rocked her world. After a few more agonising minutes, she finally spoke.

"The town is full of werewolves," she murmured, and then her eyes widened. "Oh, my God! I saw a werewolf, didn't I? That day I told you I met a large wolf; that was actually a werewolf, wasn't it?"

"Um." I cleared my throat again. "Yeah, um. That was me."

"Wait. What?"

"I was the wolf you saw," I repeated.

"You." She shook her head, still absorbing the information. Her eyes brimmed with tears. I wanted to hold her, but was unsure how she would react, and I was still sort of hurt from her earlier rejection. She closed her eyes and tried to take deep breaths. When she opened them, she wiped a lone tear from her cheek. "I'm sorry."

"What for?" I asked, perplexed.

"Being a mess."

"One single tear is a mess. Really?"

"No, I'm barely holding it together, so I'm sorry in advance."

I shook my head at her, dumbfounded. "Clem, your whole world as you knew it has been thrown upside down. Not only have you found out about the existence of werewolves, but your eyesight also miraculously healed itself. I think you're allowed to lose control a little bit. Feel your feelings. It's safe to do so, and I'm not going anywhere."

Silence returned, and Clementine stared contemplatively at the trees. I wondered how to help her through this. I was also anxious about her necklace burning a hole in my pocket with about a thousand questions linked to it alone. She appeared to be shutting down. Or maybe this was just how she coped with stress; maybe she internalized.

The necklace would probably help.

Reluctantly, I reached into my pocket and palmed it.

"You left this at my house," I said, handing her the piece of jewellery.

Her control crumpled, and tears cascaded down her face, which made Lucian growl protectively.

"The fucker broke her heart," he muttered angrily.

"Thank you for bringing it to me. I would have died if I lost it," she said as she clasped it around her neck.

A pang of jealousy surged through me. I pushed it back as far as it would go and watched as she hastily wiped her tears.

"Love conquers all?" I asked.

The unknown boyfriend obviously still had her heart. I tried to tame Lucian, who was growling and sending more jealous feelings to the surface.

"Yeah, but that's not exactly true," she mumbled.

"What do you mean?"

"It was my mother's. Love didn't stop her from dying," she said sadly.

Lucian stopped pacing and looked at her in horror. His ears flattened, and he hung his head low in shame.

"Oh. I'm sorry." A sombre silence stretched on for a few minutes.

"It was a gift from my dad to my mom. They fell in love under a full moon," she offered. "It was a symbol of their love.

She gave it to me about an hour before she died and told me that she hoped I would find the same all-consuming love that she had with Dad." Her eyes were glassy with emotion, and Lucian was whining in my head.

I didn't know what to say, so I reached out and wiped another tear that had fallen onto her cheek. The tear dribbled over the tiny fissures in my finger, creating a slight buzzing sensation. Her scent wafted around me. Instinct told me to put my finger to my mouth and lick her tear. She was watching me with her large eyes, and I didn't know if I could answer the question that would come if I tasted her tear in front of her, so I forced myself to wipe it on my t-shirt instead. Lucian whined. I cautiously put my arm around her and waited. After a half-second, she leaned in and sighed. A couple more tears dripped onto my t-shirt, but I think she had finished crying.

"Cedar and spice," she whispered contently snuggled against me.

"Cedar and spice?" I rumbled.

I felt her smile against my chest. "Your cologne." I couldn't see her face, but I knew her well enough to know she was blushing.

"I don't wear cologne. No wolves do. Heavy fragrances irritate our noses."

"Oh, then what am I smelling?"

"You're smelling me—*my* scent."

CHAPTER 21

CLEMENTINE

I was smelling his scent.

A wolfless half-breed could smell scents, heal her eyes, and hear things that she shouldn't be able to hear?

"I don't understand.' I pulled away from him and looked up at his beautiful features. His warm eyes found mine. "Every person has a unique scent. It's usually subtle. Most of the time, you really have to sniff it out to get it."

"Dad smells like pine," I murmured, looking at the chopping block.

I had assumed it was because of all the wood chopping he had been doing, but what if I had picked up his natural scent?

"Yeah, he does." Liam shrugged. "Not that I go around smelling your dad." He gave me a cheeky smile.

I threw my face in my hands. Silent laughter started erupting through me. My whole body shook with it. This was so surreal. Werewolves were real—my father, my brother, my new friend, this town–all werewolves.

Maybe I'm in shock? Maybe I needed to commit myself to a mental institution?

"Hey, are you okay?" I felt a warm hand on my back. So, I

looked over at him, giggling quietly. "Oh, I thought you were crying again."

"Nope, just waiting to wake up from this dre– Oh my God!" The laughter stopped as fast as it had started. *The recurring wolf dreams! What if the dream was my subconscious trying to tell me about werewolves?*

"What?"

"I've been dreaming of wolves for years. It's always the same. A wolf chases me down and leads me to my death. What if it's been my subconscious trying to tell me about my heritage? What if it's a premonition?"

"I highly doubt it was a premonition," he mumbled. "Lucian would never allow that to happen."

"Lucian?"

"My wolf."

"Your wolf. Lucian. Right."

He said nothing.

I watched his eyes and noticed the way the gold seemed to flicker. My dad had silver around his irises, but it didn't come and go as Liam's did. At the most, it brightened, but the ring was a permanent feature.

"Lucian is the gold in your eyes, isn't he?"

"Um...yeah."

"How come I don't see Lucian all the time like I do with Dad's wolf?"

"We aren't merged." I raised an eyebrow in question. "Our souls need to become one. It takes time for that to happen. I can't take over being alpha until that happens."

"Wait. What?"

The gold seemed to be swirling with a lot more intensity. Like this wolf spirit was watching me from the depths of Liam's soul.

"I'm the next in line to be alpha."

"Of course, you are," I frowned, shaking my head, still processing, albeit too slowly for my liking. "What do you mean he would never allow it to happen?"

"He's fond of you. He has a knight-in-shining armour complex when it comes to you."

"Is that why you've been so nice to me?" Pain erupted through my heart, and I felt a wave of sadness wash through me.

"What? No. Of course not! I like you too, Clem. We're friends," he rushed out. "I'm just trying to explain that my neurotic wolf wouldn't let anything happen to you. He's your guardian angel, so to speak."

I nodded but remained a little guarded. I turned the conversation back to werewolf talk to avoid discussions that would play on my insecurities.

"Does it have anything to do with blood-hate? Is that why he's so protective of me?"

"Your dad told you about that?"

"Not really. Not in much detail, but he mentioned it."

"Yeah, some werewolves have a pure-blood complex and don't like half-breeds. They don't like what they don't understand," he said honestly. "But you don't need to worry about that. Lucian won't let anything happen to you."

"I think it *is* happening to me," I murmured.

"What do you mean?"

Damn, I need to remember that wolves have super hearing. I sighed. "There was that guy and the two girls the other day. I swear I could taste bleach in a coffee. And what about the thing that happened last night?"

"Wait! What bleached coffee?" His eyes flashed with large rings of gold, and his voice became so gravelly that I felt my crotch clench of its own accord. However, before I could acknowledge the feeling, my mouth rambled on.

"And then I felt like someone was watching me from the trees. I swear I could hear someone out there. Feel them. It's stupid and probably nothing, but it feels like a lot of bad stuff has happened in the space of a week."

"When did you feel someone watching you?"

"The other day, just before my first work shift."

He jumped up and started stalking toward the trees, removing his shirt. "Stay here."

"What are you doing?" I called back as I stood on the back step. I watched the hardened muscles ripple down his back as he rolled his t-shirt into a ball in his fist.

"Shifting. I can smell better as a wolf. The scent might be gone, however." He disappeared into the bush.

"Liam!" I called. "Liam!" I called again. After a few minutes, I cautiously walked over to the bushes and peered into the treeline.

"Liam?" I asked nervously.

I saw the flash of a tail go behind a large tree, and a couple of seconds later, Liam popped out, shoving his arms into a t-shirt. His athletic shorts were loose around his hips, giving me a quick glimpse of the alluring arch of his hipbones.

"Sorry, Clem, the scent is gone. Next time it happens, call me, okay?"

He came toward me and pulled me into an embrace. I inhaled his comforting scent and nodded.

"It was possibly nothing."

"Lucian trusts your instincts, and so do I. Now tell me about this coffee."

We started to walk out of the bush.

"Just leave it, Liam. I just won't go back there."

"Clementine, I need to know who is doing this stuff so I can stop it."

"I probably just imagined it."

"Once again, Lucian trusts your instincts," he growled.

His eyes flashed with gold before he directed me toward the house, his hand pressing lightly into the small of my back.

"So, the coffee?"

"Just leave it."

"Clementine, there aren't many cafés around town. I can probably figure it out."

"I'm asking you to leave it."

"Like the roofie?"

I looked around anxiously. My father had wolf hearing. Was he listening to this conversation?

"Your dad isn't here," he said, shaking his head.

Shit! Were werewolves mind-readers too? "What do you mean?" I squeaked.

"He mind-linked me and told me he was glad you had a friend to help you through this. He left to go check on your brother."

I shook my head at his revelation.

How the hell had I missed that? "Mind-link?"

"Yeah. We use a kind of telepathy to communicate with members of the pack. The more powerful you are, the more wolves you can connect with at once. Only the alpha and luna can connect with everyone at once." I stared at him. "Basically, it's a wolf spirit connecting with another wolf spirit."

"So underage werewolves can't mind-link?"

"We call them pups and no."

"Can you try and mind-link with me?" I asked.

His expression went vacant for a moment, and then he shook his head with a sad gaze. "Lucian says there's no connection. You need a wolf spirit to do so. Also, you need to be a member of this pack."

"I thought being born into it would make me one."

"No, it doesn't work like that. All pups go through the initiation ceremony at sixteen."

I shook my head in amazement, trying to comprehend this new world. "So, if you can mind-link, can you read minds? Like my thoughts?"

He snorted a laughter and shook his head. I felt my face warm. "No, Clem. I can't." Well, that was a relief. "I know what you're trying to do, you know." I raised an eyebrow. "You're trying to get out of talking to me about your attacks."

"No. I'm just trying to learn about your world. If I'm going to be a part of it, I need to know."

"And the attacks?" he queried, eyes glowing with gold. I didn't answer him, not directly.

"Dad thinks I should be gone on the next full moon."

"I heard."

"What do you think?"

"I think you must do what is right for you."

"What does Lucian think?"

"He's of two minds. He thinks you being far away from harm is a good idea, but he hates the idea of not being able to protect you."

"He wants me to stay?"

"Yes, so he can keep an eye on you."

"But doesn't he want to go and run and chase deer and stuff?"

Liam laughed, and the sound made me smile shyly. "He can do that any time."

"How often do you shift and run?" I asked curiously.

"Once every few days."

"Can I see you shift?" I looked at him.

"No, Clem. Not today."

"Why not?"

"Give your brain time to process this." He paused. "You're

doing well with the news. Exceptionally well if I'm being honest."

"Maybe I'm in shock?" I smirked, then shook my head. "I guess it just kind of makes sense, you know? I never really fit in anywhere. I was always a bit of an outsider. I was a little rounder than most other girls my age, so the bullying was relentless. It wasn't just the girls either. I was a target for the guys too."

His brows furrowed. "What do you mean?"

I took a deep breath, searching his eyes before replying. I don't know why, but I trusted him. I just hoped I wouldn't regret it.

"There was a game at school. A points thing where a guy would receive a number of points for each girl he managed to do things with. Kissing would be worth so many points; touching below the pants would be another number; sex another number. Each girl had a different point level.

"I'm not entirely sure how the rules of the game worked, but I fell victim to it, unaware. This popular kid at school targeted me, and to cut a long, horrible story short, I got him a lot of points. Fat girl virginity was the highest amount of points you could get, apparently." Liam's eyes flashed a dangerous gold.

"To make matters worse, I allegedly made growling noises in my sleep, an occasional bark too. Well, you can imagine the rumours that floated around my school the next day. I wasn't just the fat girl whose hair was thick and grew ridiculously fast or the girl who was shy and awkward. I also made dog noises in my sleep." I shook my head and looked away from Liam's gaze, my face hot with embarrassment. "Anyway, that's why it kind of makes sense to me. The dreams, the barking in my sleep, the hair growth, the not fitting in anywhere. So, I guess I'm ready to accept that I was born different than everyone else."

Liam said nothing, but I could hear his harsh breathing. I took a deep breath myself and turned to look at him.

"Liam?" I asked timidly.

His eyes had gone feral, and he held his fists so tight that his knuckles had gone white. A low snarl ran out of his mouth, and brown fur started to sprout and thicken on his forearms.

Oh, fuck!

CHAPTER 22

LIAM

"Liam?" Her voice sounded far away, and I tried to anchor myself to it, but Lucian was feral with anger. I tried to focus on her scent, anything to take away the shift, but I knew it was too late. The burning and itching were too much, and I knew I was shifting. I felt the first pop of a bone moving and gritted my teeth.

Fuck, I really can't shift. Not like this. I need to run into the trees and hide.

The problem was, I didn't think I could make it to the tree-line, let alone beyond it on time. It was taking all of my concentration not to shift right here. It was taking all my energy not to rip through my clothes, land on all paws, and charge into the forest. And as much as Clementine said she wanted to see me in my wolf form, seeing somebody's bones break and realign themselves was not something you could ever unsee, no matter how quick the shift may be.

I felt a cooling sensation run over me. It confused my senses, and my sprouting fur instantly started to recede. Lucian stopped stalking long enough to tilt his head to the side. He was as confused as I was. I looked down at my fists—small delicate thumbs circled them as tiny hands tried to encase my fingers. My eyes trailed up the cream-coloured arms, over the shoulders and to Clem's large doe-eyes, who had bravely—or—stupidly touched me in the middle of a change. She kept making small circles with her thumbs, a cool tickling sensation zapping us from her fingertips. I closed my eyes and inhaled her scent.

"Liam?" she whispered.

Lucian growled and shook out his fur. I could taste his anger on my tongue.

"Give me a minute," I growled a little harshly. "I'm trying to calm Lucian down; trying to stop the change." I took in a few deep breaths, and the soothing sensation stopped. "Please don't stop doing that," I purred. It instantly started up again in slow, deliberate, cooling circles.

After a few moments, the need to shift dissipated. The burning had stopped completely, and my bones had stopped moving. My heart had stopped hammering in my chest, and my blood had stopped bubbling.

Lucian collapsed onto his front in a tired heap, panting and making very little noise. I opened my eyes and saw large turquoise orbs full of concern. I pulled her roughly into a hug, lowering my head into the dark hair nestled at the crook of her neck, inhaling deeply before pulling away.

"Did you honestly just touch me in the middle of a shift?"

"I didn't know what else to do."

"Do you know how dangerous that could have been?" I barked.

One of the first rules around werewolves was not to touch them as they shifted. It was far too dangerous.

"I don't think you would have hurt me," she levelled.

I gaped at her for a second. But she was right. Lucian would never have allowed anything to happen to her. He would have forcibly rolled away before his teeth and claws came into contact. But still... I shook my head, looking down at her hands which had left mine, but I could still feel the echo of her touch.

"How did you do that?"

"Do what?"

"Stop the shift. Calm the beast."

Her face went pink, and she gave me that shy smile of hers that made my heart flip.

"I used to suffer from panic attacks, and my mom would rub circles into my hands to ground me," she said softly. "I just grabbed your hands out of instinct and gave it a go. I'm glad it worked."

"Me too. Or you may have been a chew toy," I grumbled.

"Hmm. Well, maybe then I could shift."

"What?"

"You know, because if I get bitten...I could shift?" she said with an amused tone to her voice.

"No, Clem. That's not how it works."

"Oh. Well, that's a shame. I was going to ask you to bite me."

"You– What?"

"Kidding!" She laughed.

But I had a feeling she wasn't kidding at all. "You want to be able to turn into a wolf?" I asked softly.

She took her plump lower lip between her teeth, worrying it for a few moments before replying. My eyes traced the movement. "It's just... I've always felt out of place in the human world. And now, I don't really have a place in this world either."

"You'll always have a place in this world," I said earnestly. Lucian rumbled in agreement. "Thank you for helping me."

"No problem. Um, can I ask what sent you into–"

"The change?" I offered. She nodded. "I didn't like hearing someone hurt you; that they used you like that. I wasn't kidding when I told you Lucian was protective over you. He was losing it, listening to the story. And I don't have full control over him yet. He's a little hotheaded."

"Okay. I'll refrain from telling stories like that in the future," she said.

There was no flippancy or joking tone to her words. When my eyes met hers, I understood that she was being sincere.

"Wait. There's more?" I growled.

"Um, maybe?"

I closed my eyes and started taking deep breaths again as Lucian growled.

"You should tell me then. Rip the Band-Aid off."

I opened my eyes and found her watching me, her eyes flashing with cool and controlled anger. "What part of me makes you think I'm an open book, Liam?" she snarled.

Shock washed over me. Even Lucian retreated slightly at her sudden waspish tone.

"I didn't mean it like that."

She crossed her arms, which pressed her already ample cleavage to breaking point in her dress, and glared at me. Even though she only seemed irritated, I quickly realized that I never wanted to feel the full burn of her anger. I could foresee the aftermath of what her angry eruption could look like, and she was a force to be reckoned with.

I placed my hands up in a peace-keeping gesture. "I swear. You don't have to tell me anything you don't want to. I just meant that if you were going to tell me more, then just do it quickly so I can control Lucian." She stared at me for a few moments, her turquoise eyes hard and unyielding, then she gave me a stiff nod. "I'm sorry," I said, reaching out for her hand. I didn't think she would let me hold it, but she placed her palm inside mine, and I was amazed at how tiny and delicate it felt. The cooling sensations had stopped, but a small energy was still coming from her.

"It's okay. I didn't mean to snap. I just find it hard to trust people."

I sat down on the step and tugged her hand so she would sit with me again. She gracefully landed on the step next to me. I didn't let go of her hand. I enjoyed the feeling of her fingers intertwined with mine.

"I have never been able to stop a shift from happening," I confessed, trying to get her to understand the gravity of what she had managed to do. "Sometimes, I've managed to reason with Lucian or calm him down enough that he doesn't force the change, but I've never been able to stop it from happening when he's been so enraged, especially when the shift had already started." She looked at me, confused. "The shift was already happening, Clem. I could feel my bones realigning. You stopped it."

"I didn't do anything. I just wanted you to know I was here."

I gave her a soft smile. "I think that was enough."

"How is Lucian now?"

"Calm." I nodded at her and proceeded cautiously with my next sentence. She was still guarded. "Are you okay? Speaking of those memories must have been painful."

"The memories don't go away, Liam. You just learn to live with the crap life throws at you," she said without emotion.

I felt saddened by her remark. I wished that I had known her back then. I knew I would have protected her from all those assholes, even before I got the strength from Lucian. It would have been me and Clem against the world.

I turned to Lucian, *"And to think, it could have happened. We could have grown up as friends if Alpha Jed hadn't been such an evil piece of shit. Clem could have grown up with me, and she would have never had to feel afraid, bullied or...or—"*

"Be sexually assaulted?" offered Lucian with an angry flick of his tail.

"I don't think she was sexually assaulted. I think she consented without knowing what she was consenting to." I tried to reason with him as a sick feeling bubbled in my stomach.

"Which is the same thing!" he growled. *"Why do you think I was losing my shit? The minute we find out the prick's name–"* he started pacing again.

"Where did you go just now?"

"Sorry?" I asked her, confused.

"Your eyes went vacant like you were having an absence seizure."

"I was chatting with Lucian." I felt my wolf press forward.

"Hi, Lucian," she murmured timidly, and I felt him wag his tail in response.

She lifted her other hand toward my cheek as if unsure of what or why she was doing it, then gently put her fingers on my face and cupped my scruffy jaw. It tickled, but I didn't move away from her fingers.

"Thank you for looking out for me." As fast as her fingers were in my beard, they were gone, leaving an echo of her touch. Lucian grumbled.

Clem's cheekbones had a dusting of pink as she looked away from me again. I looked down at our intertwined fingers and smiled softly. She sighed. We sat for a few more moments in the quiet, and eventually, she got up, announcing she had to go shower. I nodded and told her I would wait around for her, but she shook her head, saying she was okay.

I'd been dismissed.

That was probably a good thing because the moment she said that she was going to shower, Lucian sent flashes of creamy skin sprinkled with water droplets into my mind. He didn't stop there either. I had images of her running a washcloth over her large breasts and the curve of her hips. And now I really needed to run. Otherwise, I was going to ruin our friend-ship by asking to join her in the shower.

Lucian gave a wolfy chuckle as I stepped into the bush and stashed my clothes under a tree. I heard the shower turn on, and closed my eyes. Gritting my teeth, I took a deep breath before shifting into my wolf form, letting out a cheeky howl, knowing she would hear it.

CHAPTER 23

CLEMENTINE

THE SOUND of the howl made me jump out of my skin. I turned and looked in the general direction of the backyard. *Idiot*, I smiled fondly. I turned my head to see if I could hear anything else, but all I could make out was the shower running.

The water was scalding hot by the time I stepped into it. My entire life had changed within twenty-four hours and learning about everything had exhausted me physically and mentally. The aftereffects of the Rohypnol were unapparent. There was no queasiness or hangover-like symptoms now—just pure exhaustion. I simply wanted to burn the essence of the day away with this hot shower, climb into bed, and sleep for a million years.

I pushed my face right into the spray of water, then lowered my head, letting it hit the back of my neck, groaning as the heat hit my muscles. Eventually, I grabbed the soap and loofah and washed myself in slow, soothing circles.

After my shower, I dressed in shorts and a comfy threadbare t-shirt and headed toward the kitchen. My stomach was starting to growl, and I realized that I hadn't eaten since dinner last night. I preheated the oven and proceeded to make homemade pizzas, nibbling on the shredded cheese as I did.

When the first pizza was ready, I put it in the oven and proceeded to make the second, adding part of a ghost pepper to the sauce this time. I heard a growl quickly followed by a whimper from the backyard. Frowning, I looked out the large window. I couldn't see anything, but I swore I had heard something. The sounds of thundering footsteps and twigs breaking caught my attention. I stepped through the mudroom and down the back steps.

"Hello? Liam?" I called out. No answer. I walked toward the treeline and peered in. "Is someone there?" I stepped in a bit further and placed my palm on the trunk of a large tree. I looked around. Someone was there. I could sense them. It made the hairs on the back of my neck stand on end, and I called out again.

With still no answer, I couldn't shake the feeling that someone was watching me. I sniffed the air but could only smell the wet forest—the decaying smell of moss and lichen. I was sure if I had a wolf, I would be able to smell traces of other stuff, including any persons who had walked past this tree in the last thirty minutes. Hell, I would have been able to scent Liam. But I got nothing. I listened, trying to tilt my head to see if I could hear anything, but all I could hear was the gentle breeze rustling through the trees.

'Call Liam,' the quiet voice in my head said. I shook my head defiantly at my conscience, flipped my middle finger to the imaginary person in the forest, and stalked back toward the house. I could no longer be afraid of the big bad wolf. Or wolves in this case. It was more than possible that just a few wolves were running past our property. Pack members had every right to run through this forest. It was their land, and I was the outsider.

Furthermore, I wasn't going to call Liam whenever I suspected someone was out there. I had my dad, and eventually, my brother, who would keep this place safe. And I was mortified at the thought of Liam coming all this way just to tell me that it had only been a deer or a squirrel. Nope. I wasn't calling him.

I walked back into the house just as the oven timer went off. Pulling the first pizza out, I rested it on the stovetop, then put the second one in and restarted the timer.

"I hope there's enough for us!" Vinny said, stomping through the mudroom, removing his boots, and sliding on his socks into the house.

"That depends." I smiled. "How much do werewolves eat?"

He grinned. It was nice to see him smile. I hadn't seen him this happy since long before Mom had gotten sick. Dad came in behind him, sniffing the air. He gave a low growl of appreciation at the smell.

"Better make three or four pizzas for future reference. We could easily demolish one or two by ourselves." Dad chuckled as I started to slice the first pie. I had never really seen my father eat excessive amounts of food, but I wasn't surprised after coming to terms with the fact that he hid such a large portion of his life from me. It was just one more thing to hide so I wouldn't ask any questions.

I slid a slice onto a plate for myself and indicated they could help themselves. I started to nibble at the pizza as my dad put a portion on his plate, and my brother placed four slices on his.

"How are you doing with this all?" Dad asked me as a stringy bit of cheese hit his chin.

"I'm okay."

"You know you can ask me anything, eh?"

"Yeah, I know." I turned to my brother, digging into his pizza as if he had never seen food. "What about you?"

"I think it's fucking awesome."

"Language!" my father cut across.

My brother rolled his eyes. As much as Dad growled about our language, he never really enforced it, probably because he was known to excessively drop colourful language himself.

"Although, it's a little weird that Dad is now allowing me to fight," Vinny finished.

"Fighting and training are entirely different things, Vincent."

"I can't wait to meet my wolf."

"When will that happen?" I asked Vinny, who had just taken a large bite of pizza and was panting around the steaming clump of crust and toppings in his mouth.

"Around his sixteenth birthday usually. Although, it can happen anytime in his sixteenth year," Dad answered for him before shoving the rest of his pizza slice in his mouth, not caring about the temperature.

Vinny nodded excitedly, his eyes flashing with the silver that I now knew to be attributed to his wolf. "I'll hear him first, then sometime after that, I'll be able to shift."

"I'm happy for you, Vinny."

"Maybe you will hear yours too. You've already been having the same side effects as me. I know you're hearing things you shouldn't." He gave me a pointed look.

"No, that won't happen. I have no wolf," I said sadly.

The oven timer pinged, and I stood up and took the second pizza out. Leaving it to rest on the stovetop, I turned back to my brother, who looked confused about the situation.

"Your sister hasn't got a wolf, but that doesn't make her any less of anything. She's still your sister," Dad said kindly.

I saw his nostrils flare, and he turned back to Vinny. "Sniff the pizza. See if you can figure out what she put on it."

"If it's Clem, it'll be a ghost pepper." He rolled his eyes, and I smirked.

"I'm trying to help you hone your senses. See if you can smell it out on the pizza."

"Nope. I'm just planning on avoiding that thing. The chili is already making my eyes water. She definitely has no wolf. That shit burns! No wolf can handle that!"

"Really?" Dad challenged with a mischievous twinkle in his eye. "Clem. A large slice, please." I smiled and dolled him a hefty portion.

"You're both nuts! I'm glad your ass holes are going to burn, and mine isn't. Who the fuck likes that spicy shit?"

I placed the pizza in front of my dad, who bit into it with theatrical flair.

"Nuts!" my brother repeated. "My condolences to your butts."

Dad started laughing hard, and even I found my cheeks twisting into a smirk. It was one of the things my dad and I had in common. We both loved our spicy food. The hotter, the better. My brother and my mom hated anything to do with it.

"So, besides a wolf, what do you want for your birthday? It's only five weeks away," I remarked.

Vinny shrugged. "I think that'll be enough. I'm so glad I'm not crazy."

"Well, you still might be a little crazy," I teased.

He flipped me the finger and shook his head as I placed a spicy slice of pizza in my mouth, instantly feeling the joyful tingles of the spice lapping at my palette.

The pizza didn't last long either. Dad wasn't kidding when he said that werewolves ate a lot. I always chalked it up to the fact my brother was a growing teenager, but now, under my new filter on the world, I could see that it was because of his genetics. He finished the rest of the first pizza and even braved a slice of the spicy one. After three bites, he called us crazy and abandoned the slice to chug glass after glass of water. My father took the rest of Vinny's portion and then finished the entire spicy pizza without batting an eyelash.

I managed to fit in three slices of pizza before it all disappeared.

Dad helped me clean up the kitchen while Vinny ran off to shower.

"Hey, Dad."

"Hey, Clementine," Dad mimicked.

"Did you smell any other wolves when you came home?"

"I smell other wolves all the time, Clemmy. The bush is full of wolf scents. Why?"

I ignored his direct question. "Should I be worried about it?"

He shook his head, giving me a calculated appraisal. "It doesn't hurt to be a little cautious. As I said, I haven't run with this pack in a long time."

I took a deep breath. I couldn't tell my dad. Not until I was sure there was something to tell him. But I could make his life a bit easier.

"I've decided that I'll leave on the full moon."

"Oh?"

"Yeah. It makes sense for me to be away. Can I borrow your truck? I'll head back to Vancouver for a few days. Get out of your hair for a bit."

"Maybe check out the university again, eh?"

I shook my head. "No." He had to let that go. "But there's no need to worry. I'll find something to keep me occupied."

"Oh, and what were you thinking?"

"I was thinking of either finding a band and becoming a groupie, or maybe just robbing a bank at gunpoint. I haven't decided yet." I shrugged nonchalantly.

"Okay, let me know if I need to hook you up with some weapons. I know a guy."

"Thanks, Dad. I knew I could count on you for my law-abiding-misdemeanours."

CHAPTER 24

LIAM

MONDAY ROLLED AROUND FASTER than I would have liked. I tapped my foot against the empty chair in front of me as I listened to the professor at the front of the hall drone on about economics. Lucian was snoring softly in my head.

I found it hard to concentrate. My mind kept wandering back to Blackfern Valley. Clem hadn't so much as sent me a text message since I left her place on Sunday. I thought she may have checked in, but when I rolled over this morning and checked my phone, there were no messages or missed calls from her.

I told myself I was worried for her safety, and it was normal for me to want her to check in after she learned about were-wolves. Her entire life had been thrown into disarray, and she needed someone to help her navigate this world without humans. Even looking around this small lecture hall of sixty-odd students, only three of them were human. Humans that didn't know they were sitting in a room full of werewolves.

There were less than one-hundred humans that lived in the Kempthorne area. And less than a dozen of them attended Kempthorne University. Humans naturally avoided areas where there were large populations of werewolves. There was some unknown force that tended to stop them from mingling with packs, but it seemed there were also a few who deviated from the rule or where said force didn't apply to them. Lucian told me that these humans felt a pull instead of a push. I joked that maybe they were the human mates of wolves coming to the one area where a large proportion of packs joined together. He didn't correct me. He just shrugged as if it was nothing of significance. If it's the reason that there were so many humans around, Fate sucked at her job because I hadn't heard of one wolf finding a human mate in Kempthorne.

The large clock on the wall flicked onto ten to the hour, and Doctor Jay finished his class, reminding us about the exam coming up on Friday. A universal groan rang out amongst the students as they put away books into their bags and started to meander out of the room. Lucian grumbled as he woke in the back of my mind and stretched while yawning.

I left the lecture hall and walked straight into the burning sunshine, thinking about Clementine. I pulled out my phone, ready to send her a message, gently reminding her that I still had her back, when something caused me to stop dead in my tracks. A girl with pitch black hair around her shoulders sat on the grass under a large tree, facing away from me.

It can't be. There's no way that's Clementine.

I started to move forward, sniffing the air. Honeysuckle and pear floated toward me, and I felt myself growl with happiness. I hadn't expected to see Clementine at Kempthorne University.

"Clem?" I called as I walked over.

"Hi." Her turquoise eyes found mine, and she gave me a sweet smile. I felt my heart twitch. Seeing her stunning eyes without being obstructed by her glasses was going to take some getting used to.

"What are you doing here?"

"Dad." She rolled those stunning orbs. "He kidnapped me and brought me out here while he's doing a job here at the University." I looked around and saw her dad's truck parked in a loading zone. Stevens Electric was written on the side panel, gleaming proudly in the sun. "Don't they have electricians in Kempthorne?" she asked as I sat next to her on the grass.

I smiled. Warmth was spreading around my body, but I think it was more from her presence than the blistering sun above. "I'm sure none of them is as good as your dad," I joked.

She made a scoffing noise and closed her eyes again. Her long dark lashes brushed against the skin of her cheeks. I could see her nostrils flare a little.

"What are you smelling?"

Her cheeks went pink instantly, and she opened her eyes. "Coffee, textbooks, and now…you."

I chuckled as her blush brightened. Lucian wagged his tail happily. She closed her eyes again, enjoying the warmth of the sun.

"I think I know why your dad wants you to attend Kempthorne University," I said.

"You mean other than to try and turn back the clock to before my mom died?" She didn't open her eyes, but I could taste the sadness that laced her words.

"No. You would be safe here. I mean, you would be safe in Vancouver too; there aren't many wolf packs that border cities. It's probably why your dad picked Vancouver to begin with," I rambled. "But you would be safe here. This university is predominantly werewolves, but there are a handful of humans."

"What the heck are you talking about?" She opened her eyes and looked at me again.

"There is a bit of a folktale behind this university. Well, it's a story about Kempthorne itself."

"There is?"

"Yeah." She looked at me expectantly. I pounded my backpack into a makeshift pillow and laid down, looking up at her. She was still in her relaxed sitting position, her arms locked behind her, and her legs stretched out into the sunshine. "You want to hear it?"

"Liam." She rolled her eyes, and I chuckled, watching the campus slowly empty of students heading to their next classes.

"Kempthorne is ancient and has the oldest of Pack Law running through it. Kind of like a life force," I said. It was hard to describe something like this. You couldn't explain it; you had to feel it. "There is no one pack who owns this region.

"Long ago, there was a pack known as the Kempthorne Pack. Their alpha was benevolent at a time when major wars were raging between packs. Lots of packs either died off or merged with others. Most of the war was about territory or belligerent assholes who wanted to make a name for themselves."

Clementine shifted and started picking at the grass absentmindedly as she listened to the story. I continued. "A big war broke out right here where the university now stands. A rival pack took the alpha's only daughter, and they tried to use her as leverage to make him join the war. Even though he was benevolent, he marched into the rival pack's camp to retrieve his daughter by negotiating for her release. He did this solo, without a plan or his pack to back him up. What he saw haunted him.

"His daughter was being used and abused by the pack's warriors. He soon realized there would be no bargaining, no hostage return situation. She wasn't being kept in good faith. She was being brutalized. Fed so much aconite that it was slowly poisoning her, leaving her too weak to fight. His benevolent nature never wavered, though, which is extremely hard for a werewolf. Werewolves are notorious hotheads, super protective, and their animal instincts usually will override their human ones.

"The alpha still refused to join the war. He was captured, of course, and put into the cell next to his daughter. Day after day, he watched as they abused her. Sadistic wolves were torturing her right next to him, and he couldn't do anything," I growled, feeling Lucian getting outraged over the story.

Clem's eyes were on me. Those two large aquamarine pools of hers were full of curiosity. "That's horrible. What happened next?"

"Well, he begged them to stop each day, but they wouldn't. Then, the begging turned into warnings that they had to stop. They wouldn't. He vowed that if she died, her spirit would rule through this land; that an alpha could never be in charge of it. Still, they didn't cease. Instead, they took it one step further and sacrificed her at the height of a Solar Eclipse. When her final drop of blood hit the ground, the alpha's command was sealed, and the wolves were forced off the land. No war has ever been fought here ever since."

"What happened to the alpha and his pack?"

"They disappeared. No one knows what happened to them," I said honestly. I noticed her give a little shiver, and smiled. "You're feeling the power from the land now, aren't you?" I ran my hands over the goosebumps that had appeared on her arm. I could feel vibrations underneath my fingertips.

She nodded. "That's an amazing legend."

"The power that runs through it is ingrained in this earth's very essence. There is no longer any alpha or one pack in the region. To this day, no alpha can claim this land. It means that the land is safe from blood-hate and pack war. It's physically impossible—the biggest alpha command known to date. The ground has remained neutral—this it's Switzerland if you will."

I took a deep breath and smiled. "Soon after, Kempthorne University opened, and the Canadian packs started sending their members for higher education here. Many rival pack members walk around this campus, but they physically can't act on their opposing views."

I looked around the grounds. The campus was empty as people were already well into their next classes. I saw Doctor Jay running across the campus, late as always and chuckled.

"What's funny?"

"That man there, with the ginger man-bun and goatee?" I pointed. She followed my finger and nodded. "That's Jason Dixon. He's one of the economics professors here. And notorious for being late."

"He seems a bit frazzled."

"Always is. He's a great guy, though. We call him Doctor Jay."

"Because he has his PhD in economics, I'm assuming?"

"No. Well, yes. But we call him Doctor Jay as a nickname. It's his DJ name. He spins around here on Friday nights. You should come check it out with me some time." She smiled but said nothing. Then she looked at her phone and frowned slightly. "What?"

"Dad is taking longer than expected. He bribed me with lunch as part of his kidnapping ruse. I'm due at work at three." I looked at the time on my phone and noticed it was indeed lunch time. My stomach rumbled.

"Text your dad and tell him you have a ride back."

"Don't you have class?"

"Nope. My afternoon is free. Let's get lunch, and I'll drive you home."

CHAPTER 25

CLEMENTINE

LIAM STOOD up and reached his hand out to me. He flashed me an award-winning smile that made my insides turn to Jell-O. I wiped my hand on my shorts then placed it in his, allowing him to help me off the ground.

The static electricity instantly started the moment my hand touched his. I was beginning to enjoy the sensation. After I was on my feet, I took my hand away from his, picked up my bag and then waited for it to be offered again. He didn't repeat his offer.

"Come on." He grinned as he threw his arm around my shoulder. "Look how little you are! You fit!" He chuckled.

I jabbed him in the side, which made him chuckle more. His side was as hard as the rest of his body—not an ounce of fat anywhere. I had already accepted that he was a marbled god, but it made me push back my insecurities.

"Have you already had lunch?" I asked shyly.

"I had food before my class, but I'm due for my second lunch." My brows raised. "I had a sandwich before, but it was more like a snack. I'm hungry; let's grab lunch."

I climbed into his car and felt my cheeks warm again, for no reason other than the fact I could smell his scent surrounding me, which I enjoyed it a little too much. He easily pulled out of the parking lot, and soon we were on our way into the town of Kempthorne.

"What do you want to eat?" he asked.

"Something light is fine."

"Clementine, I'm a werewolf. I don't do light."

"What about your sandwich earlier? Isn't that considered light?" I teased.

"Um, that was three sandwiches. Leftover roast turkey and roast chicken with stuffing, gravy, cranberry sauce, and a bit of salad. I wouldn't exactly call that light, eh."

"Well, if that's what you ate earlier, we should definitely get something light now," I said, maintaining my teasing tone. He scoffed, then pulled up outside a restaurant and parallel parked with ease.

"That was impressive."

"My parking skills impress you, huh?" he offered a friendly grin before opening the door and climbing out. I followed him out, the door groaning on its hinges, and joined him on the pavement.

"Yeah. I bet it impresses all the girls. You should use it as part of your pickup lines. 'Hey, baby, come see how I can parallel park.'" I gave a stupid wink, and he burst out laughing.

"It's the wolf genetics, baby. It makes me super agile, super attractive and difficult things like parallel parking are as easy as making you blush." He winked playfully, and as if on command, I felt my face warm again.

"Does it make you super modest too?" I asked, and he grinned instead of answering, flashing me those perfect white teeth. "Well, I have no wolf and am pretty good at parking myself," I countered, then rolled my eyes, trying to stop myself from blushing deeper.

He scoffed. "Sure, you are," he said, tucking me back under his arm, leading me down the main street. "Are you even allowed to drive? Do they even make booster seats available for the driver's seat?" I jabbed him in the side, and he chuckled again. "So violent, Clementine!"

I laughed. I couldn't help it. Liam made me feel at ease, and laughter just came naturally when I was around him. We walked into a sushi place, and I grinned. I didn't think Kempthorne would have sushi, let alone a sushi train. We were seated at a booth, and I gave Liam a genuine smile as I picked up the tablet on the side and started pressing the buttons.

"You like sushi?"

"I love sushi. I went to Osaka with my mom after I graduated high school. It was a surprise to celebrate surviving that chapter in my life and getting accepted into UBC on a full scholarship." I smiled as the various memories played in my mind. "We went into a lot of sushi places there, and many of them had a set up just like this."

"The owner is from Kawasaki or something," he offered.

"Oh, if he's Japanese, I'm sure this will be a super authentic experience."

I was still playing around with the buttons, and eventually, I picked a couple of salmon rolls, California rolls and Tempura shrimp before I handed him the tablet. He made some selections and pressed a button at the bottom to send the order to the kitchen.

"How was class?" I asked, trying to converse with him while I waited for the sushi to come down the mini train track.

"Lucian fell asleep and was snoring through it, so I found it hard to concentrate." He gave me an exasperated smile.

"Does Lucian fall asleep a lot during classes?"

The gold around his eyes flickered, and I knew Lucian was listening.

"Only economics and calculus. I took a sexual reproduction course as an elective option in my first year. He was awake through the entire thing, but that may be because we were looking at many pictures of naked bodies."

I couldn't control the laugh that came bubbling out. "I took a course like that. It was mostly about sexual dimorphism and sexual selection due to body figures and facial features like symmetry and hair."

I felt my face warm again, but thankfully, the sushi arrived and provided a sufficient distraction. I pulled our food off the little cart and pressed the button to send it back. Opening the bowls beside me, I piled pickled ginger and wasabi onto the side of my plate.

"Do you miss it?"

I looked across at Liam, who wasn't looking at me but watching me put my wasabi into my bowl of soy sauce with interest. "A little, I guess. But I'm not ready to go back to university yet. Dad pushing me to do so doesn't help either."

"No, I meant looking at porn in class?"

I threw a piece of ginger at him, and he laughed. "It wasn't porn! It was mostly about face symmetry and stuff," I insisted.

"Oh, so it was face porn! Let me guess, you liked the guys with facial hair, eh?" he said with a wink.

My face was already so red that it was impossible for it to get any redder. Rolling my eyes as a dismissal for the topic, I used my chopsticks like an expert, and popped a sushi roll into my soy sauce bowl, then placed it in my mouth to avoid answering the question.

After I filled up on my sushi, I sat watching as Liam ordered a truckload more. I tried to convince him to cover them in wasabi, to which he just shook his head after placing a small amount on his chopstick to taste it.

Well, at least he didn't cry.

He chatted with me as he loaded roll after roll into his mouth. I'd only known him less than a week, but I could admit he was becoming a really good friend. I could be honest that I liked him a lot, too. I didn't have the tendency to feel comfortable around people very often, but he'd made it easy. Effortless. He was, in fact, Mister Nice Guy.

Finally, he indicated that his next order was his last one, and I pressed the button that told the waitress to bring the bill.

"I need to ask Tina for leave the weekend after next, or to at least swap my shift," I said, reaching for the bill.

"Is that so you can accompany me to see Doctor Jay?" he asked, snapping up the bill and swatting my hand away. He placed his credit card in the little black folder and gave it to the waitress as she passed.

I glared at him but answered his question. "No, and I doubt he would be performing anyway. The full moon is that weekend, and I've decided not to be here."

Liam placed a final piece of sushi in his mouth, and his warm brown eyes had tiny flecks of gold. He chewed slowly. Deliberately. "Where are you going to go?"

"Back to Vancouver."

He gaped. His eyes were instantly rimmed with brilliant bright gold. "But that's so far."

"That's kind of the appeal."

"Kempthorne is closer. You'd be safe here in Kempthorne. All the other humans don't disappear around a full moon, here."

"I have a friend in Vancouver that I'd like to go visit. In fact, I could make it a regular thing and visit each full moon just to make it easier on Dad and everyone else."

"Who is this friend?" His voice came out in a deep growl.

"My friend, TJ," I said. "My only friend, really. We both studied medicine together."

"I think you should stay."

"Why?" My brow furrowed in confusion.

The waitress returned with Liam's credit card, and we got up to leave.

"I just think you should stay."

"That isn't a good enough reason. Dad says it might be dangerous."

"Lucian and I will protect you," he snarled, sounding insulted.

"You shouldn't need to protect me," I murmured, opening the restaurant door, and turned toward the car. "I'm a big girl, and TJ has an excellent couch."

WE CLIMBED INTO THE CAR. And drove in relative silence back to Blackfern Valley. I could see that Liam was conversing with his wolf, and by how he gripped the steering wheel, I didn't want to interrupt. It was apparent that he was having an intense conversation with Lucian about something. So, I left him to it, and hummed along to the music on the radio. Before long, he dropped me off outside Lupus' Bar and Grill.

"Thanks for lunch, Liam," I said as I reached for the door handle. "And for the ride to work."

"I can give you a ride to Vancouver," he blurted.

I almost fell out of the vehicle in surprise.

"No need. I'll take Dad's truck." A low, frustrated sound came from Liam, and I turned back to see his eyes flick with gold again before he closed his eyes. "Don't worry so much, Liam. TJ won't let anything happen to me. I'll be back in one piece before you notice."

Getting out of the car, I waved then walked into the restaurant.

CHAPTER 26

LIAM

I watched her walk through the door of Lupus' and blinked a couple of times. My stomach was in knots, and Lucian wasn't helping. He'd been agitated ever since we left Kempthorne.

I parked the car into a vacant spot, then proceeded to follow her into the bar. I stopped at the wooden door with the glass panels and looked in. When I peered through the glass at the front door, I saw her hug Ryan hello with a smile that lit up her entire face. Lucian growled in response. I didn't enter. Instead, I observed her from the door for a moment, tuning my hearing to them, once again trying to convince myself that I wasn't spying; I was simply keeping her safe.

"So, a little birdie tells me you have a Red Riding Hood fetish," Ryan teased.

"Why, are you the big bad wolf?" she flirted back.

My chest tightened as Ryan laughed and flashed her a grin that I had seen work a thousand times on the she-wolves in the area. She rolled her eyes, then gave him a smaller, more reserved smile.

"The whole town is a rumour mill, you know," Ryan commented.

"I'm sure the rumours were flying the moment my half-breed ass stepped out of my dad's truck." She shook her head and moved around, so I was now looking at her back.

"Well yeah, but this time you've really started giving them something to talk about."

"And what's that?"

"Um, your eyesight? And the fact that you and your brother now know about us. But mostly, your eyesight. You miraculously wake up one morning, healed like a werewolf, but you know, you aren't one."

She continued to set up the bar for the afternoon, while conversing with Ryan. "I'm a bit dumbfounded about that myself, but I must admit, it's really nice not to wear glasses."

I could see Ryan's face and it was full of excited animation, but he wasn't interested in what she was saying, he just ploughed ahead with his gossip like a fourteen-year-old girl. "There's also the rumours that are circulating about *who* you woke up with." Ryan waggled his eyebrows.

Crap!

I should have known that taking her from the party like that would have spurred some wagging tongues. I felt guilty that the town was talking about her, but a small part of me felt smug that the rumour was about us together.

She instantly went on the defensive and turned her head slightly so I could just make out the features of her side profile. "Nothing happened!"

Her face was ruby red, and Lucian wanted to charge in there and stop the conversation.

Ryan lowered his voice to a whisper. "Then why are you blushing? Why do you smell like him? And why is he hanging out outside the bar right now, keeping an eye on you like a creeper, huh?"

Lucian snarled at Ryan, who flicked his eyes toward me and

offered me a cheeky grin, then a wink. Clementine's head whipped around, and I pressed myself against the wall like a kid in elementary school, trying not to be caught eavesdropping. My heart pounded in my chest and ears.

The door opened, and Clementine stood there with her arms crossed. Her neck strained as she looked up at me, but at that moment, I was the one who felt small.

"What are you doing?" she asked.

I gaped at her for a moment, feeling my ears and face burning.

Busted! "Nothing. Just ensuring you got to work okay," I coughed out.

"Well, I'm fine. You can go now."

There was such a finality to her words that I felt like she had slapped me across the face. I could feel Lucian pushing forward, and I knew he wasn't going to leave without a fight. But if I had to, I'd force him.

There went my plan for studying in the bar for the afternoon. I couldn't do that now. She would think I was spying, or worse, that I was possessive or stalking her, even if I piled textbooks on the table and knuckled down to work. The only thing I could do right now was leave. Lucian was pacing in my head and growled as that idea floated to him.

"Lucian enough!" I pleaded with him. *"Clementine is safe here with Ryan."*

"It's his fault she knew we were spying!"

"We shouldn't have been spying in the first place. She's a grown woman."

"She's human, and—"

"She's a human who knows about werewolves, so she's more alert than before. Besides, Ryan purposely changed his work schedule to keep her safe."

Giving her a single nod, I forced myself out of the front

doorway and back toward my car. Lucian tried to take control and force me back toward the bar. I felt sweat drip down my brow as I pushed him back with all my strength.

"If you keep acting like this, you'll scare her away, Lucian!" I growled. He stopped. He didn't want to scare her; he just needed to be near her and keep her safe. *"She's a strong person, but there's only so much crazy a girl can take,"* I advised. *"She needs time to adapt to our world and get used to you. Give her a bit of space, eh? If you keep pushing, she may not come back from Vancouver."*

That did it.

Lucian slumped over in defeat and whimpered at that possibility. I rested my head against the driver's door's cool glass and heaved a heavy sigh.

"Did you get him under control?" I looked up and spotted Ryan heading toward me.

"Yeah, but he isn't happy with you, so keep your distance."

Ryan smirked. "Sorry, man. I was just playing around. Are you okay?"

"I'm good, bro. I just didn't need her catching me like that. It was super embarrassing."

"She's already forgotten about it, I'm sure. When she came back, she was muttering something about pathetically possessive and protective werewolves, so I think she has Lucian pegged."

"Yeah. I told her that he had an ingrained need to protect her. That's why he was spying on her."

"She knows it wasn't fully you, bro, don't sweat it. What set Lucian off this time?"

"She's going away for the full moon."

"Really? Interesting." Ryan's eyes twinkled mischievously. "You know, mates are—"

"Shut the fuck up, Ryan. This isn't what you think it is." I ran my hand over my face in exasperation. He chuckled and shook his head. "She's going back to Vancouver. That's what set him off. I think he's worried that she won't come back if she goes."

"If you say so!"

I sighed and shook my head at Ryan. Damn stubborn friends. "Lucian doesn't like the idea of being away from her. It's hard to be her knight-in-shining-armour when she's more than a day's drive away."

"Did she indicate that she needs help?"

"No. She wouldn't even let me drive her. She said she was staying with her friend TJ."

"Oh, dear! Beautiful, independent, headstrong true mates will be every alpha's downfall," he teased.

I rolled my eyes, although a flash of her stunning turquoise eyes and long black hair flashed through my mind.

"Seriously, Ryan, let it go. If she were my mate, surely she'd want to hang around here on a full moon. Something would be telling her to stay here and find me," I reasoned.

"She's human. How do we know what they feel if anything at all?"

"Yeah. She's human. So she can't be my true mate," I said a little forcefully.

"If you say so." He smirked again. "Hey, by the way, Sophie said she has a general idea of who had the Rohypnol at the party but has no concrete evidence."

"Clem doesn't want me investigating it."

"Why not?"

"She didn't say, but she was adamant that I drop it."

"Are you going to?" he asked, raising his eyebrows as if knowing the answer.

I scoffed. "No."

"Didn't think so. So should I text Sophie and tell her to keep digging?"

"Yeah, but tell her to–"

"Be discreet. Yeah, I know." He rolled his eyes and pulled out his phone, quickly sending a message.

"Clementine told me someone has been stalking and tried to poison her."

"What? When?"

I shook my head. "She told me someone put bleach in her coffee the morning before her first work shift."

"What the hell?"

"She also warned me off on looking into that too. Said she couldn't be even sure if the stuff was happening to her or if she'd imagined it."

"I don't see how you could imagine someone putting bleach in your coffee. What did you say?"

"That I trusted her instincts."

He nodded. "Stalked, roofied, and bleach in a coffee? What's next?"

"No idea, but it needs to stop." Lucian grunted in agreement.

"I'll keep an ear out and an eye on her."

"I know you will."

"I should get back in there. I'll see you at training tomorrow?" he asked, presenting his fist.

I grazed his knuckles with mine. "Yeah. Lucian likes using you as a chew toy." He laughed and started toward the bar. "Hey, Ryan." He turned back. "Keep a fucking close eye on her, eh."

He raised two fingers to his brow and saluted me before walking into the establishment.

I climbed into the driver's seat and took a deep breath,

closing my eyes. I opened them again and turned the ignition, ready to drive home.

"*You want to know something?*" Lucian asked as I put the car in reverse.

"*What?*"

"*You told Ryan it was me who was out of control and spying on Clementine in the doorway, but we both know that isn't true. It was all you this time.*"

CHAPTER 27

CLEMENTINE

"I'm going for a walk!" I called out on Wednesday afternoon as I exited the mudroom and over the back lawn where Vinny and Dad were wrestling. Or at least that's what it looked like.

"Now brace your position, just like I taught you. I'll come in from the left, and you need to counteract my weight."

"Right," Vinny said, bracing himself into a low crouch.

I watched for a few moments as Dad slammed into him with the full force of a freight train.

"And here I thought you always wanted a son, yet you're obviously trying to kill him," I teased as Vinny was pummelled into the ground. "Vinny, just kick him in the gonads. He'll go down like a sack of potatoes."

"Vincent, do *not* kick me in the gonads," Dad warned, and Vinny laughed, then dusted himself off. "I'm just trying to go through some training techniques with your brother. Where are you going?"

"For a walk. Through there." I pointed to the trees.

"You're going into the bush?"

"Um, yeah."

"You're a city girl, Clementine. Do you even know how to walk in a bush?"

"Well, there's only one way to find out."

"Why the sudden interest in the bush?"

"That damn dream is still haunting me, but I know about werewolves now, so I'm unsure what my subconscious is trying to tell me."

"Tell me about this dream again?"

I had opened up about my dreams to Dad after he told me about my heritage, hoping to get some answers. I'd asked Vinny if he had any dreams about wolves too, and he shook his head and told me that he didn't know what I was talking about. Dad, once again, used the tagline of not knowing enough about half-breeds to give any concrete answers.

I sighed. "It started off as a black wolf chasing me through the streets around our neighbourhood in Vancouver. The black wolf led me to the edge of the river before taking a running leap at me, and I woke up just before I landed in the water.

"Then, a couple of months ago, it changed to me running through the bush, and a brown wolf chasing me. I was pushed over a cliff and down to the river below. Two different wolves, two different locations. Both ended with me dying in a river." He scratched at the rough dark stubble starting to coat his chin, looking perplexed. He had nothing. "I think the dream wolf wants me to go in there. Maybe. I don't know. It all sounds crazy."

"Do you want us to come with you?"

"No. You keep training Vinny. I think I need to do this alone."

"Be careful."

"Always am."

"If you meet any werewolves–"

"Don't worry, Dad. I'll kick them in the gonads," I said as I disappeared into the treeline.

I walked deeper into the trees, past the large trunk Liam had changed behind, and past the low shrubs that were sprinkled with a dusting of black fur. I picked it off a low branch and looked at it curiously.

I raised it to my nose and took a sniff, but it didn't smell like anything. I let it drop from my fingers, and the soft fur floated to the forest floor. I pressed forward, my sneakered feet stepping over large roots and rocks.

It was humid around the town of Blackfern Valley, but it was like a sauna within the forest canopy. I wiped my brow with the back of my hand and kept on. Through the sound of birds twittering in the treetops and small animals somewhere deep within the forest, I could hear the gentle trickle of running water.

I walked deeper still. Nothing matched or seemed familiar from my dreams. There was no track, no hunters' cabin, and no broken ladder that went up to an old tree stand. It was just a dense, hot, sticky bush.

The forest went quiet. The birds had stopped, and I couldn't even hear the sound of running water anymore. It was like I had gone deaf. Then, I heard the loud sound of a twig snapping. It was like a gun had gone off. Spooked, I ran. I picked up my pace, jumping over logs and tree roots. I whipped past lichen-covered trunks and slightly damp undergrowth, and kept running, in a direction I couldn't register. All I knew was that I had to keep moving.

I heard a loud, deep growl, and turned my head to see if my dream wolf had followed me. There was nothing there. Unfortunately, I forgot to stop running as I did, and I tripped over a large root that protruded from the forest floor. I twisted my ankle and then scraped my knee as I went down. Placing my hands in front of me was useless, but I did it by pure instinct.

I heard the growl again, and picked myself up and ran—or hobbled—as fast as my body would allow. Pain ricocheted up my ankle, and I cried out, tripping once more, tweaking my ankle even worse. To add insult to injury, I also scraped my face on a rock this time. I scampered up and kept limping on, feeling around my pocket for my phone and not finding it. I must have dropped it somewhere.

Will Dad be able to hear me if I scream out loud?

And I tripped again.

Before I could get myself back up, a wolf with fur the colour of straw jumped out of the overbrush and flattened its ears.

That's what did it.

I screamed as loud as I could. In seconds, the first beast was joined by another. This one had a coat the colour of graphite. It surprised me as it jumped out of the thicket.

I scrambled backward, backing into a tree. It started huffing as if it was laughing at my predicament. It bared its teeth at me, its blue eyes glaring, and a low snarl came from its throat.

A third and fourth wolf joined the duo, one the colour of creamed honey, the other the colour of rust. My heart raced, and I'm sure they could smell my fear. I let out another blood-curdling scream.

This is it. I'm dead. I had finally followed my dream to my death. *Thank you very much, subconscious!* I closed my eyes. Any moment now, I was going to be ravaged by wolves.

I waited. And waited...

I opened my eyes to find the wolves gone. Looking around, they were nowhere to be seen. Those werewolves were playing chicken with me, and I had lost. I sat there as big fat tears started to pour down my face. Lowering my head, I sobbed into my hands. Nothing was going to stop the flow. I was both relieved and terrified, and these tears seemed more than appropriate at the moment.

Hearing a whimper, I looked up and spotted an enormous tawny wolf peering at me. His eyes were the warmest brown with rings of pure gold. *Liam.* I wiped my eyes and felt myself shudder in relief.

He cautiously approached me, one small step at a time. When he realized I wasn't afraid, he gave a little huff. His wet black nose tickled as he sniffed my face and gave me a lick. Then another. He was lapping up my tears. Oh God, this was weird.

"Liam." I cringed and pushed my fingers into the thick fur around his neck to push him back. His fur was warm and gave me as much static electricity as his human form did. I looked into his deep brown eyes. "Thank you."

I threw my arms around his neck and breathed in his cedar and spice scent. It was stronger in his wolf form. He grumbled, and it vibrated throughout his body. His warm fur calmed me, and I pulled away so I could look at him again. He was stunning. Warm browns, reds and subtle tones of cream blended into his coat.

He tilted his head in my direction, gave me a nudge with his snout, then quickly bounded away. Surely, he wasn't leaving me here? I tried to stand, and my ankle gave out, making me groan in pain.

"You're hurt." Liam's voice came out gravelly, and the sound vibrated into my soul.

I looked up to see his hard chest, small dark blond curls, strong shoulders, and smooth arms. He was human and made his way toward me, barefoot and–

Oh, phew! He has shorts on.

My face burned.

He saw where I was looking and smirked. "I stashed shorts

in little plastic bags all over the place the other day. Good thing too." He winked.

"Lucky you stashed one close to here." My voice wobbled.

He approached me again, took a knee in front of me, and clasped my chin between his fingers, tilting my face, then studied me. I was sure I was a mess. *Yup, definitely a mess*, I thought as he took a twig out of my hair, flicking it behind him.

"What happened?" he asked.

"I had the dream again," I whispered. "I decided to come in here and see–" I shook my head. "A few werewolves spooked me. I tripped. Fell. That's all."

He nodded, but his eyes flashed with gold. He didn't say anything, but I could feel the rage permeating the air around him.

"I'm okay, Liam."

"A little scraped up, actually," he stated, his eyes combing my face.

"And a sprained ankle. But I'll be okay."

"Can you walk?"

I shrugged. "Probably not."

He looked at me, a face full of concern and all I wanted to do was lean in and kiss the look off his face. I had no idea where the urge came from, but I pushed it back, reminding myself that I needed to keep my guard up, especially around him. This was Liam. The same Liam who had a line of women after him— most of which who were in his league.

"I'll carry you out."

I laughed nervously. "You can't carry me, Liam."

"I've done it before," he argued.

"No," I growled as I looked at my ankle. It was throbbing.

I pulled down my sock and saw blue splotches instead of my usual creamy skin. I winced. This was not good. He made a low grumbling noise when he saw it, and his eyes flashed gold again.

"Okay, I need you to find me two decent sticks. Liam! Are you listening to me? Liam!" I growled.

His eyes had gone vacant, and I could see he was conversing with Lucian again.

"Stop it! I'm okay. Look, I need to make a splint. Can you find me two sticks?"

He looked at me again and nodded. I pulled off my left shoe and started unravelling the shoelaces.

He returned a few moments later with a few options and watched me as I selected a couple of sturdy ones. I placed two of them as best I could against my right ankle and tried to use the shoelace to tie it in place, swearing each time they shifted.

"Can I help?" he asked, gingerly taking my foot and placing it on his knee as he knelt on the dirty forest floor. I could feel the tingling sensations around my ankle and closed my eyes.

"Thanks. You need to wrap it as tight as you can."

"Got it," he grumbled.

A few moments later, my right foot was encased in a makeshift splint, and my left foot was covered in a sock that was no longer white. He followed my eyes to my feet as he helped me up. I attempted to bear weight on my injury gently, but a shooting pain shot up my ankle. I mewled a little bit and started taking deep breaths through my nose. He growled and slinked his arm around my body, taking my weight.

"I wish you would just let me carry you," he grumbled.

I rolled my eyes and started moving forward with him supporting me, hearing him mutter about headstrong, independent women.

CHAPTER 28

LIAM

My paws pounded through the bush as I cantered around, chasing a rabbit. I was supposed to be studying for my economics test, but I needed to run. I spent all Monday afternoon and evening filling my brain with the necessary information for Friday's test.

After my morning training on Tuesday, I spent the entire day at Kempthorne University. I didn't leave Kempthorne until late, as my classes ran late on Tuesdays. By the time I got home, I was too exhausted to study. Wednesday held no physical courses for me, so I woke up early with all intentions to study, and the plan soon went out the window.

I got through an hour or two and then went to find something to eat. My dad had come into the pack house kitchen and made himself a sandwich. He had been performing his alpha duties all morning and was keen to get out and work with his hands. So, after we finished our food, I went outside to help him do some work. He was renovating a cottage at the back of the pack house.

Our pack house was set out differently than many other homes I've visited. While other pack houses tended to be large

estate houses or mansions with enormous wings and ostentatious rooms, ours was quainter.

The main house was a large four-bedroom home with a
large living area, kitchen, and office. The whole second floor
was the alpha's quarters. The pack house was big enough to
hold small meetings with the beta or a few warriors, but if a
more significant get-together was needed, it was held in the
amphitheatre, located next to the training grounds.

Across the driveway from the pack house was an identical
four-bedroom house but on a slightly smaller scale. The beta's
house was laid out in much the same way as ours, but it had no
open-planned living area. Its kitchen was a lot smaller, and
there was no office. Our current beta used the smallest
bedroom as his office.

Then, there were a handful of guest cottages scattered
around the property, nestled back into the bush, looking like
something out of a fairy tale. These were for when we had
guests of the pack, and currently, my father was renovating the
smallest one for my mom and dad to move into one day, when I
took over as alpha.

So being the world-class procrastinator I was, I decided I
would help my dad with his renovations. After an hour or so of
helping my dad, stress and anxiety kicked in, and I told him I
needed to return to my studies.

That's where I stayed for the rest of the afternoon until I
heard the annoying sounds of my brother stomping through
the house—school was over for the afternoon. I listened for a
bit longer, and he made no motion to go to the training ground,
which meant that my brother was staying in for the remainder
of the day. I would never get any studying done with him slamming about like that.

So, after stretching, I decided to enjoy an afternoon
outdoors.

THE RABBIT DARTED in front of me again, and I chuckled internally as I chased it, backing off and letting the poor thing catch its breath every now and again. I was just about to stick my nose into the undergrowth to see if I could entice the critter out again when I heard a blood-curdling scream.

The scream made my hackles rise. My paws started galloping toward it, and my nose sniffed the air as I moved forward. Then I heard her scream again. Growling, I pushed myself faster, homing in on the only smell I cared about at that moment—the one fragrance that invaded my entire being. There was a mixture of odours in the forest, loads of different werewolf scents, but right now, all I needed to find was *her*. Clem had screamed, and I had to see if she was alright.

I saw her backed against a tree, breathing heavily. Her honeysuckle scent was saturated in fear. Tears streamed down her cherub face, and her cheek was red, this time not with a delicate blush but with smears of crimson blood. Her hair was messy and littered with leaves and twigs.

I gave a little whimper as I moved forward slowly. She raised her head, and the tears in her eyes made the aquamarine swirl and glisten like pools of water. Recognition hit her instantly as I continued my approach. She gave me a small smile that made my heart thump as I watched her wipe away her tears.

I wanted to taste them. Leaning forward, I gave her a quick lick. Then another. The tears were salty-sweet on my tongue, and I felt Lucian rumble happily. A warm heat encased my body and tickled my senses as I kept lapping at her face. I was enjoying the tickly sensation and salty-sweet taste of Clementine's emotions.

It felt natural.

Good.

Right.

She pushed me away slightly and then linked her arms around my neck. Her scent wafted up and filled me with a warm buzz. She was okay.

But she screamed.

Something had happened, and I needed to find out what. After a couple more minutes, the smell of her fear subsided, and following one more whiff of her intoxicating scent, I trotted off to find the shorts I had stashed over the weekend.

I watched her as I stalked out of the trees, my shorts covering my manhood as I stepped barefoot toward her. I noticed how her eyes raked my body, devouring every inch before they darted away, and a red tinge complimented her cheekbones.

As I took in her dishevelled appearance again, I felt myself stir a little at her bashful nature. She looked as though she had taken an intimate tumble around in the shrubs, the way her cheeks were flushed, and her eyes were bright. Then she turned her face, and I saw her cut cheek, which reminded me that it couldn't have been further from that.

When I saw her ankle, I almost lost it. Not Lucian this time, but *me*. I was furious. The woods were full of werewolf smells but after confirming with Sophie her suspicions and detecting the tones of the same wolves, I was ready to leave Clementine and go hunt those fuckers down.

Where Clementine should have been fragile, she was anything but. Her voice was firm and commanding as she took control of the situation. I admired her for remaining calm and relaxed in an emergency. She was a natural doctor, a medic, a nurturer, and a leader.

I shook my head and helped her adjust the shoelace and sticks onto her ankle, thinking it would have just been easier to carry her out. Then, I helped her hobble forward, tucking her into me safely to support her weight. I looked at her foot, one shoe covered, one sock covered, and I grumbled. She was going to fall again.

"Why didn't you take off both shoes?" I asked.

"Because there is a chance my ankle is broken. My shoe is keeping my ankle steady and reducing the swelling. It's better to keep it from moving until we have the resources to deal with it. The sticks ensure it stays rigid and doesn't give out in a different direction."

"You're trying to walk on a broken ankle?" I snarled.

I stopped moving and looked down at her, her scratched face, her kissable-plump lips open ever so slightly as she breathed through whatever pain she was in. I took half a step back and tucked my arm under her knees, swooping her into my arms. She squeaked but wrapped her arms around my neck regardless. She started to protest, but I put a stop to it.

"Okay, Doctor Stevens," I said soft and firm as I carefully walked around an uproot. "Tell me, where in your medical training does it say if you break a bone, you should walk on it? If that's what you think then I'm glad you dropped out of medical school. You would have made a crappy doctor."

She huffed. And when I peered at her cherub face, she was smirking slightly.

We were quiet as I walked through the trees back toward my house. I needed to get her to the doctor's clinic. I could have walked her straight there, but I didn't want to cause any more rumours if people saw me carry her through town. Plus, if I could walk her to my house that meant I could have her to myself for a bit longer. I could hold her some more. She felt so good in my arms; her scent invading my senses with every step I took. It felt natural.

"Sorry, I know I'm not exactly light," she murmured, her cheeks going ruby red and her eyes filling with tears.

I huffed and didn't deem her comment with an answer. All I did was hold her tighter against my chest. How was I supposed to tell her that she felt perfect to me?

Forty minutes later, I walked out of the bush at the back of the pack house, heading straight past the cottage my dad was working on.

"Liam? What–" he started.

"Later!" I growled, then remembered my manners. I changed my tone to a softer one. "I'll explain later, Alpha."

Clem's head whipped around, and her curious eyes looked over to my dad, then back at me. I placed her down gently next to my car, opened the passenger door for her, then assisted her into the seat. "I'll be right back. Let me grab a shirt and some flip-flops," I told her.

I DROVE Clementine to the medical centre and looked around before I helped her out of the car. The street was empty, so I naturally went to pick her up again. This time, she didn't fight and moulded herself to me. Lucian rumbled with pleasure.

Unsurprisingly, the medical centre's waiting room was empty. Adult werewolves didn't tend to need much medical intervention. I was directed to take Clem into one of the exam rooms. I placed her on the gurney and helped her into a sitting position.

"Thanks, Liam. I'm sure there's somewhere you're supposed to be. Don't you have a test you need to study for?" I crossed my arms and said nothing. "Seriously. I'm okay now. I'll just call my– Oh, crap, my phone!" She closed her eyes and a frustrated expression passed over her pretty face.

"What?"

"I dropped my phone somewhere in the bush. I can't call Dad."

"I can." His eyes went vacant for more than a few minutes before refocusing on me.

"Okay, the good news is that your dad has your phone. He apparently went looking for you and found it about a click from your house. The bad news is that your dad is pissed."

"I'm surprised he isn't on his way here," I mumbled.

"He is."

She frowned. "Great."

I smiled, and Lucian sent forward an image of me kissing her frown off her face. My heart flipped, and I swallowed. I suddenly wanted to know what Clem's lips tasted like. I wondered if their flavour would be similar to her earlier tears. Before I could act on mine and Lucian's impulses, she turned to me and sighed.

"Glad to see that even werewolf doctors make you wait. It's nice to have some normalcy."

Her eyes twinkled with her dry sense of humour, and I couldn't help but laugh. A minute later, the doctor came in and began his examination.

CHAPTER 29
CLEMENTINE

MY ANKLE WASN'T BROKEN! Well, at least it wasn't broken *anymore*. After a quick X-Ray and an ultrasound on my injury, they found that I had a severely twisted ligament, some bad bruising, and a freshly healed hairline fracture. He asked me to bear weight on it, and when I stood, I was surprised that my ankle could take the pressure. The pain had been subtle and dull, but nothing I couldn't handle. There was no way I could walk on it earlier, and with a twisted ligament, I should have been at least given a moon boot and some crutches, but the doctor shook his head and told me that I was already starting to heal, so there was no point. I blinked a few times, half hobbling over to the mirror and noticing that the scrape on my face was mostly gone. Then I studied my knees. The scrapes had healed entirely, leaving a baby-pink splatter of new tissue.

What the fuck?

Liam studied me curiously. He looked like I felt: we had a million questions running through our minds.

Dad arrived before he could ask about anything, so Liam kept his mouth shut as he pulled me into a rough hug. Liam took that as an excuse to leave, reminding me he had a test to study for.

———

Friday night rolled by quickly, and I was swamped at the bar. My mostly healed ankle still ached now and again, but I simply pushed through the twinges of tenderness. I barely had a chance to breathe, let alone rest my aches. Tina had put on a buy-one-get-one-half-price cocktail night, and Ryan was getting a crash course on making decent cocktails from yours truly.

He was soon getting the hang of the cocktail shaker and started to show off like he was a mixologist in the Vegas club scene.

I laughed at his playful nature and then scanned the room. "Why is it so busy tonight?" I complained to Ryan as I smashed up large clumps of ice with a scoop.

"This place is always pumping the weekend before a full moon. All the wolves are getting revved up for it and want to party hard before the pack run. All the bars shut early on full moon evenings, and most of the pack meets up at the pack house before they go for a run," he informed.

It was still light outside, and most people were enjoying the evening sun on the patio, but the bar was filling up fast.

"What about the um...pups?" The word felt foreign on my tongue.

"Yeah, they all get into mischief usually." He winked. "A few wolves who don't want to run usually take care of them. The pups have an organized movie marathon at the theatre in town this full moon."

"Sounds like fun."

"The younger kids will probably go. The older ones will

probably sneak away and go be, um, teenagers?" He smirked at me in such a way that made me wonder what he used to get up to when he was a teenager without a wolf. "Is your brother going to Vancouver with you?"

"No, he's hanging around here with some other kids his age that haven't turned yet. He wants to watch the pack run."

"It's not that exciting to watch. Being a part of it, however..." He gave me a wink and went to serve margaritas to some ladies waiting at the end of the bar before going into the storeroom.

I smiled and shook my head at him.

Nola walked up to the bar and thrust a piece of paper in my face. I read the order and pulled out a few glasses and ingredients to complete it.

"What, you can't be happy with our alpha-elect; you need to take the beta-elect too?" her voice was waspish, and I wasn't in the mood for her angst.

"What the hell are you talking about, Nola?" I rolled my eyes and measured the spirits I needed to pour into the glasses.

"Everyone knows that you slept with *my* Liam. And now you're looking at topping it off by sleeping with his best friend?"

I felt the heat burning my cheeks, and usually, I would shy away from drama, but this time I needed to set the record straight.

"For your information, not that it's any of your business, I haven't had sex with Liam," I snarled. "And secondly, I'm pretty sure he's *not* your Liam. In fact, I'm sure the whole town knows he's done with you."

I heard her low growl and saw the flash of silver that ringed her icy blue eyes. "You may have lost the dorky glasses, but you're still a fat virgin, Clementine. If he did have sex with you, it was probably just a pity fuck."

"We didn't have sex," I repeated, feeling my face burn hotter, but this time in anger.

"Clementine, let me give you some advice. No half-breed is ever going to be luna."

"Nola, let me give *you* some advice. Jealousy doesn't look good on anyone." I placed the drinks on the tray and slid it to her. "Is that all?" I asked as politely as I could.

I bit the inside of my cheek. She looked like she was about to say something else.

"Is everything alright, Nola?" I felt Ryan's presence behind me.

Nola glared at both of us and stalked away with her drinks. I turned to face him and saw that he was carrying two large boxes of bottles to reload the small bar fridge. He placed them on the floor next to me.

"You okay?" He placed his hand on the small of my back. "I thought you might have needed some help taking care of the trash." He flicked his eyes over to Nola and smirked.

"Nope, all good here." I wiped my hands on my apron, bent down to bring the bottles forward in the bar fridge and ripped open the box to start loading the warm ones behind them. "She was just marking her territory."

He rolled his eyes. "Liam isn't even here."

My anxiety ramped up tenfold at Ryan's comment. I pushed it away as soon as it surfaced, plastering a fake smile on my face. I tried not to make it obvious that I was waiting for him to show up; that every time I looked around and didn't see him, it left an uneasy feeling in my stomach. I kept a casual eye on the door as I fluttered around, working the bar. I was keen to see him if only to buy him a drink to say thank you for carrying my fat ass out of the bush.

I knew he was busy studying for a mammoth test, and other than his spout of heroism, I hadn't seen or heard from him. But he promised me he would come hang out at the bar tonight to drown his sorrows, and I found myself eagerly watching the door.

"Oh no, her territory also extends to you, Mister Beta-Elect."

"Beta-Elect? Me? God, she's tripping."

"What do you mean?"

"Beta is like the second-in-command in a werewolf hierarchy. The current beta is Jerome Evans, and his son Murdoch is next in line."

"Then why does she think that you're the beta-elect?" I looked into Ryan's crystal-grey eyes ringed in their warm brown.

He gave a non-committal shrug. "Well, technically, it's not a position you can be born into."

"Then how is Murdoch next in line?"

He shook his head. "I'm not explaining this very well. Okay, pack lesson number three-hundred-and forty-two. Alpha blood is handed down generation after generation to those within the alpha lineage. Alpha Jed had it, and so does Alpha Josiah, which means so do Liam and Sean. Naturally, the first-born son is alpha-elect unless he renounces his title or gets killed or whatever. That's pretty simple to understand, right?"

I nodded. "Yeah, sort of like Royal Family bloodline. The kingdom generally is passed on to the eldest son." I smiled at my analogy.

Ryan tilted his head and started ripping open the second box of alcohol, handing me the bottles to stow away.

"Yeah, kind of, I guess. Beta werewolves don't have a bloodline. There is no such thing. Alphas generally pick the wolves they think have the best attributes to be second-in-command. The werewolves are usually strong and loyal and have a shit tonne of respect amongst their peers." He took a breath. "Anyway, because the beta lives at the pack house and is so close with the alpha, the beta's pup and the alpha's pup grow up together. They typically develop a brotherly bond, and that's why, traditionally the beta title is usually handed down to the son. But it isn't a position you're born into." He handed me another couple of bottles. "So that's why Nola thinks I'm the beta-elect. It's because Beta Jerome had two daughters around Liam's and my age, then he had Murdoch. Liam and I grew up together. Liam and Murdoch didn't."

"Can't a woman be a beta?"

"Not generally. Pack law is a bit misogynistic." He shrugged apologetically. "Here's a kicker, though. Most betas throughout history also have alpha blood."

"What do you mean?"

"Well, there can only be one alpha for each pack, right? But most alphas have more than one pup. The siblings have alpha powers but no title. So, male, and female sibling wolves usually either move to new packs or become pack warriors, etcetera. Eventually, the bloodline dilutes a little over time, and they aren't nearly as strong as the alpha anymore, but they make great betas."

"Are the Evans' of alpha descent?"

"No, they aren't. But I don't believe the Evans' were Alpha Josiah's first pick."

"Who was his first pick?"

"Josiah never wanted to be alpha. He thought he could handle it if he had his best friend as his beta. Rumour has it that his best friend and business partner turned him down because his best friend had fallen in love with a human and had moved to Vancouver during Alpha Jed's reign."

The bottle I was holding fell out of my hand and rolled away, luckily not shattering. Ryan stretched out to retrieve it, then handed it back to me.

"Are you saying that my dad was asked to be second-in-command? That Dad has alpha blood?"

"Asked to be beta, yes. As for your second question, I guess I will find out on the full moon when he runs with the pack."

"How will you know?"

"The size of the wolf and the amount of power that rolls off him while in wolf form, and a few other trade secrets." He winked. "I'll just be able to tell. It's instinct." My mind was swimming. Ryan smirked. "Well, your brain looks truly full and cooked. My work here is done."

"Hey, Ryan. One more question," I said before he walked away.

"Shoot."

"What the hell is a luna?"

His eyebrows rose. "Why do you ask?"

"Nola. She didn't only say you were beta-elect, but she indicated that I would never be luna. What the hell is a luna?"

"Every king needs his queen," he said, referring to my earlier comparison. "Luna is the title of the alpha's mate. The alpha and luna rule the pack together."

CHAPTER 30

LIAM

I WAS TENSE. I figured it had been the stress from my economics test. Or maybe it was something to do with the approaching full moon, but we were still a week out from it. I paced my room back and forward, deep in thought. I couldn't be this jittery around Clementine, she was bound to ask questions, and I didn't know how to answer them. I hadn't responded to her questions since I left her with her dad at the medical centre. Her text messages had been left mostly unanswered too.

This morning I received a message from Clementine wishing me luck on my test, and my entire stomach twisted into knots. I hadn't replied to that one either. Instead, I turned my phone off and drove out to Kempthorne University.

I had told her I would go to Lupus' after my test, but I couldn't bring myself to go. My mind was all over the place. My body thrummed with unwanted tension. I felt like I wanted to burst out of my skin. Lucian was lying down with his head between his paws, watching me pace but offering no guidance.

I snarled when the door suddenly opened. Sean was standing there chomping on a chicken drumstick. "Dude, I can hear you pacing from the kitchen. You're driving me nuts."

I ran my hand through my hair and pulled anxiously on a long bit of the front that was starting to flop into my eyes.

"It's Friday night. Don't you have a hot date or something?"

"No. I don't."

"Is that why you're pacing? Can't decide what she-wolf to call?"

"No."

"Well, you're in luck. Roman texted me before. Apparently, Lupus' is going off, and most of the she-wolves are there, getting cheap cocktails. So, stop pacing and go get some tail," he said cheekily through a mouthful of chicken.

Right, Lupus'.

The one place I was internally debating whether I should go to or not. Where Clementine was serving her mouth-watering cocktails. Where she could capture my attention from across the room by her scent alone. Where I could get lost in her turquoise eyes for hours. Where I could see her kissable plump lips–

Lucian's ears perked up at my thought pattern, but I ignored him, pushed the intrusive thoughts away, and then looked at my brother with interest. "Why is Roman texting you? And why is she texting you about cheap drinks at the bar? You're sixteen," I said.

"I sort of asked her out." He shrugged nonchalantly. "We were supposed to go out tonight, but she told me that Tina called her in at the last minute to work."

My brother was trying to act cool, but I could see through his act. It was a great distraction.

"You asked Roman out? Good for you, dude."

He gave me a sheepish smile. "Yeah. Our date is postponed, but she suggested we could run together."

"As in *run* together?" I asked.

"Yeah, during the pack run," he grumbled.

Usually, this was what wolves said to each other to find out if they were mates. But my brother was sixteen years old, and I knew Roman was of a similar age, if maybe a little older. They couldn't find this out for sure until they both were twenty years old. Still, the gesture was sweet.

"Does she know you haven't shifted yet?"

"Yeah, I told her. It was super embarrassing," he grumbled.

"Maybe this will give Silas a hurry up?" I said kindly.

He shrugged. "So, I was wondering…"

"Yeah?"

"Can you take me into Lupus'?" And just like that, my moment of distraction was over. My heart started pounding in my ears—the tension drowning me in waves.

"Why? You're a minor. You can't take advantage of the cocktails."

"No, but I can watch Roman."

"Sean, that's creepy," I grumbled, the irony not lost on me.

He rolled his eyes. "Not like that."

"Then what did you mean?"

"Nothing. Never mind. So, can we go?"

Panic set in. I prayed that my face was indifferent. "Sean, I'm not really interested in going out tonight."

"Yes, you are. You always are."

"I was thinking of shifting and going for a run if you want to join me?" I teased.

He flipped me his middle finger. "The moment Silas decides to show his fur, your ass is grass!" he grumbled. "I'll leave you to your pacing."

"You lied to your brother," Lucian said softly after Sean disappeared. *"You don't want to run at all."*

"No, I don't," I agreed.

"We can run, you know. I won't take you there, even though that's where you want to be."

"I don't know what you're talking about."

"You're avoiding her."

I closed my eyes. *"No, I'm not."*

His tone was still soft, as if he didn't want to spook me. *"You're the only one standing in your way, Liam. I can tell you that when I'm not around her, I miss her. A lot. And I'm pretty sure you do too."*

"I don't want to talk about it, Lucian."

He swished his tail and said nothing more.

I turned to my bed and collapsed on it, groaning into my pillow. I breathed in and out into the down-feathers. I don't know how long I lay there, but I was there for a while, trying to get the antsy feeling to dissipate, and wondered why I was feeling the full moon's pull so far out from the actual night. Clementine's scent was long gone from my room, but I kept imagining I could smell it on my pillow. It didn't calm me like it usually did.

My phone pinged from my desk across the room, and I looked at it curiously. My heart thundered in my chest. Was it Clementine checking in? I crossed the room, each footstep feeling like I was walking through quicksand. I picked up my phone and smiled when I saw Sophie's name on the screen. Relief washed over me, followed by a wave of something similar to guilt. I pushed the feeling away and opened her message.

SOPHIE:

Doctor Jay is playing some epic tunes right now. SOOO good. Get your ass here!

I smiled and checked the time. It was ten o'clock, and I did need a night out after that horrendous test and get rid of this built-up tension. Watching Doctor Jay was probably the best offer I would get. I hesitated before texting her back, wondering if I should pop into Lupus' on the way out. I decided against it.

Until I could figure out why I was suddenly so jittery and all in knots over Clementine, I had to stay away. I messaged Sophie, telling her that I would see her soon.

———

I walked into the noisy nightclub and spotted Stacey at the bar. I smiled as I walked over to her. Her blonde curls reflected the lights as they strobed around the space. It was packed with Kempthorne residents, both werewolf and human, by the smells that wafted toward me.

"What are you drinking?" she shouted over the heavy bass.

"Tequila," I shouted back.

"Alpha after my own heart." She grinned, then leaned over to the bartender and asked for two tequila shots. The amber liquid came down the bar with a slice of lime on top. Stacey was licking her hand and sprinkling table salt between her thumb and forefinger. Grabbing my hand, she licked where my thumb met my palm and sprinkled it with salt. The gesture surprised me, and usually, I would find something like that seductive, but right now, it felt incredibly wrong. And I was growing more tense instead of relaxed. The weird sensation between my neck and shoulders had come back. I rolled my shoulders to try to relieve some of the pressure, but it did little to help.

She grinned my way and handed me the tiny glass. "Cheers!" she said as she took the shot.

I mimicked her, licking the salt and slamming the glass back. The alcohol burned and tasted awful, so I bit into the lime, shuddering slightly.

"Whoo!" She applauded, then ordered another round.

Sophie came over, grinning from ear to ear as we downed our third tequila shot.

"You made it," she cheered. "Come dance!"

"In a minute," I said.

I saw a bartender shaking a cocktail shaker. She had long dark hair and big green eyes, and I suddenly felt disappointed. I shook it off and flexed my shoulders again. I put my hand up to one of the bartenders and ordered my fourth shot of tequila and a beer. It took a lot to get a werewolf drunk, but I still should pace myself.

Doctor Jay was spinning out some of my favourite tunes, so I grudgingly agreed to be dragged out onto the dancefloor. The girls were twisting and turning to the music, and I felt myself joining in. Lucian smiled as I let myself go and released the tension that had accumulated over the last couple of days.

Another four rounds of shots, and I was perfectly relaxed. I was in no way near drunk, but content. Tapping my foot to the music, I sat on a sectional couch. The girls had disappeared to the restroom, and I pulled out my phone.

There were no messages from Clementine. I tried not to feel disappointed, knowing that she was working, and the bar wouldn't close until around one in the morning. I looked at the time. It was twenty-to-two. Shit, she had already finished work. I knew that Ryan probably had driven her home afterwards, but I still felt like an ass.

I went to send her a text to apologize for not showing up, but I couldn't figure out what to say. She might already be asleep, but I needed to say something. After two or three false starts, I gave up and returned to the bar for more alcohol.

I was greeted by some drunken university friends—all werewolves—so they must have started much earlier than I did. I joined their party for a moment, smiling as they all took shots of a golden liquid with flecks of purple through it. They offered me one, and I quickly threw my head back, gulping it down. I coughed hard. It was the weirdest tasting thing I had ever ingested. It tasted sickly sweet yet burned on the way down. I looked at the shot glass and noticed there were little flecks of purple still at the bottom of the glass. Before I could ask them about it, Stacey found me and pulled me back onto the dance floor.

I was finally buzzed. My arms were wrapped around Stacey's tiny waist, and her ass grinded against my manhood. Her scent was weak, and I had to push my nose right into her hair to get a decent whiff. I was sure I could smell her subtle wolfy tones, although I couldn't place the scent. I could make out another scent on her, though—the start of arousal. I spun her around and smiled before claiming her lips with mine.

CHAPTER 31

CLEMENTINE

I SMILED at my dad as he handed me the truck keys. It was Thursday and the day before the full moon. Dad had allowed me to borrow his truck a day earlier than planned. The full moon was officially at its peak on Friday night, but Dad had mentioned that the night before and a few after the full moon were still filled with quite the raucous for werewolves, and I could tell. The whole town seemed to be going crazy.

It appeared that everyone started to go nuts a lot earlier than my father had indicated, honestly. Ryan seemed antsy. Tina was going through a deep clean of the bar and grill. Sophie was quiet, and Roman acted like she had too much caffeine in her system. Most other people were behaving oddly too. I hadn't seen Liam since last week, so I couldn't even begin to understand how the approaching full moon was affecting him, but I think it was safe to say that it was a good idea to get the hell out of Dodge.

Liam hadn't turned up at Lupus' last Friday, and I tried not to be disheartened by it. As the bar shut down around one in the morning and the mop buckets came out, Ryan turned to me and grinned. He flashed his phone toward me and informed me that Sophie, Stacey, and Liam were partying it up in Kempthorne thanks to Doctor Jay. First, I was confused because Liam had invited me this weekend to see Doctor Jay but never mentioned that the DJ was spinning last Friday. I kept my face indifferent as unwarranted hurt invaded my emotions. He had told me he would turn up at Lupus' to drown his sorrows, yet he had invited two other gorgeous women to party in Kempthorne.

I took a deep breath and plastered what felt like the hundredth fake smile across my face. I had no right to feel upset, but for some reason, I did. Even when I reasoned that it was possible, he hadn't made it back to Blackfern Valley, that he'd opted to stay in Kempthorne after his test, the foreboding feeling wouldn't pass. When Ryan turned his back, I quickly pulled my phone out of my apron pocket to check for messages. There were none. My hurt amplified. I was crushed and barely holding it together. I took a few deep breaths and busied myself away from everyone else to regain control of my emotions.

Ryan suggested that we headed into Kempthorne to join them. Part of me wanted to go; head home, throw on a great outfit, travel into Kempthorne, and dance my feelings away, all under Liam's watchful eye. I craved to show him what he was missing. The confident part of me that rarely showed her head was soon subdued by the shy and insecure side. The latter shook her head and told me that it was a stupid idea; that if he had wanted to see me, he would have come to Lupus' as he'd said he would, or he'd have invited me out to Kempthorne himself. I didn't want to appear desperate or needy by suddenly showing up.

Ryan stared and waited for my answer.

"No, not tonight, Ryan. I'm tired," I lied. "But you totally need to go ahead and burn off some energy on the dance floor.

Go show some she-wolf what she's missing," I added with a friendly wink.

"Are you sure?" He examined me closely, and I plastered another fake smile. He didn't know I had been waiting on Liam all night. And he didn't need to know how much it bothered me that he was in Kempthorne. I wasn't Nola, Cassie, or any other girl who seemed to want Liam. I was just me. I had no claim on him. And I never would.

"Yes. I'm sure. I'm not much for the clubbing scene, but you go ahead. I'll just walk home."

"I'm not letting you walk home!" His eyes flashed dangerously. The browns around his grey darkened.

"Fine. Take me home if you must, but then you should go and find some girl to party with." He gave me a small, almost shy smile that didn't match his habitual cocky demeanour.

"There is actually only one girl I'm interested in, Clem."

My heart flipped uncomfortably. "W-who?"

"Stacey." He shrugged as nonchalantly as he could, then he gave me a sheepish smile, and I noticed a little pink on the tops of his ears.

I was relieved it wasn't me. Then, I felt a little foolish that I thought, for a brief second, it could have been. I wondered if I would have felt the same if it was Liam instead of Ryan who confessed, and I frowned.

Stop it, Clementine!

RYAN DROPPED ME HOME, and I shrugged off my oversized work shirt, threw on a pair of pyjamas and turned into my bed, staring down my phone on my bedside table for roughly an hour, waiting to see if he would text me. It stayed silent, and eventually, I fell into slumber and dreamed of wolves.

I THOUGHT I would have seen Liam over the weekend, or even Monday or Tuesday while I worked, but he was a no-show then too. I tried not to let it get to me, aware he could be busy with university, but his absence was noticed, and not just by me. Nola had picked up on it, and so had Ryan.

Ryan had said that Liam was always at Lupus'. He couldn't understand why his friend had suddenly stopped showing up. I told him that he was probably studying, and that's when he let it slip that Lupus' was usually his preferred study destination. I felt like I had been smacked in the face. But as always, I hid my dismay with a small smile, and turned my back to those who knew me most.

My mind went into overdrive. I worried I had scared him away; that he was avoiding me. I wanted to reassure him that he wasn't obligated to protect me. Hell, he wasn't even obligated to be my friend. I was more than happy to pretend we hadn't even started a friendship, just so he could be his normal self. My insecurities were raising their ugly heads, and I forcibly shook myself of those nasty reticent memories.

No, I refused to believe that Liam was avoiding me. He wasn't like the other assholes I knew. One week of not seeing him wasn't a big deal. I wasn't going to let myself fall into a dark place because of that. I pushed away the bereft feeling that came over me and continued to laugh with Ryan, pretending I wasn't worried, or that I wasn't missing Liam even though it was the truth. I missed seeing his face, hearing his laugh, and his scent. I missed *all* of him. Silly, considering I had only known him for about three weeks. But being friends with Liam had been so effortless.

"ARE you sure you want to do this? It's a long drive by yourself," my dad asked nearly a week later.

"Yes, Dad. But more importantly, are you sure it's okay if I leave a day early? What about your work?"

"No one works that hard around a full moon, Clemmy. And my work is slow at the moment."

"Are we in trouble? I can try and get more hours at the bar if we are."

"No, Clemmy, we're not in trouble. Stop worrying."

I paused to look at him. His black hair was scraggy around his shoulders, and his green eyes were creased with wrinkles, but he appeared relaxed for the first time in months. Content. Blackfern Valley was good for him. It was obvious a wolf needed his pack.

"If you're sure."

"I'm sure. Text me when you get there," he grumped, giving me a brief hug before pushing me toward his truck. "And stay safe. If anything happens to you, I swear I'm heading down there and ripping TJ apart with my bare hands."

"How are you going to get there? I have your truck." I poked my tongue out at him.

His eyes flashed for a moment, the silver glowing. "You forget, young lady, I'm a werewolf. I have ways you haven't even begun to understand yet." His tone took on a mysterious quality, and I studied him.

"You would just borrow somebody's car," I laughed, and he threw me a cheesy smile that told me I nailed his 'mysterious way' on the head. I clambered up into the cab and rolled down the window.

"I'll see you Tuesday," Dad said.

"See you Tuesday," I parroted as I started the vehicle. "Unless, of course, TJ and I are in prison. Then I'll be ringing you and asking for bail money." Before my dad could retort, I rolled the truck down the driveway and gave a couple of toots on the horn, along with a brief wave through the driver's side window.

The moment I reached the border of Blackfern Valley, a strange sensation started in the pit of my stomach. It churned, and I suddenly felt extremely nauseous. Not only that, but I felt a sudden tension in the back of my shoulders and neck. I stretched a little bit and groaned. I had only just started driving; it was too early for me to seize up. Turning up my tunes, I tried my hardest to ignore the sensation.

The feeling eventually disappeared as I sipped on a water bottle and gunned my way to the main highway. Soon, the deep greens of the forest were far behind me, and I pressed my foot down harder on the accelerator. The excitement started to rush over me as I zoomed my dad's truck down the highway.

I drove for six hours before I pulled over for a decent break. I entered the Tim Hortons and ordered myself some food and a coffee. I took out my phone and was surprised there were no messages. I looked at Liam's name on my messages list, opened the message box, and saw that he still hadn't responded to the message I had sent him on Tuesday. Hell, he hadn't even viewed it.

Thank you, iPhone, for making it clear.

I opened a message box for TJ and told him that I had just stopped for a break and would be in Vancouver at some point the next day. I looked at Liam's name again and sighed. I had no idea what was up with him. I went to type out another message to let him know I was out of town for a few days, but quickly decided against it. He probably wouldn't reply anyway, let alone read it. My stomach churned at the thought, and the tension between my shoulder blades was back. I placed my phone in my bag and got ready for more driving.

I clambered back to the truck with a box of Timbits and

laughed as I almost lost my balance trying to get my short ass into the cab. Liam wasn't kidding when he asked if I needed a booster seat to drive. I smiled as I remembered his teasing me about it, then shook my head angrily. I felt like I was letting myself fall into the same trap over and over again. Liam was living rent-free in my mind, and I needed to use this trip to forget about him and focus on something else. I needed to remind myself why I needed to be on guard around guys like him.

Once more, my stomach churned, and my shoulders ached. I rolled them and took a deep breath before turning over the ignition and making my way back onto the highway, away from Blackfern Valley and toward the city of Vancouver.

CHAPTER 32
LIAM

I HAD WOKEN with the sound of drills in my head. I felt out for Lucian, and I couldn't feel him, which was my first indication something was wrong. I slowly opened my eyes but didn't recognize the ceiling I was staring at. I looked around the room and noticed a cheap Formica coffee table and a small television fixed to the wall.

"Good morning, Liam." Stacey smiled as she entered the living room, walked over to the small kitchen, and started to warm a pot of coffee.

"Oh, God! My head! What the hell happened?"

The couch I was lying on was hard and uncomfortable. I tried to sit up, and the world spun.

"You got piss drunk, so I had to bring you back here."

"Why does my head hurt?"

She smiled at me mischievously. "I believe they call it a hangover."

"Werewolves don't get drunk or get hangovers," I snarled.

The room spun slightly, and I grabbed my skull to try and stop it.

"They do if they take shots laced with wolfsbane."

"I'm sorry, *what*?"

"You took a shot with wolfsbane in it. Do you not remember?" The purple flecks in the bottom of the shot glass flashed through my memory. "Werewolves usually take a shot like that if they actually want to get drunk. Unfortunately, if you're not used to it, it gives you a hell of a hangover."

"How the hell does someone get access to wolfsbane in Kempthorne?" I grumbled into my hands.

"It's just a plant. Plants don't have any immoral notions. It grows around here," she said casually.

"It was put in my drink," I snarled.

"Not evilly. And it's such a small dosage that it weakens you enough to get drunk without poisoning you. The bar wouldn't be able to sell the shots otherwise. Besides, each time you take one of those shots, they keep a close eye on you."

She placed a mug of coffee in front of me and sat in an armchair opposite me, sipping at a bright-red cup. She gave me an appraising look. I was sure I looked like shit. I definitely felt like it.

"Do you remember anything from last night?"

I shook my head. My heart pounded in my chest and ears. *What the hell did I do?*

"Well, we had heaps of shots, we danced, we sang, we laughed and then we came back here together."

"Where was Sophie in all this?"

"She disappeared with some guy from her French class long before you took the wolfsbane shot." She took another sip of her coffee.

"So that's it? We got drunk, and you carried me home?" Relief washed through me.

"Well..." she began, obviously choosing her words with care as she cradled the bright-red mug between her hands.

"What?" I urged, taking a large gulp of the black, bitter coffee, and feeling the scorching liquid scald my throat.

"We kissed on the dancefloor, and *then* we came back here."

My eyes went wide. *Fuck.*

"But then you started apologising. I know you're Canadian, but that was a real turn-off. And what made it worse was you weren't apologising to me."

"I wasn't?" Now, I was wholly confused.

"No. You were apologising to Clementine. Something about not going to see her and not understanding why she makes you feel the way you feel. I'm not sure. They were drunken ramblings. So, when we got here, I guided you to the couch, and you fell asleep straight away."

My stomach lurched. "I'm sorry, Stacey."

She chuckled, then smirked. "At least you have the name right this time. So, what are these feelings you have for Clementine?"

"What?" I was still clawing at my head, but when I looked at Stacey, her hazel eyes danced with curiosity. My heart thumped in my chest, and I was sure she could hear it. "Fuck if I know. I was drunk."

I SPENT the next three days nursing a hangover. After the first day, I could feel Lucian's presence, but he was still asleep, snoring and growling in his slumber. That was only a tiny amount of aconite, and it had entirely taken out my wolf. When he woke up on the second day, he yelled at me for being stupid, then retreated into the far recesses of my mind in a glorious sulk.

Lucian was quiet for the rest of the week too, but the closer we got to the full moon the more impatient he became. It started with subtle hints, flashes of the forest, flashes of the full moon, a trickling stream, a black wolf, the sound of a howl. When that didn't rouse me, he changed tactics and got a little bolder as he kept flashing images of Clementine: dark hair, her long black lashes making her turquoise eyes pop...

I couldn't believe it had been more than a week since I'd spoken to her. I didn't mean to stop, it kind of just happened. And it made me feel terrible. It had reduced our friendship to feeling awkward and strained. And it was all my fault. Now, I felt this gravitational pull, a need to be near her. All I wanted to do was go see her and beg for her forgiveness.

Lucian wagged his tail when he realized I finally agreed to his not-so-subtle hints. According to her text messages, that I never responded to, she was heading to Vancouver on the morning of the full moon.

All I needed to do now was go to her house and convince her to let me take her to Vancouver. We would be able to talk about whatever bullshit we needed to on the road; re-establish our friendship. Sure, I would miss the pack run, which would suck, but I was sure there were many places I could turn and run as the full moon hit on the city's outskirts. And when we got to Vancouver, there was bound to be an area I could change if I needed to run for the other nights following the one of the full moon.

Patrick managed to live in Vancouver for twenty-something years. I bet he can tell me where to go.

With that in mind, I quickly shoved a couple of changes of clothes into an overnight bag, then dashed into the bathroom and had the world's fastest shower. I brushed my teeth and threw the toothbrush and toothpaste into my overnight bag too. Putting on some fresh clothes, I slipped my shoes on and grabbed my car keys.

.   .   .

I PARKED outside her house just after eight in the morning and ran to the front door. I knocked loudly and then pushed the annoyingly long bit of my hair back. Patrick answered and looked surprised to see me standing on his doorstep.

"Hey, Liam. What brings you here at this time of day?"

"Hey! I'm here to take Clem to Vancouver."

"Wait, what? She's already left for Vancouver, son. Didn't she tell you?"

"What are you talking about? When did she leave?" Maybe I could catch up to her, get her to take her dad's truck back home and join me in my car.

"She took the truck yesterday."

Dread weighed deep in my stomach. "But she told me she was supposed to be leaving today. And I was meant to take her."

"Sorry, Liam, she never told me those plans." Patrick looked genuinely confused. "I didn't realize you were heading to Vancouver with her. She was going to visit Travis."

"No, it's okay. I've been so busy with university and studying that I must have missed the– Wait, who's Travis?"

"Travis Jones. She calls him TJ. They studied together at UBC. Lacey told me that she was quite smitten with him once. I'm not sure how their relationship grew, but I think he's why she wanted to return."

Cold fury washed over me. Suddenly, I couldn't see straight. My eyes burned and blurred. Without even registering what I was doing, I let out a long mournful howl that vibrated through every cell of my body, and I instantly shifted.

I glanced over to find a shellshocked Patrick, taking in the features that were so similar to Clementine's before I darted off his front porch and down the back of the property toward the trees.

I had no idea which direction I was running in. My eyes stung, and Lucian was livid, fully at the helm.

"If you had just admitted that you were attracted to her, then she would still be here. If you hadn't ghosted her, she wouldn't have run back to Vancouver and into another man's arms!" I felt his anger and tasted it on my tongue. *"She might not even come back now, and it'll all be your fucking fault!"*

He went to the far reaches of my mind and slammed an impenetrable wall between us. I slowed down to a trot. Lucian was wrong. All I felt for Clementine was a friendship and the need to keep her safe. Lucian was the one infatuated with her. Wasn't he? He was the one who howled in pain when Patrick had told me of her actual plans for Vancouver. It wasn't me. Or was it?

I tried to reach out to Lucian but couldn't feel him. Suddenly, I felt very alone for the first time since meeting my wolf, and the idea of Clementine driving back to Vancouver to be with a guy who wasn't worthy of her made me want to vomit. My blood boiled with rage. I let out another howl. And when that didn't release my anguish, I let out another.

I didn't realize where I was headed until I reached the border of Blackfern Valley and kept going. I closed off my mind-link and just focused on my feet pounding through the forest. Was I honestly about to follow her to Vancouver on foot?

I skidded to a stop and hung my head in shame. I'd been running for hours and hours, but hesitantly, I turned and made my way back toward Blackfern Valley. It was the one place where I didn't want to be because it was the one place where she wasn't.

By the time I arrived, it was well after dark, and the moon was full in the sky, glowing brightly over the town. I made it back to the border and let out a lonely howl. Another couple of howls met it, and I could smell the scents of hundreds of wolves running through the bush. I heard them yipping and frolicking in the distance. But I still didn't open the mind-link. There were only two wolves in the entire pack who could break through the mental block I had put up. They had heard my howl and checked in instantly. I reassured them I was okay and told them to enjoy their run. Then everything went quiet.

I didn't join in on the pack run. Instead, I made my way over to Clementine's house and settled down against the bottom step that led into the back of her house. I sniffed the air and smelled her lingering scent, which wasn't as good as the real deal. I let out a little whimpering sniffle and lay my head between my paws, ready to spend the entire full moon at her doorstep.

Then I smelled the four different scents that made my hackles rise. I growled low as those scents came closer toward the house.

CHAPTER 33
LIAM

I INSTANTLY GOT to my feet, took three steps forward and lowered my head, letting out a rumbling growl. My nose twitched as I smelled the four wolves running through the trees. Their scents swirled around as they darted closer, then further away, only to come close again. My mouth dripped with saliva, and I was more than ready to sink my teeth into those assholes.

My hackles were rigid, and even without Lucian's beastly anger to fuel my own, I was ready to rip them all apart, even if it was four-on-one. I growled again and waited. Fury vibrated through my paws, but I held my ground and waited.

I reached back for Lucian, but he was still behind the wall in my mind.

"Come on, Lucian. We need to protect Clementine." Nothing.

I shook my head. I thought that would rouse him, but he knew Clementine wasn't here. Did the four wolves know that?

I grudgingly opened my mind-link up and was smacked with indecipherable chatter. It felt like a rubber band pinging back into place. Within a minute, it calmed into tranquillity. This happened each time a wolf joined the pack connection. They would get swarmed with disorienting white noise, causing a bit of vertigo before it went earthly-quiet again. Lucian remained quiet, and I frowned. I was stronger with him by my side, and right now, I felt alone, but that wasn't going to stop me from protecting Clementine. Or her kin.

I was sure the four wolves didn't know she was gone and were making their way here to fuck with her again. I took a deep breath and reached out through the mind-link. I searched for the pattern-scent of my best friend and found it instantly. *"Ryan!"*

"Dude! Are you okay? I thought I heard you howl earlier, but I couldn't mind-link you."

"Never mind that!" I shouted. *"Those fuckers are circling Clementine's house."*

"Oh, fucking hell! Shit, bro! Um, you know I would normally have your back, right?"

"But?"

"Rigby has gone nuts. I have no control over him. I'm not even with the pack anymore. I just feel drawn. It's like a magnet. Fuck! My heart is pounding, man."

No fucking way! I instantly knew what he was referring to and couldn't help but get excited for him. *"Go get her, man!"*

"That's just it! I can't find her!"

I had never heard him sound so anxious. He was usually a calm and collected person. Now, he just sounded panicked.

"Just stop fighting Rigby and let him find her. She will be making her way toward you too."

"If she feels it. I haven't found her yet, so maybe she doesn't?" He seemed to stumble over his following words. *"What if that means– I mean, could she be human?"*

Dark hair, turquoise eyes and a perfect pouty mouth flashed through my mind, and I instantly felt queasy. *No. No way. No fucking way! This can't happen. This isn't happening!*

I took a deep breath and tried to calm my nerves. Was

Clementine his true mate? Was it possible that it had awoken the true mate bond because her scent was all around Blackfern Valley now and he was feeling the pull even if she wasn't here? Was he heading toward Vancouver now?

Fuck!

Jealousy licked through my body, scorching every cell. He was my best friend and deserved all the world's happiness. And so did she. I forced the following words out even though they tasted bitterly sour in my mouth. *"Go fucking get her, man!"*

I then closed the mind-link to him and gave a small whimper. I shook myself to focus on what was happening outside Clementine's house. I sniffed the air again, and the forest smells wafted toward me. The wolves had moved on. Had they smelled me here standing guard? I no longer had the anger to hunt them down. Ryan's confession had taken that from me. It had taken *everything* from me. I collapsed onto the ground and watched the forest with nothing but a thick blanket of melancholy surrounding me.

As the full moon moved across the sky, its power over me dissipated, but I didn't feel the want to change back. There was no need to change. I still had zero desire to move from my spot. I anxiously wanted to hear from Ryan, but I didn't want to interrupt him and his true mate if he'd found her.

A very naked Patrick moved across the grass under the moonlight. His mate bond was glowing on the soft tissue between his neck and clavicle. Mate bonds were a small bite-mark scar in the daylight, but under the light of the full moon, they burned brilliantly and reminded me of a crescent moon. His was still intact even though he had lost his mate. I couldn't decide whether it was a beautiful keepsake of the fact he was loved so deeply or a heartbreaking reminder of what he had lost.

He saw me and gave me a fatherly smile. Walking into the

mudroom, he returned a moment later fully dressed and carrying two beer bottles and a spare change of shorts.

"Have you been here all night?" he asked as he sat on the back step. He flicked a beer toward me. I huffed in response. I wasn't ready to change back yet. Patrick gave me an appraising look before he started up again. "I'm unsure what you felt this morning when you showed up, and I told you she was gone," he said slowly. "I'm sorry I encouraged her to leave on the full moon and that you're hurting. I'm also unsure if you two simply have a powerful friendship, or if you have feelings for her, or if there is an unrevealed mate bond there–"

"Ryan's her mate," I grumbled down the mind-link toward her father, shutting him off instantly.

"Ryan?" he switched to mind-linking me, and his voice carried over with a surprised tone.

"Yeah. He's chasing her to Vancouver now."

"No, you're mistaken, Liam. She needs to be in the vicinity for the mate bond to be activated."

"She was in the vicinity. She has been for weeks."

"And now she's gone. It doesn't really work like–"

"She's a half-breed. We don't know if the bond affects her the same way. The rules may be different for her. With anyone fated to mate with her," I grumbled sadly. He studied me for a moment, sadness and uncertainty filling his brilliant green eyes. *"I'm happy for them,"* I rushed out quickly before he could start speaking to me about it. I wasn't ready.

"Are you?"

"Yeah. I am. They're my best friends. Both of them. They deserve to be happy," I said with finality.

"You deserve happiness too, Liam," he replied in a fatherly tone. I grunted.

We sat quietly for the longest time, him drinking a beer and me looking toward the forest.

"*Sean shifted,*" Patrick announced after a few more minutes of silence.

I looked up. He was picking at the beer label, deep in thought.

"*He did?*"

"*Yeah. Silas surprised the shit out of him. Then he ran off with some young she-wolf. He reminds me a lot of your father when we were pups.*" He smirked. "*He too had a few she-wolves he impressed at that age. Not meaning to, Jed was an asshole even back then, but the she-wolves did flock to him. It was like Icarus and the sun. Lots of she-wolves got burned.*"

"*Dad has indicated that you both got into all sorts of mischief. Well, until you met Lacey.*"

Patrick chuckled and shook his head. "*I bet he told you all sorts of horrendous stories of the shit we got up to. I promise you that they're all true. Then I met Lacey, and it was all over. I settled down instantly.*"

"*What was Lacey like?*" I blurted out.

For some reason, I wanted to know if Clementine was like her.

He smiled softly. "*She was my complete opposite in every way. Where I'm loud and stupid, she was soft-spoken and kind. Where I'm dark-haired and tall, she was small with blonde hair and a face full of freckles. She was my world. Clemmy idolized her—loved her mom so much.*" His voice broke through the mind-link, and I looked up to see his eyes filled with tears. Clearing his throat, he pushed back the tears. "*Clemmy has a good mixture of both of us. She is kind-hearted like her mother and sarcastically witty like me. She has an inner calming strength and is loyal to a fault. Anyone who ends up with her is a lucky son of a bitch because that girl is a hidden force of nature. Just like her mother.*"

He finished as if he knew what I had been fishing for.

"*Lacey managed to mark you,*" I said gently, knowing that

this would be a sore subject, but I was unable to stop my question.

His hand instantly went to caress his mark. *"Yes, she did."* He smiled lovingly and then looked at me curiosity in his eyes. *"Humans can mark their mate at midnight of the full moon during mating. Their teeth elongate and develop the mating venom long enough to make a mark. It disappears shortly after. Lacey could feel what I felt and had this uncanny sixth sense. But she never developed a wolf spirit, so she could never mind-link me."* He answered my unasked questions. His eyes looked sad again.

"Sorry. I know that must be painful to talk about."

"No, Liam. It would only be painful if I could no longer talk about her," he said sincerely.

I sniffed the air and smelt Clementine's little brother before I heard the front door open and close and his call out for his dad.

"I suppose I should leave you to it and head home," I said.

"Yeah. Go congratulate your brother on shifting!" I huffed and started making my way toward the trees. *"Oh, and Liam."* I turned back. *"Clementine is coming back. She's due home on Tuesday."*

CHAPTER 34
CLEMENTINE

WHEN MY PHONE RANG, I scrambled to pick it up, hoping Liam's name would be flashing across the screen. I tried not to feel too disappointed when I saw that it was my dad.

"Let me guess, you woke up in a pool of blood, and you don't remember a thing that happened during the full moon," I joked.

"No, I remember. The blood belonged to the villagers. But don't worry, I targeted all the pretty blonde girls," he replied in a dead-serious tone.

I grinned. "What's up, Dad?"

"Just checking in. Making sure you don't need my bail money."

"Not yet, but maybe next month. TJ and I spent a long time planning a murder."

He chuckled. "And how is TJ?"

"Curious."

"Curious?"

"About my life in Blackfern Valley."

"Clementine, you cannot tell him," Dad warned.

"I know that. I'm not stupid." I rolled my eyes. "How was the run?"

"Good. They started with the initiation of the pups who received their wolf spirits. There were three this time. And then the whole pack got together and got naked."

"Sounds like a cult-like orgy."

He laughed. "Yeah, but the naked part only lasts a few moments and then everyone's bones break and realign."

I grinned down the phone. "Yeah, still sounding like an orgy."

"Then we sprout fur and a tail."

I laughed. "Not helping your case, Dad." I could imagine him shaking his head and his emerald eyes sparkling with mischief.

"It was nice to run with them again." He paused for half a breath. "Although, two of them were missing."

"Who?"

"Ryan and Liam."

I blinked a few times. My heart lurched, then dropped into my stomach.

Why were the guys missing from the pack run? Were they hurt? Is Liam okay?

I instantly regretted being so far away. My mouth went dry, and I had lost my ability to speak and comprehend anything. My brain felt like it was in overdrive and at a standstill at the same time. I opened my mouth again, trying to bring words forward where none came.

"I found Liam," Dad continued.

Relief flooded through me, and with it, my ability to think and speak returned. "Oh?" I tried to sound impassive, though I could feel my emotions deteriorating my resolve.

"Yeah. He was guarding our back door like a watchdog."

Dad paused. "He was under the impression that Ryan was on his way to you."

"On his way to me? Why?" I asked, confused.

"Um. It's a long story. Has Ryan tried to contact you?" Dad asked.

I shook my head. "No one's tried." My phone had been silent the whole weekend.

"Not necessarily by phone, Clemmy. Never mind. We can talk about it when you get home. We've all missed you around here, kid."

I smiled softly. "I'm leaving shortly. Just waiting for a very hungover TJ to wake so I can say goodbye."

"You don't sound hungover."

"Oh, no. I think we can add another tick to the list of strange things I can do now."

"Really?" his voice squeaked.

"Yeah. I'm just waiting for the X-ray vision or the super strength. Then, I'm planning on buying a skin-tight leather suit and a mask and becoming a vigilante."

"Wait. First, you were talking about robbing banks, then murder, now you plan on being a vigilante?"

"Uh, yeah! I'm pretty sure I can roll those into one job."

"And becoming a groupie?"

"Um, once people see me in my leather suit, I'll be the one attracting groupies."

Dad's laughter vibrated down the line. "Okay, so I'll see you Tuesday, right?"

"Absolutely."

"Good, because I told Liam that's when you would be back."

My heart stopped. And for the second time in this conversation, my brain froze.

"Clemmy, are you still there?"

"Y-yeah, I'm here." I stumbled. "I'll be home Tuesday, Dad. I'll see you then."

After we ended the call, I stared at my phone for a few minutes. Disbelief, distrust, and a small amount of hope filled my heart. Liam had enquired about me. Or had Dad seen him in passing and just mentioned my arrival date? Surely, if Liam had wanted to know when I would be back, he would have called me himself, or at least sent a message.

I spent a few more moments staring at my phone, questions and emotions zooming around my body. No. I wasn't going to do that to myself. I wasn't going to worry over the what-ifs and the could-haves. I pushed my emotions back and decided I needed to close my feelings off and put my guard up once and for all. I wasn't going to go chasing Liam. If, on the slight chance Liam wanted to remain friends, then Liam had to be the one to fix this fractured friendship. And if not... I shook my head, not ready to think about the painful alternative.

Even after my exhausting internal emotional battle, leaving TJ and driving back to Blackfern Valley was surprisingly easy. With my steeled resolve, I managed to stop the butterflies that fluttered in my stomach each time I thought about heading home, and who I might see when I got there.

It was a complete contrast to the feeling that had been pulling at my heart since just before I had arrived in Vancouver. There was a gravitational pull that I was trying my hardest to ignore. First, it was this subtle ache that progressively got worse. I had butterflies in my stomach whenever I thought about returning home. It was a deep longing and a sixth sense telling me I should have stayed with my pack, with Liam. I swear, that the full moon was amplifying my emotions some-how, and it took all my strength not to drive back to Blackfern Valley a lot earlier than planned.

I wondered if this magnetic feeling was a werewolf thing.

Some other dormant gene that I hadn't been told about. Maybe this was the pull of the full moon? Perhaps it was the feeling a werewolf gets if they strayed too far from their pack? Did Dad constantly have to fight these feelings while he hid us in Vancouver? I had so many questions. There seemed so much more that I didn't know.

More werewolf genes seemed to appear in my physiology, yet I still had no wolf. I was pleasantly surprised that TJ and I had managed to finish four bottles of wine last night. I was even happier when he was the only one that looked like roadkill, smelled like it too, and barely moved when I told him I was leaving.

Being a good friend, I took a photo of him in his poor state to send to him later, hooked him up to an IV bag of fluids and gave him a sisterly kiss on the forehead. I also drew a rude picture on the whiteboard above his desk, giggling immaturely as I left his tiny apartment and walked to the parking structure where Dad's truck had been parked for the weekend.

TJ and I had met during our first year at UBC and instantly hit it off. Where most people had avoided me or teased me because of my chubby physique and glasses, he chose to sit next to me in class and picked me as his lab partner. At first, I thought he had pegged me as a nerd he could cheat off of, but I soon realized he was smarter than me.

He had moved to Vancouver from Quebec, and I think I had fallen in love with his French accent, kind nature, and boy-next-door good looks. I tried everything to get him to notice me as more than a friend. Everything. I'd even convinced myself I was no longer that awkward girl from high school, that I had left the bullies behind, and my confident side had bounded forward, ready to make her claim. It was very apparent, however, that he didn't feel the same way about me. Instead of being a jerk about it, he let me down gently. Told me any guy would be lucky to have me and informed me that he batted for the other team. After that mortifying experience, he became my best friend, the one other than my mom I could talk to.

The unfortunate thing was that for the entire weekend, I couldn't talk to him. Not really. I had to avoid conversations about my new life in Blackfern Valley. Had to twist the truth.

It felt seriously wrong lying to TJ, but what was I meant to do? Tell him my eyes miraculously healed themselves because of some dormant werewolf gene? Let him know I now lived with a pack of werewolves, where a portion of them wanted to hurt me because my mother was human? And if that wasn't enough of a reason to stay mum, somehow, I had been rumoured to be dating the alpha-elect, which made me an even larger target. And then I would have had to confess that the alpha-elect basically ghosted me when he was supposed to be my friend and how utterly bewildered it made me feel, because it played on my insecurities. I couldn't tell TJ any of it. So, I did what I was so well-practised at: I hid my emotions and lied.

The horrible thing was, TJ would have understood. He knew everything about me, including my unfortunate dating history. That was the reason he was drunkenly discussing murder with me. The implement of choice was a screwdriver going into someone's eye (and now that I was wearing 'contacts' and no longer squeamish about eyes, I could do the honours). He would have understood better than anyone. He would have found a way to ease my insecurities. He would have found a way to make me laugh it off and move on.

As I drove, I worried my lip between my teeth, thinking about the lies I had told my best friend. I wondered if I should have at least told him about Liam, just to ask him some advice on how to act when I saw him next. My heart flipped as I thought about seeing Liam again. I imagined his smooth arms, broad shoulders, sexy smile, and warm mocha eyes. Nervous bubbles floated around my stomach.

Crap. What the hell am I going to do when I see him?

I planted my foot on the accelerator and decided that the one-and-a-half-day drive was a perfect time to devise a plan. If I couldn't, maybe I could just keep driving.

CLEMENTINE

I PULLED INTO BLACKFERN VALLEY, with nervousness bubbling through my body. I drove straight toward my house and pulled into the driveway, cutting the engine. Grudgingly, I got out of the truck and slung my weekend bag over my shoulder, picking up the boxes on the passenger seat and closing the door. I pressed the remote lock as I trudged toward the back door. Everything looked the same. Felt the same.

"I'm home," I called out, then rolled my eyes, remembering both my brother and father had werewolf hearing. Half of the pack probably heard my announcement.

"Welcome home, Clemmy!" Dad said from the kitchen, where he was sitting at the dining table with a cup of coffee.

He smiled, and then his eyes went vacant for a moment, which he tried to cover by taking a sip of coffee. Looking back, I realized he did that a lot growing up, and I smiled. I guess some habits were hard to break.

"I brought Timbits," I said.

I heard thumping footsteps, and seconds later, Vinny was instantly on the four boxes I had placed on the dining table, grinning from ear to ear.

"What, only four?"

I grinned stupidly at him. "The nearest Timmy's is like six hours away. Learn to drive, and then you can go and get your own."

His eyes flashed with cheeky humour. "I know how to drive."

"No more grand theft auto," Dad warned. A smile flashed across Vinny's face, which matched the glimmer in his eyes. Dad turned toward me. "How was Vancouver?"

"Much the same," I offered. "How was the pack run?"

"Can I tell her?" Vinny said excitedly.

Dad gave him an encouraging smile and sipped his coffee.

"Tell me what?"

Vinny grinned at Dad before turning back to me. "So, when the full moon hit, I felt this enormous pull. Like a magnet was pulling something from deep within me," he started. His eyes kept flicking between Dad and me, the silver around his eyes glowing bright. "It was the weirdest feeling. Dad had already prewarned me that werewolves feel the full moon's pull, so I knew what it was. I wasn't expecting a calm voice telling me this was nothing compared to what it feels like to shift. The voice was in my head, but it wasn't mine." He grinned. "The full moon woke up Vali."

"You met your wolf?" I asked.

"Yeah! His name is Vali. He's pretty neat."

"I'm happy for you, Vinny," I said, ignoring the small fissure of pain that cracked through me.

"Vincent came home the night of the full moon and told me excitedly that he had met his wolf. I was surprised because wolves usually come forward sometime after their sixteenth birthday, but Vali was early. We've been teaching him how to mind-link all weekend."

A memory stirred within me. "Hang on. I thought he had to be initiated into the pack first?"

"Only to mind-link with the pack. He can mind-link with family at any time," Dad said.

I forced myself to smile. It was exciting news for Vinny, and I was happy for him. But at the same time, I was sad for myself.

I had felt some pull from the full moon and knew I had some wolf genes, but I wasn't a werewolf. I was still an outsider, but this time, I was also an outsider in my own family. I watched as Vinny's eyes went vacant, the proof that he indeed had a wolf, and they were in a conversation. He hadn't learned Dad's finesse of hiding it behind a coffee cup yet.

I felt a flash of hurt and one of jealousy. Dad twisted his body toward mine, watching me closely. I forced a grin, then went to make myself a coffee, if only to give myself a few more seconds before facing my father. Vinny grabbed a box of Timbits and disappeared into his room, leaving us to it.

"So, what else happened?" I asked, leaning against the kitchen counter, nursing the mug in my hand.

"Liam's brother Sean can now shift. And Ryan apparently found his true mate."

Bringing the mug up to my mouth, I paused with my hand mid-air. "Wait. What?"

"Yeah, that's why I was kind of ringing you. A small rumour was going around where someone thought it may have been you."

"What are you talking about?" I put the mug down on the counter without taking a sip.

"I told you that werewolves have mates. Your mother was mine, which is why we had to leave."

"Yeah. I remember. You said that it's really rare to find your true mate, that most wolves end up picking a mate instead."

"And that's true. Ryan felt the pull of the mate bond on

Friday night, and I was told he was running to Vancouver to find you."

"He never came to Vancouver. I mean, I don't know how long it would take a werewolf to run that distance, but he never contacted me to tell me he was coming."

"Yeah, that's why I called you. To find out if you felt him or had heard from him."

"No. I mean, I felt strange around the full moon. It felt like I was in the wrong place. All I wanted to do was turn around and come back. I was going to ask you about it. I assumed it's some full-moon-pack-werewolf thing." I shook my head. "I don't think I felt a mate bond. From what you've told me, if it were a mate bond, I wouldn't have been able to resist it." Dad's eyes twinkled with silver as they observed me.

"You didn't feel a mate bond, Clem," he confirmed, dipping his Timbit into his coffee. My heart twinged, but I couldn't tell if it was caused by relief or sadness.

"So, whoever told you Ryan was coming to me must have been mistaken," I said without emotion.

"I thought as much. It's also confirmed because you're here, and he's still allegedly with his mate."

"What do you mean?"

"He's gone radio silent." I gave my dad a confused look. "He's turned off his mind-link to the pack. The only people who can reach him are the alpha and luna. It's common for werewolves to turn off the mind-link when they first find their mate. They are consumed with one another for a while and are relatively no good to anyone." Dad chuckled as if he was remembering. "The only werewolves who don't do this are the ranked wolves for obvious reasons."

"Right." I nodded. I looked at my cup of coffee on the counter, deep in thought.

"Are you okay?" Dad asked.

"Yeah. I'm okay." I nodded slowly, lifting my head, and giving him a weak smile.

"If you need to talk, you know I'm here."

"I know, Dad." Dad's nostrils twitched. "I think I'm going to head to work tonight. I feel okay, and I could use the money. I spent way too much of it on wine."

Dad chuckled, then his nostrils flared, and his eyes went vacant. "There's someone here to see you." My heart started pounding in my ears. There was only one person that could be. Dad stood up and took his empty cup of coffee to the sink before giving me a quick hug and whispering, "Just give him a chance. The poor guy has been a mess. Hear him out before you make any decisions."

He stood back, gave me a knowing look, then stepped into the hallway, presumably headed for his bedroom. My mouth rounded in surprise, and a little sound came out. How did Dad know? How was he so intuitive? Had I made the wrong choice in the car?

I worried my lip between my teeth for half a second. No, I needed to do this. He had lost my trust, and it would take a lot for him to regain it. I had to protect myself.

I left my barely-touched coffee on the kitchen counter and took a deep breath, trying to calm my nerves. I would listen to what Liam had to say, but I wasn't going to get emotional.

I stepped out of the mudroom and onto the back step. Liam stood in the middle of the backyard, more god-like and beautiful than ever. My heart pounded louder than before. I took him in. His broad shoulders seemed larger, his caramel-brown hair was longer in the front and hanging dangerously close to his eyes, and his beard was slightly scruffier than usual. He gave me a smile that instantly made my knees go weak. I hadn't seen him smile in over a week, and it seemed like this was a smile only reserved for me—one of genuine happiness at my presence.

I folded my arms across my chest and slowly walked across the backyard toward him. He stepped forward to meet me, his smile never faltering.

"You're back."

He reached out an arm to touch me as if he had to feel that I was real, that I wasn't a mirage. I took half a step back out of his reach, and his smile weakened.

"I am," I said evenly.

"You're back, and Ryan is– and–" he mumbled and gave me another genuine smile, his eyes raking over my face and body, taking me in. "How was Vancouver?"

"Fine," I replied curtly.

His Adam's apple bobbed as he visibly swallowed. He pushed his hair back to where it should have been sitting.

"Can we talk?" I raised an eyebrow and gave a single stiff nod. He frowned slightly. "Did you want to go somewhere? We could grab some food. Maybe a coffee?"

"I'm good," I snapped, then added, "thanks," when I heard how harsh I sounded.

He frowned again. "You're mad at me," he murmured sadly.

He went to reach out for me once more, and I took another small step backward.

"What did you want to talk about?" I enquired coldly. *How dare he come over, looking so sexy and god-like, give me those puppy dog eyes, and... and...*

"I wanted to apologize." I didn't reply. "Clem, I'm so sorry about the last week. I was a complete and utter jackass. It's no excuse, but I was totally up in my head about shit, and the full moon was coming and– I really have no excuses. Just please know how sorry I am."

"Is that all?" I asked after a few moments of silence.

He recoiled like he'd been slapped. "I came to your house on Friday morning to apologize and spend time with you. I wanted to drive you to Vancouver, but your dad said you had already left. Why didn't you tell me you were leaving earlier?"

"Would you have responded? Would you have cared?" I asked coldly.

He recoiled again. "Of course, I would have! I'm sorry I didn't speak to you much. I told you I was going through something. I did miss you. You're my friend—"

"Am I?" I snarled.

My composure was cracking. I didn't know how much longer I could take this without bursting into angry tears of frustration. I knew if I cried, he would reach out to hug me, and I would melt into his warm arms and alluring scent. But I was resolute in keeping my walls up. I couldn't get hurt again. I *refused* to get hurt again.

"Clem—"

"Are you done?"

"Clem, please. Please talk to me. I hate this frigidness. Can't we just go somewhere and talk like we used to?"

He took a step forward, and his brown eyes were full of remorse, but I was too disillusioned to care.

"You know what? No, we can't. You had plenty of time to talk to me before I left for Vancouver. You didn't even look at my messages prior to me going, and you didn't contact me once while I was there. And now you want to talk? Seriously?"

Anger bubbled through me, and I took another step back. He frowned again, his eyebrows furrowed, and his jaw gone rigid and taut.

"Why are you being so cold? You're the one that left before we could talk. You're the one that ran off to Vancouver to go and fuck your old boyfriend!"

CHAPTER 36

LIAM

*"L*IAM*. It's Patrick. I just thought you would like to know that Clementine just got home."*

I dropped my pen onto my paper and abandoned the calculus assignment I was using as a distraction. I jumped into my car and sped down the driveway, barely stopping to look for cars at the end of the drive before squealing tires on my way toward Clementine's house.

Relief washed through me as soon as I saw her walk out of the back door, followed by a flush of happiness. She was here. Ryan wasn't her mate. My heart galloped in my chest, and I sniffed her scent deeply, which stirred up even more indescribable emotions as I took her in.

She was dressed in a brightly coloured loose-fitting top that showed a modest amount of creamy cleavage and black yoga pants which hugged her delicious curves. Her dark hair had grown since I had seen her last and was now sitting just below her shoulder blades, and her turquoise eyes were piercing as they found mine. She was stunning. And she was standing right in front of me. The signature splash of red across her cheekbones manifested, and her lips were stained pink. She wasn't wearing makeup, so it couldn't have been lipstick. Maybe it was strawberry lip balm or something? I wanted to kiss her and taste to see if I was right. Then suddenly, I was reminded that she had gone to Vancouver to rekindle things with an old flame, and all I could think about was that some other guy had been tasting those lips. Tasting *her*.

My relief was replaced with a spark of jealousy which I tried to smother as I took in her beauty and tried to get her to talk to me. The spark reignited as soon as I realized she wasn't the Clem I knew. She was cold and distant, and the only thing I could correlate it to was the fact she had spent her weekend in Vancouver with a love interest who didn't deserve her. She had lost her sweet, kind nature and was fucking some guy all weekend while I was pining for her. I know it wasn't rational, and I didn't even have Lucian to talk sense into me as he was still blocking our connection. I tried to breathe in to calm down, and her honeysuckle and pear scent hit me again, and it hit me hard, and along with her scent came hot uncontrollable jealousy.

I inwardly cringed as I heard the words leave my mouth. "Why are you being so cold? You're the one that left before we could talk. You're the one that ran off to Vancouver to go and fuck your old boyfriend!" *Shit! If looks could kill, I would be six feet under right now.*

"What?" Her tone was deathly quiet. Her words full of venom. Her turquoise eyes widened, then narrowed into angry slits. That should have made me back down, but her cold demeanour wasn't what I'd expected. I had come to apologize, to gain back her trust and friendship. Yet she was being a bitch. She wasn't even willing to hear me out. She had closed off completely— entirely hostile.

I was so livid. I didn't know if I should shout some more at her or kiss her. Hard. I looked at her plump pink lips again and felt myself stir. *Damn it!* I wanted to kiss her. I wanted to kiss away her anger. I wanted to make her forget TJ ever existed. I wanted to show her how much I missed her. Because, God, I missed her! I should have used this moment to apologize again and take the opportunity to take back what I'd said. To grovel and earn back her trust. But I had no control over my mouth. My jealousy was in charge, and Mister Nice Guy was nowhere to be found.

"Your dad told me that you and TJ were an item and that you were going back to rekindle an old flame," I snarled. "How was it, Clementine? Did he fuck you, then dump you? Is that why you're here now?"

Her eyes filled with tears, and I instantly regretted what I said. My stomach felt like it held lead, and my heart filled with an indescribable piercing pain. I thought I felt the wall around Lucian start to weaken, but I was so focused on the hurt scribbled over Clementine's expression that I ignored it.

What I wasn't expecting was the hand striking my face. She had hit me with enough force that my head snapped to the side. I was surprised she had the strength to be able to do so. At the very least, my werewolf strength should have broken her hand. I was shocked. My cheek stung with a warm buzz across the skin.

"You sanctimonious prick," she said and spun on her heel.

It took me a moment to clear my head, but I scrambled after her. "Clementine, wait!" I called after her. She ignored me. "Clementine, *please*. I didn't mean that! I don't even know why I said it. No! I know why. I was jealous, and hurt, and– Please, Clem, just talk to me."

She spun around and looked up at me with cold fury. "I think you should leave."

"Clem–"

She took an angry step toward me. "I thought I imagined it. I kept telling myself that you weren't the kind of asshole to ghost me. Do you know how much that shit hurts?" She swiped angrily at a single tear that had escaped, then seemed to regain her cold composure. There was so much fury behind her words. "You have this grandiose complex, Liam, and I want no part of it. You think you're God's gift to women and expect me to fall at your feet. Do you think I'm stupid? I know the real reason you showed up here. It has nothing to do with our supposed friendship. You only showed up because you think I mated with Ryan. The idea that I could have had a mate brought you here. You needed to check if it was true. Because if I had a mate, then I wouldn't have space in my life to worship you. Am I right?"

I gaped at her. Where the hell had this all come from?

"You're not my friend. You're just like every other person I have ever met. You have insulted me, hurt me, and you fucking blame it on jealousy as if that's a good enough reason? You felt jealous? Over a guy you've never met. A fucking *gay* man at that!"

She turned toward the house and slammed the screen door behind her.

The sound of the screen door slamming mimicked the feeling of me getting slapped again. I stood for a moment, stunned.

What the hell just happened?

What had happened to the sweet, shy girl with the dry sense of humour? Her dad wasn't kidding when he called her a force of nature. I had gotten her borderline angry before, and I had always imagined her anger would burn brightly. And this small snippet of it had left me with third-degree burns.

Arguing with her left me feeling unfulfilled. Empty. Fighting with her sucked all of my air out and left me unsteady. I was dizzy on Clementine. Thinking back to the way her eyes sparked with a fiery intensity and the way her voice took on a gravelly tone as she put me in my place, my dick spasmed.

Holy shit, I'm actually semi-turned on by her anger. How can I feel horny and ashamed at the same time?

I knew I had crossed a line when I'd asked about TJ. Her slap had spoken volumes. It had also brought me back to my senses. I wasn't expecting her to get so defensive over him. And I definitely hadn't expected her to divulge the guy was gay. I felt like a royal ass.

Before, I had it all planned out. I was going to take her to a place where we could talk, ask her calmly about her relationship with TJ, apologize for all the shit that had gone down and slowly open up and explain what was going through my mind. But when I saw her, my entire plan was obliterated by her hot anger and my stupid jealousy. How the hell was I supposed to get her friendship back now? I blew up at her about her sleeping with her gay friend. And from what I knew about her, her only friend.

I dropped my face into my palms and groaned. She said that I was like every other person she had ever met. I had turned into one of her bullies—an asshole.

Fuck me. How the fuck am I going to fix this?

The back door opened, and my heart somersaulted. I looked up from my palms to see Patrick standing there. He gave me a look of pity, and I felt more ashamed, knowing he had heard every word.

"Clementine asked you to leave."

"Is she okay?" He looked toward the house and tilted his head, listening.

"She's in the shower. She isn't as secretive as she thinks she is either, despite using the faucet to hide her tears."

"I didn't mean to make her cry," I exclaimed.

"I know you didn't."

"I don't know how to fix this, but I need to, Patrick."

"Start by giving her some space, Liam. She doesn't trust easily. You broke her trust. It's going to take time to rebuild that."

I didn't want to give her space. I wanted to barge in there and make her listen to me. I wanted to push her against a wall and kiss her with enough heat that it would burn away her icy hatred toward me. Giving her space was going to be impossible.

"Okay," I conceded, then I turned to leave.

"Oh, and Liam." I turned back. "You break my baby girl's heart again, and I break you. Alpha-elect or not." His eyes flashed dangerously, and I knew he was serious. It could have been taken as a challenge if I was an alpha, but I wasn't, and I deserved it.

"Trust me. If I break her heart again, I wouldn't even put up a fight."

I walked away from her house even though every fibre of my being told me to return to her. I felt back in my mind and wasn't surprised to feel Lucian there.

"Lucian, I know you witnessed that entire confrontation." He looked over at me and huffed. *"I know I deserved that and a lot more."* He growled. *"Now, I need your help in gaining back her friendship."*

"You want more than her friendship," he said exasperatedly.

"I do." I sighed. I couldn't lie to myself—to my wolf anymore. *"Seeing her made it crystal clear what I want. It smacked me in the face when I saw her walk out the back door. Then it hit me even more so when she actually smacked me in the face."* I walked down the road toward my car. *"I'm a fucking idiot. There's no way anything is going to happen between us now. And at this stage, I'll settle for her friendship because I don't think we can be any more*

than that after what I've done." Lucian came forward and swished his tail. "*I can't lose her, Lucian.*"

"*You won't. You just need to remind her of who you are and earn her trust back. And then you have to keep it.*"

"*Trust me. Once I have her trust back, I'm never letting go.*"

CHAPTER 37

CLEMENTINE

I WALKED BACK into the kitchen, freshly showered and ready to head to work. All I needed was to make a quick sandwich, and I could go to a place where I could be distracted from my downward-spiralling thoughts.

"He's gone," Dad said as I nervously looked out the kitchen window at the backyard. My heart sank a little.

"Good," I said crossly.

"Are you okay?"

"I'm fine."

"You can talk to me, Clem."

I smiled and nodded, "I know." I proceeded to pull out the ingredients for a sandwich.

"I'm sorry you're hurt, Clemmy," Dad continued.

I stopped buttering the bread for half a moment before I started swiping my knife across the bread again, encasing my emotions. "I'm fine," I repeated, wishing he would drop the subject.

"For what it's worth, I think Liam genuinely cares about you."

I bristled. "If that's true, he has a really shit way of showing it."

"Well, he was here in our back yard for the night of the full moon and every night after, waiting for your return. He didn't join the pack run at all."

I shook my head at the revelation. "Too little, too late," I said bluntly.

"Yeah, I know. That's why I told him to give you space," Dad said. "You have every right to be angry, Clem. Just don't stay angry for too long." He kissed me on the head and walked out the back door, leaving me to my sandwich and my delicately spiralling thoughts.

"WELCOME BACK!" Tina greeted me as I walked into Lupus' Bar and Grill.

"Thanks." I smiled. "I thought maybe I could work tonight. I know you said we would be pretty quiet, but I would love the work."

"If you're up to it, sure!" She smiled. "I have something for you. Follow me." I followed Tina into the office, and she pulled out a box. "This just came in." Inside were brand new women-sized uniform t-shirts. "I got you a few of each size."

"These are great, Tina. Thank you."

"No problem. Kimmie is covering the bar tonight. So, I only really have a waitress spot open. I can put you behind the bar with Kimmie if we get busier, but I don't suspect it will get too chaotic."

"That's fine. I'm more than happy to waitress."

"Great. Are you available tomorrow?"

"Yeah."

"I have no idea when, or if, Ryan is coming back. Do you

mind helping me out tomorrow? The pace should start to pick up by tomorrow."

"Yeah, that's fine."

"Can you also ask Liam to be here?"

My heart stopped, and I instantly put up my emotional wall and made my face impassive. "What? Why?" Her hazel eyes found mine and gave me an appraising look.

"You realize that Ryan changed his shifts to work with you, right?"

An uncomfortable lump formed in my throat. "Why?" I choked out.

"To keep an eye on you. To make sure no blood-hate bullshit came into my bar," she said without a flicker of empathy or emotion.

Of course, he did. "I-I don't know." Then I rushed forward. "Look, it's two days. The pack members should be used to me by now. Besides, I now know about werewolves, so I'll keep my tongue in check, and you suspect it's going to be quiet, so there's no need to call in reinforcements." I smiled. Tina gave me a stern appraisal before she finally nodded.

I took the box of t-shirts into the restroom to try a few. I started with a size ten, and it was way too big. I took it off and looked at the cut, trying to determine if it seemed larger than average. It seemed the correct measurements to me. *Strange.* I put on the size eight and found that it was still slightly baggy, but much closer to the correct size than the ten. Eight was often a little snug on me, and I needed to move up a size for comfort. It was hard being in between sizes. I looked at myself in the mirror again. Was TJ, right? Had I lost weight?

I dug around in the box and looked at the other sizes. It appeared that she had done a bulk order on various sizes. I found a six and tried it on. It looked awful, clinging to me tightly and it gave me more rolls than a bakery. I frowned at the unattractive folds.

Well, I obviously haven't lost that much weight. I replaced the too-tight t-shirt with the ten and looked at myself in the mirror once more.

I readjusted the chain on my mom's necklace so that it was placed more comfortably while I worked. Digging around in my purse, I found my name badge and a spare hairband. I swept my hair back and tied it roughly off my face. I preened and primped for a little bit, and when I was satisfied that I looked somewhat presentable, I walked out to start my shift.

I dropped the box and purse inside the office door and tied my apron around my waist as I walked into the main area. My name badge had unclipped itself, and the pin stabbed me right in the boob. *Ouch!* I quickly adjusted it before looking up and around the quiet bar.

I frowned when I spotted Liam sitting in my section. It appeared that he was back to his studying and was busy scribbling away, his nose inches from the paper and books scattered around him. A beer was on the table next to him, barely drunk.

Crap. Did Tina call him?

I tried not to feel betrayed and decided to ignore my predicament. Ignore him. I walked up to April, and demanded, "Swap sections with me."

She gave me a disgusted look. "What?"

"Swap sections with me," I repeated slowly and deliberately.

"Why would I–" She looked over and saw Liam. Her smile turned gleeful, and her brown eyes sparkled at the prospect. I could see her predatory thoughts as she raked her eyes over him. I had an unexpected urge to claw her eyes out, but before I could even contemplate where the feeling came from, she replied, "Sure, I'll swap with you."

"Fine." I nodded and moved to her tables.

I felt Liam's eyes on me as I walked clockwise around my section, tidying up chairs and wiping down surfaces, but I refused to give him the satisfaction of looking in his direction. I told him to leave me alone, and even my dad told him to give me space.

So why the fuck is he here?

Half of me wanted to go over and have it out with him. Call him on his bullshit. The other half of me wanted to hide away and cry for the next week. I did neither. Instead, the tabletops got extra attention, the wooden chairs were unnecessarily wiped down, and the salt and pepper shakers were refilled.

Tina wasn't kidding when she said that it was quiet. Even though it was approaching dinner time, there were only a handful of people in the place. I busied myself with mundane tasks in a strict attempt not to look at Liam, whom I could hear talking with April. He seemed to be slightly dismissive of her, which annoyed me.

So, he hasn't just dismissed my feelings. He's dismissive of everyone's—what a jackass.

A few people had entered and sat in my section, I walked over and took their drink order, and as I walked away, my avoidance was thwarted. I accidentally looked up and saw big, beautiful mocha eyes with rings of pure gold penetrating mine. Glaring at him, I thrust my chin high and walked away. I made it to the large French doors that led to the outside tables and slipped out. I needed a couple of minutes to regain my composure. No one was out here, so I leaned against the railing and took deep breaths. I was hoping work would distract me from my problems, not shove them in my face. My hands went to my necklace, and I gave it a good squeeze, wishing not for the first time my mother was here to help me navigate this chapter of my life.

I walked back through the French doors and noticed Sophie come in. She made a beeline for Kimmie to grab a glass of wine before heading over to talk to Liam. I shouldn't have been surprised; they were friends.

Wait! Are Sophie and I friends? Or was it all fake? I didn't know anymore.

I felt a gentle buzz that told me I was about to have a panic attack and started to fiddle with my necklace again. Dark thoughts began to invade my head. I considered walking out, renting a car, and never coming back. I took a deep breath to regain my composure, and before I could decide if I was going to run, a couple of guys walked into the bar, found a table, and seated themselves in my section. I let go of the breath I was holding and walked over to take their orders, plastering on a fake smile.

It went on like this for another hour or so. Liam never left. He ordered food and proceeded to work on whatever university assignment he was doodling on and kept watch over me protectively. I growled to myself and closed my eyes. I knew that his wolf had an innate need to protect me, but it wouldn't work anymore. Liam needed to back off. Like seriously, or we were going to have major problems.

And it turned out those problems would come to a head sooner rather than later, as April made a beeline for me, her annoyance flickering on her model-like face.

"He's asking to speak with you."

"What?" I snapped.

"Liam is asking to speak with you."

"He's in your section," I countered dispassionately.

"He told me to switch back."

"That's not up to him."

She rolled her eyes then arched a perfectly manicured eyebrow at me. "You really have no idea how pack hierarchy works, do you? It doesn't matter that this is Tina's establishment, and she makes the rules. He's the alpha. The boss. *Everywhere.*"

I shrugged. "Well, he's not *my* alpha."

"You disrespectful little—"

"No. Don't even go there. Respect needs to be earned. Maybe when he actually earns the title, I'll show him some respect, but at the moment, he's just like every other asshole in this stupid inbred fucking town," I snapped, finally losing my composure.

Her brown eyes went wide, shimmering with jade-coloured rings. "Clementine, I don't want to be pulled into whatever tenth-grade drama that's going on. He's asked to speak to you. Just grow a pair and go serve Liam. Now!"

Without knowing it, April had said the wrong words before she stormed off.

CHAPTER 38
LIAM

I settled down to study in my usual booth at Lupus'. I could smell the honeysuckle and pear scent as soon as I stepped through the door, and knew she was here. I opened my books and ordered a beer, trying to get through the massive workload thrown to the class just before we went on a summer-midterm break. I'd usually have held it off until the last minute, but because I needed the distraction while Clem was in Vancouver, doing my assignments seemed like a perfect choice. Now that I had started, I just wanted to get it over and done with.

Instead of studying at home or in the library at the university, I decided to go back to my regular routine of studying at Lupus'. I was hoping Ryan would have returned by now, that I'd walk in and see him working the bar, but he hadn't yet. I was hoping I would meet his mate, see how happy he was and forget the shit thoughts I had about him over the weekend. And I was hoping he could give me some advice on how to get Clem to talk to me.

Clem appeared with a large box in her hand, which she quickly placed inside the office before making her way into the seating area, tying her apron around her waist. Her hair was tied back, and my eyes instantly went to the curve of her neck before they slowly raked down her delicious curves, displayed for everyone to see.

She moved her fingers from the apron strings and fidgeted with her name badge, making her creamy cleavage peek gently out of the top's neckline. Tina had supplied her with a uniform that fit a little too well.

I felt Lucian press forward, growling possessively. She hadn't looked up at me yet, but I needed it to look like I wasn't watching, that I wasn't stalking. I knew she wanted space. I would respect that, no matter how hard it was to do. But I couldn't bring myself to leave.

I focused as hard as possible on the equation in front of me. I stared at it, and the words eventually started to blur. I felt the moment her eyes located me. Lucian stirred and swished his tail. We were both hyperaware of her. I started tapping random numbers into my calculator, making it appear as though I was busy, as I turned my hearing over to Clem.

"Swap sections with me," her voice cracked.

"What?" April sounded annoyed.

"Swap sections with me," she repeated a lot clearer and calmer this time.

"Why would I– Sure, I'll swap with you." April no longer sounded annoyed but intrigued.

Lucian huffed, but I continued to tap nonsense into my calculator. I heard April bound over but kept my eyes on my nonsensical work. I didn't want April to wait on my table. I wanted Clem to. That way, she was forced to talk to me a little bit.

"Hi, Liam! Do you need anything?" April gushed as she came over.

I grudgingly looked up and noticed that she had purposely pushed her breasts up. I wanted to roll my eyes, but I refrained and gave her a polite smile. "No, thank you, April. I'm good here."

"Oh, okay. Just holler out if you need anything."

"Will do." I dismissed her, flipped a page in my textbook and tried to tune back into Clem.

"So, is it true?" April asked, trying to put an alluring tone into her voice, evidently not having left my table.

"Is what true, April?" I asked.

"That Ryan felt the pull of his mate bond."

"Yeah, he did. I'm sure he'll be in contact soon," I affirmed.

"Wow. Imagine that. I turn twenty soon, and I can't wait to find out if my mate is around here. It would be magical to know that a person is made just for you." She flicked her brown hair off her shoulder and watched me with evident interest in her brown eyes. I smiled kindly at her, not missing the hint.

"I wish you all the happiness in finding your mate," I said, trying to dismiss her again, flicking another page absent-mindedly.

"Well, I should know by the next full moon. Maybe we could run together?" I looked up from my work, ready to reject her suggestion. "Just think about it," she added with a wink as she sashayed away.

Lucian shook his head and chuckled. I looked up and watched Clem busy herself with cleaning tables. She was facing away from me, and I was lost in a trance as I watched her apple bottom for much longer than I should have. She straightened up and stiffened as if she felt my eyes on her, but she refused to look back. Instead, she clenched, then unclenched her fists, and moved to the next table.

I frowned. She was still mad. How long was she going to stay that way? I took out my phone and texted Sophie, asking her to join me for a drink. She responded instantly and had turned up at Lupus' within twenty minutes.

"You look like a puppy who's been kicked," she commented as she put her glass of wine on the table.

"I have been."

"Oh?"

I didn't answer. I was too distracted with keeping an eye on Clementine. She looked around the room, following my gaze and spotted her giving a cheery grin to a couple of good-looking guys who had just arrived. I growled a little louder than I realized, and Sophie's eyes snapped back to me in shock.

"Okay! Tell me what happened. No, wait." She put her index finger up toward me, indicating for me to hold on for a moment, and then took three large gulps of her wine. She then moved her index finger up in the air, signalling Kimmie for another drink. After taking another large swallow of her current glass, she smiled. "Okay, now tell me what happened."

I sighed and gave her a general rundown of what had happened. Her face contorted as I told her the story and eventually landed on rage, pity, then indifference.

"Well, let me tell you one thing that I can only tell you now because you're currently not my alpha." April chose that moment to arrive with another wine for her and another beer for me. We waited for April to leave before Sophie continued. "You're a fucking idiot! What the fuck, Liam!" She reached out and smacked me hard just in case her annoyance wasn't portrayed in her tone. She whacked me again, the swirls of her wolf apparent.

"I know I am, Sophie! Stop hitting me and help." She took another gulp of wine, finished her glass, and placed it to the side. She pawed at the next glass and held it between her fingers delicately.

"I should have known something was off with you when we were partying in Kempthorne. Man, I was so wrong. I thought you were into Stacey." An uncontrolled expression must have flashed over my face. Sophie smirked. "Yeah, she told me about the kiss. She didn't give me any more details, no matter how hard I begged. So, I concluded that you both either really liked each other, or decided it was a terrible idea."

I groaned into my hands and decided it was best not to get into that conversation right now.

"Sophie, how am I going to protect Clem from the bullshit of this town if she won't let me close to her?"

She gave me another pitying look. "Don't worry. Ryan and I have it covered." She pressed her lips into an annoyed expression. "Well, I have it covered until Ryan returns." I glared at her, and she rolled her eyes. "Okay, let me think." She took another large gulp of wine and gazed over to Clementine, who was busy serving someone a beer. I sighed and offered another piece of information as Sophie contemplated how to help me.

"She's fierce with her anger. She shouted at me and told me I have a superiority complex, and I just wanted her to worship me. She said I didn't care about her and that I only cared about being worshipped by her. It was so precisely worded that I feel someone must have done this to her in the past."

"What do you know about her past?"

"Not a lot. She doesn't really open up to people. I know she was bullied a lot growing up. She never really had any friends. She finds it hard to trust and let people in. I fucked up and acted like every other person who's bullied her. She's never going to forgive me." I groaned and stacked my books to the side. There was no point pretending to study now.

"But she has never gone into specifics?" Sophie questioned.

"Only once. I won't tell you what she said because that's her business, but I'll tell you, Lucian almost lost his shit right then. I almost lost control." Lucian grumbled.

"But you didn't."

"Only because Clementine managed to calm me down." I

took a sip of beer and looked over at Clem again. She was doing her best to ignore me. She had only looked over three or four times, and when she did that, her disgust was evident.

"I think I know what you have to do." Sophie smiled. I snapped my eyes back to her, eager to listen. "You said she's been a loner and bullied her entire life, right?" I nodded, cringing at Sophie's bluntness. "Well then, you can't leave her alone."

My brows furrowed. "What?"

"No, think about it! She's never experienced the one thing we all need. A good friend. The kind that when you're angry at someone and tell them to fuck off, they'll still be there. If you want to regain her trust, show her you aren't going anywhere. Make sure she knows you're there for her. Try to strike up random conversations. Not about your issues, but trivial crap. Things like the weather or the latest Canucks defeat. Just find some neutral ground. Do you know what I'm saying? Eventually, she'll realize that you can be trusted to stick around. Because at the base of all this anger, she's probably just afraid that you won't be here. So, show her you will be. Even if she repeatedly tells you to fuck off, stick around and talk to her."

"I don't know, Sophie. Her dad says to give her space."

"You should never get advice from a girl's father on the best way to talk to their daughter. Dads don't know. You need to ask her mo–" Sophie stopped herself and instantly looked sad. She glanced over at Clem and shook her head. "Trust me. Don't give her space. Space is the worst thing you can give her right now. If you give her space, she will stop caring. You don't want her to do that. Don't let her have the chance to grow indifferent to you."

I bit my lip and looked at Clem, who was laughing at something those two good-looking guys were saying as she placed a food order between them.

"Are you sure?" I asked.

"Yeah, positive. I took a psych paper last semester. I'm basically a trained shrink now." I arched my eyebrows at Sophie's flippant humour. She responded by giving me a stupid grin before continuing. "Seriously, it's simple: Don't be an asshole. Be her friend."

"Okay." I nodded slowly in agreement. Honestly, I was willing to try anything, and this sounded a lot better than giving her space. "Hey, Sophie?"

"Yeah?"

"I love you, but fuck off, eh?"

She grinned at me before she downed her wine and placed it on the table. "Good luck with the studying." She leaned over and tapped her manicured fingernail on the textbooks. "Clementine doesn't know we are on a break, does she?"

"Sophie–"

"Yeah, yeah. Fuck off. I got it." She laughed, stood up, and added, "You're paying for my wine, by the way. Consider it payment for your therapy."

Chuckling deeply, I reopened my textbooks, taking a sniff and enjoyed the honeysuckle and pear scent that permeated the air, pausing to look up and admire her. Even furious, she was breathtaking.

Now all I had to do was force my friendship on her. But first I needed to switch my waitress.

CHAPTER 39

CLEMENTINE

When April walked off, I felt indescribable rage. Liam had summoned me to serve on him, proving what I had shouted at him earlier. Clad in impenetrable armour, I walked straight up to his table, each of my steps echoing loudly over the wooden floor. He didn't even look up or register I was there. His caramel brown hair had fallen onto his page as he scribbled away.

Cold fury rolled through me. He summoned me, and now he wasn't talking to me. For what? To prove that I was indeed a slave to his needs, that he could get me to worship at his feet, to follow him around like a lost puppy. What was the old saying? Treat them mean and keep them keen?

Asshole! "You know, universities have libraries for that purpose," I snarled.

His head snapped up, and he gave me a small smile that made my heart flip. It was a slight twitch of his soft-looking lips, but it was still a smile.

"I know. But this has always been my place to study."

Except for the week, you were ghosting me.

I felt a sharp sliver penetrate my armour. Maybe it wasn't as hard as I thought. I could feel the infliction that the shard caused, but my anger seared it closed. I wanted to shout at him, but this was my place of work, and I was not one for confrontation. So, I stamped my anger and tried to put on my best customer service façade.

"What can I get you?" I snapped, pulling out my notebook from my apron.

"I just wanted to see if you're okay." His warm brown eyes were full of sincerity. Old Clementine would have been floored by his tone. She would have rolled over and exposed the soft underside of her belly. She was naïve and stupid. Thankfully, I had learned my lesson.

"Never better. Is that all?" I crossed my arms over my chest and noticed how his eyes seemed to dart downward, pausing for a second on the generous cleavage displayed before they met my eyes again.

"Lucian came back," he announced randomly. His voice was a little gravelly. I raised an eyebrow at him. "He left shortly after you did." He cleared his throat, seeming like he was scrambling to talk, as though he was simply trying to fill empty air. "He sometimes punishes me by hiding away for a period of time." I didn't say anything. "He's happy to see you back here just as much as I am." I could see the gold illuminating his eyes. The gold seemed to be more prominent somehow. Instead of appearing randomly, it blended into thin rings around his irises.

"About that," I said, trying not to get absorbed into the beauty of his eyes, which appeared to change every time I saw him.

"Yes?"

"I know that it's Lucian's need to protect me. I'm asking him—and you—to stop."

Liam's eyebrows furrowed. "Stop?"

"Yes. I don't need a fairy-god-wolf, a knight-in-shining-armour, or whatever it is you described him as. I want him— I want *you* to stop."

"Clementine. You need to understand that it's impossible." He pushed a warm brown lock out of his eyes in a fidget. His jaw was hard, emphasized by his freshly-groomed beard. I took a breath, and his once comforting scent felt like it was suffocating me.

"No. Liam, please. You need to understand," my voice broke. "I can't do this. Not anymore."

His eyes softened, and his face filled with remorse. "I'm sorry, Clemmy. I really am. I'll spend the rest of my life apologising to you if that's what you need. But I'm not going anywhere. That's a promise. I'll always be here for you."

My heart beat uncomfortably against my ribcage, and I could feel the tears building behind my eyes. I watched as his nostrils flared, and the golds of his eyes flickered with uncertainty as he reached for my arm, which was still crossed protectively over my chest. I took a step back, creating a canyon between us—a chasm of physical distance mirroring my attempt at an emotional one. I just couldn't let him touch me. When he touched me, I became dazed and confuddled. When he touched me, I exposed my soft underside.

"Please don't cry," he murmured, lowering his hand. I glared at him, swallowing the emotional lump in my throat. I wasn't crying, but I was close. Before I could deny anything, he continued, "I can smell the tears you're trying to keep back. I don't like being the cause of your sadness."

Great. Just great. How was I supposed to hide my emotions if he could smell them? I took a deep breath. His scent swirled around me, but I did my best to disregard its effects.

"Liam. Let me be very clear," I said softly. "My world does not revolve around you. If you proceed to come into my place of work, I will be polite, but don't mistake that as friendship. You are not my friend. Now, if there's nothing I can get you, please allow me to go back to work."

I pivoted on my heel and escaped into the office for a moment, hyperventilating quietly. The heavy cedar and spice scent followed me, and I gave myself one moment to let my guard down and enjoy it. I allowed it to bring down my heightened anxiety. Then, once calmer, I left the office and gazed over to his booth.

He was gone.

I THOUGHT I would only have to endure Liam's unwanted company at work, but he was everywhere! From the grocery store to the local park, I kept running into him. I hoped that university would keep him in Kempthorne, but obviously he wasn't going, and he was purposely seeking me out. I was considering going to Kempthorne just to hide from him.

I hated that each time I saw him, I had to stuff my emotions in a box, bury them deep and put a rigid wall around it to ensure I didn't get hurt again. Each time he saw me, he would offer me a small smile and try to break down my walls, one tiny dust particle at a time. Slowly, the wall would start to crumble, but as soon as I was alone again, I would rebuild the damn thing, adding rebar and barbwire to make it stronger. I hated the fact that Liam made me feel like this. I despised the confusion and emotions that stampeded through me whenever he got close. I loathed the fact that he made me feel vulnerable. And I detested the fact I was still desperately attracted to him.

It would be a hell of a lot easier if I hated Liam, but I didn't. I cursed the fact I still cared for him. I abhorred that I could pinpoint him in any room by his alluring scent. And I disliked that his scent still affected me; it calmed me, angered me, and made me pulse at the apex of my thighs. And most of all, I was offended there was nothing I could do about it.

RYAN STILL WASN'T BACK, making my shifts seem longer and slightly unbearable. Once again, Liam had come in, but as I was behind the bar, I didn't have to serve him. He was surrounded by books again, but he barely looked up at me this time. I didn't know whether I felt happy or saddened by this fact.

I looked up from the mojito I was making and saw darkened shadows under his eyes. He ripped his fingers through his hair and yawned. I frowned as I looked down at the little planter of mint and plucked some leaves for the drink's garnish.

Is he not getting enough sleep?

I scowled at where my thoughts had gone, looking hard at the mojito. I observed the cool drops of condensation trickle down the outside of the glass and pool onto the grey counter. I really needed to distance myself from him. What did I care if he wasn't getting enough sleep?

"Did that mojito say something to offend you?" I jumped at the voice. Gazing up, I saw that Liam was now at the bar. How had he crept up on me?

"You're the only one that offends me," I muttered under my breath. Liam chuckled softly and graced me with that sexy smirk of his. Damn it, I forgot about werewolf hearing—*again*. I put the mojito on the tray, which already had two glasses of beer and a glass of wine. April swung by and picked it up, giving Liam a sultry smile as she did. My scowl deepened. "What do you want, Liam?"

"Can I get a beer?"

"Sure. But you know you can ask your waitress to get it for you, right?"

"But if I do that, I don't get to talk to you."

"Exactly." I pulled the handle of the tap toward me. "I suggest you go and find someone else to talk to because I'm not interested."

"I like talking to you, Clem."

I smiled internally and felt small butterflies flutter, but I squished them fast. "You mean you like the sound of your own voice," I said dryly as I pushed the beer toward him.

He laughed. "See, there! Why would I want to talk to anyone else? Your dry, quick-wit and sarcastic humour make me laugh and want to converse with you."

"Well, unfortunately for you, it takes at least two willing people to have a conversation, and I'm not willing, so please take your beer and leave me alone."

CHAPTER 40

LIAM

WE WERE GOING HARD at training, pounding into the dirt as we fought and tousled with each other. My brother Sean was stalking me on all fours. He was a dirty blond wolf with sandy-coloured highlights through his fur. His eyes were ringed with light gold, making the browns in his hazel eyes stand out. His wolf was smaller than mine, but that was to be expected considering his age.

Sean was attending his first lesson fighting in wolf form, and he was giving it everything he had. He charged forward, his tail waving high in confidence, feigning at the last moment and snapping at my back leg. I dodged and snarled, snapping my teeth at him, before ramming my side into him, trying to knock him off balance. He growled, and I tried it again. He rolled gracefully out of the way, kicking dust at me as he did.

He charged again, but I managed to get a mouth full of neck fur, and I gave it a gentle but firm shake, snickering to myself as he tried to kick me off. I shook him again, and he grumbled, lowering his body in submission, like a pup admitting defeat to an older wolf. It was short-lived, however, because as soon as I released him, he started to charge and faked me out again, bouncing forward and snapping at my face. I used my paw and smacked him down, chuckling.

Jaws were snapping, saliva was flying, and hackles rose. But it wasn't aggressive. It was instructive and a necessity. My brother needed to be able to defend this pack, and so did I. There hadn't been a war in Blackfern Valley since Alpha Jed was usurped, but as the warriors constantly told us, that didn't mean there wasn't one coming, and if we didn't train now, we were worse than dead. And as the sons of Alpha Josiah, we needed to lead by example as for most other things in our lives. We were groomed to show the pack we were worthy of them, that they could put their trust in us. It was a shame I couldn't show Clementine I was worthy of her attention, and she could put her trust in me.

We roughed around like this for a few hours, and eventually, Sean's coat was covered in dirt and blood and looked bedraggled. He shifted back, panting with exertion, and his body was sweaty. He threw me a grin and grabbed his towel from the side of the training grid. His shoulder wound was already healing. I didn't mean to take a chunk out of it, but he made a snide comment through the mind-link and unfortunately, he ended up running into my teeth shortly after the statement. Funny that.

I changed back, grinning at him like an idiot. Today's session had been a lot of fun. And I managed to burn off some of the frustration I had about Clementine. It had been almost a week since she returned home, and she was still in no way closer to opening up to me nor allowing me to be her friend again.

Ryan wasn't much help either. He returned home on cloud nine and kept saying that I needed to leave Clementine alone and forget about her. He stated that if it was meant to be, it would be. Like I could forget about her. Somehow, the curvy little woman became the thing that kept me up at night. She was the singular thing I couldn't get out of my head. So, I often sat in the trees behind her house, watching and guarding her while she slept. I knew it was creepy, but I told myself that I was just keeping her safe. There were still people who wanted to hurt her.

It was nice to see Ryan happy. He had found his mate on the night of the full moon, followed her all the way past Kempthorne and halfway to the next town over. She had felt the pull of something but got spooked and ran the other direction, but eventually, her wolf made her turn around, and they'd found each other.

She had moved to Kempthorne two years ago, but it made sense that he hadn't found her until now. As if it wasn't hard enough to find a true mate, the distance in which a wolf can smell their mate is about sixty kilometres, give or take, and Kempthorne is about eighty kilometres away from Blackfern Valley. That's not to say that the wolves who live in Kempthorne didn't run toward or within that sixty-kilometre radius on a full moon. She and her friends often ran the boundary line of our pack's land, occasionally darting over it. The reason that he hadn't found her until now was that she'd only turned twenty the week before the full moon.

She had kept her birthday primarily quiet and only told one of her friends, who had been outraged at the idea she wasn't doing anything to celebrate her twentieth. Her friend dragged her out to the bar to party—a bar where Doctor Jay was spinning at.

***

I was sitting at Lupus', feeling displaced. It was a Sunday afternoon, and Clementine's scent was nowhere in the bar.

Ryan sat next to me and dug into his poutine, watching Stacey come through the door with a bounce in her step. She smiled cutely at him before she sat down and swiped a particularly cheesy fry from his fingers before it made it to his mouth. She placed it in her mouth and licked her lips. His face turned all mushy as he watched her chew on his food.

"Ugh, guys! Stop with the mushy shit. Some of us are trying to wallow here," I whined.

Stacey smirked. "Do you really want to wallow? Or do you want to know what I just learned?"

"What did you learn?" I grumbled.

"I was just on the phone with Sophie. She was talking to Clementine. It turns out her dad has taken her brother camping. He offered for her to go, but she laughed in his face and told him she wasn't interested. She hates camping." She waved her hand impatiently as if what she had said wasn't necessary. "So, her brother and dad left yesterday."

"Okay?"

Her hazel eyes twinkled mischievously. "So, she's alone in her house. She was inviting Sophie over for dinner, but it might be a good opportunity for her friend Liam to show up instead."

"Stacey, I could kiss you!"

She laughed. "Yeah, not again!"

Ryan growled, and I gave him a sheepish look. He knew about the kiss. I had no idea that at the time I had kissed her, he had started crushing on her. It turns out he wasn't just crushing on her, he'd felt the mate bond's gentle pull before the full moon. I felt like a total asshat and apologized profusely once I'd learned this. No apology seemed to cool his beast however, and for the first time, I saw him lose control of his wolf, shifting and snarling at me. His teeth had glistened with saliva, and his hackles made his enormous brown wolf look mountainous.

He had once told me that he couldn't go against his alpha.

And I saw the internal battle that he'd waged with himself. One moment he was mad, the next, he was whimpering and submitting, only to hackle up and snarl again. It hurt me to see him like that. I had done that to him. I had already lost Clementine. I couldn't lose him too.

So, I did something he never expected. I shifted and submitted to him for the first time ever. I could feel his hot breath by my neck, ready for a fight, but I was submitting, and this time, it wasn't a fake-submit like in training. I was genuinely begging him to forgive me. He shifted back and gave me a single nod. I took that to mean he forgave me.

He may have forgiven me, but he wasn't going to forget anytime soon. Stacey realized the same thing and quickly put her hand on his, rubbing her fingers over his knuckles and looked adoringly into his eyes. He smiled softly at her and pulled lovingly at one of her blonde ringlets before brushing his lips against hers.

I suddenly felt like I was intruding on a private moment, and my heart ached. I was happy they had found each other. It looked like the fibres of their bond were already starting to knot and tether them together. I had a feeling they would mate and mark at the next full moon, which would make their bond impenetrable, and I assumed that Stacey would join our pack shortly after that. I didn't want to ask Ryan if he planned to move away with her. It would be weird not to have him around. As Stacey had a few more years of studying, it made no sense to rush for the answers to those questions. Only time would tell.

I chuckled to myself as I left the bar. *Looks like he'll be meeting his favourite athletes after all.*

I was enjoying walking in the early evening air, and Lucian was rumbling happily. We'd been getting on a lot better lately. I felt more connected to him than I have in weeks. And suddenly, something occurred to me.

"Hey, Lucian. Are we ready to merge?"

"I think we are close. But there's one more thing we have to do first."

"What's that?"

"Something important."

"Want to give me a hint?"

"I don't know any more than you do. We'll just know what we have to do, at the right moment. It'll be instinctual."

"Do we know when we'll have to do this mysterious chore?"

"Soon."

"Right. As helpful as always, buddy!" Lucian chuckled and went quiet again.

Clem's house was just around the corner on the next street. I started to plan what I would say when I saw her. How would I convince her to let me in or to at least open the door and talk to me? Maybe I could take her to dinner. I knew she liked spicey food and sushi. I knew I couldn't take her to Lupus' for dinner, and the only other places to eat in town was a chip truck and a pizzeria. There was an all-you-can-eat barbecue place in Kempthorne, though...

"I smell smoke," Lucian grumbled. I looked up and saw a dark cloud rising against the blue sky. I could hear the crackling of flames. Someone's house was on fire and I started to run.

I sniffed the air again.

Fuck, is that gasoline?

I heard a loud pop as I turned the corner and saw Clementine's house glowing in a foreboding, hazy orange.

My blood froze.

"Clementine!"

CHAPTER 41

CLEMENTINE

HE HAD RUN into the house like an idiot, screaming my name. I watched in horror as Liam opened the door and dived into a house full of orange and amber flames. Dark black smoke billowed out, and I stood there frozen in shock, shrouded safely across the road. The cell phone in my hand still glowed from my use. I had already called the emergency services.

I heard a pop and shattering of glass breaking, and felt my entire world stand still. My world may have stopped, but I hadn't. On autopilot, I ran toward the house, shouting Liam's name like a lunatic. I was looking through the windows, trying to see him, but I couldn't. Panic rattled through me.

He has to be okay!

My rational mind had already departed. I was ready to run into the burning building; consequences be damned. My body was zinging with the need to save him. I screamed his name again and approached the back door.

A large tawny wolf came barrelling out of the house and tackled me to the ground, growling deeply. I hit the grass hard; the wind knocked out of me. But I couldn't help but smile softly as I lay underneath his gigantic furry body. The warmth was borderline unbearable, but it felt right. It felt *good*. Relief washed over me. Liam was okay. His long snout nuzzled into the crook of my neck, and I felt his body move. It was an oddly warm, wriggling sensation, followed by cracking and popping that was utterly different to the sounds of the bonfire happening behind us. When he pulled his snout away, I was looking at Liam's human form. His mocha eyes were gentle as they searched mine. His creamy skin glowed in the orange ambience. I absorbed him for a moment, aware that he was stark naked and lying on top of me.

"You're okay. You're safe," he said, more to himself than me.

I felt myself clench at the purr of his tone. His muscular arms were wrapped around me protectively, and his body was smooth against the exposed part where my shirt had ridden up. His nose was inches from mine. His brown eyes were ringed with a perfect shade of gold. His breath tasted sweet as he breathed heavily. My entire body tingled, and my breathing hitched when I felt something else pressing against the inside of my thigh.

"And you're an idiot?" I snarled, trying to throw ice-cold water on the heat that was growing between my legs. "Who the fuck runs into a burning building, Liam?" I glared. I was too aware of his body, of his hardened length. Nothing was able to distract me, or dampen the heat between my legs, which was making my folds slick with wetness.

"I thought you were in there," he said softly, his eyes flickering with too many emotions to pinpoint one. His nostrils flared, and I felt him as he growled. That rumble vibrated into my wetness, and I struggled to suppress a moan. My mouth had gone dry.

"You're still an idiot," I croaked, trying to regain my composure.

"When it comes to you, yes, without a doubt," he said,

watching my mouth with such intensity that it made me lick my lips.

I felt his dick twitch against my thigh, and my sex responded in turn. He started to lower his face toward mine, and I felt my breathing stop. He surely wasn't going to kiss me. Not now. Not with my house still burning in the background.

"Liam," I said as his mouth was millimetres away from mine. "Get off me." My voice was a breathy whisper, and I felt his dick spasm.

He opened his eyes, the browns swirling with bright gold. "I don't think I want to," he said in a low tone. "And I don't think you want me to either."

He ran his nose over mine, and I felt myself clench. He was right. I didn't want him to move, but I needed him to. This was too much. I could hear the fire engines in the distance. My house was still burning. I smelled gasoline and knew that someone had set fire to my home. I had only popped out for a moment and returned to find an inferno.

"Liam," I croaked, fear and lust warring through me.

He pulled back, and his nose twitched again. Instantly, his eyes were browner and less gold, and he gave me a soft sigh. "I'm glad you're safe." He pulled back a little further and then gave me a soft kiss on my forehead. "Wait here. I need to go find some clothes."

He stood and started to walk toward the bush, brazen and proud with his dick standing at attention. My eyes were drawn to it. He was large, thick, and unashamedly rigid. I admired the veiny shaft that ended in a crown of dark blond curls. All I could think was how much I wanted that enormous cock to fill, stretch, and claim me. My panties were drenched, and my womanhood throbbed.

I was afraid, but next to that fear, I was so aroused. He turned around and looked at me again, his eyes full of swirling gold, his nostrils flaring. He stared into my gaze, and I felt my cheeks burn. Was it the rush of adrenaline that made him hard like that? Or was it me? I looked away bashfully, and when I looked back, Liam was already beyond the treeline and out of view.

THANKFULLY, the fire department had arrived and managed to put out the fire before the entire house had come down. I called Dad and told him what had happened, but I was instantly homeless. Sophie had offered to take me in for the night, which was good because I was pretty confident that if I'd stayed with Liam as he had suggested, I would have done something I would have seriously regretted.

Dad and Vinny arrived the following morning. They had left the mountains the moment after I managed to get a hold of them and had travelled all night. Dad's eyes were alert as he pulled me roughly into a hug. He growled as he sniffed the air. He didn't appear to want to let me go. Vinny didn't escape his overbearing hug either. He pulled Vinny in and growled again before reluctantly leaving us and heading over to talk to Alpha Josiah and Liam, who were standing back slightly. Liam's eyes were protective as they watched me, and he occasionally nodded at whatever his dad was saying. Each time I caught his eyes, I would blush as more confusing feelings continued to swirl to the surface.

Dad, Vinny, and I entered carefully and looked around in horror at the blackened and charred timber frames. The house had been gutted. I sifted through and found a few photo albums and random knick-knacks that had managed to survive the blaze. Thankfully, the fire hadn't managed to make it to my closet, and some of my clothes had remained untouched. The clothes stunk of smoke, but they were still intact, unlike the rest of my room which was black and covered in ash and soot.

The house was uninhabitable, and Liam's family had quickly put us up in one of the cottages on their property. Dad had explained that it was the pack house, and even though it was where the alpha and beta lived, the pack house belonged to the pack.

Being this close to Liam irked me. At least at my old place he wasn't right next door, and I could avoid him. I was able to hide away in my own company. Now, if I stepped outside, I could easily run into him. And even though we were in a better place than we were a week ago, I had a stronger need to avoid him.

I still couldn't believe my body's response to his. It's not like I had never been aroused before, but my past experiences paled in comparison, to the powerful surge of hormones I'd experienced last night. It had to be the rush of excitement and danger of what was happening. It was the only explanation. Yet, I couldn't stop replaying the primal look in his eyes. And every time I remembered that lustful animalistic gaze, his smooth body and how Liam's mouth had almost captured mine, I felt myself getting wet all over again. So yeah, I needed to avoid him.

I adjusted my mom's necklace as I looked at myself in the mirror in my new bedroom and sighed. I ran a comb down my dark hair, slightly annoyed that it was no longer sitting nicely around my shoulders.

I heard a knock at my door, and Liam barged in.

"You know the etiquette is to wait for someone to acknowledge your knock before you storm in, right?" I smiled softly. I tried not to admire his new haircut and loved how the caramel brown seemed to highlight his eyes.

"I have news."

"And that news allows you to break bedroom etiquette?"

"Bedroom etiquette? Oh, darling, I never break bedroom etiquette," he purred. I felt a low buzzing start in my core.

"What's your news?" I said weakly, placing the comb on the dresser and wiping my suddenly sweaty hands on my shorts.

"I came up here to tell you that the alpha has announced a meet. Your brother said most of his blood-hate harassment has settled since he got his wolf spirit, but yours is still continuing. You've been here a month, and you're still being targeted. He's going to end this blood-hate harassment you've been experiencing by making an example of the person who set fire to your house." His eyes flashed gold.

"You know who set fire to my house?" I asked quietly.

He nodded. "She's going to be banished," he growled. "I would have chosen a different punishment. This wasn't some form of rebellious arson. This was attempted murder. You could have died." His eyes were swirling with gold. When I spotted the signs of his agitated wolf, I instinctively reached for his hands and rolled my thumbs gently over the rough skin. He made a rumbling noise.

"So the meet is set for tomorrow. Alpha has sent out a command for everyone to turn up to the amphitheatre, but I've convinced him to let me take you away from here while it's happening."

"Take me away. Why?"

"Yeah. I want to take you away from here. We could spend the day away to keep you safe." He grabbed onto my hand and interlinked his fingers with mine. I forgot the strange static electricity I felt whenever we held hands. It seemed stronger now somehow. "Say yes," he murmured, watching my lips with intensity.

"Okay, but..." I worried my lip between my teeth.

His eyes darkened and sparked with gold. "But?" he prompted.

"Who was the person who set fire to my house and why?"

"We know why. She's deranged," he rumbled angrily.

"But who was it?"

He looked at me and gave my hand a gentle squeeze. "Cassie."

CHAPTER 42

LIAM

AFTER AN ICE-COLD SHOWER, I walked to the alpha's office and rapped my knuckles against the smooth wood. My dad had summoned me, and I had a feeling it had something to do about the meet.

"Enter," his voice vibrated through the wood.

I opened the door and wasn't surprised to see Patrick sitting on the hard leather couch. My father looked exhausted, and Patrick's eyes glowed with silver. He nodded at me as I entered and turned back toward my father.

"Alpha, with all due respect, you don't know that. You told me my children would be safe in your pack and look what's happened. My daughter's been stalked, attacked, and poisoned. She was roofied, and someone tried to burn her alive." Patrick's eyes flashed even more dangerously. "If it weren't for my son's need for this pack, I would be taking them both away. As soon as this meet is over, I'm going to tell Clementine that she needs to leave."

"What?" My blood went cold. "You can't do that!" Lucian's hackles raised.

"Yes, I can. She's my daughter, and I will not put her in any more danger. It was a mistake to bring her here. They don't target Vincent because he has a wolf. He's different but still one of them. Clementine is an outsider and being here puts her life in danger."

I snarled, Lucian's anger merging with mine. Dad put his hand on my shoulder and gave it a gentle squeeze. It was the only thing stopping me from charging forward.

"You know that no one will try anything after the meet. Once we make an example of Cassandra, no one will dare," my dad said in a confident tone.

"The only way to stop this is to put out an alpha command."

"What?" The gold rings of my dad's eyes flashed. "You know I can't do that."

"Can't or won't, Josiah?" Patrick countered.

My dad ignored the disrespect that was being administered. "I won't, Patrick. You just have to take my word that your children will be safe."

"She's not safe. Next time, these assholes may succeed in actually killing her." Patrick's voice broke, and I saw Clementine mirrored in his features at that moment. Their eyes crinkled the same way when they were upset. His jaw was set hard, just like hers did. He was crushed and trying to stay strong. Yes, she was so much like him.

"I can keep her safe, Patrick," I said desperately.

"You can't be with her all the time, Liam. No matter how much you want to be. She's human. This world isn't right for her." He gave me a knowing look before he continued. "I know you care for her deeply, but she can't be your luna. That would be a death sentence for her. There's a reason why no human has been luna before. You can't choose her as a mate. You need to let her go. I'm so sorry." He sounded so bereft and defeated.

Mate. I shook my head, trying to ignore the strange feeling that word gave me. Lucian started whimpering in my mind, and I felt conflicted about where my train of thought was going.

"I-I-I…" I struggled to get out the next words. Lucian encouraged me with a gentle nod. He was in complete agreement with my decision. "I'll renounce my right to be alpha. Sean can lead the pack. And if Clementine chooses to leave, I'll leave with her."

Patrick's emerald eyes went wide, and Dad looked aggrieved.

"Liam. No," Dad said softly. "Don't make any decisions like that yet. Not until after the meet, at least."

"I told her I would always be there for her. I'm not going back on my word."

"And no one is asking you to," Patrick said.

"But you are. You're asking her to leave." We all looked at each other in silence. We had reached an impasse.

"Let's not make any decisions until after the meet," my father murmured.

"Fine, but I would like to be excused from it."

Dad's eyebrows rose. "Oh?"

"I would like to take Clementine away from here. Keep her safe. And keep my promise. Patrick is obviously worried about retaliation at the meet, so let me take her away to ease his anxiety. Let me keep her safe."

Dad exchanged a look with Patrick before looking at me and nodded.

"Thank you, Alpha." I turned to leave.

"Liam, wait. That isn't what I wanted to talk to you about. Cassandra has requested to talk to you."

I spun and looked back at my father. "What?"

"She has asked to speak with you. She wants to explain. It's the duty as alpha to hear these things."

"Fine," I said reluctantly. I didn't want to hear what the woman had to say, but I would do it.

I walked through the pack house grounds toward the cellblock. Once again, where most pack houses had a cold and dark dungeon in the bowels of their large ostentatious houses, we didn't have anything like that. Instead, we had a stone jail block where warriors were stationed when we had prisoners. I nodded at the guard and walked straight down the stone corridor.

"You wanted to see me," I said, looking at Cassie's long red hair and big blue eyes ringed in purple. Her gentle scent burned my nose.

"Thank you for coming to see me." There was a short moment of silence as Cassie simply looked at me. "What's going to happen tomorrow?" she asked.

I gazed at her. "You will be banished publicly, then escorted by the warriors to the edge of the pack territory. You will be executed if you step foot on pack territory again."

Her eyes widened in fear. "But what about my parents?"

"They will be allowed to join you in your banishment. If they choose to leave, they cannot come back either. But if they stay, they will have to live knowing that you betrayed the pack."

"I didn't betray the pack, Liam! I just—"

"You just what, Cassandra? You ignored the warning at the last meet when we were told that half-breeds were moving into town. You were told that Clementine and her family would be treated as part of the pack," I said calmly. I was far from calm. I was furious.

"Just let me explain," she whispered.

"You want to explain how you burned a house down to try and kill an innocent girl? I smelled the gasoline, Cassie." A powerful wave of alpha energy overtook my body at the memory of seeing the hot orange flames blazing out of Clementine's house. I started to pace to try and keep myself calm. "Was this blood-hate? I never saw you as a bigot, but the alternative theory is unfathomable. There's no way you're that much of a psycho."

"I didn't want to hurt her, Liam." Her eyes filled with tears. "I overheard Sophie saying that Clementine's family was out of town, and I thought–" she stopped and took a shaky breath. "I honestly just wanted to scare her."

"You set her house on fire! You tried to kill her!" I screamed, losing the small amount of composure I had left.

"No!" She shook her head. "You don't–"

"You deserve far worse than banishment," I snarled. She bowed with the small wave of alpha energy vibrating off me. "You've been stalking her through the bush for weeks! You fucking broke her ankle! You set fire to her house!"

"They made me do it," she whimpered.

I stopped pacing and looked at her. She looked deflated and suddenly reminded me of the Cassie I had gotten to know from school. I shook my head. "They didn't make you do anything. You chose to do it. The only one that can make you do anything is the alpha. You should be thankful that he's only chosen to banish you. If I were alpha, you would be fucking dead!" I spat venomously.

"You love her, don't you?" she said through eyes full of tears. I didn't answer. I just stared at her, my eyes glowing with the power of my wolf. "She should have stayed away! It would have been safer for her if she'd stayed away."

I had heard enough. Pivoting on my heel, I stormed out of the cells. I turned back toward the pack house, but smelled Clementine's scent as soon as I reached the garden path's crossroads. I took a deep breath of it, and suddenly all I wanted to do was be near her again.

It had been a hard few days living next door to her. I didn't think there could be a scent as intoxicating as her natural honeysuckle and pear until I smelled her arousal the night of the fire. Now, all I could think about was that intimate scent of hers. It was seared into my memory.

I would instantly get hard whenever I remembered how her hair fanned around her head on the ground like a dark halo. The way her turquoise eyes shone brightly under her dark lashes and her tongue came out and licked her perfect pouty mouth that seemed to beg to be kissed would also get a rise out of me. But those memories were outstaged by the smell of her heat. My dick would get painfully hard with the memory, and I ended up spanking one out every time one of those came up, which was often.

It had been a few days, and Clem would give me her sexy, shy smile and blush beautifully when she saw me, but other than that, there was no mention that we had been moments away from kissing. What hadn't gone unnoticed by me was that there had been no mention that she was as affected by me as I was by her.

Many times, I wanted to throw her against a tree trunk and taste her lips. I wanted to hear her gasp, the breathy little sounds I imagined she would make. I wanted to burst into her room and finish what we'd started the night of the fire when she smelled so delicious and had stared at me like…like she wanted me.

It had been torture. She was so close, yet I couldn't touch her. And oh, how I wanted to do just that. I wanted to know if her skin felt as creamy and soft as it looked. I wanted to discover what sounds I could coax out of her as I brought her to the brink of pleasure. But I knew she still didn't trust me, and I needed to earn that back before I could do anything else. So, for now, I was spending a lot more time with myself, and ice-cold showers were the next best thing when that didn't work.

I TURNED toward the cottage she had been inhabiting for the last few days. The closer I got to it, the stronger the scent was, and I took a few moments to revel in it. My fear of losing her diminished as soon as I spotted her front door, knowing she was behind it. I excitedly bounded up to the door and opened it, making a beeline for her bedroom.

I paused for a millisecond at the room's door, remembering to knock just in time before my need for her urged me through the door.

She looked at me through the mirror. Her dark hair was a smooth river down her back. Her eyes met mine, and her cheeks were already dusted in their signature pink. I sniffed the air and smelled the undertones of subtle arousal.

What was she thinking about before I barged in?

It took all of my resolve not to cross the room and kiss her deeply, to see if I could intensify my new favorite scent. Lucian rumbled happily at the thought, but I took a deep breath and smiled instead.

CLEMENTINE TOOK the news of Cassie's betrayal in stride. The idea that the woman had tried to hurt her—wanted to kill her even—infuriated me, but Clem didn't even bat an eyelash. I wanted to ask her what she thought, but instead, she changed the subject back to our date.

Yes, I was calling it a date. However, I wasn't going to say that to her for fear of making her retreat into the shell of a person she'd been since her return from Vancouver. I didn't want her to distrust me all over again.

"So, what are we doing tomorrow?" she asked, looking down at our joined hands and slowly pulling her fingers away.

My heart instantly felt heavy. I didn't want to let go of her hand. She moved over to the loveseat positioned under the window and sat down. She tilted her head, indicating I could join her. My heart started to beat a little faster. She wasn't rejecting me.

"I thought we could go for a hike," I said, sitting beside her.

In another life, I could see us kissing on this couch, but for now, I had to behave. If only she knew how hard it was to be a gentleman around her.

Her brows rose. "A hike? Really?" I knew she was a city girl and didn't really like nature. She most definitely wouldn't like to hike through nature with me, but there was something I wanted to show her. Something I wanted to experience with her, and the location I was thinking of was the best spot to do it in. "Not a big one. It just takes an hour or two...uphill."

"Liam–"

"Come on! Trust me, this beautiful clearing is at the top, and I will pack a picnic." I smiled shyly at her.

"A picnic?" she tilted her head, and I watched her mouth twitch as if trying to suppress a smile. "Okay. But two hours will be more like four hours with me."

I winked. "Don't worry. If you get tired, I'll just carry you."

"You can't carry me, Liam."

"I have before. Twice, if I remember correctly." She rolled her eyes, and I couldn't help but feel delighted at the familiarity of this conversation. "Do you want to know a secret?" She looked at me expectantly. "I like carrying you."

"No." She shook her head fervently as if I was lying. "I'm too heavy, Liam."

"I think you're perfect," I admitted earnestly.

And as I'd hoped, she blushed that brilliant shade of red I'd grown to miss.

CHAPTER 43

CLEMENTINE

T̲H̲E̲R̲E̲ ̲W̲A̲S̲ a knock at the front door the following morning. For once, it appeared that Liam was adhering to door-knocking etiquette. I took a deep breath before I opened the door.

"Are you ready to go?" He was dressed in light-coloured cargo shorts and a grey t-shirt that emphasized the marble-like muscles underneath. I ran my eyes down him but frowned when I saw the hiking boots on his feet. I was wearing sneakers.

"I don't own hiking shoes," I mumbled, feeling a little anxious.

He nodded and ran his eyes over my clothes as if assessing their suitability for the hike. "Sneakers will be fine." I wore a breathable, moisture-wicking athletic top in pale blue and a pair of black shorts. Simple but comfortable. His eyes seemed to linger on the V-neck of my top.

"Is this okay? Is it suitable?" I asked about the rest of my attire.

His eyes snapped to mine, the gold rings swirling. "Yeah. It's not a hard or long walk," he croaked.

I sighed as I stepped out the front door. Looking around, I

saw lots of people heading toward the amphitheatre. "I thought the meet wasn't until this afternoon."

"It isn't. But this is normal for a meet. People come in early, turn on the barbecues and have a bit of a party first."

"Oh. Are you sure you don't want to stay?" I asked, trying to keep the hopeful tone out of my voice.

"Nice try." He flashed me a humoured grin. "Let's go."

We walked toward his Civic, and I looked around the pack house grounds as the smell of propane and sausages started to fill the air. As I turned to climb into the car, I stopped dead in my tracks and saw a large figure with dark hair and icy cold blue eyes. Nola and her sister were on his arm, laughing obnoxiously at something he'd said. A cold feeling washed through my body as his eyes connected with mine, and his lips turned into a sneer. I hadn't seen Lincoln since Liam had chased him off in my first few days here, and suddenly, I couldn't wait to get away—from here—from *him*.

LIAM CUT the engine of his car and grinned. We were somewhere in Kempthorne but far away from civilization. I looked at the timber archway that indicated the start of the hiking trail. The little blue square with the white pictograph of a keen hiker glared at me from within the small rectangular green sign with its white border. Liam had convinced me to go on a hike. How had this happened? Oh right! His big brown eyes and his sexy smile had robbed me of my ability to refuse.

This hike was going to rob me of my dignity. If I didn't die because of how unfit I was, I would die from sheer embarrassment if Liam decided to carry me.

"*He thinks you're perfect,*" echoed a voice in my mind as if I needed a gentle push in the right direction.

"Are you ready?" Liam asked, flashing that same sexy smile, his brown and gold eyes looking softly at me.

"I guess so," I said, getting out of the car, my sneakers crunching on the gravel and dirt below. Liam smirked which made his eyes twinkle as he opened the trunk of his car to start unloading gear. He showed me a tan-coloured baseball cap with a large red maple leaf on the front.

Just in case other hikers had no idea where we're from, I suppose.

He gently placed the baseball cap on my head, his fingers leaving tingles in their wake as he smoothed out my hair. "I would hate for your pretty face to get burned," he said in a tone that made my stomach knot. "Although, we might be unable to tell with the amount you blush," he added with a wink, and my face warmed on cue.

Liam gave me a small red backpack to carry, and I looked at it curiously. There was a neon blue tube coming down the shoulder strap. He gave me another sexy smile that made my stomach flip again. He helped me put it on. "Hydration pack," he murmured.

Hydration. Right.

He placed a boxed-shaped bag on his back which I instantly recognized as a modern picnic basket and locked his car with his key fob. He motioned toward the timber archway and held out his hand for me.

"What about bear spray or a bear bell?" I asked, suddenly aware we were going for a hike in the forest.

"You mean a dinner bell?" he laughed. "Bears tend to avoid areas where there are werewolves. Haven't you noticed that there isn't any sign of bears around Blackfern Valley?" He threw me another sexy smile. "But don't worry, I'll shift into a big wolf if we happen upon a bear and protect you with my life."

"How heroic," I said, rolling my eyes. "We should totally

add this to the list of things you can use to impress girls. One: he can parallel park. Two: he'll save you from a bear."

His eyes snapped to mine, and he gave me a small smile as he grabbed my fingers and started to pull me along the trail. "I don't need to impress girls," he murmured. "Just you."

My heart started hammering in my chest, but I didn't answer him as I was sure that he hadn't meant for me to hear that.

Before long, the gentle trail started to incline. I could feel the sweat building at my nape and in the canyons of my sports bra. It was sweltering. I was going to die. I was already panting and making sounds that sounded like a dying animal. I took another deep suck on the tube, never more grateful for the ice-cold water swirling over my tongue.

"How are you doing, Clem?" Liam enquired, looking back at me from a little further up the trail.

"Did I ever tell you how much I hate hiking?" I growled through my laboured panting.

"You're doing great, Clem. And remember, I can always carry you," he said with a wink. I scowled at him and kept pushing on.

The canopy of the trees got a little thicker, and I could see some game trails heading off to the side and looping around. I was getting an odd sense of déjà vu, but I knew I had never been here before, so I was unsure where the feeling was coming from.

Liam kept us on the main trail, occasionally letting us take a break so I could catch my breath. He never once complained that I was taking too long or criticized me for being unfit. Instead, he seemed to enjoy the walk and the conversation we were having as we headed to the place he wanted to show me.

As we got closer to the mountain top, I found a hidden reserve of energy and pushed ahead of Liam. It was as if the top called to me. I felt a gentle magnetic pull, something powerful about the destination. I was sweaty and hot and felt a little nauseous, but I was determined to make it up this mountain.

We finally made it to the clearing at the summit. I'm sure most people would have called it a hill, but it was a mountain to me. I looked around in awe at the clearing. It was covered in tiny purple, blue and white alpine wildflowers. There were a couple of stray pine trees near the edge of the grassy area, which was knotted and gnarled. I walked closer to the edge of the clearing and saw a gentle serpentine river in the valley below. A soft breeze danced around me. The small meadow was beautiful, as was the view beyond it. There were mounds of rolling hills covered in pine trees and the sliver of a glistening blue lake further in the distance.

"This place is beautiful," I said in a breathy tone.

"Told you!" He smiled as he lay a small picnic blanket on the soft grass. "But there's another reason I brought you here."

"Oh? And what's that?" I readied myself for whatever blow he was about to deliver.

He smiled impishly. "You'll see." I frowned, then took a deep breath. He grabbed my fingers and pulled me toward his picnic. "Trust me, you'll like it."

He sat down and tugged gently on my hand. I plopped down next to him and smiled as he brought out a couple of beer bottles, grapes, strawberries, crackers, cold meats, and cheese.

"I know this is supposed to be with wine, but I don't know anything about the stuff, and I didn't want to pick a bad one," he said apologetically as he opened the beer and handed it to me.

"This is fine." My stomach started to bubble. *Is this a date? No, surely not!*

I nervously picked a strawberry and took a bite. It was juicy and sweet but did nothing to calm my nerves. I took a swig of the beer Liam had handed me, its suds tickling my nose. I was about to open my mouth and ask him if this was indeed a date when suddenly his phone beeped, and he grinned, turning off the alarm.

"Are you ready?" His brown and gold eyes sparkled with excitement. He reached into the bag and pulled out two pairs of sunglasses, perching a pair on his face before he turned and placed the second pair onto my nose. He gently pulled me, so his arm was wrapped around my waist, and I was cuddled into him. His scent invaded my nostrils, and I didn't try to escape his affectionate embrace as I looked to where he pointed—the sky. No, not the sky. The sun.

Why is he pointing at the sun?

There were a couple more moments of nothing happening, and then I saw it. A dark shadow moved across the sky.

Holy crap! That's the moon!

It was a solar eclipse! I watched as the sky darkened even though it was still early afternoon. The sun started resembling a three-quarter moon at first, then a half, then a crescent moon.

I started to feel strange. The nausea I had earlier got stronger. My stomach churned, and my body felt uncomfortable. I realized I hadn't eaten anything and concluded that the feeling must be due to low blood sugar. I looked around the picnic blanket for a knife as the moon finally moved in front of the sun. A black sphere rimmed it in white gold. It was absolutely stunning, but I knew I couldn't give it my full attention unless I shoved food into my mouth.

"Liam. Is there a knife for the cheese?"

"Yeah, in the bag," he commented as he watched the eclipse.

I leaned forward and reached into the bag, palming the tiny

blade. The steel bit into my flesh, and I yelped in surprise, pulling my fisted hand out and cradling it.

"Are you okay?" Liam asked with concern evident in his tone.

"I just cut myself on the damn knife. It was so stupid and careless," I murmured.

"Let me see," he commanded. I opened my hand, and the wound started prickling as crimson blood appeared at the surface.

"It's not too deep," I said, examining it. "I was just trying to get something to eat. I felt strange and thought it might be low blood sugar," I murmured, watching the blood pool on my hand, run down the creases and drip onto the grassy meadow.

Drip. Drip. Drip.

By the seventh drop, the nausea subsided and was replaced with searing, burning heat. My entire skin began to itch. It felt like a million fire ants were running over my skin and biting me.

I threw my hat off my head and unclasped my necklace, throwing it, and my sunglasses into the bowl of the hat, as I started to scratch at my skin.

Am I allergic to the flowers? What the hell is going on?

My blood erupted into fire in my veins. When I felt the first snap of my bones breaking, I let out a blood-curdling scream of agony.

CHAPTER 44

LIAM

I watched, stunned, as Clementine's eyes flashed with flecks of bronzy yellow, and she started to scratch at her skin like she had a fever. Lucian gasped in shock as he witnessed her bones begin to snap. Her arms dislocated, and her legs bent backward as she fell onto all fours.

She was shifting.

But she doesn't have a wolf spirit! She's human! And she's definitely shifting into a wolf. What the hell is going on?

"*Holy shit! Her wolf just woke up. I can sense her!*" Lucian said in awe.

Snap, crack, pop, snarl!

Clementine's honeysuckle and pear scent was saturated in fear and adrenaline. The human smell had weakened and was almost completely gone, and her underlying canine scent became more prominent. I witnessed the pure child-like fear in her turquoise and amber eyes as fur the colour of midnight sprouted over her forearms. She cried out in pain again.

"Clementine, listen to me. You need to breathe through this." Another scream, as her nose started to protrude and morph into a snout with a wet black nose before it flicked back to her cute button nose again. She was fighting it. If she fought it, the pain could kill her. Resisting the first change could kill anyone.

I raced forward and looked into her eyes as they flashed a swirling amber with the agony she was experiencing.

"You're shifting, Clem. You can't stop the change. Listen to your wolf. Let her take the lead." A guttural growl left her sweet mouth, and I knew she wouldn't stop fighting. The more she resisted, the more it would hurt. She was going to die. Cold terror exploded through my body. I needed to help her. "Clementine, stop fighting it. Trust your wolf."

All I wanted to do was hold and comfort her as she went through this, but I couldn't touch her. Touching her was dangerous. She stared at me, her eyes flashing with bronze and turquoise. I stared right into them, unflinching. "Trust me," I whispered. "I promise you, I'm not going anywhere. Just let go and trust me." She blinked, and I instantly saw the trust in her eyes. She stopped screaming. Stopped fighting. Her silence was short-lived, however.

Another scream echoed, followed by the sound of her clothes tearing. Her body realigned with loud popping sounds, her nose elongated, and at the same time, her fluffy tail sprouted. Within a blink of an eye stood a medium-sized wolf with dark black fur. Her pelt glistened, and I could see tones of bluish-black and midnight-onyx blending through her wolf's coat. Clem opened her eyes and stared at me with her stunning aquamarine ones. They were now ringed with a pale amber.

She did it!

And she was fucking amazing! So stunning. She made a wheezing noise, then flashed her teeth at me before getting up and running.

"Fuck! Clementine, wait!" I yelled as I yanked at the laces of my boots and kicked them off. I ran after her, stripping off my clothes and shifting on the fly. Following her scent as she darted through the trees, it didn't take me long to catch up, as I dashed ahead of her quickly to cut her off. She feigned to the side and ran again, darting toward a game trail to the side, sprinting hard on four legs.

Her scent wafted around me as I saw the flash of her tail flick through the trees. I weaved around an old tree ladder that was falling apart and kept running after her—scurrying down the path and weaving in and out of the trees. She was surprisingly fast as she looped around and tried to throw me off her trail. She skidded past a derelict cabin deep in the woods, but her scent had veered off in a different direction when I reached the cottage. I heard her scurrying down the path to my right.

I growled playfully as I aimed for higher ground, stalking her from above. When she stopped, I braced myself. Her ears twitched, and she sniffed the air. But it was too late. I pounced on top of her from above. We started rolling down the mountainside slope before landing in some twigs and leaf litter, right on the edge of a deep stream.

Fairly quickly, I realized she wasn't playing. Clem was fighting me. Her teeth snapped, and her hackles were raised. I backed up and sat on my hind legs, tilting my head as I watched her. She was panting hard as she lowered her head, her ears flattening against her skull. She was incensed. I don't think she recognized me or knew what the hell was going on. She growled ferociously and showed me her large canines. The sweet smell of her honeysuckle and pear seemed out of place on this aggressive she-wolf.

"We need to help her through this," Lucian mumbled.

"Yeah, we do," I agreed. *"Can you reach her wolf?*

"No. She's not pack, and she's too agitated right now to even attempt it. We could try releasing alpha power?"

"I don't want to spook her any more than she is. Let's use that as a last resort."

"What do you suggest?"

Instead of answering, I inched forward submissively, hoping the animal inside her had enough instinct to recognize the act. She growled a deep warning tone that anyone listening would have understood it to mean, 'back the fuck off.' I ignored it and edged closer.

She attacked, but I didn't respond. I let her snap her jaw around my neck. An instant buzzing vibrated through my skin when her teeth met my flesh. I could feel her canines grazing through the thickened fur around my jugular. One large bite and a shake, and I would be seriously injured.

She pulled back when her teeth broke my skin and whimpered a low, miserable noise. She nudged her muzzle into where her teeth had been moments before and started licking at my minor neck wound. Then she looked straight into my eyes and nuzzled her snout against mine in a way that I could only describe as affectionate. Clementine was back.

I stood up, rubbed myself along her flank, and then tucked her under my chin, rumbling with affection. She rumbled back, and I felt elated.

She seemed to enjoy sniffing and darting around the forest on our stroll back toward our picnic. Her favourite thing to do was run and crash into piles of crunchy leaf litter, rolling over the top of them before bounding away and rubbing her scent over every other tree. Lucian and I chuckled as we watched her play. I wish I could have mind-linked her to find out what she was thinking, but for now, her excitement over her wolf was enough.

I nudged her side and guided her back to the clearing, keeping her flank and admiring her wolf, which barely reached under the shoulder level of mine. Much like the human side of her, she fit perfectly.

She tucked down on the grass near our abandoned picnic, exhausted from her first change. I growled lowly and snuggled down next to her, enjoying her scent's tingling warmth. I felt a seismic shift and a click as Lucian, and I finally merged. Grinning at Lucian, I lay my snout on her shoulder blades and drifted off to sleep.

SHE FELT SO good snuggled into my arms, her hair tickling my nose. I opened my eyes and edged myself back a small amount.

Oh shit!

Somehow, while we slept, we had shifted back and were now cuddling naked. Clementine was tucked up, facing me, her head under my chin, her face serene in her sleep. Her black hair waved out over the side of her body. Her large mounds were perfectly wedged under her arm, so I could only see the edge of her nipple.

I was instantly hard. My God, she was beautiful. I reached out and ran a hand over her side, admiring the soft and creamy skin under my fingertips. I continued to draw my fingers down and over her hip bone. Tiny electric tingles buzzed at my fingertips. I studied her face as she gave a little moan in her sleep. My dick twitched in response, thickening at the sound. I wondered if I could get her to make the sound again, and I couldn't help myself. I ran my fingers over the curve of her hip and felt her gently thrust into me in her sleep. Her warm thigh rubbed against the head of my cock, and I shivered in pleasure.

Oh, fuck me!

I needed to put some space between us before I gave into my arousal. I reluctantly leaned over and gently kissed her creamy shoulder before I disentangled myself from her, then pulled my shorts on. The moment my clothing covered my manhood, she moaned in her sleep and rolled over, her glorious tits on display. They were more than a handful in size, creamy, with perfectly pink taut nipples. Her beauty added to my arousal. My already bulging erection got painfully hard, tenting against my cargo shorts, and I left a small wet patch at the front. I looked at her lying on her back and stifled back a growl as I followed the smooth skin of her perfect rack, to the soft tissue of her stomach and down to the thick dark curls in the v of her legs.

All other she-wolves I had been with had waxed it clean off or left me a play trail, but with Clementine, her pussy was perfectly womanly in her simple bikini wax. It truly suited her personality and turned me on immensely. All I wanted was to shove my nose into it and taste the treasure beneath. I wanted to lick her folds and coax more of those erotic noises she'd been making out of her.

"She's not going to be happy with you if she wakes up exposed like this," Lucian murmured as he gazed lovingly at Clementine, the colourful wildflowers crowning her head.

I nodded in agreement and plucked up the picnic blanket. Walking over to her, I committed her naked beauty to memory before gently laying the soft picnic blanket over her.

Hovering over her, staring at her beautiful cherub face and perfectly pouty mouth, I could no longer resist. I lowered my head, gently caressing her lips with mine. They were soft and supple, and warmth spread throughout my body. I pulled my lips away and admired her again before I lowered my head and teased her lips some more. My mouth covered hers, and my tongue darted out and gave the crease of her mouth a gentle lick as I moved my lips against hers, tasting her.

I wasn't expecting her to open her mouth in a moan or to

deepen the kiss. My tongue explored hers, and she gave a sexy little mewl that almost made me lose control completely. Our mouths fused in the heat of passion, and I reluctantly pulled back, breathing hard. That kiss had been amazing. I'd finally gotten my taste, and I was officially addicted.

"Did..." her voice was coarse. "Did you just kiss me?"

I opened my eyes and looked into hers, which flickered with amber flecks. "Um, no?" I lied sheepishly.

Her brows rose; she obviously didn't believe me. "Oh, okay." She looked to the side. "I must have been dreaming then."

"Yeah, I think you might have been," I agreed, although my throbbing erection begged for her eyes to trail downward to know it had been otherwise.

"That's a real shame because that was one sexy kiss." Then the little minx grinned playfully. A proud Lucian preened. And I couldn't help but return her cheeky little smile.

I started to lower my face toward hers, waiting for her to grant me permission this time. She reached her arms out and tangled her fingers into my hair as she pulled me down on top of her, her lips crashing desperately onto mine.

CHAPTER 45

CLEMENTINE

His lips sent tingles all the way to my core. Was I truly lying here kissing Liam with only a picnic blanket hiding my naked body from him?

Who is this confident girl?

Normally, I would usually be shying away from this sort of affection, but Liam's kisses had awoken something in me that oozed with confidence. His mouth skilfully teased mine as he deepened our kiss. And even though his hands remained up around my face and hair, I felt my folds start to dampen.

My entire body reacted to his kiss as his arousing tongue fought for dominance in my mouth. I couldn't get enough. I wanted to feel his hands run down my porcelain skin and enter the heat between my legs to relieve the ache that was building. I arched one leg out of the picnic blanket and over his hip. I felt the hardened rod between his legs perfectly align with my clitoris, and desire ran through me. He growled into my mouth when he felt my leg straddling his hip and gently thrust himself against the blanket between us. I gave a little moan in response.

He slowly pulled away, delivering the gentlest and sweetest

intermittent pecks to my lips. The golds of his eyes were a perfect solid ring, and I just knew he had merged with his wolf.

"As much as I love the idea of spending the rest of the afternoon kissing you," he kissed me deeply again, causing me to moan and thrust up against him, "you must be starving. You shifted for the first time. That usually leads to binge eating straight after." He pecked my lips again.

"Yeah, I am hungry, now that you mention it." I nodded, looking into his brown eyes, admiring the thick and solid ring of gold. "But not for food."

His nostrils flared and his eyes flashed with lust, as he let out a deep rumble. "Behave," he growled playfully, giving me a peck on the nose before kneeling to reach the picnic basket, his god-like torso glistening in the sunlight.

All the nausea and pain I had felt earlier had subsided, and my body felt loose and free. There was also this hollow part in my mind that hadn't been there before. It was new. I felt around the edges of it and was surprised when a sweet voice giggled, then said, *"Hey, that tickles!*

"Oh!" I exclaimed into the hollow space.

When I reached back in, I noticed a pitch-black wolf sitting there swishing her tail at me. She gave me a saucy wink and motioned her head out of the hollow space as if she wanted me to look back into the real world.

Liam was back with the picnic bag, which he placed beside us before he propped me up into a sitting position and tucked himself behind me. He kissed my bare shoulder, then started grazing his teeth up toward my neck, nibbling and kissing softly on the soft flesh between my neck and shoulder, making me shiver with delight. I clenched my legs shut and stifled a moan.

"Are you talking to your wolf?" he murmured as he continued to trail kisses down my neck and shoulder.

Oh, my God, he's so good at that. Who knew that that soft spot between my neck and shoulder was so erogenous?

"It turns you on because that's where the mate mark goes," said the sweet voice in my mind.

My eyes snapped open, and I looked back at Liam, trying to ignore the intruder in my mind. "Did you mention food?" I asked, gently pulling away and reaching into the bag. I heard a deep growl behind me and snapped my head back. I watched as Liam's eyes moved down my naked back.

"Yes, food. But I think you should probably get dressed first."

"Um, Liam. My clothes were shredded." I rolled my eyes. "Hold on."

I stood up and gently wrapped the picnic blanket around me, knotting it at the side of my breast and where it ended at my knees. I tied a couple of the funny tassels together to ensure that the gaping hole between my chest and knees was reasonably covered. A wave of vulnerability washed over me. Liam had seen me naked. He had done the honourable thing by covering me up, but he had still seen my naked flesh with all its imperfections: the cellulite, the stretch marks. He now knew how ugly my body was.

I turned back to look at him. "Is that better?" I asked shyly, trying to push the negative feelings invading my mind away.

"Not even close," he growled, staring at the cleavage my makeshift dress was pushing out.

I readjusted myself nervously before sitting back down on the grass and popped a strawberry in my mouth.

He started to dish out our picnic, and we sat quietly, eating. I watched him as he piled ham and cheese onto a baguette I delicately stuck to the fruit and allowed him to eat his fill. I admired how his arm muscles bulged and rippled over his shoulders and the smooth, light tan he was exhibiting. He was a total contrast to me. Where I was soft and plump, he was ripped and muscly. Whenever he caught me looking at him, I would blush, making the gold rings in his eyes brighten as he ran the backs of his fingers over my cheek.

We sat in silence as we ate. Every now and again, he would offer me half of his next sandwich, to which I would shake my head and nervously nibble on the fruit and an odd cracker. He frowned, but never said anything.

"I can't believe you shifted," he finally commented.

"Neither can I."

"How? How is that even possible, Clem? You were human." He leaned in and sniffed the crook of my neck. "You are definitely a werewolf now, but how the fuck did that happen?"

"My w-wolf said it was the power of the eclipse." She hadn't shut up about the eclipse and its mysterious powers while I ran with her. "She's been trying to come through since I was sixteen, but my human side was too strong."

"Just like the legend," Liam murmured. "Something amazing can happen at the peak of a solar eclipse." He shook his head in awe.

"I also said a whole lot of other crap, too. Remember?" my wolf teased.

"Not now," I mumbled to my wolf.

"I know you don't believe me, but you'll see."

I looked at Liam, who was watching me converse with my wolf with interest. "What's her name?" he asked curiously.

I suddenly felt my cheeks burn. "I never asked her," I admitted. I looked back into my mind, and she smiled. Her name whispered over to me. "Her name is Circe."

"Well, I, for one, am stoked that you've found her."

"Even if it meant missing the eclipse?" I teased.

He chuckled. "Well, I wasn't going to say anything, but way

to ruin our date, Clementine!" He grinned and started putting stuff back in the bag.

I opened and closed my mouth like a fish as I gaped at him. *So, this* is *a date!* I felt my mouth twitch into a shy smile and struggled to find something to say after that revelation. My mouth had gone dry, so I cleared my throat and tried to change the subject. "I see the eclipse helped you and Lucian merge."

"Nope, that was all you."

"Me?" My eyes widened.

"Yeah, you." He gave me an affectionate smile, and the gold of his eyes glowed. "I needed to help you through your first shift. To help you accept the change and bring you back from when the animal instinct took over. The first change is hard enough when you have a wolf guiding you through it. But you never received the instructions from elder wolves or Circe in advance." He took a deep breath. "Resisting the first few changes can kill you. When I saw you going through it alone, I was scared you wouldn't accept Circe. That you were going to–" He closed his eyes. An odd salty smell in the air lasted for a second or two before Liam opened his eyes again. "Lucian always said there was something about you. I guess this was what he meant. It's why he was always so protective over you. He could feel you needed us on some level. And this is what we needed to do. We needed to help you accept Circe and bring you back."

I instantly remembered the panic I felt when Circe tried to break free. I remembered the way my heart started beating loudly. The way my bones bent, broke and dislocated. The pure, white-hot burning in my blood. The way my nails had thickened and sharpened, and the claustrophobic feeling that came over me as my nose elongated. I literally couldn't breathe, and my lungs burned. I felt like I was dying. And I guess I was because I was fighting the shift.

Warm emotion ran through my body, and I looked at Liam fondly as he continued to pack up our picnic. He had done so much for me, and I didn't know how to express my gratitude.

"Hey, Liam." He made a humming noise which I took to mean he was listening. "Thank you for helping me through that shift and bringing me back when I forgot who I was."

"I told you, Clemmy. I'll always be here for you. You don't have to thank me for staying true to my promise."

"You mean that, don't you?" He nodded solemnly. I looked at his brown and gold eyes and smiled at his honesty. I slowly edged forward, my heart thumping in my throat as I looked at his lips. Then ever so slowly—to give him a chance to back up and reject me—I gently touched my lips to his. His hand instantly reached into my hair as he pressed forward a little harder and returned my kiss.

Circe fluffed herself up and grinned.

I HOOKED my mother's necklace around my neck and placed the baseball cap back on my head, laughing at how silly I must look having a picnic blanket dress on with a baseball cap. I found my tattered underwear and shorts and frowned when I discovered my pale blue top was in tatters. I had liked that top.

"*Next time, strip before we shift,*" Circe suggested unhelpfully. I picked up all the bits of clothing I could find and placed them inside the picnic bag. Thankfully, my sneakers were still somewhat wearable despite the hole in their sides.

"*Thanks for saving my shoes, Circe.*" I rolled my eyes. She laughed a wolfy chuckle, and I made my way over to Liam, who was frowning at his phone. "What's up?" I asked.

"Nothing," he said, quickly deleting whatever he'd just read.

Distrust and suspicion instantly reared their ugly head. "Liam?" I asked again, giving him a measured look.

He gazed at me, his eyes taking in my facial features before he shook his head. "I had about fourteen missed calls from Cassie. She wants to talk to me, but I deleted and blocked her number."

I bristled a little, then took a deep breath. Girls were always going to be messaging him. It was something I would just have to accept. I had no claim over Liam, no matter what my wolf had implied.

"Maybe you should talk to her," I said quietly.

"No. I really shouldn't. Besides, I deleted her number already."

"Just mind-link her and find out what she wants."

"Can't. She's no longer pack. That tie has been severed."

"Liam. What if it was important?"

"No, Clementine! She fucking tried to kill you. How can you even think I would talk to her?" His voice came out with a protective growl, and I knew he had made his mind up with the stubborn set of his jaw. "Are you ready to go?" he asked. I nodded as he took the picnic bag from me and put the hydration pack inside it before placing it on his back. He looped his arm around me, tucking me into his side. "You still fit," he murmured as he kissed the top of my hat.

It didn't take as long going downhill, even with me in a makeshift dress and ruined sneakers. When we got to the car, he opened the trunk and started digging inside it, pulling out an oversized blue t-shirt and a pair of shorts.

"These might be a little more comfortable?" he asked, handing them to me. I smiled before turning away and pulling the shorts on underneath my makeshift dress. I pulled the t-shirt down over my head and untied the picnic blanket, letting it shimmy down my hips. Hearing a low groan, I peered over my shoulder at Liam. His eyes watched me with a predatory look.

"Shake that ass like that in front of me again, and I just might have to smack it," he growled low, and my womanhood clenched at the thought.

Then he directed me to the front passenger door and helped me into the car.

CHAPTER 46

LIAM

It took all my self-control not to take Clementine right there in that clearing. If she were any other she-wolf, who was showing me such apparent signs of arousal, I would have been removing my shorts in a flash. But with Clementine, I made a physical effort to restrain myself, keeping my hands permanently in her hair to ensure they wouldn't travel between her legs. I would have been a goner had I touched the heat of her desire. Absolutely lost—to her.

She deserved better than a quickie in the clearing on top of a mountain. Even if it were multiple quickies, she deserved someone who would take things slow and worship her. From what I knew of Clementine, she had never had that. Hell, now that I thought about it, I had never given anyone that either. I frowned at the realization.

I took a moment to gather myself as I grabbed her some food. When I turned around and looked back at her, her eyes were glazed over, and her face was peaceful. My dick twitched as I took in the image of her messy hair and her slightly flushed cheeks. Lucian huffed proudly; we had done that. Slowly, I returned to her and inhaled her scent like an addict.

I was a sucker for punishment and couldn't resist her. Clementine's skin glowed under the sun, and the tantalizing smell of her arousal hung in the air. The little mewling noises she had made as I kissed and nibbled against her neck had almost made me come against the rough material of my cargo shorts. Instead, I took a deep breath and tried to calm my inner beast. My animal instinct told me to claim her and make her mine. I could feel my teeth elongating, which wasn't surprising, although it was the first time it had ever happened.

Even though I couldn't mark her officially until the full moon, I could still put my claim on her. The venom wouldn't solder a bond as the mating mark would, but it would infuse my scent with hers, even more so than just fucking her senseless would. It would eventually wear off, but I couldn't see myself letting that happen once I smelled myself on her. Lucian desperately wanted me to graze her with our venom, letting all the other wolves know she was mine. He was rumbling deep inside me, but as we were now merged, he accepted my decision without fighting me.

Pulling myself away was the hardest thing I ever did, and my balls weren't thanking me for it. They demanded release and denying them made them too sensitive to touch. Even the rough material of my cargo shorts was too much pressure against my cock, but I would endure it for her. Honestly, I would endure anything for Clementine.

I pushed the food toward her but noticed she didn't eat much. She seemed nervous and almost shy again. Werewolves needed to replace depleted resources quickly, especially after a shift, but all she was doing was picking at the strawberries and looking at me with those beautiful doe eyes. I tried not to let it worry me. Maybe half-breeds didn't need to eat as much as full-blooded werewolves? I was sure that Circe would encourage her to eat when needed.

We made it to the car quicker than I had anticipated. I sighed with relief as I found her something to wear other than that alluring blanket she had tied around herself. Knowing I could reach into it and feel her bare ass or tease her pussy during the entire time we were in the clearing, then walking down the hill had not helped my blue-ball situation. I hoped if I got her some clothes, it would help my desperation for her. I was wrong. Not only did she shake her ass in my general direction but seeing her in my clothes and smelling my scent on her from our make-out session, only brought one word to mind. *Mine.* I felt my teeth elongate again, and all I wanted to do was arch her over the hood of my car and smack her ass while I massaged her clit. I craved to make her orgasm. Growling possessively, my reaction made her sweet scent of arousal flood my nose. She wanted it too.

Fuck!

I painfully adjusted myself before getting into the driver's seat and turned the ignition. I reversed the car before directing us out of the parking lot and toward the road. Her scent surrounded me to an almost unbearable level in the closed confines of my car. It made me want to pull the vehicle over and abandon my chivalrous notions. I cranked the A/C in attempt to blow it away from my nostrils and gripped the steering wheel tightly.

"So, when we get back to Blackfern Valley, you'll probably want to take a shower," I said, looking over at the bashful beauty sitting in the passenger seat. She shot her turquoise eyes over to me in surprise, then confusion at my statement, and before she could ask, I continued. "I know you probably want to go and see your dad. But, um..." *How do I word this delicately?* I grimaced as I concentrated on the road ahead. I decided just to rip the Band-Aid off. "Werewolves have a keen sense of smell, and your father won't only know that you spent the afternoon making out with me, but he'll know it aroused you." I glanced over, and sure enough, her cheeks were their signature pink.

"You can smell my arousal?"

"God, yes! And it's driving me insane," I complained, white-knuckling the steering wheel. I looked back at her and saw that her eyes were vacant, and her nostrils twitched. Her cheeks went redder.

She was scenting her own arousal. But I didn't expect her to clench her legs and groan in embarrassment. I almost crashed the car at the sound.

"Not helping, Clementine," I growled.

"Sorry," she murmured, clearly embarrassed. I could feel her shutting down, so I reached out and grabbed her hand, holding it against the top of my thigh as I drove.

"That smell is the most intoxicating thing in the world to me. And smelling myself on you mixed with it, well, there's a reason I'm gripping this steering wheel so tightly. It's taking all my strength not to pull over and take you in the backseat of this car."

She smiled shyly and looked out the window, hiding her pink cheeks behind the dark strands of her hair. Then her head snapped back to me, her eyes wide. "Wait! Do you mean anytime I– You– My dad– Oh, my God!" Her sentence broke as she joined the pieces together. She let go of my hand and buried her face behind her palms, mortified, and I couldn't help but chuckle. She whacked me hard. "It's not funny!"

"It's kind of funny," I offered, sniggering.

She whacked me playfully again, and I flashed her a charming smile as we both cracked into embarrassed laughter.

I PULLED up at the pack house, and before I could even lean across and taste her lips one last time, she was out of the car and running into the little cottage. Less than a minute later, I heard the sound of the shower being switched on and couldn't help but laugh to myself. I made my way into my house to have my ice-cold shower.

When I got out, I dressed quickly and headed to the alpha's office, rapping my knuckles against the wooden door.

"Enter."

"Hi," I said, making my way to the leather couch and collapsed onto it with a grunt.

Dad looked up from his laptop screen and smiled. His eyes combed my face with pride, twinkling with the pale gold around his irises. "You and Lucian have finally merged, I see," he said smugly as he closed his laptop.

"Yeah. All I needed to do was help a half-breed through her first shift under the peak of a solar eclipse. Then *bang!* Lucian and I merged," I said as casually as I could.

Dad gaped for a moment. "Clementine shifted?" His voice was full of wonder.

"Into a beautiful black wolf." I grinned, remembering the bluish-black tones and midnight weaved through her fur. "I told you I smelled a wolf on her."

"That's astounding." I nodded in agreement.

He pulled out a crystal decanter and poured two glasses of maple whiskey. He came over to the couch, handed me a drink as I scooted over to let him sit. Grinning, he said, "We can start your stage three training as soon as you like. And when you're ready, we can announce your inauguration date."

"So eager to get rid of the alpha status, huh?"

He chuckled a rich laugh before he took a swig of his whiskey. "I know you were a little heated earlier when you said you would renounce it. Is that still the case?"

"I just need Clementine to be safe. And now that she has no reason to leave, there's no need to give up my status," I said, slowly sipping on the whiskey.

"You like her a lot, huh?" Dad asked. I looked at him with a deadpan stare but didn't answer. "You realize that now she has a wolf, she would be able to become luna. If you choose her as your mate, she would ultimately become luna of this pack."

"I guess that would have to be her choice," I murmured, feeling my anxiety rise. I swallowed the lump in my throat with a big swig of the drink in my hand.

He eyed me before continuing. "There's no rush. You need to be ready for it. Both with the inauguration and whoever you choose to be your mate. And if you need advice, I'll always be around to support you, son." He sighed but gave me a smile that made him look half his age. His eyes twinkled a little mischievously as he chuckled again. "But truthfully, I'm fucking ready to retire."

I smiled at Dad and noticed the stress hidden in the depths of his eyes, behind the twinkle of humour. "How did it go today?" I asked, knowing that this would be my job soon enough.

"As well as I could have hoped for. There were a few outcries, but I silenced them soon enough."

"What were the outcries about? Who made them?" I demanded, my eyes tinting ever so slightly with the anger I felt.

"Relax. They were a few misinformed wolves. I always expect there was going to be one or two who are disgruntled. I'm glad they felt they could raise their concerns with me. It helps enormously with keeping the peace."

"Dad, you're the alpha. You make the final decisions. They shouldn't be disgruntled. Your word is law, alpha command or not."

"Watch it, Liam. I may be their alpha, but they are still

allowed a voice," he reminded me. "Not giving people a chance to express their concerns leads to anarchy. I listened to their concerns, reassured them, and punished Cassandra Worthington for her crime against the pack. Not against a half-breed, but the pack. I don't expect anyone will try anything against the Stevens' anymore. They have seen I will be ruthless if I need to be."

I gave Dad a single nod and downed my glass, hoping that his version of ruthlessness was enough.

CHAPTER 47

CLEMENTINE

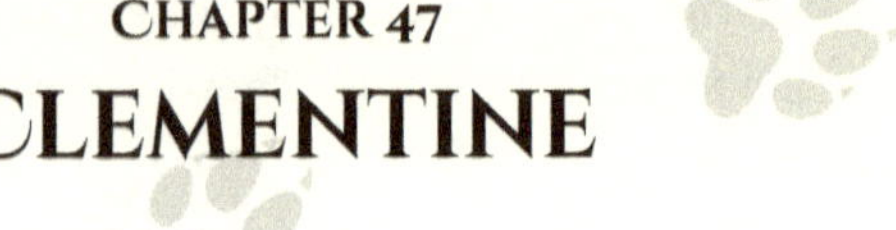

I WALKED INTO LUPUS' with my head held high and smiled when I spotted Ryan behind the bar.

"Hey, Ryan!" I exclaimed as I took my position behind the bar, purposefully letting Circe flash through my eyes at him.

"Nice wolf." He grinned, and I couldn't help but cackle in glee. "I heard you and Liam went off and watched an eclipse together."

"Yeah, and then the eclipse landed me with Circe." I rolled my eyes, and he laughed. "I heard your future in-laws are coming to town."

"Where did you hear that?"

"You would never know this, but your sister loves to gossip."

"Oh, I know! Who do you think told me all the sordid details of your trip up the mountain?" I blushed, and he chuckled deeply. "Wait, *were* there sordid details?" he asked, taking in my demeanour.

"I don't know what you're talking about," I said seriously. He chuckled again.

. . .

It was a standard Friday night, and the bar was pumping. Liam sent me a text message, telling me he would swing by later and we could have my dinner break together. He had seen me yesterday and was eager to see me again. I smiled at the thought and tried to ignore the nervousness that bubbled in my stomach.

Stacey showed up and took a seat at the bar. Her curly blonde hair was perfect, and her hazel eyes shone with happiness. She grinned, then congratulated me on my wolf before turning her attention to Ryan.

The sexual tension between those two was astounding. The air had shifted as soon as she'd arrived and locked eyes with her mate. She and Ryan flirted shamelessly as he worked. They seemed always to be slightly touching and bantering, and soon, I could smell the subtle tones of her arousal. But unlike me, Stacey wasn't ashamed about it. She was bold as she leaned across the bar and whispered something erotic in Ryan's ear. His eyes flashed as she sashayed toward the back.

A few beats later, Ryan announced he was going to the storeroom to get more alcohol. I rolled my eyes at the pretence and couldn't help but smile at their antics, trying my hardest to tune out the giggling and growling sounds coming from the back a few minutes later.

My smile was short-lived as Nola came marching up to the bar, her blonde hair pulled back into a tight ponytail that swung from side to side as she walked. She looked around and grinned maliciously.

"No more guard dog! It seems he's been neutered."

I rolled my eyes. "I don't need a guard dog, Nola. That was Liam's and Ryan's decision, not mine." I took her order pad and started pulling a beer from a frosty tap.

She tilted her head and studied me, her icy-blue eyes

rimmed with silver. "I thought you would have left by now. I heard your father was going to make you leave," she stated as she loaded her tray with the beer I'd just poured.

I stiffened. How did she know my dad and I had discussed me leaving? After we walked through my house's charred remains, I was seriously contemplating it and had even started looking for apartments in Kempthorne. That way, I would be close and relatively safe. But when I said as much to Dad, he shook his head and told me that if I chose to leave, it would need to be much further than Kempthorne. He made it clear I could still be targeted if I stepped outside of the town's boundary, indicating that out-of-sight-out-of-mind was a better approach. I had made the decision to move back to Vancouver the morning of the solar eclipse. I had even texted TJ to ask him to house me while I looked for an apartment, only for my entire world to flip again. I wasn't human anymore. I was a werewolf, and a werewolf needed a pack.

"I'm sorry?" I asked. I could feel Circe pace in my mind, but she huffed at Nola as if she wasn't worthy of our attention.

"How many times must you be told that you're not wanted around here?" she hissed.

"Oh, I assure you, I'm wanted, and I'll be initiated into the pack this full moon."

"So what? You fucking get Cassandra exiled, and you think you can take her place?"

"She burned down my house, Nola! She did that to herself. Besides, shouldn't you be happy that Cassandra is gone? She was your competition, wasn't she?" I poured a glass of red wine and added it to the tray.

Circe snorted. *"As if this amoeba could ever get Liam."*

"You think this is about Liam?"

"Isn't it always with you she-wolves? How many of you

have warned me off him, yet he hangs around, kisses me, and wants to fuck me until my toes curl. I think we can safely say that he doesn't share your opinion," Circe said impatiently through my voice.

I looked back at her in shock. I had no idea she could talk through me like that. She swished her tail, looking bored. I really wish she hadn't told Nola my personal business. I didn't need more rumours floating around. I needed people to accept and allow me to be a member of this pack. And that wasn't going to happen if the cliquey she-wolves were spreading rumours. Nola's eyes flashed dangerously, the silver rings becoming bright with anger.

"What's the matter, Nola? Scared of a little competition?" Circe snarled through me, bringing herself forward into my eyes.

"You may have a wolf now, Clementine. And you may have stroked some chubby-chaser curiosity from Liam. But you're a fleeting conquest. You'll never be luna. No one is going to follow a half-breed whore!" Nola spat, turning on her heel and taking the tray with her.

"Wow, your wolf is badass," Ryan said from behind me.

I spun around, not having realized that he had returned. He grinned as he set down a box. A fresh set of teeth marks and a purple bruise were on his neck, and he smelled strongly of Stacey. His eyes were twinkling with humour as he looked at me.

"I can't believe she just said all that. Liam and I are just friends–" I started.

"She was putting another she-wolf in her place. It's a sign of dominance. She-wolves tend to be snarky, revving each other up until one eventually snaps. Male wolves are a little snappier from the get-go, but mostly, it's all just showing teeth and hackles. She was baiting Nola, trying to get her to snap so she could put her in her place."

"Why would Circe do that? I have no idea how to fight. I have no idea how to shift! Is she trying to get me killed?" I cried. "I have no clue how to be a wolf. It's only been a day!"

"Nola wouldn't touch you, and Circe knows it. She probably was sick of you being stepped on by these she-wolves." He looked toward the door and smiled before looking back at me. "Your alpha has arrived. Go show Nola who you really are, Clemmy."

Circe chuckled deep inside me, and I felt her give Ryan a saucy wink through my body.

"How the hell do I control you?" I growled.

"Hey, I've been trapped behind a big fucking wall for the better part of five years. Let me have some fun!" But even as she said that, she moved back into my mind ever so slightly, and I turned to see that Liam was making a beeline straight for me. My nose homed in on his scent, and I naturally smiled. "Hi," I said almost breathlessly.

"Ready for food?" he asked. "I thought we could get out of Lupus' for a bit."

"Yes, please!"

I came out from behind the bar and waved at Ryan before tucking myself under Liam's arm and letting him guide me out of the bar and grill. When I looked back, all the she-wolves looked at me with a murderous glint in their eyes, and I felt I had unconsciously declared war against them.

I suddenly felt very nervous. We walked away from Lupus', but I was deep in thought.

Sensing something was up, Liam looked at me curiously. "Why are you biting your lip?" He gently tugged my lower lip with the pad of his thumb, the golds of his eyes brightening. I have no idea what possessed me to do it, but I darted my tongue out to taste his thumb, then I puckered my lips and sucked on it, swirling my tongue over the rough skin seductively. Actually, I did know what possessed me to do it. I glared back at Circe, who tried to make herself look innocent.

"Um, sorry, that was Circe," I mumbled, blushing. "I don't know how to control her." I wrung my fingers together and looked at my feet.

"Don't control her too much," he purred. "I like that she makes you brave. It's fucking sexy." He then pushed me against the wall of a building and kissed me hard.

His mouth tasted like minty toothpaste, and I felt the tingles start low in my belly as his tongue massaged mine. I moaned into his mouth as the fresh mint, and his natural scent swirled into my nose and straight to my groin.

"I would have liked to say that was Lucian, but it was all me." He grinned cheekily. "Come on, let me buy you dinner."

We walked into a small pizzeria with only enough room for four tables and a drink fridge. He went up to the counter and ordered two large pepperoni pizzas and a side of garlic bread before directing me to sit at one of the small tables.

"This place isn't much, but it does pretty decent pizza, and Winter makes a delicious strawberry cheesecake."

"Winter?"

"She works here. Her dad owns the place," he said. "I thought you wouldn't want an audience as we ate, and other than Lupus' there's only this place or a chip truck. Unfortunately, we don't have time to go out to Kempthorne."

"You thought correctly. And this is fine."

"How are you doing with everything?"

"I'm okay."

"What did your dad say when you told him?"

"He was pretty happy. He started to show me how to mind-link him and my brother. My brother and I will be initiated into the pack on the next full moon. That reminds me, I need to text TJ and tell him I'm not coming anymore." I pulled out my phone and opened a message window for my friend.

"You were going back to Vancouver?" he asked with a slightly defeated tone to his voice.

"Yeah. I decided it was for the best. That way, you lot could run, frolic, howl at the moon and be at peace. But I guess there's no point now that I'll be howling at the moon too." I finished writing my text message and hit the send button.

"Did you want to run together?" he asked, his voice wavering slightly.

I looked at him and wondered why his cheeks had a slight redness. Circe puffed herself out and nodded eagerly at me. "Um...sure, I guess. I have no idea how any of this pack-run stuff works. Having a friend to show me the ropes would be good."

Before Liam could reply, a willowy brunette delivered the pizza and garlic bread to our table. She smiled fully at Liam, and Circe rolled her eyes. The girl was beautiful with big brown eyes and red lips. I tried to ignore the feeling of inferiority as she blatantly flirted with Liam for a few moments.

I took a slice of the pizza, covering it in tabasco sauce, which was already on the table as Liam and the young she-wolf chatted. I tried to push any negative thoughts away. Circe huffed her annoyance, trying to reassure me that Liam wasn't interested in this stick figure of a girl, then proceeded to remind me of the conversation she had with me on the mountain. I ignored Circe too and patiently waited for the intruder to leave our table.

I nibbled at my pizza delicately as Liam helped himself to a large slice. He was right. The pizza was pretty decent. I allowed myself two slices and the crusty part of the garlic bread before I announced I was done. Circe rolled her eyes. She knew I was again comparing myself to the other girls in the pack.

Liam frowned. "You need to eat more than that."

"No, honestly, I'm fine."

"Clementine, that's barely enough for a human, let alone a werewolf," he grumbled. "What's going on?"

"Nothing."

His eyes narrowed into slits. "You need to eat, Clementine. Werewolves can withstand a lot of things, including lack of food but even then, there is a limit. Your fast metabolism will cause your stomach to eat itself, heal and eat itself again. Your strength with eventually waver. But it's not your hunger, or strength you need to worry about; it's your mind. A werewolf without food can be dangerously feral. This is why pack wolves are big on eating; keeps your body and mind fit and ready for training – which in turn makes you hungrier. You'll be starting training soon and will end up eating more than you ever have. Your werewolf side needs the fuel. Honestly, there's no reason to be embarrassed by the amount of food we need."

"What if I don't want to train?" I said.

"You have to. It's Pack Law."

"I'm terrible at exercise, Liam. Do you not remember how I almost died walking up that mountain?"

"I told you I would carry you."

"And I told you I'm too heavy."

"And I told you you're perfect."

I blushed hard as he took my hand and kissed my fingertips softly. Circe fluffed herself up at the attention. She was glowing with adoration.

"Ready to try some of Winter's strawberry cheesecake?" Liam asked. "It's the best cheesecake in all ten provinces and three territories."

I couldn't help but smile at him, remembering our conversation the first week we met about the best poutine. "Hard claim."

"It's true." His eyes twinkled roguishly.

"And how do you know this is the best cheesecake in Canada?" I played along.

"Winter told me," he said with a cheeky wink.

CHAPTER 48

LIAM

I FOLLOWED Clementine's alluring scent into Lupus' and saw her chatting behind the bar with Ryan. I noticed her straight away; her soft earlobes, flawless skin and piercing eyes. The crown of her head had a beautiful, glossy braid that weaved and looped back into her ponytail, which showed off the soft spot between her neck and shoulders. Her necklace emphasized her subtle cleavage, and I grinned, remembering the gorgeous full breasts I knew were hidden beneath the black t-shirt. But mostly, I noticed how she smiled radiantly at me and made me feel like the luckiest guy in the room. Lucian puffed himself up proudly as we went to collect her.

As I tucked her selfishly against my side and turned to leave, I spotted the way all of the unattached she-wolves looked enviously at her, and I couldn't help but feel proud. They were fucking jealous of the woman they constantly sneered at and called a half-breed. Maybe they had finally realized that she was worth tenfold of them all.

I wanted to take her anywhere else, but Blackfern Valley was limited in its food options. I knew that with her shy nature, she wouldn't want an audience as we ate, especially now that no one watching could deny the chemistry between us. So, I directed her to the pizzeria and ordered two large pizzas and a side of garlic bread. The pizzas were massive here, so they would easily feed us both, and if I got hungry later, I would just get the poutine at Lupus' while she worked.

Dinner went far too quickly, and it was time to walk Clementine back to work. As we left, I tucked her under my arm again, smiling at the perfect fit. Sniffing her hair, I enjoyed her scent as we walked through the darkening streets. The sound of our footsteps was the only noise that bounced in the surrounding humid air.

We made it to Lupus', but before she disappeared to go in, I found myself pulling her arm and leading her away down the side of the building. Before she could ask, I pushed her into yet another wall and gently kissed her. Her lips tasted of cheesecake, and I growled as her strawberry-tainted tongue found mine.

At first, the kiss seemed shy and sweet. Then it became a little more desperate and sensual. Clem's wolf flashed in her eyes, making me realize that Circe once again was giving her a little boost of confidence, and it fucking turned me on. Lucian pressed forward a little more in response, and the smell of Clementine's arousal was instant.

I was hard and pressing myself against her, behaving much the predator not allowing his prey to escape. Her hands were pinned above her head, and I enjoyed the whispery little noises she made as I started to kiss up her jaw toward her earlobe. I pulled it between my teeth and gave it a gentle suck. She shivered in delight. Her scent and mewling noises made me heavy with need, and I had no idea how I would stop and let her go back to work. I was either going to take her back to my house or make her surrender here in the alleyway.

A light buzzing in the front of her crotch shocked right

through me. I groaned as I realized that she was getting a call. I reluctantly pulled away, and Clementine, whose aquamarine eyes were bright, and her face flushed with crimson, scrambled to pull her cell out of her apron pocket.

I looked down at the glowing screen and noticed an unflattering photo of a guy with blond hair. Usually, a strange guy's photo popping up on a she-wolf's phone while we were making out should have made me a little territorial. It didn't. The poor guy should have been handsome, but he was obviously hungover, which did not make him look attractive at all. I cringed as if I could physically feel his pain. 'TJ calling' flashed over the guy's nose. I nodded to indicate that I was okay with her answering. She grinned at the photo and did just that with a smart-ass comment, chuckling away. I pulled back a little further, telling myself that it was a good thing her friend had called because I was one step away from breaking my chivalrous promise to take things slow. I felt my wolf-teeth start to retreat with each deep breath I took. The scent of her arousal was waning too, and slowly, my own subsided.

When I felt calm, I listened to her quiet conversation, and grimaced when I was able to connect the dots. When she spoke about heading to Vancouver, I thought that she was talking about heading there for the next full moon. The thought then, had made me incredibly uncomfortable as I briefly relived what had happened last time. But as she spoke to TJ, it sounded like this latest trip to Vancouver was supposed to be more permanent.

Lucian growled lowly as we continued to listen.

No! She isn't planning on leaving permanently, is she? Had her dad convinced her to leave? When was this decision made? And why the fuck hasn't she told me?

She ended her call and gave me a sweet smile which I couldn't return. She had planned to leave me all over again.

Hurt and anger singed my tongue, and I felt a fissure crack through my heart. "You were moving back to Vancouver? I thought you were just going back there for the full moon." My voice sounded hollow.

Her eyes widened momentarily, and she shook her head. "No. It was going to be permanent." Her voice broke slightly.

"Were you going to tell me?"

"Yes, I was going to tell you yesterday."

"That's big of you. Telling me this time at least," I snarled.

"Why are you pissed at me?" She looked genuinely confused.

"You were going to leave."

"Yes," she spoke slowly as if trying to rein in her anger. "I *had* decided to leave. I *had* been thinking about it for a while, but the fire cemented it. I didn't feel safe here, so I was going to leave. I was going to leave so no one else could hurt me. I was going to leave so I could stop being a burden on my dad, on my brother, on the alpha. And on *you!*" she said with soft anger. "I was going to tell you yesterday, but then I kind of got side-tracked with a wolf, and my priorities have changed."

"Glad to know I'm a priority," I snapped, mentally licking my wounds. She arched an eyebrow and flicked her ponytail back in annoyance.

I knew I was being unreasonable. It was the first time she had opened up to me and admitted that the fire or the people in this town scared her. She'd been so quiet about everything up until now, refusing to let me look into everything that's happened. I should have taken the time to talk to her, to show her that I was there for her and let her feel supported through this, but I was angry she was running away and heading to another man for the support I should be giving her. Even if TJ was gay, it still hurt.

And as soon as that thought came into my mind, I

encroached on her space like a predator, making her back up against Lupus' wall for the second time. I captured her bottom lip with my teeth gently before I kissed her possessively. She moaned into my mouth, and I instantly got rock-hard again.

"You aren't going anywhere! You're mine, Clem. Mine!" I growled dominantly, panting hard from the kiss.

"I don't belong to anyone," she whispered, giving me a stubborn look. Her turquoise eyes were hard and unyielding. I growled once more. She was mine; she just didn't know it yet, and I was more than happy to educate her.

My mouth covered hers, kissing her roughly. She crumbled against me. I assaulted her tongue with mine before pulling back and giving her soft, quick kisses on her swollen lips. Her eyes flashed, and I could see the internal battle between her wolf and herself in the depths of those turquoise pools.

"Your wolf is telling you otherwise, isn't she? She wants to submit to me," I asked in a gravelly tone.

The scent of her heat gave her inner turmoil away. I felt my teeth elongate, and I knew I wouldn't be able to resist marking my territory. I kissed her again and started peppering small kisses across her jaw and down her neck. She moaned beautifully, which made me return my tongue to hers. Her sweet strawberry-tainted tongue caressed mine, and I rumbled deeply.

Mine.

I jerked when I felt her hands rubbing my cock through my jeans. Her fingers were stroking the head in slow, erotic circles. I pulled back and looked at her, her eyes flashing with amber.

"Are you sure you don't want to submit to *me?*" she asked seductively. I shuddered into her touch as she gently pushed away from the wall. I wanted more. I *needed* more. As she stepped forward, she pivoted me, and the wall was now against my back as her hand pawed at my junk. I thrust my hips forward and gasped as she undid the button of my jeans with a *pop*, then started to unzip slowly. Humid air blew up against my thickened cock, and her hand grazed against the skin of my shaft. I threw my head back and closed my eyes. Her fingers gripped it with the perfect amount of pressure, and I felt my toes start to curl in anticipation. Then she suddenly stopped. "Well, I better get back to work now."

She gave me a cute little wink and walked away.

Fuck! I think Clementine just won this round.

I looked down at my open jeans with my hard-on saluting proudly on the outside. Yes, Clementine definitely had won that round.

CHAPTER 49

CLEMENTINE

"*W*HAT *THE HELL,* C*IRCE*?" I growled as I walked into Lupus' Bar and Grill.

"*What?*" she asked innocently.

"*What do you mean 'what?' What was that all about?*"

"*He was trying to dominate you! Usually, I would be down for the big bad alpha to be dominating all over us, but not like that. He needs to know that he can't just walk all over you. Not like that fucking asshole in Vancouver did. I'm all with TJ on that, by the way; a good old screwdriver to the eyeball would sort him out!*" she continued on her tangent. "*Anyway, you have me now. No guy is ever going to walk all over you again.*

I glared. "*You made me pull his penis out in public!*"

"*And now he will worship the ground you walk on. You can thank me later.*"

"*He's never going to talk to me again!*"

"*Stop being so dramatic! I told you he is endgame!*" She swished her tail, then winked.

This wolf was delusional, and she was going to get me killed. She rolled her eyes at me again as I returned to my position behind the bar.

"How was dinner?" Ryan asked.

"Fine," I said, washing my hands in the sink and readying myself for the rest of my shift.

"You know you're going to have to wash more than your hands if you want to get his smell off you," Ryan whispered before he moved away to serve someone.

Circe fluffed herself up. *"I think we smell good. Should we see what everyone else thinks?"*

"Circe!" I growled.

Circe baiting the other she-wolves was a terrible idea. The pain of the first shift had been so intense that we needed a decent rest before we could try it again. Otherwise, the second shift would surely kill us. She told me that we could only shift if our life was being threatened or if we were in the company and comfort of our mate because he had the power to heal us. She said she would let me know when we needed to shift again, but for now, it was a good idea to avoid stressful situations that could lead me to want to shift.

And here she was, putting my head on the chopping block! I was pretty sure baiting she-wolves was considered stressful and life-threatening. She was seriously trying to kill me. I bet she had already picked out a lovely ceramic urn for my ashes too. Maybe a few sad songs for the three or four people attending my funeral. She chuckled at my dramatic thoughts.

Nola was the first one to notice. She sniffed the air as she approached the bar, her eyes flashing with silver. Her gaze narrowed into slits as she thrust her order pad at me. I spotted tiny tear marks on the order pad, and when I looked at her fingernails, I saw they had gone thick, black, and had become sharp. I quickly met her eyes and raised an eyebrow. She was stoic, her face was rigid, and her eyes glowed with fury. I could see she was physically trying to stay calm, but she hadn't taken a breath the entire minute she was standing there.

"Breathing helps," I offered as I cracked open a new bottle of wine.

"What?" her voice felt like sharp knives.

"To calm down, you need to breathe," I murmured as I loaded her tray with three glasses of white wine and started making a CC and Dry.

"She can't breathe," Circe murmured, tilting her head in observation. *"If she breathes, the scent she detected on you will be unbearable, and she'll shift. She's barely holding it together,"* Circe said smugly.

I placed the final drink on the tray, and Nola made a growling noise in her throat as she spun away, taking the tray with her. It wasn't just Nola who seemed to be doing everything in her power to control their anger. I could feel a low buzz while I worked—like a swarm of angry bees. Stacey and Roman were the only she-wolves in the bar who didn't seem to care. I wanted to hide from it all, but Circe refused to let me. She made me hold my head up high and smile.

<hr>

FINALLY, my work shift ended, and Ryan drove me toward the pack house. There were few streetlights in Blackfern Valley once you got out of the center of town, and the pack house was a little further away than my previous home. We passed the last dusty amber glow of the last light, and the ambience changed into a more foreboding atmosphere. Ryan's high beams reflected off the tree trunks and odd house as they popped out of their little alcoves in the bush.

Ryan always offered me a ride home after work. Truthfully, I was more than grateful. With the tension in the bar, I was sure that any number of she-wolves who'd been tonight's patrons would have jumped me on my way home had I been travelling alone. I would have had to shift to defend myself, and I didn't know how to do that. Hell, I didn't even know how to shift of my own volition.

"Ryan, how do I control my wolf?" Circe huffed.

Ryan chuckled in a deep baritone. "Unfortunately, it takes a little longer than forty-eight hours to learn that."

"Circe is going to get me killed."

"How so?"

"She likes the idea of antagonising the other she-wolves." I shook my head and bit my lip. "You saw how they all treated me before I got a wolf. And now that I have one, and, uh, something with Liam…" I sighed and redirected my speech slightly. "Those she-wolves are crazy. I mean, Cassie burned down my fucking house."

I looked at Ryan's profile as he drove and noticed how his lips drooped into a frown. "Have you told Liam your concerns about Circe? About the she-wolves?"

"No. Um, Liam and I had a fight?"

He smirked as he pulled into the pack house's long driveway and drove toward the roundabout area at the end before stopping, then flicking on the dome-light in his car.

"I wouldn't sweat it too much. No one is going to touch you after the meet. No one would dare piss off the alpha."

I worried my lip between my teeth. "Circe said the next shift could kill me. And then she goes and antagonizes all these wolves. I'd have said she was being cocky because she knew I was untouchable, but there's no way that's the case. She's just simply cocky, and reckless. If the next shift doesn't kill me, the she-wolves sure as hell will."

Circe rolled her eyes as if I was being overdramatic.

"Talk to Liam. He wants to know this shit, Clementine. You need to trust that he'll be there for you. He'll put the other she-wolves in their place, so Circe doesn't have to." He smiled softly. "And in regard to your shifting, once you start to get some strength behind you, you'll be able to shift again. Your wolf will be able to talk you through it, as will any other werewolf around you. Soon, you'll be strong enough to shift without hurting as badly, and it'll become second nature. Come to the training grounds tomorrow at one, and I can help you start to build some strength—tame your beast."

I got out of the car and waved as he drove away. I took out my phone and turned on the flashlight feature. I looked at the gravel garden path that led to the cottage we were staying in, but instead of walking that way, I turned toward the main house, creeping through the garden until I found a window that smelled of cedar and spice, thankfully on the bottom floor. I shimmied the window open and hoisted myself inside.

The bedside lamp illuminated instantly when my feet hit the carpet, and Liam sat up, the sheet slipping off his marbled body and pooling around his waist.

"Clementine?" he said, his voice full of sleepy wonder.

"Hi," I whispered, walking over to his bed.

He groaned, looking at his phone on the bedside table. "Clemmy, it's two-thirty in the morning."

"I know, I'm sorry," I mumbled as I sat awkwardly on the edge of the mattress. He reached over and pulled the blankets back, indicating that I should at least get comfortable if I was going to wake him at this hour. I slipped under the comforter and turned onto my side to face him as he lay on his back. I looked into his confused brown eyes.

"Circe is a lot to handle," I whispered. "I'm sorry she did that to you earlier."

His eyes softened as I apologized. "Don't apologize, Clem. I like that your wolf boosts your confidence and isn't afraid to put me in my place." He took my fingers into his hand and brought the tips of my digits to his mouth, where he brushed them softly with his lips.

"Yeah, but she's still going to get me killed," I mumbled. "The other she-wolves were unhappy that I came into the bar smelling like you, and she thought it was fun to antagonize them."

"I'm sorry I didn't follow you back in. I needed a moment." He smiled sheepishly. "Then, I got stuck doing alpha stuff so I couldn't come back. I promise you they'll get used to us."

"*Us?*" My voice wobbled.

"You and me. Whatever this is. They'll get used to it. They'll have to." His eyes were full of sincerity, and I found myself smiling shyly.

There was an *us*.

I should have been nervous, but I wasn't as I leaned in and covered his mouth with mine. His hands instantly went into my hair as I licked his lips and asked for entry. He opened his mouth with a soft grunt as my tongue gently darted out and caressed his. I bravely ran my hands over his hard chest, feeling the tight smooth muscles as I continued to kiss him. He gently pulled away from my mouth and peppered me with tiny kisses. As he kissed my cheek, my eyes roamed his body, and I noticed a sizeable tenting under the bedsheets.

He rolled onto his side to face me properly, which hid his erection, but I purred, knowing I had done that to him. His hands found my hips, and he gently stroked the bare skin at the hem of my t-shirt as he moved back in to kiss me again. Tingles ran all over my body as I inched closer to him. I needed more.

"Clementine." He breathed between kisses. "I'm trying to be a gentleman here, and you're making it incredibly hard."

I smiled. "Hard, eh?" I joked.

I felt a little swat on my behind. "Behave," he growled playfully.

"Or what?" I baited.

He grinned as he took my bottom lip between his teeth and nipped harder than I had anticipated. Then he soothed it with his mouth. Gentle tingles ran over my lips, and I sounded my instant agreement to his biting.

I let my hands explore his arms as I deepened the kiss, gently rocking forward and pushing him onto his back before I began kissing down his chest, grazing with my teeth and nipping at his skin between kisses. I felt him rumble with pleasure beneath me, and I smiled against his heated flesh. He was enjoying this just as much as I was. I could scent the start of my arousal as soon as it started budding deep in my stomach, and the idea that he liked this as much as I did made me ache between my legs.

Next, I began to kiss the sexy muscle of his Adonis belt which peaked out from the bedsheet, but when I got to the edge of the sheet, he jerked and pulled my body back up toward him. I looked into his lust-filled eyes and instantly knew I hadn't done anything wrong, but I raised a brow in query.

"Um, I don't wear boxers," he mumbled.

"To bed?" I asked, feeling the heat creep up into my cheeks.

"I don't *own* boxers," he clarified.

"You don't own boxers," I repeated. *Mister Nice Guy likes to go commando?* I suddenly remembered that he wasn't wearing anything earlier under his jeans, and I knew my cheeks had flushed redder.

"Too restrictive," he explained.

"You mean to tell me the only thing covering your cock is this flimsy bedsheet?" My voice was rough as I felt Circe's excitement merge with mine. I gently reached my fingers down and grazed the tent of the sheet, feeling his velvety head through the soft cotton. He jerked a little but didn't stop me as I started to roll my fingers over the top of his cock.

"Clementine..." he whispered in awe, closing his eyes and arching himself up to meet my hand.

"Liam," I whispered back. His eyes opened and flashed gold as I continued to rub him through the sheet.

"Please," his voice cracked. "Please don't stop." Then he wrenched back the sheet covering his manhood, springing his enormous cock free, and I stared at it in wonder as I watched a drip of precum bead at the end.

Oh!

CHAPTER 50

LIAM

I WAS NOT EXPECTING Clementine to clamber through my window and sneak into my room in the early hours of the morning. I woke up when I heard the window open, and my hackles had risen defensively. As I turned on the bedside lamp, her honeysuckle scent wafted over to me, and I felt Lucian rumble softly, which instantly calmed my defensiveness.

She looked at me like a doe caught in the headlights, nibbling on her delectable bottom lip as she made her way nervously over to my bed. I rumbled lowly as I watched her worry her lip through her teeth, and blood started heading south as her scent infused my bedroom.

Clementine's hand felt like soft velvet on my cock. I shivered into her touch. My plan was to take it slow, but that plan went out the proverbial window the moment she held my girth with both hands. I thrust into her grip.

Wow! Where did she learn to do that?

I groaned, curling my toes, and enjoying the light electric sensation coming from her slow movements. Growling, I couldn't help myself as I smashed my lips against hers. A cute little mewling noise came from her throat as she enthusiastically returned my kiss. Her fingers ran over my head in soft erotic circles. I growled again, remembering that all I wanted to do was taste her and coax noises out of her.

I moaned against Clementine's lips and rolled her over, grabbing both her hands and pinning them to either side of her head. I nibbled gently on her lip as I pulled away and looked into her eyes. Hers were ringed in a perfect amber, and her breathing had become laboured with our passion. I took a moment just to appreciate her. She looked at me curiously, those gorgeous aquamarine eyes penetrating deep with lust.

I wanted to take things slow, to worship her the way she deserved. I wanted to taste her and hear those moans and whimpers. I braced myself over her and started kissing down her neck, giving gentle nibbles which made her body arch up in pleasure. Her fingers flattened against the bed. The mewling sounds mixed with her laboured breathing made my rock-hard cock pulse.

My God, she's intoxicating.

I continued to kiss down over the top of her t-shirt and hated the barrier. I wanted it gone.

I held the edge of the hem and gave it a gentle motion that I wanted her to take it off. She bit her lip and slowly nodded. She edged herself up and slowly moved her work shirt up and pulled it over her head. I groaned when I saw her ample cleavage spilling out of a white cotton bra. No lace, no frills. She hadn't prepared for me to see her, and for some reason, the innocence of it all made it more erotic. Her face was crimson, and she lay back down. Her erotic scent swirled around me and made my canines elongate.

Her necklace fell into the divot between her breasts, and jealousy surged. That's where I wanted my tongue. I removed the moon from between her cleavage and started to kiss over her large breasts, massaging one mound in one hand as my mouth paid attention to the other. Her nipples pebbled through the soft cotton as I teased them through the bra with my teeth and hand. My tongue travelled down the flesh of her cleavage to the cute little bow embellishing her bra. She arched her back in pleasure, letting out a sharp gasp.

Good girl.

I gently kissed my way over the cotton-covered mound and down onto her stomach. I felt her stop breathing. Her body went rigid. I looked up at her from my position against her stomach and saw the uncertainty flicker in her eyes for a brief second.

No, baby. Don't get self-conscious.

I kissed her stomach again, keeping an eye on her reaction. She warred between uncertainty and lust. I followed the length of her soft belly with my tongue and grazed my teeth over the top of her hip bone. She moaned in pleasure, gripping the bedsheets beneath her, and my dick thickened and pulsated at the sound. I continued my assault on her, kissing, nibbling, and making her moan. She was so fucking responsive, and I hadn't even touched her heat yet.

Grazing my fingers over her shorts, I slipped my fingers up a leg hole. She was drenched, and I could feel so much heat coming from her core. Her scent drove me insane. The thought of her untamed desire almost made me lose control and rip the rest of her clothes off.

I withdrew my fingers to ensure I didn't tempt myself further and started kissing back up her stomach toward her plump and delicious mouth. My tongue found hers, and the slow and sensual worship increased in pace. I ran my fingers down over the skin of her stomach, enjoying the sensation of her warm, soft skin against my rough fingers. I toyed with the space between her navel and the edge of her shorts, tickling as I softly moved my fingers over the surface. Her hand had moved from my bed and was now running down my bicep and the length of my arm, electricity echoing everywhere she touched.

Suddenly, she grabbed my hand and shoved it roughly into the top of her shorts, popping her button and zipper in the process, before her fingernails clawed the muscles of my back, and she scraped at my skin with lusty need. I pulled away from her irresistible lips and saw her eyes ringed with a perfect shade of amber and filled with undeniable lust. She knew what she wanted from me, and I was happy to oblige. Inching her thighs wider, she groaned as soon as I located the nub of her sensitive clit. Her sweet arousal clung to and coiled in the air between us.

I rubbed her clit with my thumb in circular motions, and her body responded instantly. I watched her swollen lips ring into a perfect 'o' shape as I slid two fingers along her slick folds and entered her warm tunnel before pumping into her heat. She moaned in pleasure as I began to build up a rhythm.

Her hips ground into my hand as my rhythm increased. The soft sounds of my fingers in her pussy, and her laboured breathing were the only sounds in the room. She pulled my head down to hers and kissed me hard. I could feel her warm, wet pussy pulsing and squeezing my fingers as the pressure started to build. And my beautiful, responsive Clementine was about to make all the sounds I had been dying to hear.

Panting for breath, she pulled away from my mouth and let out a loud and sexy moan.

Oh. My. Fucking. God.

Hearing her being pleasured like that was going to make me shoot my load. I covered her mouth with mine to quieten her down as she climbed, exploded, and convulsed with her orgasm. Her body shook with pleasure underneath mine.

I released her mouth and stared into her blazing eyes only when her quivering ceased. Her cheeks were flushed with the sexiest pink I had ever seen.

So fucking beautiful! I slipped my fingers out and placed them into my mouth, sucking on her juices. *So fucking sweet!*

"Liam?" her voice was barely a whisper.

"Yeah, baby?"

"Your turn."

Her hands found my cock again, swirling the dewy moisture around, and I shivered into her touch. She pushed me back onto the mattress and gave me the sexiest little smile I had ever seen. Her teeth started nipping and kissing down my stomach, her tongue darting over the corded muscles. I groaned in pleasure as her hand pumped in rhythm with the kisses. Suddenly, the tip of my thick cock was in her mouth, and I jerked in surprise.

Fuck!

I ran my fingers through the ends of her ebony ponytail, which tickled my stomach, as her small hand gripped tight around the base of my penis, and she fucked me with her mouth. I growled and jerked against her soft lips.

It took all my patience not to take charge and pound her mouth hard and fast. The gentle caress of her tongue as she pumped herself back and forward over my cock was driving me insane. Her tongue slid around my shaft, up and down, up, and down. I arched into her mouth a little more, wanting all of it. She responded, and I felt her throat open a little more to take in my length. She flicked her eyes over and looked at me, her perfectly plump mouth locked around my girth. She was fucking me with those bright, turquoise eyes as she fucked me with her mouth. It was erotic as hell!

I arched. Every time I arched, she would relax her throat and take me deeper into her mouth.

Does this girl have no gag reflex?

I groaned deeply and felt her lips twitch against my girth, which suggested she was giving me a cheeky smile. I wrapped her ponytail around my fist and started to pump myself gently into her mouth. She slid up and down over my dick, her mouth, teeth, and tongue driving me crazy.

I felt my balls tighten and closed my eyes, seeing stars forming behind my lids. I released her ponytail and pawed at her, wanting to hold onto her flesh and grip her tight as my toes curled and my balls tightened further. Her tongue didn't stop. The tightening continued, and my dick became even harder.

"Oh, fuck, Clemmy!" I groaned. "I'm going to come." She kept the pace of her assault, and within seconds, I thrust hard against the back of her throat, groaning, and shooting my load. Her mouth milked my cock as she licked every last drop and swallowed.

Good fucking girl!

I lay there panting. Clem's head hit the pillow next to mine, and I rolled over and kissed her mouth hard, tasting myself on her. My dick flexed at the flavour, but it was more than satisfied, and I could already feel it starting its descent. She returned my kisses softly and reluctantly, as if she was almost unsure.

How can she be so unsure? She just had my dick in her mouth!

I gripped my hands into her ponytail and kissed her roughly, trying to show her how much I lusted for her. She moaned, and I pulled away, satisfied.

"That was...uh. Wow!"

She didn't say anything, and I could tell she was deep in thought. She just watched me quietly as her brain buzzed. I leaned forward and gazed at her in pure admiration. I kissed her again, softly this time, planting smaller, softer kisses down her collarbone and over the part where I hoped she would let me mark my territory someday. She shivered against me and gave me a gentle moan which made Lucian growl possessively at our perfect, passionate little Clementine.

"I should go," she whispered.

I shot her an incredulous look. "No, you really shouldn't."

"I shouldn't?" she asked softly. She seemed so unsure, with her shy nature taking hold.

"Fuck, no!" I growled as I pulled her into a cuddle and draped the sheets over us. "You belong here. Stay."

Lucian grumbled in agreement.

I marvelled at the fact that I wanted a girl to stay in my bed for the first time ever. In fact, I didn't want her to ever leave it. Her warm body was tucked into mine, and she felt perfect. *She* was perfect.

Looking at her one last time, I admired her softness and femininity before I reluctantly leaned back to turn off the light. Returning to her seductive warmth, I protectively tucked her into my body, kissing her shoulder gently. As her breathing evened out and the tension in her body relaxed, I too fell into slumber.

CHAPTER 51

CLEMENTINE

I STIRRED IN MY SLEEP. The first thing I noticed was the underwire of my bra digging uncomfortably into my breast, and I knew I had made the mistake of falling asleep with my bra on.

The second thing I noticed was tiny butterfly kisses over my shoulder and down my arm. The soft scratches of facial hair gave me goosebumps as the light kisses continued, soft and sensual. I stifled a moan at how good it felt.

The third thing I noticed was a heavy weight draped around me and a large hard object against my ass. I shifted slightly and rolled onto my back to find the warmest brown eyes looking down at me before soft lips enveloped mine.

"Morning, beautiful," Liam murmured, giving me another quick kiss.

"Hi," I said, feeling my cheeks heat under his gaze.

His fingers reached out and stroked my cheekbone before they moved from my face, then gripped hard onto my hip, tilting me forward and rolling me until I was facing him. The bedsheet barely covered his morning erection. I let out a gasp, but not because his dick was situated against my thigh and was already making me wet, but because my underwire chose that moment to dig into my boob again.

"My bra is hurting me," I mumbled as I shuffled away from him slightly, clawing at it, trying to get some reprieve.

"I can help with that." And I felt his warm hands trace up my spine to the clasp at my back. Within a second, the clasp was undone, and then he gently removed the straps from both shoulders, pulling up the bedsheet to allow me to cover myself as he removed the garment. His calloused touch heated my skin as he pulled it out from under the covers. I looked deep into his eyes as the sound of the bra thumping gently onto the carpet hit my ears.

His mouth covered mine again in soft kisses, and his fingers played with my ponytail. Circe smiled and stretched before collapsing into a relaxed heap as if she was enjoying the feel of his gentle fingers in my hair.

"I like waking up next to you," he murmured softly.

"You do?" I asked shyly, tucking the sheet around me tightly and then placing my hands under my warm cheek as I faced him.

He hummed and nodded. "Very much." His fingers played with strands of my ponytail as he watched me with a look of pure awe on his face.

"What's the time?" I suddenly asked him.

"A little after ten. Why? Worried you'll have to sneak out through my window?" he asked teasingly and gave me a wink.

I took a hand out from under my cheek, and pushed him playfully. "No! I'm joining the pack training today," I mumbled shyly.

"You are?"

"Yeah. Ryan said he's going to help me tame Circe."

Circe growled. *"I don't need taming. What I need is right here, pressing into your thigh."*

"That'll be good. I have some alpha duties to perform today. Otherwise, I would join you and help out."

"You want to train with me?"

"Any excuse to get you hot and sweaty." He grinned.

I whacked him playfully again. "That sounds gross, Liam."

"Not at all. Your scent could never be gross." He grinned before leaning close to my ear and whispering seductively. "Besides, some of the positions you get into in training are extremely erotic. Rough-housing with you on the ground, copping the odd feel and scenting you as you try to deny your attraction..." I shivered in delight as his tongue and teeth grazed my earlobe. "It's a major turn-on. And afterwards, the idea of you in the shower, washing soap down your delectable body–"

I gave an involuntary moan as he trailed off and moved his attention to my neck, his lips leaving echoes of tingles as I felt warmth spread through me. I felt his dick twitch against the side of my leg, and I assumed he was imagining what he was describing so coquettishly.

"What time is training?" he asked between kisses.

I had no idea where I got the voice to answer him as my mouth had become parched. "One o'clock," I said in a breathy whisper. His eyes flashed wickedly, and I felt my body shiver in delight. I liked it when he looked at me like that.

"Good. That means I have time to ravish you. I'm going to worship every inch of this skin until you have to leave."

He gently pushed me onto my back, and I felt the sheet slip slightly. Liam gave me a sexy smirk as he tugged the bedsheet a little further, kissing down my shoulders. My nipples popped out of their covering, and his mouth started to descend onto my breasts with a hunger unrivalled. His tongue found my nipple, and I gasped.

"Liam!" I moaned as my fingers gripped his hair. He grumbled and continued his assault on my nipple, his tongue and teeth sending sharp pings through the bud and down into my heat. He gave a gentle snarl as the scent of my instant arousal sat heavy in the air.

"You're going to be the death of me," he murmured as his lips found my other nipple.

I arched my back as his teeth grazed the nub into a tight bud. He pulled back and blew on it softly before his mouth returned, kissing, and sucking ever so gently. I moaned as he pulled away again.

"But fuck it! At least I'll die a very happy man."

***

I WALKED past the amphitheatre onto the training grounds and bit my lip. The males were on a grandstand to the left and blatantly checking out the beautifully toned and fit she-wolves, who were all in circles, gossiping and stretching their calves out, bending over, and admiring the attention, while they pretended to be unaware.

I felt eyes land on me as I walked across the dirt-covered ground. My hair was in a tight braid down my back, and my clothes stuck to me like a second skin. Nervousness bounced through me with every step I took. My fingers gripped my water bottle tightly. I tried to look at my feet as I walked over, but Circe wasn't having any of it. She made me hold my head high and gave me an extra bounce to my step.

I looked around the area and tried to find a friendly face. I saw Ryan talking to another guy with a similar size and build.

Are all warriors this massive?

Ryan grinned widely when he saw me and nodded at his friend before he motioned me over. I felt my insides squirm as the figure turned, and cold blue eyes raked over my body before his mouth twitched.

Lincoln.

Circe snarled deep inside my mind, and I knew she must have flashed briefly through my eyes as Lincoln's twitch turned into a deadly smirk. Ryan bounded toward me and met me half-way. He was only wearing workout shorts, and I marvelled at the golden colour of his enormous bare chest. His gentle scent was mixed with Stacey's sweet smell, and the bitemark on his neck was worn proudly like a beacon, telling me he was taken.

"You made it." Ryan's friendly smile didn't chase away the cold dread cemented in my stomach.

"What is Lincoln doing here?"

"He's a trained warrior. He's scheduled to help with training."

"Oh. I didn't realize," I said coldly.

"Don't worry about him. How are you feeling?"

"Nervous."

"About Lincoln? Or about the training?"

"Fuck Lincoln!" Circe snarled menacingly through me, making Ryan laugh.

"Let me get these guys started, and then you and I will find something gentler to do, okay? We'll ease you into it."

I nodded. "Okay."

It made sense he wanted to ease me into things. Just because I had a werewolf didn't mean I would be instantly fit and fighting ready.

I stood back and watched as Ryan let out a high-pitched whistle and called everyone in to start their routines. Lincoln gave me another slimy smile as he walked around people who had begun to pair up, correcting stances and whatever else it was that pack warriors did. His hand would touch the she-wolves as he bent over them and corrected their stance, looking back at me as he felt my penetrating stare on him. He would smirk again. I resisted the urge to flinch. Circe paced in my mind, keeping an eye on him at all times. My skin was starting to itch and tingle.

A few moments later, Ryan was bounding back to me and noticed me rubbing my arm. He looked directly into my eyes, blocking my view from Lincoln.

"You alright, Clem?"

"Fine. Just a little jittery," I stated.

"Okay, let's get started and see if we can keep Circe in your skin."

My eyes snapped to his, and he motioned me to look down. I followed his gaze and noticed that my skin was red and splotchy. My arm hair was thickening into tufts of deep black before it thinned out, only to thicken up again.

"You aren't ready to shift again yet. It's too soon. Liam would kill me if you got hurt," he mumbled softly, then started making a large production of breathing through his nose and out through of his mouth. I began to copy. After a few deep cleansing breaths, the itchy feeling subsided, and I gave Ryan a single, grateful nod.

"Okay, let's get started," Ryan said, taking me by the hand and walking us further away from the group. I looked over my shoulder and saw Lincoln still leering at me.

"Clemmy. Eyes on me," Ryan instructed.

I snapped my eyes up to Ryan's and gave him a single nod. He took my drink bottle and put it on the ground near us.

"We are going to start with punching. Show me your fists." I grimaced slightly and put my fists up. He covered my hands with his and corrected my thumb placement. "Okay, do you snowboard?"

"Do I look like I snowboard?" I quipped in a snarky tone.

He chuckled. "I was just going to ask if you were a goofy foot or a– look, never mind. Put one foot in front of the other." He kicked at my leg to get it to move. "Most people think that punching is in your arm strength. But it's mostly in where you plant your feet. You have your feet right, and it doesn't matter how weak you are, you can still land a solid hit." He placed his hands on the backside of a red foam board.

"Aim for the black 'x' on the pad. I want you to hit with your right fist. Tuck it in next to you, and twist and hit with your knuckles as you bring it out."

I felt foolish, but I hit the board.

"Okay, and again." I hit it again. "You need to loosen up a little. Stay light on your feet and let the punch flow from your hips and into your fist. If that makes it easier, you can imagine this is Lincoln's face."

I snorted a laugh and started hitting the board with a little more energy.

"Good, now cross over with your left fist. Good. Left. Right. Left. Right."

We went like this for at least forty minutes before his eyes glazed over. He spun around and nodded to whoever mind-linked him. "Okay, break time."

"Break time?"

"Yeah, there's a ten-minute break, and then we switch up what we teach. The group is going to do some balance training after the break. I need to set up the gear, so get yourself some water, and I'll come to collect you for balance training."

"Okay."

I looked around and noticed most people were leaving to get a drink. A few others were laughing on the grandstand, and a group jogged around the training grounds.

The mixture of sweat and arousal swirled around me, and I knew some people would be hitting the showers together after-wards. I blushed, remembering what Liam had told me earlier that morning, and suddenly, I felt very hot and needed a drink of water.

I sipped from my water bottle, trying to calm myself, and after a moment, I dropped the container, stretching my arms out behind my back, then bending over and trying to loosen up.

"Well, it must be your ass he's into because it's definitely not your face," said a soft velvety voice from behind.

I twisted and looked directly at the gorgeous and ruthless face of Lincoln James. My heart pounded, and my adrenaline level spiked. I snapped my body up and took half a step back, clenching my fists.

I wasn't stupid. Forty minutes of learning how to punch wasn't going to save me. Lincoln was a fully trained pack warrior. He was deadly and unforgiving, and I wouldn't stand a chance. Lincoln sniffed the air, and his eyes darkened. For the first time, I noticed the icy green that ringed his deadly blue. He lowered his dark lashes and glared at me.

"You reek of Liam," he complained. "What an interesting flavour of the week you are. Have you been keeping his bed warm at night, little half-breed? Sharing some of that body fat for heat?" I recoiled slightly, but Circe growled, trying to give me some courage. Her hackles were raised, and she was baring her teeth to Lincoln. "I missed you at the meet. I thought it was compulsory for everyone, but the golden boy managed to whisk you away. And then poor Cassandra was booted out because of you. All because you moved to town and decided to climb into bed with Liam. Tut. Tut. Tut." He waggled his finger at me.

"What do you want, Lincoln?" I asked. I thought my voice would come out weak, but it was firm.

"I just wanted to check out Liam's new half-breed toy." His velvet voice seeped through my ears and into my consciousness, gentle and caressing.

Circe lowered her head, snarling quietly.

His eyes travelled over me slowly. He was drinking in every part of my body, and it made my skin crawl. His eyes snaked over my legs and hips, roamed my cleavage for an extra minute before looking at my neck, and he sneered maliciously. Then he gave me the same look he'd given me the first time we met, and cold panic washed through my body. I felt my heart pound in my throat.

Circe snarled again. But the roughness came from between my clenched teeth instead of the sound only being in my head. My fear brought her forward, and she was not letting me back down.

His eyes snapped, and he flashed me a smile, but his expression was still cold and calculating. "There she is. I thought I saw her when you first got here. The mysterious wolf that I've heard about. Want to come out and play little wolf?"

I snarled again, and his malevolent grin widened. "Liam hasn't even tried to mark you. It just goes to show that you really are just a toy. And the good thing about toys is they're meant to be shared."

CHAPTER 52

LIAM

IT WAS so hard to concentrate on the tasks my father had assigned to me for the afternoon when my head was back in my bedroom and between Clementine's legs. The scent of her arousal was seared into my nostrils. I could still hear her pants and moans; still taste her pussy on my tongue.

Fuck!

I adjusted myself for the twentieth time. I really needed to stop thinking about this otherwise, I would abandon my work, go down to the training grounds and steal her away.

"Liam, are you listening?" Dad growled.

My head snapped up, and I nodded quickly. *What were we talking about? Oh right, the warrior shifts on the perimeter.*

Beta Jerome's job as head of the warrior squad was to keep our boundaries secure, but I needed to know the job too. It had been three years since a rogue had ventured this far, and that was by accident. He was trying to find Kempthorne and got turned around. There hadn't been a fight. The warrior just gave him directions, and he was on his way.

"Your mind is all over the place today, Liam."

"I know. I'm sorry."

"Clementine?" he asked softly.

"What?" I cleared my throat.

"Well, you're lost in thought. You keep adjusting yourself, and you smell like her, which makes me think she stayed the night last night?" Dad's eyes twinkled.

I ran my fingers through my wet hair.

Well, that shower didn't work as well as I had hoped. "Um. Yeah." I smirked. I needed to change the subject and quickly. "She left to go down to her first training session today. I think having an uncontrollable wolf scares her. She's used to being in control," I surmised.

Dad nodded. "It's good that she wants to train. The stronger she gets, the easier everything will be on her. And if you choose her to be your luna, then she'll need the strength behind her."

I nodded along but didn't comment on his probing.

"Have you spoken to her about being luna?" Dad asked.

"Decided to drop the subtle probing, Dad?" I retorted.

"Hey! You can't blame me for being curious. This is the first she-wolf that's got you tangled in knots. And your mother and I still have that bet going, remember?"

"Right. The bet." I rolled my eyes. "Sorry to break it to you, Dad, but Clem and I are just having some fun." My stomach churned at the lie.

"Well, in that case, head back in the game, Liam! You can go have *fun* with Clementine later." I rolled my eyes once more. "You get this work done, and I might let you sneak off early. You could see how much she has learned from Ryan and Lincoln in her first couple of hours."

My blood turned ice-cold, then heated with rage. I stood up faster than I thought possible, and suddenly, I was sprinting toward the training grounds.

Dad's surprised voice mind-linked over. *"Liam. Where the hell are you going?"*

"I'm not letting Lincoln anywhere near her."

"Liam–"

"Dad, you said being alpha is mostly following your gut instincts, and my instincts are telling me to head to the training grounds."

I rounded the corner, and the grounds came into view. My eyes immediately found Clementine standing out in her yoga pants and a bright pink V-neck athletic top. Her thick hair was pulled back into a braid that ended in the middle of her shoulder blades. She was standing regimented, with her head held high, her eyes hard, and her fists clenched as she stared down the sizeable male wolf trying to intimidate her. I snarled as I raced forward, the natural need to protect her coursing through my veins.

"What the fuck is going on?" I snapped.

Lincoln's face turned, and he grinned. "Just talking to your new toy here."

Toy. The word insulted Lucian deeply, and he snarled angrily as I stepped closer to Clem. Her scent was laced with adrenaline, but little fear. *Good girl. Don't let him intimidate you.* Her eyes flashed to mine, and she gave me a look of understanding before they flicked back to Lincoln and her cute nose wrinkled in disgust. *Wait, did she just hear me?* I reached out and tried to find her pattern scent, but I was hit with nothing.

I saw the wolf swirling within the depth of her turquoise pools. I felt anger zing on my tongue, but it didn't taste like mine. It tasted almost sweet, like her.

"Toy?" I spat venomously.

"Your half-breed plaything. I was just saying how toys are supposed to be shared. You walked in just as I was about to get a taste." Lucian's snarl joined with mine.

"He's baiting you," Clementine whispered. "Ignore him."

"Yes, Liam. Ignore me. Go back to the hole you crawled out

of and let me show the half-breed what a real wolf is like." He licked his lips and looked at Clementine with cold indifference. "It's obvious she's just a bed-warmer for you. She reeks like you, but she's not significant enough to wear your mark. She's free game, really. But don't worry, you'll get her back again once I've handed her around to my buddies like the whore she is."

My vision blurred to red, and a loud snarl came out of my mouth as I moved forward with unseen speed. Lincoln met me blow for blow, and each hit sounded like a cannon had gone off. Clementine's screaming was drowned out by the sound of blood in my ears when I was suddenly pushed away.

Ryan stood between us, Rigby's power flowing through him. His nails were long and dark, piercing my chest with one hand and Lincoln's with the other.

"Clem, get Liam out of here," he commanded, and soft hands found mine. She started tugging, attempting to lead me away. The feel of her softness gave me small tingles, which was enough to help me put one foot in front of the other and change my focus from killing Lincoln, back to keeping her safe.

We made it to the edge of the trees and disappeared into the forest. She was still talking, but I couldn't focus on what she was saying. The sound of blood rushing through my ears, and the need to kill Lincoln still warred with my need to protect Clem.

"He wasn't going to touch me with all those witnesses, Liam. You know that! It was just a display of dominance. He was baiting you." Big turquoise eyes were looking up at me with an untamed emotion I had never seen run through them. "Go shift and run off your anger."

The emotion in her eyes floored me. I was instantly hard as I took her flustered demeanour in. I grabbed her roughly by the arms and slammed her into the nearest tree, kissing her as if she was pure air and I was struggling to breathe.

He was about to touch what was mine! Nobody touches what's mine. My teeth elongated, and my focus moved to the sexy spot on her neck. The sensitive area that persuaded the most alluring sounds out of her pretty mouth.

The need to mark her was overwhelming.

I kissed the sensitive spot and bit down. She gasped in shock as my venom entered her system. I sucked and nibbled and tasted her blood. It tasted of honey and almonds. Her scent started changing, and even though she still smelled of honeysuckle and pear, my scent was mixing with hers, coagulating and sinking in deep. She groaned as I removed my teeth and continued to lick and suck, leaving my mark on her skin. It was a bright purple bruise, but the teeth marks were glowing with the power of an alpha's claim.

I gently kissed my way up her neck and back to her mouth, grinding my painful erection against her core. She moaned in pleasure as the scent of arousal flooded my nose. I ripped at her top, tearing it in two as she found the button of my pants, pulling them down and springing my cock free. I sucked down her chest, growling at the sports bra hiding those glorious tits from me. I popped them out one at a time, sucking and nibbling each magnificent mound. Her hand found my cock, rubbing her covered pussy against it like a bitch in heat.

I grunted in pleasure before I returned to marking every inch of her chest in rough purple bruises when her hand removed itself from my cock and pulled at her yoga pants and panties until they crumpled into a heap at her sneakers. She stood on them awkwardly as she removed them from one leg completely. I pulled back and looked at her, admiring how her marked breasts were trussed up, spilling overtop of her sports bra, and shifted to the glistening dew drops stuck to the black curls between her legs.

I grinned as I suddenly wanted another taste. I went to

lower onto my knees to get said taste when suddenly she clawed at my arm and pulled me toward her again.

"Not that," she breathed in desperation. "That." She pointed at my cock, before she pulled me toward her.

"You want–"

"You to shut up and fuck me against this tree, Alpha!" Her eyes swirled with amber as she thrust her wet folds against my smooth head.

Oh, fuck me!

I hoisted her up by her hips as her legs wrapped around me, positioning herself over my cock and lining it up with her opening. She slid down at the same time I pushed up, and I needed to hold myself there for a second if only to let her tight little pussy adjust to my thickness. She gasped and moaned against the feeling.

I groaned as I started pumping into her. Her beautiful breasts bounced in my face, making my teeth seek them out while I held onto her hips for dear life. The sounds she made as she moved against my cock made me tremble. Warm. Wet. Tight. *Mine.*

I gasped. "I'm sorry, baby, but this is going to be quick."

"Make me come first!" she ordered roughly, tugging my hair, and making me look at her. The amber swirls darkened as her orgasm approached. Her channel got tighter, and I knew that the friction against her clit must be helping, so I kept going the way I was, fucking her hard against a tree, trying to hold off my release for as long as I could.

She shivered, and her pussy squeezed my cock as she rocked against me. Her moaning intensified, and when she called my name, she exploded, coming all over my cock. Two thrusts later, I joined her with loud groans and grunts of my own.

It took a few breaths to get myself together before I gently slid out of her pussy and lowered her back to the ground and kissed her gently. She placed her boobs back into her bra and pulled up her yoga pants.

"Well, there goes my plan to take it slowly with you," I mumbled. I pulled up my pants and looked around at her torn top that littered the forest floor. "Sorry about the top," I apologized sheepishly.

She smiled. "You more than made up for it."

I saw my mark glowing against her neck, and rubbed it gently with my thumb, "Sorry that I marked you without your permission."

"You marked me?"

"Yeah, in the heat of the moment." Her face contorted with confusion, then understanding. In an instant, all emotion was wiped off her face.

"I'm sorry, Clemmy! I needed to tell the world you're mine. You're not my toy or bed warmer or flavour of the week. You're mine."

Clementine's face remained stoic as she registered what I was saying. She said nothing but stared at me. I could see the emotions brewing behind her eyes.

"My mark will keep you safe," I promised her quickly, trying to ease her evident distrust. "When I'm not around, my mark will remind people that you're mine."

"I thought the scent of our fooling around would have done that."

"That will rouse the wolves. The mark will put them in their place." I murmured, feeling as guilty as fuck but also insurmountable pride when I saw my mark glowing on her skin. She still said nothing. I took a sniff, and Lucian rumbled with happiness. "I love the smell of my scent on you. Before I even marked you, you smelled strongly of me. I love the fact my scent is mixing with yours. It's a real turn-on." I moved my fingers around her hips and pulled her close, whispering into her ear, "I noticed you changed into those delicious yoga pants and that sexy top that unfortunately met its demise. Did you not think of showering before you went to training?"

I was getting hard again and couldn't keep myself from sniffing at her neck, a deep rumbling escaping me. *Damn, she smells good.*

"Really, Liam? You were playing around and making me orgasm more times than I ever have, giving me less than ten minutes to get changed and get to the training grounds, and you expected me to shower your scent off me?" she said with disbelief. "I could barely even walk after the way your tongue imprisoned me."

I grinned down at her playfully. "You like my tongue?"

"I liked your tongue this morning," she corrected, pushing me back slightly. "Just like I liked your cock five minutes ago. It's done now. I'm heading home. Try not to kill Lincoln if you see him." Her voice sounded hard. Then she started to walk away.

"Wait, Clementine!" I grabbed her hand, and she spun, looking at me. "You're pissed at me."

"No. I just need time to process," she mumbled.

"Process what?"

"Are you really that dim?" she asked. "You took away my choice, Liam! I'm now bound to you forever. When my dad marked my mom, he made it sound romantic. This feels cheap."

"No! No! Clemmy, this isn't a mate bond. That can only happen on a full moon. This is a territorial marking. It just infuses our scents and tells everyone you belong to me. It warns other wolves to back the fuck off." She stared at me like I had grown an extra head. "I'm not explaining this well. Fuck."

"No, I think you are. Basically, I'm a piece of meat—your property. I guess I should be glad you didn't piss on me. Your possessive streak knows no boundaries!"

"Mark me back," I said in a rush. "Bring Circe forward and bite me right here." I pointed to the soft part of my neck.

"Nope, I'm good." She took another step away. "I would never mark you without your consent."

"Clementine, you have my consent." My tone was desperate.

"Well, you didn't have mine."

My heart shattered as she turned and walked away from me, the scrapes on her back left over from the best sex I have ever had were already healing.

CHAPTER 53

CLEMENTINE

I HADN'T GONE VERY FAR, MAYBE twenty metres ahead of him. I stepped onto a well-worn trail and stopped to get my bearings. I heard Liam's frantic heartbeat as he quickly caught up to me. It was beating incredibly fast.

"Clementine, please! I'm sorry." I spun around, facing him. His eyes were wide, and his cheeks were flushed. "I can explain! Well, I can try to. All werewolves have instincts buried so deep that even the most mature and calm wolf will crumble under the weight of instinct. All wolves struggle with it, Circe included. The instinct to mark someone you are...fond of is one of those overprotective instincts. You're the first she-wolf who has woken that possessive side in me. It's been awake since our first kiss or maybe even before that. Suddenly, all I could think about was marking you. When Lincoln said you were free game, my animal instinct took over. It's a drive to protect, to make it clear that you are not a toy and are very much taken. My human side knew it was wrong, but Lucian's instincts were too strong for me to hold him off."

"I thought merging with Lucian was supposed to calm this idiotic behaviour."

"I told you, when it comes to you, I'm an idiot, and I'll probably always be," he said sheepishly, running a hand nervously through his hair. "You'll understand it better as you and Circe grow. I wanted to let you get used to being a wolf first. Then I was going to ask you to bear my mark. I'm sorry the instinct became too strong when I sensed you were in danger. I'm so sorry, Clementine. Please don't hate me," his voice croaked.

I stared at him and crossed my arms over my exposed stomach before I replied. "You have to understand where I'm coming from, Liam. I've never really had a relationship. Not one that I would count anyway. I was made a mockery my entire life. The first time I had sex was a school joke. My second time, the guy was as toxic as fuck. He was my first boyfriend, and I worshipped him."

I took a deep breath and explained further. "We dated for about a year, and during that year, he treated me like he was doing me a favour. He broke me down and ruined me. It started as small, tiny, razor-sharp comments designed to crumble my confidence piece by piece, but at the same time, they were designed to tie me to him—to control me. He started making my decisions for me, just small ones so I wouldn't notice at first. But TJ did, and he gave me a fucking pamphlet on abusive relationships. That's when I started making excuses. Brady would never hit me. He was a good man. He was going to be a doctor, and doctors didn't do that."

I took a breath as I tried to push the memories back. "TJ tried to tell me that emotional abuse was just as dangerous as physical abuse. I ignored all the signs. I mean, why wouldn't I? I was in a relationship, and someone cared for me. Then Mom got sick, and Brady told me I was spending too much time with a dying woman. He was getting nasty, possessive, and irrationally angry. He was trying to get in between my mom and me, so I ended it." I shook my head as Liam's face drained of colour, making the golds of his eyes pop as his eyebrows furrowed. "So, you have to understand that for you to go and do something that takes away my right to choose, no matter how instinctual it was–"

"Clem–"

"If you took away my right to choose, what makes you any different than the two guys I've been with?"

"I *am* different. I swear! I didn't do it to hurt you or to control you. I did it because I– I–" he fumbled with his next words, his voice waning and cracking. His cheeks turned pink, and his eyes glowed with desperation. He couldn't come up with an excuse.

I shook my head. "It doesn't matter why you did it. I'm still learning this werewolf thing. I want to believe you. I do. But–"

"Ask Circe," he suggested. "It's instinctual for her too. She can explain it better than I can, I'm sure of it."

"Unfortunately, my wolf is rolling around happily and looking at you with lovey-dovey eyes, so she's no help to me right now. You made my wolf submit," I grumbled.

"She wanted it?" Liam croaked out his question.

"Yeah, she did. But that doesn't mean *I* did," I said softly, looking at my feet.

"Does she want to mark me?"

Circe's ears perked and she grinned, nodding enthusiastically.

"Yes, she does." I nodded. "But I don't. Right now, I want to go home and have a shower. I want to have time to process this, Liam."

I looked up and witnessed the emotions dance over his expression. He looked so lost.

"Clem, if you mark me, you'll understand what this mark is, and maybe you'll feel better about the whole thing. Please mark me."

"I don't want to mark you, Liam. I want to go home." My voice was flat and lifeless. I was exhausted.

"I don't want you to be angry. I don't want you to hate me."

"I don't hate you, Liam," I said honestly. "I-I just need time to process."

He looked as though I had kicked him. "Okay. Take the time you need," he murmured, looking absolutely crushed.

I wanted to comfort him, but I steeled my heart and reminded myself this was a tactic that Brady had used repeatedly. I wasn't going to be manipulated. I needed some space to reflect, and I was going to get it. But even though I needed space, I instinctively reached up and kissed Liam on his cheek before turning away and forcing myself toward my house.

I HEARD Dad pulling up in his work truck and went onto the back porch to meet him. He had an excited smile on his face as he saw me.

"Hey, Clem! Alpha Josiah and I just went down to the house and removed some of the debris. We think once we remove the bad timber, we can start on rebuilding. I know you didn't like that house, so I went to an architect, and he's drawing up some new plans. Something modern for us to live in."

"Sounds great, Dad. I'm sure you'll be really happy there," I said dispassionately.

"Uh oh. What's wrong?"

"Maybe me moving away is still a good idea."

"What brought this on? Last time we spoke, you were ready to be initiated into the pack." He ran his eyes over my face before he found the purple bruise sticking out from the edge of the t-shirt I put on the moment I got home.

"Wait, is that a hickey?" he exclaimed, then his eyes sparked with mischief. "Clem, do I need to give you the birds and the bees talk?"

"Dad, I went to med school. I'm pretty sure that I know how that all works."

"You did drop out. Maybe they don't teach the reproductive stuff until your final year?" he quipped cheekily. But he frowned when he saw my face, and his playful banter stopped. "Okay, kid, let's go inside and talk."

I turned and walked into the house, my body shaking as the tears started to threaten. I entered the large kitchen and made two cups of coffee, placing them on the table and breaking out some maple cookies. A tear rolled down my cheek, but I quickly swiped it away. My dad's nose twitched, and instantly his eyes snapped to mine. He took another sniff, then he squeezed the bridge of his nose with his fingers and closed his eyes for a second.

"It's not just a hickey, is it?" He opened his eyes, and both colours were calm and collected.

"No." I stretched the neck of my t-shirt and showed my dad Liam's teeth marks.

"That's an alpha mark," he said with controlled emotion. "I didn't realize you and Liam were involved. I knew he liked you, but I didn't know you were together."

"We aren't," I glossed.

I didn't want to admit to my dad that we were something. I had let my guard down, and then Liam had gone and marked me without my consent. I didn't know how I felt about him now. I didn't know how I felt about anything.

"Your scent tells me you are involved, and that mark tells me he's serious about you. It's giving me a very big 'fuck off' vibe. Any werewolf you come across will notice it, and any male werewolf will feel its aura and steer clear."

"He did it without my knowledge about what it meant. Or my consent."

"I see," Dad said curtly.

"Do you?" I asked bitterly. "You're a werewolf, Dad, and according to Liam, it's normal for werewolves to mark she-wolves like cattle."

"I may be a werewolf, Clem, but I'm also your father, and I raised you in the human world. This is all new to you, and your cultures are clashing. So, the best thing is to sit and talk about it then try to navigate it," he said softly. "How did it happen?"

"Lincoln James got under his skin. He made a disgusting comment to Liam that I was free game and that he and his buddies were going to have some fun with me. Liam didn't like that, so a fight broke out. I pulled Liam away, and the next thing I know, he's going all vampire on my ass and biting my neck," I grumbled. I pulled at my t-shirt again and showed Dad the bright white teeth marks against the purple bruise. "I hope he's had his rabies shots."

Dad smirked before answering. He seemed to be choosing his words with care. "That makes more sense than you realize. He's very protective of you and has been since we moved here. Werewolves are territorial by nature, and the need to protect the things they care for is written into the essence of their being. You'll notice it when Circe finds something she loves. She'll fight tooth and nail to keep that love safe. Perseus found that instantly with your mother and is still protective over you and Vinny because of it. There are some things that the rational human side can't stop. Your human side could be screaming about common sense and consequences and trying to stop your animal side from reacting, but nothing will stop it if it means that much. *Nothing*. It will make you do all sorts of stupid things, like running headfirst into a burning building, for example." He took a sip of his coffee. "Did I tell you that I wanted to fight Alpha Jed when he threatened to murder your mother?"

"What?"

"I was going to challenge him to be alpha. He threatened my mate, the animal instinct took over, and all I wanted to do was kill him. It's tough to fight a wolf's instincts. Perseus' instinct was to wipe Alpha Jed from this earth. It was the only way to keep his mate safe. Thankfully, your mother managed to talk me down and convinced me to run. She said that she didn't want to see me die for her. Alpha Jed taunted us for the first two years down the mind-link before he got bored and eventually left us alone. He was baiting me. Trying to get me to come back and fight him. Blood sport was Alpha Jed's favourite game."

"You really did have a death wish thinking you could fight an alpha," I smirked, then nibbled on a maple cookie.

"That's what your mother kept telling me each time I tried to leave Vancouver and go defend her honour. It was Perseus' instinct. I couldn't help myself. Lacey had to hold me back multiple times. Once, she silvered me to a chair and threatened to feed me aconite."

"You really thought you could have taken on an alpha?" I asked.

"We come from a long lineage of powerful werewolves, Clementine. There's alpha blood running through us— anciently old," he replied. "But no, I would have died taking on an alpha. Alpha Jed not only would have murdered me, but he would also have made it a slow, cruel, and painful show to the entire pack. Then, just for shits and giggles, he would have sent the warriors out to find Lacey." He growled deeply, and his eyes flashed.

"We come from alphas?" I asked as Circe started preening herself in a regal manner.

"One of our ancestors was an alpha. A long, long, long time

ago. A small sliver of alpha blood lives in my veins. Not a lot, but it was enough to keep you and Vinny in line as children," he said with a smirk.

Dad took a sip of his coffee and watched me closely. "So, Lincoln acted like a predatory asshole, baited Liam, and Liam reacted. You attempted to diffuse the situation, and Liam's wolf reacted the only way he knew how—marking his territory to keep you safe. Is that about the sum of it?" I glared at Dad due to the crass and dry manner he'd described it, but he summarized it pretty well even though he'd left out the part where I felt commandeered into my predicament and had no choice in the matter.

"Yeah, I guess," I conceded. "But it's still not right, Dad. He should have asked me first."

"He should have, and his human brain knows that and is probably drowning in guilt. But his wolf doesn't think of the consequences. His wolf just acts on instinct. The good news is that you're not bonded to him through this mark. Most territorial marks are gone within two or three days. Since Liam has alpha blood, it may take a little longer, but it will dissipate. I should warn you that Liam's animal instincts may not want that mark to go, however. He may be eager to mark you the moment he senses it waning. You must tell him what you want and expect when it does vanish. When Circe gets stronger, she'll put him in his place if he displays any dominance that she doesn't like."

"Fat lot of good she did. She submitted to him right away when he marked me. And now she's looking like a love-sick puppy."

"She may have been swept up in the moment, but at the end of the day, she's your wolf, Clemmy. She lives in your mind. She is you, and her instinct is to protect you."

Circe gave me a single nod.

"I just don't want to be owned by anyone. It doesn't sound healthy. I mean, what if I meet someone else and I decide that I want to be with that person? What if I want to leave and travel? I don't want to lose options anymore."

"You have this all wrong, Clemmy. There are two different bonds for werewolves. You are tied together by the full moon's light with the mate bond. It's like a gigantic pull that leaves you breathless. You basically become one person. You will feel each other's thoughts and emotions. It tethers you together and amplifies your love, but you do not become a slave to the other person. And you can always reject it if you decide that you don't want it. I heard that hurts like a fucker, but it can be done." He looked at my purple bruising on the edge of my t-shirt. "The mark you have is a territorial marking, and none of the afore-mentioned feelings need to apply. All it does is mixes your scents to create a powerful aura. This is like a big beacon that warns other wolves away. It's also an aphrodisiac to the wolf that marked you. But mostly, it puts other wolves in their place. She-wolves can also mark male wolves in the same way. As I said, she-wolves have animal instincts too."

Suddenly, I remembered Ryan's mark and how I felt it gently telling me that Ryan was off the market. That must have been the aura of Stacey's mark. Then I remembered how Liam was basically begging me to mark him. I thought he was doing it out of guilt but was it possible he was doing it instinctually? Did he want to wear my mark, letting people know he was mine, and to keep the other she-wolves away?

"He wanted me to mark him too," I murmured.

Dad's eyes twinkled playfully. "That's like the human equivalent of promise rings. You guys are definitely going steady now! That's so cute!"

I flipped him the bird, and he laughed harder.

CHAPTER 54

LIAM

AFTER PACING my room for hours and scenting Clementine over every surface of it, I decided to head to the training grounds early to get rid of some of my snowballing possessive energy. It had been two nights since she had been in my room, but her scent was still infused. I kept hoping that she would sneak through my window like she did the other night, but she hadn't shown up. I was apprehensive I had fucked something up for good when I marked her.

Is this the end?

Lucian was agitated and wanted to seek her out but agreed that we could wait a little longer and that being dominant over her wouldn't help our case. I was unsure how long I could wait, but hopefully the exercise would help.

I WALKED past the teenage-level class currently in session and moved toward the large hall just off the side of the grandstand. A small area housed the pack training equipment at the back of the hall. It also had a couple of squat cages, weight machines and punching bags. The rest of the room was left purposely empty for pack training, although it was only used in the winter when it got too cold outside to train.

Whack, whack, whack, swing, whack. The punching bag swung with each brutal hit I mustered—the dust sprinkling like confetti with each blow.

"Lighter on your feet," came Ryan's voice as he walked across the training-gym floor.

I shifted my weight and kept punching harder and harder.

"You alright, bro?" Ryan asked, approaching carefully, sensing the frustration radiating off me.

"I marked her," I muttered between punches.

"You marked who?"

"Clem."

"Good job, bro! I was wondering when you guys would finally make it official. What is it, like two months since she's been here? You move slow, Alpha! When she first moved here, I said some stuff in passing that upset Lucian and the way you reacted, I knew she had already gotten under your skin. I was like, 'this will take two weeks, tops', but two months? Bro, two fucking months!" He chuckled with excitement. "When she came to the training ground the other day, your scent was all over her, so I knew it was only a matter of time before you got serious with her. It's great news to hear that you finally mar–"

I spun around and pointed to my flawless neck. Lucian huffed, placing his head between his paws in a massive sulk.

"Oh. She didn't mark you back?" His tone went from excited to confused.

"No, she didn't. I asked her to, and she refused."

"Why?"

"Because I'm a fucking idiot," I snarled in frustration as I hit the bag. "She looks like a fucking sexy-as-sin goddess, and she makes me feel things I've never felt before, but I keep forgetting she's a pup in this world. She has no idea what shit means. I fucking marked her without her knowledge. I knew it was wrong." I hit the bag with more ferocity. "I had planned on doing it so differently, but when Lincoln–" I snarled and continued to pummel the bag so hard, it swung back and forth. "Instinct took over, and suddenly I'm all over her, and I marked her. I saw the disbelief roll through her, the emotions, the distrust, and then I saw her close off. So, I tried to explain it, and when that didn't seem to clarify things, I asked her—no—*begged* her to mark me. I thought she would understand it better if she felt the power of it. That it would kickstart her instincts. As soon as the words left my mouth, I realized I wanted it. I wanted to let the entire pack know I was hers and only hers as much as she was mine. But she said no. There was no emotion to it. Just the word no. What am I meant to do with that? I wasn't expecting such indifference from her. And now, I haven't seen her since. I fucked up, man!"

"That's heavy, bro." He nodded sadly. "Although, I kind of get why she refused."

The punching bag swung back toward me. I caught it between my palms and looked at him expectantly.

"I assume she's severely overwhelmed. A year ago, she was studying to be a doctor. Then she lost her mom, and her whole life was uprooted and restarted. To top it all off, she discovered she's a fucking werewolf. She feels like she's the most hated person in the pack because of her mixed heritage and your friendship with her. And now, you're declaring your claim over her? That's a lot for a timid twenty-year-old girl to take. She's just trying to find her feet in this world, which won't happen if you keep knocking them out from under her. So maybe you should swallow your pride and hurt and try listening to what she needs." I sighed, giving Ryan a single, thankful nod. "Or," Ryan gave me a cheeky grin. "It could be that she's just interested in you for sex and nothing more. Maybe she doesn't have feelings for you." I snarled menacingly. Ryan put his hands up to defend himself and stepped back into a submissive position.

"Hey, man! I'm on your side. But think about it. How many she-wolves have been in your bed, fallen for you and hoped to be your luna? How many hearts have you broken because you didn't reciprocate their feelings? As wonderful as I'm sure you are, it's possible she doesn't want a relationship with you."

I glared at him as Lucian paced in my mind with his hackles raised. I started hitting the bag again so I wouldn't hit Ryan's face. There was no way Clementine was just using me for sex. Not. Fucking. Possible

He grinned knowingly, then continued, "I'm just saying, instead of acting impulsively and...I don't know...asking her to be your luna and completing the mate bond with her next week, give her time to adjust to being a werewolf. Let her work out how she feels on her terms." I cracked a sad smile in Ryan's direction and nodded. "Just as an FYI, I'm rooting for you two. I have been since the beginning. So, stop fucking it up!"

My alarm beeped quietly. I stopped hitting the bag and stepped back, shrugging my shoulder at Ryan as we made our way toward the training ground for level three training. I was finally merged, so I was officially ready to learn how to use my wolf in my human form.

"Stacey texted me earlier. It's official. Her parents and brother will be in Kempthorne for the full moon."

"You don't think they are going to cockblock you, right? Like, get in the way of your mating and shit?"

"Fuck! They better not." He chuckled. "I'm marking that girl the moment that moon reaches its peak. Then, I'm spending the rest of the run deep inside her. So please, bro, no mind-linking. And I'm sure she'll tell her family the same."

We walked through the grounds and saw that the teen training class had ended. I spotted my brother and a young she-wolf chatting quietly by the grandstand and smirked. Looking around, my eyes landed on the treeline edge Clem and I had disappeared into, and I felt warm emotion stir. Less than twenty metres in, there would be the tree that scraped her back when passion had taken over between us.

"Head in the game, man!" Ryan pushed me playfully.

I'd been staring at the bush for so long I hadn't noticed that training had started.

Right. Let's do this.

THE SOUND of the window opening made me look up from my laptop. I was sitting at my desk, finalising my assignment when the scent of honeysuckle and pear sifted through the window. My heart hammered in my chest.

She came back!

"And you growl at me about bedroom etiquette! There's a door, you know," I teased, pressing the save button on my document and spinning to face her.

"But this way, I can practice my breaking and entering skills," she whispered, her eyes glinting with humour.

"You definitely need practice," I confirmed with a small smile.

My eyes feasted on her beauty. Her dark hair had been freshly cut and was around her shoulders, framing her cute cherub face. Her soft curves were wrapped in a delicious black wrap dress. She wore no jewellery or makeup, and her scent still smelled strongly of my mark which shone proudly on her neck.

I stood up and crossed the room, pulling her into a hug so I could inhale the scent deeper. "Hi," I murmured into her hair.

"Hi," she whispered back.

I kissed the top of her head and felt her smile against my chest. "I've missed you."

"Me too."

"What brings you here?" I pulled back and watched her face as I gently ran my fingers down her spine. Then I slowly brushed my lips against her pouty mouth. She returned my kiss gently but didn't deepen it. That didn't matter to me; her shy kisses were still a turn-on. Even with the softest of them, all I wanted to do was throw her on the bed.

"Circe needs to run." That surprised me enough to stop thinking about what I was about to do to her on my bed.

"No. It's way too soon," I said firmly, Lucian's protective instinct rolling through my voice. Looking into her eyes, I saw Circe flashing within them. Clementine held up her arm, and I noticed how her skin bubbled, and her hair started to thicken.

"Circe knows it's too soon, but she needs to. And…we need you. I don't think I can do this by myself."

"Yeah. Okay. I'll help you through it. Let's go into the bush." I tucked her into my side and walked her through the house to the French doors and out into the backyard, which blended into the trees. When we arrived, I pulled off my t-shirt and saw her nervously attempting to untie her wrap-around dress.

I stepped forward and placed my hands over hers, gently kissing her mouth as I fiddled with the strings, untying them. I slipped my hand inside to wrap her in my arms and stroke her back calmly, only to discover she was naked underneath.

Fuck me!

She moaned into my mouth as the dress slipped off her shoulders and pooled at her feet. Pulling back, she smiled softly at me and took her flip-flops off, her bright pink toenails winking back.

"Just take your time, Clemmy. Listen to Circe. I'm right here."

She nodded as she tried to cover her beautiful naked body. I glared and pushed her hands away from their protective posture. She smiled shyly, then instantly straightened her back with a little more confidence. When she took a deep breath, I felt her nervous energy disappear. I really wanted to hold her in my arms, but I couldn't touch her as she shifted. It was too dangerous. So I stepped back.

Lucian guarded her protectively as her skin started to bubble again. The tension was brewing, and my nerves were on edge. "Oh, and Clem, if you die, I'm going to be fucking pissed," I snarled softly, running my eyes over her body, and ending on the mark in the soft flesh above her collarbone.

She blushed beautifully and chuckled nervously. "Circe says we won't die." She bit her lip as another wave of pain went through her. "Please, just stay close," she whimpered.

"I'm not going anywhere."

Then, the snapping and cracking sound started, and she cried out in pain, falling onto all fours. Her eyes swirled with amber as her bones began to break. I got down and kept my eyes on hers the entire time.

"Just breathe, Clemmy. Breathe. Don't fight it."

It was taking a long time. Sweat beaded her body as if she was overrun with fever. It was another ten minutes before her fingers turned into claws and her hands and feet shortened into paws. Her gorgeous silky hair moulded and merged around her neck, with the thick fur sprouting all over her body. There was another loud crack and pop and another whimper as her snout elongated and her teeth lengthened.

She was almost there. She just needed one final move-ment, and she would be a wolf. There was another sickening pop as her back cracked, her tail sprouted, and her ears perked off the top of her head. It was half an hour before Clementine lay there panting in the skin of her wolf. Her beautiful black fur still held my scent in this form, and I glowed with happiness.

"Good girl, Clemmy! Well done! Rest for a minute. I'm going to shift, and then we can go explore," I said as I brought forward Lucian to change. My shift took less than a minute, and soon I was nuzzling her snout with mine.

She rumbled underneath me and gave me a gentle lick before standing up a little wobbly on her feet and rubbing herself along my flank. Her scent coated mine, sending warm sparks fluttering over my fur. She gave me a gentle nip, then darted off into the bush, yipping excitedly. Lucian and I exchanged a cheeky grin and chased after her.

We had no mind-link with each other as we dashed and darted around the trees—only instinct. Her teeth would graze me playfully as she pounced from above, then would dart off again. She whimpered when I tackled her to the ground and growled playfully, only to kick me off and lunge at me in return. We were in tune with each other as we frolicked, hid, pounced, ran, and tousled. Our wolves instinctually knew each other's moves and habits without having a conscious mind-link. It was a good hour before I noticed signs of her fatigue. I guided her back to the pack house as she flanked me happily.

Her shift back took less than five minutes. Her hair was messy, and her eyes were bright from her run. I felt my cock stir. She quietly looked around for her dress to cover up her body. As she attempted to wrap it across herself, I pushed her against a tree and pressed my nose into her neck, inhaling her scent.

"You did well, Clem," I said as I gently kissed her mouth and placed my hands around her bare waist. She shivered at my touch. "Do you want some food?" I smiled against her mouth, kissing her again.

"No."

"What do you want?" I asked seductively. My dick twitched in anticipation.

"Sleep. I'm exhausted."

"Okay then, Sleeping Beauty. Come to bed with me."

"Liam..." she went to scold me before she succumbed to a dainty yawn.

"Just to sleep. I promise. I can keep my hands to myself on occasion." I pulled my hands away and helped her tie her dress before I dressed in my clothes, directing her toward my bed, where she belonged.

CHAPTER 55

CLEMENTINE

I PANICKED when Circe told me she needed to run. Cold fear rippled through me, which was then replaced by a burning tingle throughout my nervous system. She told me to stay calm and find Liam, that I would be less nervous with him around. After the next hard spasm of pain, I succumbed to her suggestion, ripped the Band-Aid off the stupid mark on my collarbone, changed my clothes, and slipped out of my window to find him. The idea of seeing him was making me a little giddy with nervous excitement.

Although I had messaged him, I hadn't physically seen Liam for two days. I had spent my time practising punches with Sophie. I found that punching was a good way of releasing my stress, but talking to Sophie was even better, and there was a lot to talk about. When I told her about how I had received my mark, she groaned into her hands and shook her head exasperatedly. But she had also laughed when she saw my attempt to hide it, telling me that although the Band-Aid was masking the bruise, the aura was still detectable to werewolves. I grumbled as I smacked my fists into her training pads, releasing my anger and compartmentalising and steeling over memories threatening to tear me apart.

Liam's scent instantly comforted me, and the sharp barbwire and burning sensation settled into a low buzz, at least for a moment. The pain of my shift rolled through me, breaking my bones in hot bursts. My lungs constricted so that I couldn't breathe, and my heart pounded so hard that I thought it would burst through my ribcage. But I didn't feel like I would die—not this time. There was a low hum radiating off Liam the entire time I shifted; a hum that made me feel safe. And when he turned and rubbed against me, I felt that hum a little deeper, like it was stitching its way along my body and into my subconscious.

After our run, he tucked me into his bed and held me close. There was no heated passion or need to rip our clothes off. It was just blissful tranquillity as he cuddled me. His warmth radiated into me as he whispered words I couldn't make out. It didn't matter; his voice resonated and lulled me to sleep.

Circe stretched out and rumbled at his touch, and just as I drifted off to sleep, I heard her say, *"Told you he's endgame."*

My stomach made a considerable gurgling noise, and my eyes snapped open. It took me a second to work out where I was. The heavy scent of cedar and spice surrounded me, and I smiled. My arm was wrapped around his torso, and my legs were tangled with his. I revelled in the comfort and the warmth and attempted to close my eyes again when my stomach gurgled for the second time.

His body started vibrating with a low chuckle. "I think you're hungry, Clem," he said in a sleepy tone. His eyes were still closed, but his fingers started gently rubbing over my skin, giving me goosebumps.

"Yeah, I should probably go home and eat." I yawned, trying to pull away from him.

"Or we can go into the kitchen and make breakfast," he suggested, holding me tighter. "I could bring the food in here, and we can have a picnic in bed." His voice was thick and gravelly, and I tried to ignore the way his voice vibrated into me.

"That will just put crumbs between your sheets," I said.

He chuckled and kissed my head. "Isn't that what a washing machine is for?" His hands roamed over my hip as he shuffled me slightly, and I accidentally grazed his morning erection. His eyes instantly opened, and he looked down at my face. His eyes were bright, clear, and mischievous as he smiled. "The idea of bringing food to you is becoming more appealing. Especially if it means you end up naked. Food, nakedness... Yeah, I like the sound of that."

I rolled my eyes and made a motion to get out of bed.

"And where do you think you are going?" he asked, grabbing, then pinning me back down and rubbing his nose against mine.

Circe hummed in adoration.

"Well, you're taking too long to feed me."

"Am I?" My stomach gurgled again in answer. He chuckled and gave me a quick peck on the lips. "Okay, okay! Let's go get some breakfast."

Untangling himself from me, he rolled off the bed. There was no embarrassment on his part as he pulled up his shorts to cover his manhood. I felt myself blush when he caught me looking and winked at me. I got out of the bed and adjusted the wrap dress I slept in to ensure it was covering everything before I followed him out of his bedroom and into the kitchen.

He pointed to the kitchen island breakfast bar, and I sat on a stool as he started to take items out of the fridge. "Omelette okay?" he asked.

"That's fine." I nodded as I watched him move around the kitchen, making us both breakfast.

He placed two frying pans on the stovetop, and the scent of cooking egg soon filled the air. To ease my grumbling stomach, I started to pick at the ingredients on the island's granite countertop.

"Hey! Keep your hands off!" He playfully whacked at my fingers.

"Well, feed me faster," I snarled jokingly.

"Restaurant quality meals take time."

"Wow. You would think with how many times you would have needed to make breakfast the morning after, you would be a pro at this by now." I rolled my eyes and snuck another mouthful of shredded cheese.

His eyes snapped to mine. "Well, considering you are the only she-wolf I have ever made breakfast for..." he smiled shyly as he added the ingredients to the half-cooked egg and got a spatula out.

"You've never dragged another girl from your bed and made her an omelette?" I probed.

"No, Clemmy. I haven't," he said in a soft voice. "But hey, if it means you'll stay the night more often, I'll make you an omelette every fucking morning."

"Well, hang on! I have to taste it first. If it's terrible, I might just run the other way."

"You better run fast then because I'll be giving chase. And you know, I'm an alpha, so I'm fast," he jested as he piled a massive omelette onto my plate.

I smirked.

. . .

Taking my first bite of the omelette, I chewed slowly. Smirking at Circe, I stood up and started walking toward the front door. "Yup, just as I thought. Terrible."

Liam's eyes flashed gold as I slowly made my way to the door, baiting him. Circe grinned.

"I told you I'll chase you! But what I never said, was that when I caught you, I'd punish you until you begged me to stop."

Circe fluttered at the thought and egged me on.

I rolled my eyes and smiled tauntingly. "Oh, okay, Big Bad Alpha."

"Clementine," he warned playfully.

As he stepped out from behind the kitchen island, my smile split my face. I raced to the door, but before I could get my hand on the handle, his arms were wrapped around me, tickling my ribs. I started giggling as my feet were lifted off the floor.

"Okay! Okay! I yield! Put me down!" I said through fits of laughter.

He carried me back to my seat and plopped me down with a soft kiss on my cheek. Then he slid victoriously onto the stool next to me. "Did you want to do something today?" he asked, wolfing down his omelette with impressive speed. I guess I wasn't the only one who'd been hungry.

"Sorry, I can't."

"Oh?" he enquired gently.

"Yeah. It's Vinny's sixteenth today. I need to get home and spend the day with him. Maybe he'll shift or something. I want to be there for that." I frowned slightly. "It's a shame I won't be able to run with him."

Liam's fingers gently rubbed the crease between my eyebrows. "It's unlikely he'll shift today, so you probably won't miss out on anything. And as you get stronger, you'll be able to shift more regularly. Speaking of which, can I make you another omelette?"

"No, thank you. I'm fine."

"Clementine, you shifted last night and didn't eat anything afterwards. One small omelette isn't enough to sustain you."

"That was a small omelette?" I asked in disbelief.

"Yeah, it was. So let me make you another."

"I'm honestly full." Then my stomach gurgled in protest.

"Your stomach says otherwise."

I frowned and looked up at Liam as he made another two omelettes. I peered down at my empty plate and bit my lip. His hand gripped my chin gently, making me look at him. "We have fast metabolisms, remember? I told you we need to eat more. There's nothing to be embarrassed about. All wolves around here eat more than their fair share."

"Yes, but they're all fit and beautiful, and I'm like this," I whispered.

He roamed his eyes over my body and his gaze softened. "You're beautiful. I love your curves," he said in a sincere tone. "Please trust me when I say you have nothing to worry about there." He leaned across the island and gave me a quick kiss. "I mean, I could always take you back to the bedroom and show you physically how my body reacts to you if you need a reminder." He said in a low tone that resonated through my core. His eyes darkened, and I could feel the butterflies start low.

"Nope! You are not going to distract me with your devilish sex skills today. I told you I'm busy."

He cracked a grin, and a few minutes later, he slid another massive omelette onto my plate. I sighed and looked at him again. He gave me a small encouraging smile as I took a small bite.

"Happy birthday, Vinny!" I squealed as my brother finally made an appearance from his bedroom. His wheat-coloured hair was sticking up in all directions, and his pants hung low on his hips as he tugged on a t-shirt.

"Thanks, Clem," he said as I threw my arms around his middle. His muscles seemed harder and he'd gotten a little taller ever since Vali appeared. He wasn't in any way massive, but he was toned. His arms awkwardly patted my back.

"You smell like Liam." He pushed me away with a tiny glint in his eye. "He helped you shift last night, eh?"

"How did you–"

"Vali told me he could sense your wolf needed to run. Vali said that you needed help. I was about to knock on your door and check on you when I heard you jump out the window."

"Don't sneak in and out of windows to see your boyfriend, Clementine. Use the front door like a normal person," Dad said, coming into the living room with a chuckle as he hugged Vincent and wished him a happy birthday.

I felt the gentle tickle in my mind as Dad's voice came across. *"I'm glad you managed to find someone to help you shift last night, Clem. I'm sorry I wasn't here to help you."*

"That's okay, Dad. Circe said she wanted it to be Liam."

I looked up and saw Dad's head tilt curiously. He didn't say anything but stared at me oddly.

"Come on, Vinny, let's show you your birthday present." I grinned at my brother and took him by the hand, leading him to the front door.

There was a heavily draped item in thick, army-green sheeting on the garden path that led into the forest and back toward the main house. Vinny looked at it curiously, and Dad nodded for him to go ahead.

"When I was your age, I hated the idea that everyone around me could shift and I couldn't. Perseus didn't want to run until closer to my seventeenth birthday. Josiah, Jed, and a girl I was dating were running around shifting and howling at every free moment. So, your grandfather decided to give me his old dirt bike. It was a rust-bucket of a thing, but we spent time together doing it up, and eventually we got the bloody thing to work," Dad explained as Vinny started unwrapping his gift. "So, I thought you and I could do the same thing." Underneath the sheet was a beat-up-looking yellow dirt bike. "It took me a while to track a decent one down, and I didn't think I was going to get one in time, but last night I got lucky, and I had to go get it." There was silence as Vinny looked at the bike.

"Well? What do you think?" I pressed excitedly.

Vinny turned to look at us both and his face cracked with an excited grin. "This is great! Now I don't have to keep stealing your truck!"

CHAPTER 56

LIAM

CLEMENTINE'S MARK was almost completely gone. I'd noticed the bruise and my teeth marks had faded when I picked her up for our date. My scent was still infused with hers, but it wasn't nearly as strong. I felt Lucian growl any time a male wolf looked in her direction, including the waiter who seated us at the barbecue restaurant in Kempthorne. She never paid attention to anyone else as she animatedly told me about her brother and dad working on a dirt bike and how he finally managed to get the engine going, only for it to sputter out and die again.

As time passed, Lucian paced my mind, and my eyes kept drifting the length of her neck to the soft part where my mark once shone proudly. I shifted uncomfortably in my seat as the waiter delivered our beers, and Clem flashed him a shy-but-sexy smile. He returned it, but once he caught my eye, he instantly submitted and scampered away. He wasn't a member of my pack, but he wasn't stupid enough to agitate me either. Even in a place like Kempthorne, where I couldn't physically do anything, his nature told him to back down and submit.

I did everything in my power to keep calm as she took a sip of her beer and continued her conversation. The meat was frying on the hot plate in front of us, and she seemed oblivious that the sizzling of the meat was mimicking my irritation.

"I need to ask you something," I said.

She paused bringing a piece of meat to her mouth, and raised an eyebrow. "Shoot."

"Are we ever going to discuss marking each other?"

Her turquoise eyes widened, and a light pink stained her cheekbones. "Oh. Um. I suppose we should." She put her meat on her plate and bit her lip.

Lucian growled deep; his feelings were identical to mine. I wanted to bite that lip. I wanted to pull it into my mouth and nibble it before grazing my teeth all over her soft skin. I wanted to hear her moan, to scent her arousal and bury my nose in it. Lucian grumbled again as I adjusted myself. My gums were tingling, and when I tried to take a deep breath, her scent curled into my nose, making my teeth sharpen.

I gently tugged her chin to make her release her lip and look at me. Her eyes showed no hint of her wolf; they were as clear as the first time I'd seen them. Her long dark lashes fluttered a little as she tried to look away as if the intensity of my gaze made her uncomfortable. It only lasted a brief second before those stunning eyes were back on mine, and her emotions were sealed away.

She stayed quiet and shy, which reminded me so much of when I'd first met her. But I wasn't going to allow her to retreat into herself. We were having this conversation, or I would have to leave so I didn't mark her against her will again.

I took my hand from her chin and gripped my beer bottle, taking a swig before I continued, "I noticed your mark has faded. I can barely smell myself on you anymore. I have to say it's making Lucian uneasy. Especially with all these other male wolves sniffing around." I glared at the waiter who walked past again.

"Don't you think you're being a little irrational? No other wolves are sniffing around." She rolled her eyes, and I let out a small growl.

"Don't roll your eyes at me! I'm being fucking serious. You have no idea how hard it is to sit here and resist my urge to take you against a bathroom wall and mark you again," I snapped. My voice was thick with anger.

She looked at me in surprise. Her eyes flashed momentarily with amber, then clouded for a brief second as she conversed with her wolf, and then she sighed sadly. "Dad said that might happen. I was hoping it would take a little longer for your urge to mark me again to come back."

That dampened my anger and my instinct. Surprised, I stared at her.

My voice came out softly. "You talked to your dad about our marking?" I reached out and grabbed her hand in mine. Maybe everything was going to be okay.

"Yeah, and he did pretty well with that conversation. I used to talk to my mom about this sort of stuff." Her voice wobbled slightly. "Well, obviously not this stuff exactly." She shook her head and continued, "Anyway, Dad tried to help me navigate my new culture and its views against my old one."

Lucian's ears perked up. "That's good. That means you're a lot more open to the idea, right?" My stomach gave an excited flip. This girl had been under my skin for weeks, and we were finally getting somewhere in our relationship.

"I'm sorry. No." She shook her head, and Lucian whimpered.

"What? Why?"

"Because even though I understand the concept, it still feels wrong."

"Why?" I tried to keep the anger out of my voice. I really wanted to understand.

"Because you're doing so to stake some wolfy claim. I'm a person, Liam. Please don't make me feel like I'm less than that."

"But you would also have a claim on me. It would tell people we're serious about each other. That I'm serious about you!" *Surely, she has to know how much I care about her?*

"You shouldn't need a physical mark on the skin to prove that to anyone."

"It will keep you safe from—"

"Other male wolves? She-wolves?"

"Yes. Exactly," I said sadly. I thought she would understand this, but she seemed more stubborn than ever. Clem pulled her hand away from mine and shook her head, amber rings flashing around the aquamarine colouring. Her eyes were clear and determined.

"Liam. I know the mark is designed to put other wolves in their place. I understand the territorial instincts of a werewolf. I know it's the building blocks of your—*our*—species. I'm hoping that by explaining how I feel to you, you can resist your ingrained urges for a little longer. I don't want you to lose yourself to your instincts with this marking thing. Everything is still so new to me, and I'm not ready for us to mark each other yet." Her voice lowered to a whisper. "I'm not ready to lose myself while trying to keep you happy."

"What if we compromise?" I suggested as diplomatically as I could.

She arched her perfect ebony brow. "You want to compromise?"

"Yeah, what if you mark me this time? I'll wear your mark, and I'll do so proudly. Then, once your instincts kick in, and you realize that you want it too, I'll mark you so long as you're okay with it."

"Liam." Her voice was soft but unyielding. "I was raised human. Do you think I'll rewrite my entire life philosophy in the six weeks I've known about werewolves? Do you think six weeks is enough time to adapt to being one myself? I know nothing of this world. I'm not ready."

"What does Circe think?" I asked, no idea if she'd been able to converse with her wolf logically yet.

"She respects my decision. She knows I'm trying to learn how to navigate this world, and she knows my reasoning for not wanting to be someone's possession."

"We would be each other's *possession*." I wiggled my fingers at the use of her horrendously insulting word.

I didn't want to own her. I wanted to be with her. Lucian frowned as he heard my soft and gentle tone turn rough, desperate, and ugly. She heard the tone too, and her eyes hardened.

"I know you may not understand or like it, but I need you to respect it," she said with soft directness. "If you can't under-stand that I'll walk away right now. I'm not going through this bullshit again."

Lucian flattened his ears and whimpered. He didn't want Clementine to leave. This thing between us couldn't end before it had even begun. I studied her face, realising that her words weren't an empty threat. She would do anything to protect herself.

I couldn't push her. I knew she was timid; that she had been through a lot. My thought process was causing Lucian to pace and snarl protectively. The idea that anyone could hurt her was abhorrent, but I knew that she had been treated badly multiple times before. Her ex had manipulated her insecurities and broke her so severely that she wasn't recognisable even to herself.

Over the years, Clem took all the crap that had been thrown at her, and she had buried it deep. She avoided conflict and internalized her feelings, making it hard for anyone who cared about her to know what she was thinking or feeling. Everything she did, she did to protect herself. But the one thing I didn't want her protecting herself from was me. Acting like an ass wasn't going to get me anywhere. It was just going to confirm and trigger her survival instincts. If that happened, I was going to lose her. I couldn't. Taking a deep breath, I inhaled her scent to try and calm myself.

"I promise you it's not like that at all. You said he was manipulative and abusive and found ways to tear you down. You have to know I'm not like that. I want to build you up and support you. I don't want to tear you down. I've told you time and time again that I'm here for you. Whenever you need me, I'll be here. Fuck, Clem, I just helped you shift, and I never once left your side. You can always trust me to be right there. Always," I begged her to understand.

"If you're on my side, don't force me to mark you. I don't think it's an unreasonable request. I just need time. Please." I suddenly remembered what Ryan said, knowing this was exactly what he had talked about. I had to listen to what she needed. A wave of guilt came over me, and I closed my eyes. Her voice breezed over me as she added, "I'm not saying the marking will never happen. I'm just saying not yet."

"Okay," I said, defeated, and I opened my eyes again. "Okay. I promise I won't mark you unless you allow it. It's going to be fucking hard to resist my instincts, but I want you to trust that I will never force you into anything you don't want. I never want you to feel like you're my possession. I want you to feel like you're my equal. I wish you could see yourself the way I see you." I took a breath and added, "I promise I won't manipulate, trick, or force you into anything. You have my word that I'll wait. I've never really been in a relationship either, Clem, but I want to be with you. I'll do anything for you, even fight against my own nature, just so we can be together."

Her face held a soft expression, and I knew then that my words were the epitome of truth. She was more than worth it. Lucian agreed with me wholeheartedly and promised to do everything in his power to never lose control with her. Ever.

I picked up her hand again, brought her fingers to my mouth, and gently brushed my lips against them. She nodded and gave me a shy smile that made me feel twenty feet tall.

"But if I scent one male wolf targeting for your affection, I may have to give into other instincts and fight for you." I gave her a playful smile. "And you know, it might just be a battle to the death."

She rolled those beautiful turquoise eyes at my teasing. "That won't happen, Liam. No other werewolf has ever been interested in me. You have the monopoly on that."

If only.

CHAPTER 57

CLEMENTINE

THE NIGHT of the full moon was approaching, and I was feeling the overwhelming pull of the wolf instincts I'd been told about. I understood why wolves started to go a little crazy leading up to the full moon. Circe was jittery as the moon phase closed in, and she wasn't helping my nerves. Over the last few days, she had been snarky and grumpy, slamming a wall between us every time she had a temper tantrum.

Liam was trying his hardest to fight his marking instinct out of respect for me, catching himself a few times before his teeth grazed my neck again when we'd get hot and heavy. He told me he understood and would wait for me to be ready, but the closer we got to the full moon, the more difficult his instincts became to fight. So, between Lucian and Circe, I had two grumpy wolves on my hands.

When Circe's wall was down, and she saw Liam's anguish, she would try to reason with me. When that didn't work, she would snarl, and suddenly I was overcome with a wolf instinct I had been warned about: the one where she might break free from me, ready to bite into Liam's neck and claim him as hers. The couple of times this had happened, Liam had restrained her and also fought his own instincts simultaneously. Her voice bled through mine, begging him to let her mark him, to mark each other. His eyes flashed every time as he diffused the situation, trying his hardest to stay true to his word. Respect blossomed for my alpha and some other emotion I couldn't place.

FINALLY, the evening of the full moon arrived. I was nervous as I stood with my brother in front of the amphitheatre. Vinny and I were with Roman's kid sister, waiting to be initiated into the pack. My brother chatted with her in low tones as people started to fill the area. I wanted to fidget badly, but Circe kept me from doing so. Even though the moon was low in the sky and pulling at her, she held back her instinct to shift. This was more important.

There were about five hundred people in the crowd. Most of them I didn't know. I looked around, and besides my dad, I couldn't spot a friendly face. Ryan had gone to Kempthorne for a few days to meet his in-laws and was running with Stacey out there. Sophie decided to go to Kempthorne too and run with her 'boyfriend who wasn't really her boyfriend'. I couldn't see Roman, but I assumed she would be out there as her sister was on stage. I scanned the crowd and spotted Kimmie and April gossiping behind their hands, looking at me. I saw Nola and her sister glaring in my direction, and Lincoln gave me that disgusting slimy smile of his that always made me fidget off the feeling of disgust that would always overwhelm me when his attention was focused on me.

I looked for Liam. He'd promised me he would run with me tonight. Circe was confident he would be here, but I couldn't help but feel anxious. I'm sure Dad wouldn't mind helping me shift and run with me if Liam stood me up.

The doors to the pack house opened, and out walked Liam's brother and Luna Sierra, followed shortly by Liam and Alpha Josiah.

Liam's gaze met mine, and he smiled as he came up on stage to take his place next to his family as Alpha Josiah's voice seemed to boom across the amphitheatre.

"What a great turnout for tonight's pack run!" Everyone cheered. "I'm pleased to announce that we have three pack members who have discovered their wolves and will be initiated into the pack this evening. So, let's not waste any time, because I'm sure you all feel that moon and want to get out there! Indiana Andrews, please step forward."

Indiana beamed beautifully as she stepped toward her alpha. I watched as Alpha Josiah said a few words to her before he sliced her hand with a ceremonial dagger and gripped her small hand within his. She shook violently for a few seconds before Luna Sierra pulled her into a motherly hug and helped her off to the side.

My brother was called upon next. He said his vows with the alpha and then shook his hand. Vinny didn't shake violently, but he did stiffen before moving to the side of the stage, to join Luna Sierra and Indiana.

"Clementine Stevens," Alpha Josiah called. I nervously looked around, seeking my father, who beamed at me with pride. My eyes then met Liam's, who gave me a look of pure adoration as I stepped awkwardly toward his father.

"Liam walked you through this, eh?" Alpha Josiah asked. I nodded, too afraid to speak. Alpha Josiah continued. "Our blood will mix after you pledge your loyalty, and your mind will open up to the pack link. It will feel weird, but it lasts only a few seconds." I nodded again.

"Do you pledge fealty to the alpha and every future alpha of this pack?"

I looked back briefly at Liam and smiled tenderly. "I do." Circe's voice mixed with mine as we said our vows.

"Do you pledge loyalty to the pack and accept all other members as your pack?"

"I do."

"Do you agree to do your best by this pack and abide by Pack Law?"

"I do."

"Do you, Clementine Stevens agree to become a member of the Blackfern Valley Pack?"

"I do."

The sharp blade sliced my palm, and Circe started humming deep inside me. I gripped the warm, calloused hand of Alpha Josiah and instantly felt an electric trickle flow between our blood and the sealing of my wound. A second later, my head felt like it had exploded with white noise. It wasn't painful, but it was disorienting. After a few seconds, it passed as Alpha Josiah had stated it would, and I smiled as his very voice tickled its way into my mind.

"Welcome to the pack, Clem. I want you to know I approve, and you and Liam have my blessing." I blinked stupidly at him. *"Go off and have some fun."*

Alpha Josiah turned his attention back to the pack and announced the start of the pack run just as the full moon moved upwards in the darkening midnight-blue sky. I walked toward Liam, who grinned at me as he wrapped his arms around my waist. I felt the full moon's pull get stronger, and my skin tingled. Circe was beginning to get restless.

"Ready to go for a run?" His voice was velvety soft as I heard him for the first time in my subconscious. I wanted to reply through the mind-link, so I did just as my dad had taught me. I reached out with my mind and found a golden pattern, the same colour as the rings of his eyes. It was laced with authority,

cedar, spice, and a smattering of unsurmountable power. It was definitely Liam; his scent was infused in the pattern, making a clear bridge connection between us.

"I'm more than ready." I thought back toward him, and he grinned, placing a gentle kiss on my mouth. I frowned and looked around at the pack members who could have witnessed his display of affection. Liam knew I was concerned about provoking the she-wolves, so him kissing me so openly felt strange. However, when I spun around, I only saw flashes of tails as the run had already begun.

My skin began to burn as the moon got brighter and higher still. I needed to shift. Spinning around, I looked for my brother to let him know I was going to run, but I didn't find him anywhere.

Liam's laughter trickled through the mind-link. *"He just disappeared with Indiana. Your brother has game."*

"My brother... Indiana... Right."

"Come on, Clem, let's get you out of those clothes." Liam winked, and I blushed then rolled my eyes at him.

I pulled my underwear off under my summer dress before removing it from over my head in one swoop, then let it drop to the wooden floor of the stage. Liam stood watching me protectively. I was at my most vulnerable while I was shifting, especially being so new at it, so there was no way Liam was going to shift first. We had no idea how long the shift would take, and even though he could protect me in wolf form, he seemed happier to wait for me to shift first. I smiled at his caring and protective nature, thinking that maybe I was starting to enjoy how closely he looked after me.

"Are you ready, Circe?"

"Fuck, yeah! Just breathe and allow me to come forward. Listen to the moon, and don't fight the pull. It'll be easier this time; the full moon will help too, as will having Liam here."

I felt the heat surge across my body as I fell onto my hands and knees. My bones snapped, and I let out a guttural cry as my blood boiled. I could feel the sweat bead over my body, and I started to pant. The tingles over my skin became fires, then I noticed the hair thickening. I opened my eyes and looked straight into comforting brown and gold orbs as Liam's voice came across the mind-link.

"Remember to breathe. The moon will pull Circe out. Don't fight it. I'm right here. Always."

Instead of focusing on the pain, I shifted my focus to the low hum emanating from him. I allowed the hum to roll over me as my body convulsed. There was a brief suffocating feeling as my snout burst forward and my ears pushed themselves onto the top of my head, but I didn't focus on that. I focused on Circe's soft instructions and the golds of Liam's eyes. With one last shake of my fur, I stood up and grinned at him.

"That was really quick! That took less than five minutes. Do you need to rest?"

"No, I need to run." And I ran toward the trees, looking back over my shoulder, taunting him. Liam flashed me a smile and pulled off his shorts, running after me and shifting on the fly.

"Didn't I tell you not to run from me? I'm an alpha and fast, and I'll catch you!"

"Oh, Big Bad Alpha," I taunted as I darted around a tree. *"Come and get me!"*

He let out a playful howl before tackling me to the ground. His teeth found my muzzle, giving me a gentle, playful shake. I giggled through the mind-link, and he let me up, sitting back on his hind legs. I could feel the power radiating off him, and I suddenly knew what Ryan meant when he said that wolves could just tell. I hadn't noticed it before because I'd allowed Circe to take the lead and do whatever was instinctual for her, but now that I was aware, I was awed. Liam wasn't even trying to be threatening. He wasn't purposely using his power. It was just there, and I naturally wanted to simultaneously be near and away from it.

"You okay?" he broke through my chain of thought. He tilted his wolfy head as he looked at me quizzically.

"I can feel your alpha power. I never noticed it before. It's a little overwhelming. I'm just trying to get used to it," I replied.

"You have a small amount too."

"I do?"

"Yeah. It's just a little trickle that tells me there's something more in you." Circe fluffed herself proudly. I rolled my eyes.

"So, what do I need to know about this pack run?" I asked, flanking him as we started to trot through the trees.

"Nothing really. Just do what you normally do on a run. Just stick within the territory and follow your instincts."

"So what if my instinct tells me to run from you?" I bantered.

"I think I've proven I can catch you. You've sensed my power; you don't stand a chance." His eyes twinkled as I rubbed against him, enjoying the low humming and the deep scent of his fur.

"Well then, Alpha, catch me if you can." I darted off deep into the trees.

The pull of the moon was powerful. There was an almost magical feeling as it rose higher into the sky. Not only did I feel its magnetic force, but it also lit up the forest in a blue-white light making the flora I had once hated seem more beautiful. I could feel Liam's low hum around me like a security blanket, even though he wasn't close. We were playing hide and seek. It was a childish game, but it was fun in wolf form. Every time we found each other, the hum would roll over us, zinging through my fur and weaving itself deep inside my subconscious.

I was hiding again and chuckled lowly as I felt him zip past. My snout was sticking out of the low brush, and he was pretending he didn't know where I was. I felt the tug of the moon as it reached its highest peak, and suddenly his scent became overpowering, and the low hum from Liam became loud in my ears. The gravitational pull was too strong to resist as I barrelled out of the brush.

Liam stood in the middle of a small clearing; the moonlight was glowing above his head, but a soft luminosity seemed to be coming directly from his fur. Circe looked at him in awe; the soft light from him made him look even more beautiful, powerful, and regal. He was the magnet, and I was being drawn in. As I stepped slowly toward him, he stepped toward me. A pull of gravity forced us together. I felt a click, and suddenly I understood what the feeling was.

"Circe?" I asked in a small nervous voice.

A coiling mix of emotions came from her. She was enraged as much as she was excited.

"I fucking told you! I told you from the moment I was awakened. I fucking told you! You refused to listen. You refused to admit there was something more than physical attraction under the surface. I told you that he was important to us. I told you that we could fully trust him, and that he would never hurt us. I told you that Liam wasn't going anywhere. I told you he was endgame! Now, do you believe me?" Circe snarled before pushing me forward and forcing the shift back to my human form.

Liam let out a howl before his body vibrated, and he shifted back too. He stared at me with pure emotion. I couldn't place it, but it floored me. I shifted within seconds, and before I could even stand, he pulled me off the ground and wrapped me in his arms. His fingertips left delicious sparks as I felt a strong magnetic connection stitch between us.

"Mate!" he growled, sounding more wolflike than ever before. Then his mouth desperately descended on mine.

CHAPTER 58

LIAM

I skidded into a small clearing created by fallen trees just as the full moon reached its peak and felt the instant gravitational pull coming from behind me. I twisted around, knowing that my mate was nearby. My heart thundered in my chest. There were a lot of she-wolves running around the forest, but I knew none of them was my mate as I had run with them all before. Only two new twenty-year-old she-wolves were in this forest, but I already knew which one it would be. My heart told me what I had known for weeks but refused to admit in the event I was wrong.

Lucian pushed us forward, sniffing the amplified sweet scent of honeysuckle and pear that almost made me fall with the pure weight of the emotions I felt.

Her glossy black fur glowed as she stepped out of the brush. At first, I thought it reflected the moonlight, but then I realized it was coming from her. The magnetic force was pulling me forward, and I felt electric tingles erupt over my fur. Lucian gazed adoringly at her; he was awestruck. I felt a click as the mate bond slotted into place. *Mine.*

"Lucian. Clementine–"

"She is perfect. She's our perfect little mate. Our perfect luna."

I couldn't believe I had finally found her. I let out a howl of excitement which echoed around the forest, and I shifted back into my human skin. I stood tall and naked with the moonlight glowing as I watched her body vibrate and shift back. Her dark hair sat in messy waves over her shoulders. She still glowed under the magic of the mate bond. Her skin was flawless, and her pouty lips were a blush-pink. She was so fucking beautiful.

"Mate!" Lucian's voice bled into mine as I embraced Clementine and kissed her deeply.

The kiss was more potent than normal, sending energy pulses around my body. Every sense was heightened as her tongue found mine, and she moulded against me. Her nakedness pressed against mine, and I felt myself stir as her body warmth tingled and weaved with mine.

I reluctantly stopped kissing her, inhaling her scent, and then rumbled happily. I wanted to take her here in the clearing and complete the mate bond while the full moon was still at its peak, but I knew I needed to give her time to adjust and understand what had just happened.

Pulling back slightly, I gave her a small smile and observed every emotion in the book dart across her turquoise eyes, her expressive face.

"Say something," I whispered. I needed to hear her voice.

"I-I don't know what to say," she replied softly.

"Do you understand what just happened?" I asked nervously.

"You're my mate," she mumbled.

"Do you know what that means?"

She looked so overwhelmed. Her turquoise eyes were wide, but I couldn't scent any tears behind them. I ran my fingers through her hair, each stroke sending waves of euphoria through me.

"It means that the moon put us together for eternity. It means we are true mates. It means we were made for each other," I explained.

She smiled softly, and I felt my heart flutter in my chest.

"Come on, let's go home and talk properly."

She looked at me and shook her head as if clearing a fog. "I-I-I thought that you were going to want to mark me."

"Clementine, believe me when I tell you I want nothing more than to do that." My voice came out roughly. "But as I promised, I'm not going to do anything you aren't ready for. I've waited my entire life to be bonded with you, so I'm happy to wait a little longer. We can only complete the bond at midnight when the moon is at its highest peak. The moon is already starting to move; I can feel it. I'm not going to rush our bonding so I can mark you before it moves too far. I want us to take our time, and I want you to be sure it's what you want. The bond will do everything it can to bring us together, but it's ultimately a choice."

She reached up and kissed me tenderly. Sparks flew from where her lips met mine and down the bond into my soul. I groaned into her mouth and forcibly opened it, deepening the kiss. I was surprised that the mate bond had already increased my sensitivity to her. My senses were in overdrive. The tingles of her hands around my neck and at the base of my hair zinged everywhere and filled me with warmth. There was the subtle taste of almond and honey on her tongue, and I instantly recognized it from when I marked her. I felt my gums tingle as Lucian grumbled at the taste and glanced warily toward the moon. Then he pushed himself as far back as he could go like he had done every time the instinct to claim her appeared.

"Seriously, I need to get you home. There are too many male wolves out here, and you are fucking delicious," I murmured as I brushed my lips against hers. "And as much as I love you naked," I kissed her again. "You need to shift so we can go back."

I looked up at the moon just as it went into its next phase and heard the howling of wolves in the distance. Clem jumped slightly at the chorus of howls and looked up at the moon. The power of the peak was over for another month. The moon would no longer force unmerged wolves to shift, and there was now no chance of completing a mate bond.

I looked at Clementine, and although she still had a slight aura that made her stand out to only me, the glow that acted like a beacon and pulled me in had stopped. As if she felt me watching, she looked at me through her thick lashes before she turned away and shifted with ease. She gave off a mighty howl, which was met with curiosity from the other wolves in our surroundings. Looking over her shoulder, she gave me an expectant look.

I stared at her in amazement. She had shifted instantly as if it was as natural as blinking. I followed suit and rubbed against her, enjoying the sparks before following her back through the trees toward the pack house.

We made it back and shifted. Dressing quickly, I guided her back to my room. As much as I wanted to throw her on my bed and see how intense the mate bond amplified our passion, I had promised her we would talk.

"You shifted without any issue back in the clearing," I stated the obvious as I took her hand and led her to my bedroom.

"I didn't even think about it. I just told Circe we needed to go, and she came forward instantly."

"That must be the mate bond. It's already working," I said, stroking her cheek adoringly with the back of my fingers before opening the French doors and motioning her inside.

"Apparently, it's been working for a while." She smiled shyly.

"What do you mean?"

"Circe said some stuff to me when I first shifted. She told me that it wasn't moving to Blackfern Valley that started to wake her up. She said that it was being close to you." She blushed under my fingers. "I told her she was being stupid, that it was the solar eclipse that had brought her forward. She told me that when my blood soaked the earth under the peak of the solar eclipse, it had only helped her break through the wall, but something woke her up and was calling to her well before that. She was convinced it was Lucian. She could feel Lucian healing her and calling to her. She said she didn't know why, but you were important and, that you were 'endgame'. Actually," she giggled, "she really loves to use that word."

"She could feel we were true mates," I said, my voice thick with emotion.

"No, she never said those words. She said she could feel you were important, and I needed to trust you." Clementine's eyes flashed with amber rings. "You woke her up, and you started to heal me. It was you who healed my ankle. It was you who healed my eyes. It's the only thing that makes sense. I lived with a werewolf for twenty years, and neither my dad nor a dormant Circe had ever managed to heal me before. I met you and–" She shook her head.

"The mate bond started working," I concluded.

She turned and looked at me. Her eyes sparkled as the amber flashed in and out. She reached up and ran her fingers through my beard. I moaned into the sensation, pulling her against me to kiss her. My thickened cock pressed against my shorts. I groaned into her mouth and pulled her lip between my teeth, teasing it softly. The kiss consumed us, a mixture of mate bond intensity and the heavy scent of her arousal filling the air.

"I know you wanted to talk about this," she whispered. I could feel her tingly breath on my lips. "But I think we should just talk after." I pulled back and looked at her. There was something seductive in her tone, and it shone in her eyes too.

"*After?*" I asked, my voice husky with excitement.

"After," she confirmed, pulling her dress over her head and shuffling herself backward on the mattress to lay down seductively with her head on my pillow. The only item of clothing she still wore was a pair of pink boy short underwear, and I felt my mouth go dry right before I followed her in a trance toward the bed.

***

"I THOUGHT all true mates would bond together under the full moon the moment they realized what was happening," Clementine said, coming out of my ensuite wearing my t-shirt. Her sexy pink boy short panties played peak-a-boo from beneath it with her every step. I forced myself to focus on her words rather than the instant pride and arousal I felt by seeing her in my clothes. She joined me on the bed, the scent of my mint toothpaste mixing with her naturally delicious aroma.

"There aren't many true mates out there. It's incredibly rare. I can count only a handful of true mates on my hand. And only one set of them bonded under that first moon, and that was my parents. Even your dad and mom didn't bond straight away."

Clem made a cute snorting sound. "What did you expect? There's no way Dad would try to kidnap my very human mother, tie her up and beat on his chest like a silverback gorilla. Actually, knowing my dad, he probably did do something like that. He probably threw leaves up in the air and hooted too. Or whatever the werewolf equivalent is. My parents were constantly harassed by your sadistic uncle even after they moved away from Blackfern Valley. So, it surprises me that they managed to make the bonding mark at all. Good thing they did, or I wouldn't just be a half-breed. I would be a half-breed and a bastard," she said sarcastically, humour glinting through her eyes.

Lucian cocked his head at her dark humour and gave her a small huff of amusement. I reached out and tapped her playfully on the nose.

"Okay, something a little more recent. You know that Ryan and Stacey are true mates." She nodded soberly and tucked her legs up under her. "Stacey ran when she felt the bond. She fought every inch of her instincts and ran the other way. When Ryan finally found her, it was about an hour after midnight. He and Stacey have spent the last month with the bond tethering and linking them together, making them stronger as a couple."

"She must have been strong; I had no chance when I felt the pull."

I smiled and gave her a quick kiss. "Neither did I," I admitted. "With Stacey, I think she was mostly scared, but her wolf won out, and she sought out Ryan eventually."

"I can understand being scared," she said with such raw honesty that I stopped running soothing circles over her back. I felt a tiny sliver of uneasiness lick against the bond before it disappeared into an abyss. I knew the bond would allow us to feel each other's emotions, but I wasn't expecting it to have started already. From what I knew, it took time, emotions trickling through small amounts before the floodgates opened upon marking.

"I'm here for you. Always."

She smiled and leaned in to give me a sweet and tender kiss, but any emotion she felt remained private.

Lucian grumbled and nodded. I needed to tell her the next part. I didn't want to, but I had to. She had a right to know.

"I need you to know that you still have a choice in this." Her doe-like eyes found mine. "The mate bond is designed to bring us closer. It'll connect us in an indescribable way. But at the end of the day, to mate with me is a choice." I swallowed a lump in my throat and looked away. "You can choose to reject the bond." My voice cracked. "To reject me."

She palmed my cheeks between her silky soft hands and made me look at her. Her eyes shone. She didn't say anything but slowly brought my face down to hers and brushed her lips against mine. Sparks flew from the kiss as she shared her emotions with me down the mate bond. I couldn't fully identify the sentiment, but it comforted me, and I knew she was telling me that she wouldn't reject me once the time came.

Lucian rumbled happily as I was saturated with this unnamed emotion, desperately clinging to it and committing it to memory as I rolled her onto her back. Sparks zapped between us, and I gently pulled my lips from hers. I gave her another gentle peck before tucking her in close.

In the distance, we could hear the sounds of wolves howling as the full moon shifted across the sky once more. The moon's soft light tried its hardest to seep through my curtains as if it wanted to remind me that it was the reason for my happiness. Clementine stifled a yawn, and I kissed her shoulder gently.

"Sleepy little mate." I cuddled her against me and gave her another kiss on her shoulder. "Go to sleep. We need to talk about telling our parents, but that conversation can wait until tomorrow." Then I chuckled softly.

"What's so funny?" she asked.

"My dad owes Mom twenty bucks."

CHAPTER 59

CLEMENTINE

When we woke in the morning, I had mind-linked my brother and father, asking them to come to the pack house. I was surprised to discover I was able to open a link to both, like a three-way phone call. Their pattern scents had merged into one, and the connection bridge was wider than usual.

"Most wolves can mind-link up to ten people at once. The stronger your wolf, the more minds you can access in a single attempt," Liam explained, trailing gentle kisses down my neck and over my bare shoulder as he ran his hands over the material of my summer dress. "I don't think I like you in clothes," he added, his playfulness tickling down our bond.

"Well, tough! I'm not parading around your house naked in front of your parents."

He grinned wickedly before he pulled me toward the alpha's office. It was larger than I thought it would be. A massive mahogany desk was situated toward the end of the room. One entire wall contained bookshelves; there was a black leather couch, and a couple of armchairs tucked cosily around a small coffee table. Liam directed me to the couch and tucked me in next to him. He was so close that our skin touched, sending delicious hums across my body.

Sean sat in an armchair when we arrived. My dad and brother entered next, and Vinny took a seat in the other armchair, fist-bumping Sean while Dad stood behind him and smiled softly at Liam and I. Alpha Josiah and Luna Sierra, stood behind the large mahogany desk. When Dad looked to them, they shared a quizzical look with him.

"Liam, you called a meeting?" Alpha Josiah asked in a levelled voice.

"Open your wallet, old man. You owe Mom twenty bucks," Liam said cheekily. Luna Sierra looked at both of us and squealed in delight, jumping up and down on the balls of her feet. Sean grinned at his brother, whereas my brother looked confused, and my father looked mildly intrigued.

"Um, Liam is my true mate," I whispered to my family.

Vinny's eyes widened in surprise, Dad's lips twisted into a smirk, and he gave me a nod. I knew that look very well.

"You knew?" I asked him incredulously.

Dad nodded. "I suspected. Yes." Then he explained. "The way he acted around you was more mate bond than your standard boy-girl crush. How he howled on the last full moon when he discovered you had gone to Vancouver was another. That howl was one of mourning. It made me wonder if the mate bond had started to form between you both because his reaction was quite extreme for such a short time of you both knowing one another. It was all speculation, of course, but if mating came to fruition, I knew it would be an issue because you were human. When Liam later announced he'd reject his alpha title to be with you," I snapped my head toward Liam, who met my gaze unflinchingly, "my suspicion grew. I told Alpha Josiah my thoughts, only to find that both Liam's parents shared my suspicion. And then you went and changed the rules.

You shifted. And you shouldn't have been able to shift. You were human, Clem."

"That was the solar eclipse," I explained softly, looking at the three parents in wonder.

They all grinned as if they were in on the world's biggest secret. Liam didn't look nearly as shocked as I did. I could feel his calmness down the mate bond, and I knew he had suspected we were mates on some level too.

"Yeah, it was. But your wolf was drawn to him. She needed to seek him out for your second shift. It's known that a mate bond is healing. It's what convinced me that Liam was your true mate. I think you knew it deep down too. Circe would have told you things that made you suspect, or, in your case, deny whole-heartedly." He gave me a knowing look and grinned. "But you were drawn to him from day one. What you two have is extremely special, Clemmy." A salty scent was in the air, and Dad's eyes became glassy. I instinctually got up, walked over to him, and wrapped my arms around his middle. "Your mom would be so proud," he whispered into my ear as he returned my hug.

It had been a few days since the full moon, and people were slowly getting back into their routine. I was going through a defensive sparring session with Sophie at the pack training ground. Liam didn't want me training with Lincoln anymore, so my training was randomized to avoid his classes. To make it easier, he told me that Sophie would be my training partner in every class to ensure I always had a friend while I developed my fighting skills.

I told him he was being ridiculous; that Sophie had university classes and a life. He had growled and said that it was this, or I wore his mark. We argued for a good forty minutes. Both of our wolves were agitated, the mate bond twanging and pulling tight, making our argument turn sexual. But even then, he kept his promise and didn't mark me. He gave me a large handprint on my ass cheek and love bites all over my breasts though, but he never marked me.

I didn't know the instructor giving the lesson, but he seemed pretty happy to let Sophie and I do our thing. I suspected it was more than likely he had been told to be happy about it.

Sighing, I tried to focus on the defensive moves Sophie had taught me as she punched.

"He was way more into me than I realized. We ran together, he asked to mark me, so I broke it off," Sophie said between jabs.

"I'm sorry, Sophie," I replied as I blocked her next attack.

"Yeah, but I mean if my brother could find his true mate and you and Liam found each other, there's hope for me, right?"

"There's always hope," I said with a nod, ignoring the conversation I'd had with Liam a few days ago about the rarity of true-mate bonds. "What about your sister? Has she had any luck yet?"

"No, she hasn't. She's in the fucking Yukon right now. If her mate isn't there, then maybe I'm doomed."

"You are not doomed."

"Anyway, I decided I'm not in any rush. I'm only twenty, and there's a shitload of time."

I smiled as she focused on correcting my move for the twentieth time, then the instructor announced the session was over.

"Hey, beautiful." Liam's voice came through the mind-link. *"Do you want to come to Lupus'? Ryan is showing his in-laws around town, and he's asking for some interference."*

"Do you want to go to Lupus'? Your brother needs a buffer with the in-laws," I asked Sophie.

She tinkled out a laugh. "Yeah, alright then. Let's go."

Sophie and I walked into Lupus' and looked around. I instantly spotted Stacey's blonde ringlets bouncing as she talked with an older woman with blonde hair and hazel eyes and an older man with a darker shade of blond hair and blue eyes, who chuckled heartedly at what his daughter was saying. I slid into the booth next to Stacey, and Sophie sat across from me.

"Hey! Liam and Ryan will be back in a moment. They just went to pick up my brother. He got a little lost. Mom, Dad, this is Sophie, one of Ryan's sisters, and Clementine. Sophie, Clem, these are my parents, Georgia and Jake." Stacey introduced.

"Clementine!" Stacey's mom smiled at me. "I hear we are kindred spirits." I gave her a soft smile.

"I only found out recently. It's been a lot to take in."

"I bet." Her hazel eyes twinkled with kindness.

Stacey's expression suddenly went vacant, and she rolled her eyes. "Looks like my brother found the place after all. I'm just going to ring Ryan and tell them my brother is in Blackfern Valley."

"A wild goose chase?" I asked as I made my way out of the booth to let her pass.

"Yeah, my brother is good at making people chase him." She chuckled.

"I need to pee, so if Liam comes in–"

"Don't worry, Clem. The bond will tell him where you are," she whispered in my ear and then gave me a conspiratorial wink before making her way to a different area to make her phone call. I was sure she wished they were members of the same pack. The mind-link would certainly have come in handy right then.

***

THE RESTROOM DOOR opened with an angry bang. I turned to look at the door, and my heart stopped cold. My eyes ran over his blond hair and blue eyes. I staggered on the tiny dimple in his chin and watched as his eyes flickered with recognition.

"When I stepped into this bar, I thought my nose was playing tricks on me," he said in a cold, disengaged voice. My heart thumped, but not with fear. Circe would not allow me to feel fear. Instead, my heart thumped with anger. "I thought there was no way Clementine would be here, in a werewolf pack, of all places. So, I followed the smell only to find that your scent has changed. You still have your previous sweet smell, but now there's the distinctive one of a werewolf." His previously gorgeous blue eyes bore into mine. "How the fuck do you have a wolf scent, Clementine, when you were so very human the last time I saw you?"

"Brady," Circe's voice blended with mine, "what the fuck are you doing here?"

"What are *you* doing here, Clem? And why is your scent polluted with the stink of some vacuous man-whore?"

Circe snarled in my head at the insult to our mate. I took a gentle sniff of the air and realized that Brady smelled like lawn clippings and something musky with the underlying scent of canine. Horror and instant understanding suddenly flooded through me.

He's a fucking werewolf.

Brady was emotionally manipulative, possessive, and controlling. He bore all the traits of a werewolf and then some.

Circe snarled deep, and our hatred for him resonated through my body. There was no fear, only pure hate.

He took a deep sniff while his eyes roamed my body once more. He screwed up his nose, then looked at my collarbone for a mark.

"Are you keeping another wolf's bed warm, little Clemmy?" His eyes darkened with a black ring, and I stepped back. Circe snarled again. "Have you already forgotten about me?"

"I couldn't forget about you if I tried. You're a malignant tumour on my memories." He chuckled and stepped toward me.

Circe came forward angrily and growled in warning. I felt a pull down the mate bond, and I knew Liam must have sensed my emotions. I felt another tug, knowing that Liam was trying to locate me.

"You better leave, Brady," I warned, feeling my bond with Liam start to hum.

"Why? I just found out you're a werewolf. Do you know how happy this makes me?" He smiled softly. His eyes were cold and calculating, and his voice came out like honey. "I loved you once, and I can love you again. We can be mated. And you already know how to serve me so well. You'll be such a good submissive mate."

Before I could even think of defending myself, he cornered me against the sink.

"You're fucking deranged. You never loved me," I snarled.

He ran his hand down my cheek, and I felt Circe flash in my eyes. "How is it you're a werewolf, Clementine? This is going to be an interesting story to tell our pups."

"I want nothing to do with you, so, go tell your imaginary pups that!"

"Oh, baby. No one else wants you. Not even the wolf you've been fucking. If he did, his mark would be all over you. Sure, his pathetic scent is, but I'll soon change that."

I saw his teeth elongate, and suddenly I knew what he would do. I wasn't strong, I wasn't skilled, but Circe gave me a little power boost as my fist grazed his extended canines. "Get the fuck away from me!"

I felt the mate bond pull and twist as Liam came charging into the restroom. The low hum felt like angry wasps as he saw me cornered by another wolf. Brady flew across the restroom as Liam stood in front of me protectively.

"Who the fuck are you, and why are you touching my mate?" he roared.

"Really, Clementine?" Brady sneered arrogantly. "This is who you've replaced me with? Do you submit to him too?" He grinned evilly at Liam. "Bro, I taught her everything she knows. She was this shy little med student with these big bright eyes and an ass you could pound into. She was so naturally submissive. I was the TA for her class and wanted to teach her. So, I did. Repeatedly. She was such a good student. So willing to comply; willing to make me happy." His eyes found me again, and his blue gaze sparkled with need. "Sorry to break it to you, but now that she has a wolf, I'm fucking taking her back."

Liam's eyes started to glow. "You will not touch her if you want to leave here alive."

"She is mine, and I'm taking her back." Brady's dark rings flashed ominously around his irises. I stared at him in disbelief. Could he not feel the controlled power that rolled off Liam? Did his arrogance cloud his judgement that much?

"I'm not your fucking possession, Brady!" Circe's voice echoed through mine.

"Oh, Clementine. I love the way your wolf comes through. I can't wait to break her in and tame her." He gave me a wink. "Just wait right there, Clem. This won't take a minute."

"You won't fucking touch her!" Liam growled as Brady leapt into attack mode.

The sound of the fighting brought in Sophie, Ryan, and Stacey. Ryan jumped in instantly, pushing the two wolves away from each other.

"What the fuck is going on?" he snarled as he stood in a protective stance in front of Liam; in front of me.

"He has something that belongs to me," Brady spat.

"What are you talking about, Brady?" Stacey asked.

"Clementine belongs to me."

My eyes went wide in further understanding.

Brady is Stacey's brother?

"Clementine belongs to me," Liam corrected, and I felt a burst of fiery emotion come down the mate bond. "She's my true mate and is the future luna of this pack, so I suggest you leave my territory, Brady, while you still have air in your lungs and a heart beating in your chest. I don't give second chances."

Stacey's hazel eyes went wide, and the colour drained from her face. I watched her brother's face contort with rage. The look he gave Liam was murderous. Then his eyes found mine, and he smirked sinisterly.

Liam tucked me under his arm protectively and escorted me out of the restroom. I looked around and noticed about twenty pack members. They had to have heard his declaration.

Oh shit!

The only people who had known about our true mate status at this point were our close friends and families.

"They were going to find out eventually." His voice travelled into my mind, breaking my train of thought. *"Let's leave before I go back and kill that wolf for trying to claim you. He actually thought he could take you from me?"* I could taste Liam's anger on my tongue. It felt hot and fiery like a ghost pepper.

"I never thought I would see him again."

"That was him, wasn't it? That was your ex?"

"Yes. That douchebag was Brady," I said out loud as we left

Lupus' and turned toward the pack house. Liam's eyes flashed with rage, and I knew he was about to give in to the same instinct my dad had when my mom's life had been threatened.

I tried to send calm, soothing thoughts down the mate bond.

"Even though he's an arrogant son of a bitch, and Circe has wanted nothing more than to shove a screwdriver in his eye, we can't do that to Stacey."

"You didn't mention he was a werewolf."

"I didn't know," I said quietly.

"Your dad would have," Liam snarled.

"Dad never knew about Brady. I convinced myself that it was too good to be true and that if I told my parents, the other shoe would drop. The only person I told was TJ." I bit my lip. "Liam, that look he gave me when he left. I think he saw your claim as a challenge." Circe's hackles rose.

"He won't fucking touch a hair on your head," Liam roared his promise, his rage hotter on my tongue.

"No, he won't," I agreed, pulling him toward me and brushing my lips softly against his, allowing the tingles to soothe him.

The soft kiss progressed as he grabbed hold of me with desperate need. My tongue ran over his, and our mate bond sang between us, a singular word we needed to hear couldn't have been clearer to us both.

Mine.

CHAPTER 60

LIAM

Brady had left for Kempthorne with his family in tow shortly after I took Clementine away from Lupus'.

And I'd *taken* Clementine, repeatedly, in my bedroom. Her responsive little mewls drove me to the breaking point again and again. The mate bond zinged between us and made each orgasm more intense than the last. She seemed to be thirstier for our physical attraction than usual. She was more insatiable, responsive, and feral in her desire. Her wolf claimed me through the throes of passion, and my gums itched to mark her. But this was precisely how it had happened the first time; I'd felt threatened by another wolf, then reacted without thinking of the repercussions, or what Clementine wanted.

Her eyes sparkled with lust and desire every time she looked at me, and the mate bond was as solid as ever. Instead of officially marking her, I left small purple hickey's all over her delicious cleavage, a mark representing every time I had made her come. A different kind of mark to tell the world she was mine. That would be enough for now.

RYAN and I were at the training grounds. I had come straight here from university for our level-three training. He was informing me of what had happened after I had rescued my mate from Brady's slimy hands.

"He tried to explain to Stacey that he met her at university and fell for her, then she suddenly upped and left him. He told Stacey that he never expected in a million years that she would show up in Blackfern Valley or that she would be a werewolf. He said he thought Fate had brought them together again." Ryan twisted his body as I rolled into him. "Stacey trusts him fully. She's convinced this is a big misunderstanding."

"And what do you think?" I asked.

"I think he's a crafty son of a bitch. He's smarmy and manipulative. He's got his whole family convinced he's just a nice pack doctor who wouldn't hurt a fly. I don't trust him at all."

"Clem's worried he won't take my threat seriously. That he sees it as a challenge."

"I agree, bro. When I tried to play nice for Stacey's sake, I told him that Clementine had moved to her dad's pack, and her wolf was awakened because her true mate was here. I let him know that her true mate was the alpha-elect, and that I was sorry he lost his love, but he should be relieved she was happy. If he's smart, he'll heed your warning."

"And what did he say to that?"

"He said, 'why would I listen to the juvenile warning of an alpha-elect from some trashy inbred pack?'"

A red filter dusted my vision, and when I twisted my fist into Ryan, I saw that my claws had extended. Ryan noticed too and met my claws with his own.

"He definitely has a death wish!" Lucian snarled.

"I think you need to mark Clementine," Ryan said softly, making his next strategic move. I watched his footing with interest and spun at the last second, narrowly avoiding his claws. "But then again, Brady is so arrogant that he would probably ignore it and attempt to claim her anyway." I let out a soft snarl, and Lucian's hackles rose. "I admit, I'm a little concerned about this whole thing."

I looked at Ryan and saw he was holding back something he wanted to say. I stopped sparring with him for a moment and looked at him expectantly. "What is it?"

Ryan sighed before responding. "Brady said when I eventually joined their pack that I better bring him a gift." Ryan grimaced. "Then he said, 'actually, never mind. I'll get it myself.'"

"You think he's going to come after Clem again?"

"I think he has a death wish," Ryan confirmed with a nod. "He seems to think he loves her. Sorry, man."

"He doesn't fucking love her. He's obsessed with owning her."

"Yeah, that's the vibe I get too."

"He's a fucking lunatic. The pack is full of warriors who would die for their luna."

Ryan frowned before giving me a pointed look. "But she isn't their luna. And most people have only heard whispers of her being your true mate. She hasn't been around long enough to earn their trust." He spoke softly, trying not to anger me but needing to give me counsel.

"And there's still that group of wolves that Alpha Josiah is watching like a hawk. We both know they're just waiting to make their move on her, and now, there's that asshole Brady to top it all off. We both know he won't back down. The guy is crafty. He'd already started asking his sister questions about this pack under the guise of being interested in where she would potentially end up. My gut tells me he was checking for weaknesses and devising a strategy. Even though you threatened him, kicking him off the territory, your dad is still the alpha. I wouldn't put it past him to arrange a meet with him."

"Then I need to become alpha and stop this bullshit once and for all."

"Are you ready for that?"

"I've been groomed for it since I was twelve."

"But are you *ready* for it?"

"With Clem by my side, I'm ready for anything," I said honestly.

"Then you need to tell your dad. And you need to tell the pack that you and Clem are mated."

"The first part will be easy. The second, not so much." We went back into our sparring stances.

"Is she still fighting her instincts?" Ryan asked as he barrelled into me.

"No. The mate bond is opening her up a little more. But she's still the same timid girl we met two months ago. She still tries to go home at night occasionally, even though I've told her I want to wake up with her every morning. We have our dates in Kempthorne because she still doesn't want to be seen with me around the pack. I don't mind that so much because, you know, way better stuff to do in Kempthorne. And even though she'll kiss me happily in public, it's only when we are alone that she truly blossoms out of her shell. She hates anything that draws attention to herself." He went to attack me again. I hit his ribs and gently pierced his skin with my claws. He nodded to inform me that the move was good. We stood back from each other to start a new spar.

"Maybe she's embarrassed by you, bro?" I gave a low warning growl. "Kidding!"

"She's scared that it will make her a target. I understand she's just protecting herself from potential fallout. The she-wolves are crazy around here," I said, circling Ryan.

"You ain't wrong. Cassie burned down her house, then dared to try and call me."

"What?" I stopped circling Ryan.

"Yeah. She called me a few times. I told her to stop calling and blocked her number. But that bitch is as fucking persistent as she is crazy. She kept saying she needed to talk to you."

"Fucking Cassie," Lucian's voice fused with mine.

"Well, you have your work cut out for you! Not only do you have to go through your alpha ceremony, but you also have to convince your luna to go public in a pack full of volatile she-wolves. May I suggest you just call a meet, pull her onstage, rip off her clothes and fuck her right there? Then be like, 'Oh, by the way, meet your new luna.'"

I looked at him incredulously and saw how his suggestion humoured his eyes.

"Right. She won't even wear my mark, but she would totally be down for a good public fucking. Good plan, Beta Ryan." I rolled my eyes.

"Wait, what?" His eyes snapped to mine.

"Well, I'm about to be alpha, and you're going to be my beta, right? So, you really should get used to your title."

"Bro, I don't know what to say."

"Uh, usually you say yes."

"Shit." He closed his eyes.

"Do you not want to be my beta?"

"No, it's not that. I have a mate from a different pack, and I just told her I would move with her to Kempthorne while she finishes her studies. We haven't even discussed what happens when she graduates in a few years. And I know we've been best friends since we were pups, but I honestly thought you'd pick Sean."

"Sean is too young."

"He won't be too young for long. And until then, I assumed you would keep Jerome Evans as beta."

"It was never meant to be the Evans' family. It was supposed to be Patrick Stevens."

"I heard that rumour. Maybe you could ask Clementine to be your beta?" Ryan suggested mischievously. "If Patrick didn't get chased away, she would have grown up here and only been a couple of years behind us in school." A cheeky smile split his face.

"She already has a title." I rolled my eyes. "Look, don't make a decision today, but honestly, think about it. You're my best friend, and I want you as my beta."

***

Dad was at the cottage, and there was no time like the present to tell him my plan. My mom had a swatch sample book of linen, and Dad looked as though he was in pain as my mother attempted to get his opinion on the interior design.

"Liam!" Dad said excitedly, gripping onto the distraction like a lifeline. Mom smirked knowingly as my father bounded away from her.

"Hey, um. So, I was thinking. I want to take over the pack. Like now."

"I thought you wanted to wait until you graduated," Mom said, tilting her head my way.

"Why the change of heart?"

"What difference does a year make? I mean, I'm almost finished with school. There's no reason I can't finish my last few classes and run a pack simultaneously. I've been groomed for this since I was twelve. I should have taken it over on my twenty-first birthday. I've merged with Lucian. I've found my mate. I just think it's time," I rambled.

Dad chuckled. "Why do you think your mom is bugging me with the curtain colours and crap? She's pushing me to get this finished before the next pack run. She had a feeling that you would be taking over alpha shortly after the full moon. She reminded me the main house belongs to the alpha and luna of the Blackfern Valley pack." Dad's mouth twitched as he looked toward my mom. "And she said that once the moon gave you your luna, you would need the space to go at it like rabbits. She wanted to be out of the house before that happened."

"Yeah. And look, I was right. You should know by now that I'm always right. Your dad has been a typical tradesman, and now we are delayed!" Mom rolled her eyes.

"As I said when you merged with Lucian, I'm more than happy for you to take the title whenever you're ready. It's yours, son."

"Is Clementine ready to be luna?" Mom asked, flicking over to another swatch.

"I haven't even discussed it with her. She's still getting used to the idea of being a werewolf." I murmured, worry flooding me. "I don't want to put too much pressure on her."

"She doesn't automatically become luna when you become alpha, so there shouldn't be any pressure," Dad reminded me. "When you tell her that you'll be alpha, just explain what that means for her. She'll understand."

"Yeah, I know." I nodded.

"So, how quickly did you want to do this thing?" Dad enquired, shaking his head, and screwing his nose up at a bright purple swatch Mom showed him.

"If we could do it right now, I would. But I know the expected protocol."

"We could call a meet at the end of next week or tie it in with the next full moon?" Mom suggested, flipping over to a pastel purple swatch instead.

"No!" I shook my head anxiously. So much could happen in that time.

"How about the weekend then? Sunday?" Dad suggested, sensing my determination. "That will give you a few days to talk to Clem and give your friends the heads up. It will allow me to ensure everything is going to be handed over smoothly." He then whispered quietly to me, "It will give me a reason not to look at colour swatches." Mom glared at Dad and flipped to another swatch sample.

"That would work." Lucian nodded in agreement. "Thank you for allowing me to take it so soon."

"Liam, the seat is yours. I've just been keeping it warm for you. And as I've already told you, I'm ready to retire."

"Josiah, you know if Liam is going to be alpha on Sunday, we need to move out. So, no, you don't get out of this." She gave him a stern look, and Dad sighed deeply.

I laughed and went to leave. When I turned back to look at them, Dad was gazing adoringly at my mother as they shared something down a mind-link. He kissed her quickly, and she swatted him playfully with the sample book. Then she started flipping through the swatches again and holding them up against the windows. I smiled at how happy they were. It was as if it was a premonition of my future.

"Mom." She looked at me curiously. "Go for the teal blue one," I said before taking my leave.

I wanted to see Clementine before she started her shift at Lupus'. I had to leave her in our warm, scent-infused bed this morning to head to university, and even though it hadn't been that long since I'd seen her, I missed her. I wanted to feel, smell, and be close to her as often as possible. Especially with that fucker Brady re-entering her life.

I reached down my mate bond to locate her. The bond hummed and tightened as an image flashed through my mind. Fast flashes of a forest and the feeling of paws thundering came down the bond.

"She's shifted." Lucian grinned in amusement. *"Seems like our girl needed to run again."*

"Well, let's go chase her."

CHAPTER 61

CLEMENTINE

I STRETCHED as I rolled out of Liam's bed, my legs felt like Jell-O, and my body ached from being pleasured repeatedly. I smiled as I looked in the mirror and saw my flushed face, messy hair, and bright turquoise eyes flickering with amber. My wolf was preening and looked positively smitten with what we had spent the last several hours doing. We hardly got any sleep, but it was more than worth it.

I ran my fingers through my hair to try and untangle some of the knots and instantly knew it was a losing battle. I walked into Liam's ensuite and climbed into his shower, aiming the shower head lower and giggling softly at our height difference as I turned the tap handle to scolding hot.

I groaned as the hot water hit my body's sore spots. I looked at the small purple marks over my breasts and smiled. He loved marking my skin, and I realized I liked it too. I liked the raw passion, feeling wanted, feeling safe and protected. I stopped examining the bruises and looked back at Circe, who was grinning, a knowing twinkle in her eye.

Deep in thought, I scrubbed myself with his fragrance-free soap and shampoo. Getting out, I grabbed a big black fluffy towel and wrapped it around myself. I wiped the steam off the mirror and studied myself. I was so short I had to tip-toe slightly to see myself properly. I ran my hand over my collar-bone and smiled softly in the mirror. I was tempted to call Liam through the mind-link and ask him to return. I wanted to try and send visions of myself naked on his bed; images of me wearing nothing but his mark on my neck to get him to abandon everything he was doing. I wanted him to come home, fuck me hard and give me what I suddenly needed so desperately.

I could feel the heat pooling between my legs and smelled my subtle arousal.

God! Have I turned myself on by imagining him marking me?

My gums were starting to tingle, and Circe was pacing agitatedly. I was overwhelmed by her and my instinctual need to seek out our mate. Flashes of Liam popped into my head, his hard marbled abs, his sexy smile. I shook my head and pushed my instincts down.

Picking up a comb, I started to untangle my black tresses. I could discuss this with Liam later. I couldn't distract him from his busy day, no matter how much I wanted to. Circe became a little more agitated, however. I could feel her pressing against my mind, and my skin started to burn and itch.

"What is it with you?" I asked.

"I want to reach out to my mate and booty call him. But since you don't want to do that, I need to spend this energy elsewhere."

"Okay?"

"I need to run."

"We've never done it alone."

"I need to run now!"

"Just let me get out of the pack house."

I wrapped my towel tighter around myself and skimped out into the kitchen. I made it to the French doors that led outside.

Crack, snap, pop. My bones burned with each break, but I didn't have time to think as Circe pushed herself forward.

I opened the doors and groaned as the next wave of pain shuddered around my body. I fell outside onto the wooden deck and panted a little. Circe pushed again, and my vision blurred as my blood turned to lava and fur sprouted over my body. I took a deep breath as the last stage of the shift burst out of me.

It felt freeing letting Circe run. She whipped through the trees, jumped over logs, and darted around small shrubs. I giggled at her as she trotted through the stream and kept running.

We ran around for hours, looping all over the wilderness. Then we stumbled upon the pack boundary. I could feel the gentle zap telling me I was approaching the perimeter. I ran down the side of the boundary line, sniffing the air. I could smell wolves and knew that the warriors were on patrol. I was a member of this pack. I could come and go as I pleased, but meeting a warrior on duty made me a little anxious.

Alpha Josiah allowed non-pack wolves to enter his perimeter as long as they came via the main road. It was a safety precaution as well as a sign of respect. It was considered extremely rude, if not dangerous, to enter any other way. If wolves were found skulking through the forest near the boundary, well, I was unsure whether the warriors asked questions first or later.

I smelled a wolf approaching me, and sighed. I guess I was about to find out. Circe held her head high and sat on her hind legs as a small grey wolf approached.

"You're a long way from town," said a soft unknown voice.

Her eyes were hard and cold as ice. Was she a warrior?

"Just exploring my territory." I shrugged.

"Your territory? This isn't your territory," she snarled with her

hackles raised. Her nose twitched in the air, and her cold eyes narrowed. *"And Liam isn't yours."*

"Are you sure about that?" Circe's voice bled through.

"Back down! Submit to me. Know your place half-breed."

"I do know my place. My place is in bed with Alpha Liam, riding his gigantic cock and making him see stars as I fuck him senseless," Circe said. I grimaced internally. I really wished she wouldn't provoke the she-wolves.

Without warning, the wolf attacked. I felt her body smack into mine and her breath around my face. I pulled my lips back and growled at her. I had no idea how to fight, so I let Circe take over.

"He's mine, you fucking half-breed whore."

"Actually, he's mine." Circe snorted at the she-wolf. *"He was mine, over and over and over again just last night. And he'll be mine over and over and over again any other night I choose."*

"You are so fucking dead." The mind-link snapped shut, and suddenly she let out a howl. The howl was met by two, maybe three more. No, wait! It was at least five or six different howls.

Circe cocked her head and smirked before raising her hackles and lowering her head, growling at the wolf. There was a flash of fur and saliva. I felt a bite on my ear as Circe locked her jaw around the grey wolf's leg and bit down hard. The wolf yipped in pain.

Two more wolves jumped out of the bush, coming to the aid of the grey wolf. I recognized the one with straw-coloured fur and glared as her scent resonated with me. I heard the thundering of paws behind her, and I knew more wolves were on their way.

But Circe refused to let me be afraid. She wouldn't let me submit and cower. Circe was fucking livid, and I felt her instincts flow through me.

Game on, bitch!

I LAY on the leaf-littered ground, wounded and tired. Seven wolves had attacked me. Seven. And just as the straw-coloured wolf was about to deliver what I assumed would have been a deadly blow, she stopped. Her entire body went rigid, and her eyes glazed over. I looked at the other six wolves, all of their expressions identical to hers. Without warning, they suddenly pivoted and sprinted away.

I huffed as I made myself stand up and shook out my fur. I gingerly took a step forward on my paws and smiled at Circe. We had taken on seven wolves and survived. I couldn't help but feel a tiny bit proud.

She was exhausted but smiling happily at me as I took the reins and walked us forward.

Ten minutes later, I felt the low hum of Liam's presence, and I knew he was close. I sniffed the air, and his comforting scent wafted toward me. Cedar and spice.

Mine.

He barrelled into me as he came out of the brush, nipping at me playfully before bounding back and grinning. Then I saw his nostrils twitch, and he started to growl. His nose sniffed my wounds, and he growled louder as my blood-covered fur painted his nose red.

"What the fuck happened?" his voice slammed into me as he started licking at my wounds.

"I just took on seven wolves."

He stopped licking and looked at me. His eyes flashed with gold. *"What did you say?"*

"Circe and I took on seven wolves."

"Who?" his growl waved in a powerful downforce, but his alpha voice didn't work on me.

I rubbed against him, trying to calm him through the mate bond. *"It doesn't matter."*

"It does. They were told to leave you alone."

"When I was human, Liam. They were told to leave me alone when I was human."

"You got hurt!"

"I'll live."

"Why the fuck didn't you call me for help?"

"Circe's instincts wouldn't let me. She said we needed to do this."

"You could have died," his voice broke with emotion as he tucked his snout into my neck fur.

"But I didn't."

I pushed away from him and shifted back. Liam growled and followed suit, examining every inch of my skin. I reached up and cupped his cheek. He leaned into my palm and stared at me sadly.

"How am I supposed to protect you if you don't tell me when this shit happens, Clem? What on Earth was it about?"

"They were warning me off you. Just let it go. It's going to happen. You're a catch." I winked.

He glared at me, unamused. "You know I can smell them on you. You know I'll just go seek them out later." He crossed his arms.

"If they wanted to hurt me, they would have, but they all just got up and ran away. It was just a dominance thing. You must let me fight these battles, or I'll never learn to be a werewolf." I leaned forward and kissed him softly, sparks zapping our skin as he uncrossed his arms and wrapped them around me.

"I know. But fuck, Clemmy!" I kissed him again, trying to soothe his anxiety. I ran my fingers down his corded bicep, twirling the electricity of the mate bond. "I think I need to get back my advantage. What do you think?"

His eyes bore into mine. "What do you have in mind?"

I took a step out of his arms and ran my fingers over my breasts in tantalising circles before running them over the soft skin of my stomach. His eyes watched my digits with interest and darkened with lust as he saw where they were heading.

I watched him as I started to pleasure myself, fingers running over my slick, wet folds and up over my clitoris. He was already hard and standing at attention, his hands fisted at his sides. His eyes never left my body as I continued to rub my wetness against my clit. The smell of my heat hung heavy in the air between us. He growled and looked around as if he could sense someone else was close, but for the first time ever, I didn't care.

"Liam," I whispered. "Come claim me."

His mouth found mine, and our tongues battled for dominance. I'd removed my fingers from my wet folds and threaded them through his hair. He started kissing down my neck, and I felt myself curve forward as his tongue swirled into the marking spot. He didn't bite me, though. He continued his kisses down over my breasts, pulling one nipple between his teeth. I moaned in pleasure, thrusting my wetness against the velvety head of his thick cock.

He grinned and pulled the other one into his mouth, his hands moving over my hips and into my heat. "So fucking wet," he murmured before sucking on my nipple again. "I want to taste you."

He kissed his way down my body, kneeling. Gently, he lifted my leg and placed it over his shoulder as he plunged his tongue into my folds. I gasped as he licked the juices at my entrance and then dragged his tongue up toward my clit. His entire face was covered in my dark curls, and he groaned as he buried himself in more profoundly, tasting, running his tongue through my slit.

I gripped his hair as he sucked my clit, then thrust myself into his face while he gripped my ass tightly before he pulled back and said, "Do you like that, my responsive little mate?"

I moaned, and his tongue returned to its slow torture. I felt the pressure build and tugged his hair more aggressively. Shivering with excitement, I felt myself getting closer. He moaned, and the sound vibrated straight into my core, his tongue tormenting me as I climbed toward the edge of the precipice. Suddenly, it was too much, and I exploded all over his mouth, my legs trembling with my tumble over the edge. He moaned again, gripping my ass to support me as he continued to lick and lap up my nectar.

"How was that for claiming you?" He grinned before kissing me hard. I could taste my juices on his tongue, and it turned me on further.

"Oh no, you're not finished yet." I smiled seductively.

"Insatiable little she-wolf, aren't you?" He rubbed his cock against my wetness. "What do you want, little mate?"

"I want your mark."

He pulled back and looked at me. "Are you sure," he asked, his brown and gold eyes searching mine for any hesitation.

My mouth went dry, and I didn't think I could speak, so I nodded and kissed him again. His dick twitched against my leg.

"Okay, but let's do it properly this time."

He then lay me down on the leaf litter and placed one leg over his shoulder again. I moaned as I felt the tip of his cock at my opening. He grunted as he slid in, slowly, torturedly, inch by inch, filling me and stretching me perfectly.

"So. Fucking. Perfect." He growled, and he closed his eyes for a few seconds as if he was trying to regain some composure.

I gently thrust up against his large cock, and he moaned again. He met my thrust with one of his own, his eyes glowing with lust as he watched me rock against him from underneath.

I moaned as he started to rock with me, the pressure in my channel and against my clit building as he ground my hips into the forest floor. My arms ran over his sculpted shoulder blades, and my nails scraped his back as his speed increased, and he continued to rock and pound into me, claiming my g-spot as his.

He desperately covered my mouth with his and kissed me, his tongue licking my lips, asking for permission. I granted it happily and mewled against his mouth as he quickened the pace. His whole body slammed into my channel, against my clit, and it felt so fucking good—intense.

My body started buzzing with the build of my climax, the mate bond thickened and added to the pressure between my legs. Liam stopped kissing me and watched my face in awe as he kept pounding me, riding me into my orgasm.

"That's it, Clemmy. Come for me," he grunted as his mouth aimed for the marking spot. His teeth clamped down hard, and I instantly exploded over his thick cock. He moaned into my neck as he felt my channel convulse all over him. He pulled his teeth out of my skin, licked and kissed my neck softly.

Then he started to thrust again. "Oh, baby, you didn't think we were finished, did you?" He grinned impishly, readjusting me as he pulled himself into a kneeling position. I sat on his thighs, riding him. He held onto my hips as I arched backward in pleasure—my hands ran down the length of my torso and back up, over my breasts.

"Mine!" he growled as I fell back toward him and he wrapped his arms around my body tightly.

"Mine!" I repeated softly as I kissed him.

He pounded into me, hard and fast, grunting with each movement. The friction was different at this angle, and I already could feel the pressure building, the mate bond sparked and tickled between us.

I gave an immense shudder as the next orgasm shocked through my body. I exploded over his hard cock for the second time, and my teeth instantly found the soft spot above his collarbone. I bit down and tasted his blood. It had a subtle almond flavour with a dash of honey. His scent infused my nose, and I noticed how it started to change, deepen, and turn almost sweet and woodsy at the same time. *Mine.*

He shuddered and grunted loudly, calling my name as he thrust into me and released his load deep inside.

"Mate," I murmured into his hair when I could breathe normally enough to get the word out.

"Mate," he repeated breathlessly from in between my breasts.

CHAPTER 62
LIAM

SHE SLOWLY PULLED off me and gave me a sultry smile. I put my fingers up and gently ran them over the proudly glowing mark on my neck. It tingled to the touch, but there was no pain. Her saliva had sealed the venom inside. The bruise and teeth marks would last a few days before my werewolf healing would eventually kick in. And then she'll just have to mark me again, and again, until the next full moon. The idea excited me, and her turquoise eyes flashed at me knowingly.

The scent between us was deep and infused, and I couldn't be happier. I gently grabbed her by the back of her head and pulled her toward my face, kissing her deeply.

Mine.

Her instincts were finally beginning to be more werewolf than human. Even though I wanted to keep Clem's passionate nature all to myself and away from prying eyes, her provocative instincts made me feel insurmountable pride. She was so fucking perfect.

The bush had been full of werewolves. She knew that, but she didn't care. She had one thing on her mind: fucking and marking me. She wanted to show the pack her claim on me, and

I was more than willing to let her do so. She should have done it weeks ago. Then, the wolves who attacked her might have known their place.

I stopped kissing her and looked over her porcelain skin again. Her wounds from her fight were already healing, but Lucian's hackles were still up, and he remained agitated. Even marking her hadn't settled his nerves, nor had my being marked.

He knew Clem was right and had to learn how to be a werewolf, but it still made him uneasy. His instinct was to keep her safe and allowing her to get into fights was the complete opposite of that.

I swiftly remembered that the pack wolves weren't the only ones I needed to watch out for. Moments before succumbing to Clementine's pure temptation, I recognized a scent that shouldn't have been anywhere near the territory.

Lucian had wanted to investigate, but instead, we had let our beautiful, saucy little mate distract us from the fact he was sniffing around the border. In the end, it was fucking worth it. Even more so if *he* managed to hear and smell our coupling from wherever the fuck he was on the boundary line.

I sniffed the air again, and Lucian growled. His scent was still around, but as far as I could tell, he hadn't crossed the pack perimeter. The idea that he was out there, skulking around, just reinforced my need to become alpha.

"So, I need to tell you something, but don't freak out."

"Okay?" she asked, raising an eyebrow.

"So, um, I've decided that I'm going to take over as alpha."

"O-kay?"

"This Sunday."

"This Sunday," she repeated.

She got off my lap and stood up, crossing her arms over her stomach. I instantly got up and wrapped my arms around her.

She was about to shut down again, I just knew it. Instead, she surprised me when she shook her head and let out a deep breath before asking, "What does that mean for me?" she asked quietly.

"Officially, nothing. The pack will need a luna eventually, but just because I'm becoming alpha doesn't automatically give you that title. That title is bestowed upon you in an official ceremony, so long as you've accepted the role." I nervously bit my lip. "But unofficially, when the pack finds out we're mated, they'll start treating you as luna because it's inevitable that's what you'll become in all due time."

"Is there any way to not be luna? Can I just be me?"

"You'll always be you." I smiled softly and kissed her nose. Her frown made my stomach knot. "You don't want to be luna?"

"I'm not luna material. I'm not a leader."

"You were made my fated mate for a reason," I countered. "So it goes without saying that you were made to be luna too."

She closed her eyes, trying to control her emotions. "No one in this pack will accept me as their luna."

"Let's announce our true mate status first. I have a feeling you'll see how wrong you are."

"I'm not ready for that."

"A lot of people already know we're mated. And for the ones that don't, they'll figure it out because I'm wearing your mark, and you're wearing mine," I grunted, her scent heavy in my nostrils.

"Hopefully, people will think we are just fucking each other like before."

Pain seared through my chest, followed by quiet anger. Lucian growled at the insult she unknowingly slung our way. Did she think we were just fuck-buddies? Is that honestly how she felt?

"So, let me get this straight. You'd rather people think that we're just fucking, rather than telling them that we're mated and belong to each other in the most unbreakable and sacred way for our species? That's so fucking backward I don't even know how to start unravelling and understanding that."

She tried to break out of my hold, but I didn't loosen my grip. I placed my forehead against hers, and our noses touched. Minor zaps tingled between us as we breathed in each other's air. "It's always one step forward, six steps back with you, Clementine," I snarled my frustration, not removing my head from hers. I closed my eyes and tried to let the tingles of our mate bond calm me.

"I know. And I'm sorry," she said sadly. "Please don't get me wrong. I want to be with you. I love wearing your mark and want to be mated with you. I just wanted to keep this to ourselves. I wanted to be in a private bubble with you for a little while, and yes, eventually, we would have had to tackle the whole 'Luna is a half-breed' thing. But I hoped we would have more time to enjoy each other before the inevitable blood-hate came in. I'm not ready for the level of hate I'll get when the pack finds out we're truly mated. I'm barely holding on as it is."

Lucian whimpered as he smelled her tears forming. I could feel her inner turmoil, her anxiety over the situation. I wanted to take it away and rewrite it all for her, but I didn't know how or where to start. She took a deep breath, pulled her face away from mine and met my gaze head-on.

"I think it's great that you're coming into your birthright. It's fantastic you want to be alpha of this pack. So how about, for now, we just focus on *your* ceremony? My drama can wait for another day. We'll talk about it, I promise."

An unwanted scent invaded my nostrils before I was able to answer her. Instantly, I pushed Clementine behind me, shielding her nakedness from view as a graphite-coloured werewolf came through the trees. His blue eyes found mine, and he gave me a wolfish smirk.

"What are you doing here, Lincoln?"

"I'm patrolling the perimeter." His eyes seemed to focus on my mark, and he gave out a wolfy-chuckle. *"I thought I smelled sex. Who knew the little half-breed was such a passionate little minx?"*

"Back up, Lincoln," I snarled. *"Clemmy, shift into your wolf."*

"Oh, no, Clementine. Don't hide on my account. I always love a good show. Liam used to always take his conquests publicly. I'm sure he had Nola and Tammy out here the day after the full moon. They came back to me reeking of him, but that's the thing, they always come back after he's fucked each of them because they know I'll always fuck them better. You'll learn that soon enough, too."

Clementine's emotions were a kaleidoscope of colours down the mate bond. I tasted each one as if they were my own. Disbelief, resentment, sadness, anger, and distrust all appeared. He was trying to get her to distrust me and weaken our bond. The bond stayed strong, but her final emotions landed on anger and then I could no longer feel them.

Shit!

"But once again, your face is a major turn-off, so I'll be pounding into your ass. Come on, half-breed, give me a look and prove to me it's an ass worth fucking."

"You really do have a death wish! Say one more thing like that about my true mate, and I swear, come Sunday, you will no longer have a place in this pack."

His eyes met mine as he gave a wolfy chuckle. *"Uh. Yes. I did hear Clementine say something about your ceremony. But then, I also heard her say that you two are just fucking, so it sounds like this alleged mate bond might be one-sided. Good thing, too. Whores like her don't make good lunas."*

A feral snarl vibrated out of me, and I felt my nails turn into claws as I started to half-shift. He really did have a death wish. Before I could charge forward and end his miserable life, I felt a soothing sensation down the mate bond and cool fingers grabbing onto my hand. Clem gave my fingers a gentle squeeze. She didn't speak, but I felt her serenity down the mate bond, telling me not to take the bait.

Her calmness was refreshingly cold against my fiery anger. I stopped my half-shift and pushed her further backward, only opening a channel to her.

"Clemmy, please shift. I'm right behind you."

I heard a crack and pop before I felt her cold, wet nose touch my hand and give me a gentle lick. She came next to me and growled softly at Lincoln, raising her hackles, and putting her head low. Circe was giving him another warning before she flicked her tail and disappeared behind a shrub.

I glared at Lincoln and spoke loudly, Lucian's voice amplifying mine, "I'm serious, Lincoln. The next time you disrespect your future luna like that, you will fucking wish you were dead. Get back to fucking work."

And then, in the ultimate insult, I turned my back on him before I shifted. I felt his anger behind me and smirked as I bounded after my mate.

"You know that what he said was utter bullshit, right?" I said to Clem as I flanked her side. *"I haven't been with any other she-wolf since you and I started seeing each other. You're my world, Clem. I need you to know that."*

"I know."

"I felt your emotions as he said that stuff, Clem. I felt your anger and distrust."

"Toward him. Not you. I don't trust Lincoln at all. I trust you explicitly."

"That's good because the idea of hurting you, cheating on you, is abhorrent to me."

"I know. Circe keeps reminding me of that. And I can feel your sincerity through this bond. Lincoln won't take that trust away from me."

"That's what he's trying to do. He's trying to weaken our bond. He's a fucking asshole. And I've always hated him."

"I don't like him either. You know I've met his wolf before, right?"

"I know. I smelled him on you the day you broke your ankle."

"Why didn't you say anything?"

"You were human, Clem. I was protecting you. Or at least trying to. After I left you at the doctor's, I went straight to my dad and demanded his exile."

She stopped and looked at me, tilting her head. *"Really?"*

"Yeah, but Dad refused. He told me I had a personal vendetta against him and that it was clouding my judgement." Lucian huffed in annoyance. *"Dad goes on about how being alpha is to trust my instincts, and ever since I was a pup, my instincts have told me not to trust Lincoln. We've always been at each other's throats. Dad simply saw two pups with a beef. He saw jealousy on Lincoln's part, arrogance on mine, and nothing other than a typical rivalry. But Dad didn't feel what I felt when I looked at Lincoln. What I still feel."*

"And what do you feel?"

"That he's fucking dangerous."

"Yeah. I feel that too." She nodded her head and approached me. *"But don't worry, Liam. I'll protect you,"* Clem said cutely, rubbing her snout into my neck fur.

I rumbled happily at the sensation, smelling myself infused into her fur and feeling the sparks fly into my soul as the mate bond thickened a little more.

CHAPTER 63

CLEMENTINE

CIRCE GRUMBLED as I tried to cover my mark with my hair. She found it incredibly insulting that I would do such a thing. I tried to tell her that I found it unprofessional to attend work with a hickey, and she just scoffed.

"That's human thinking, Clementine. Did you see Ryan hiding Stacey's mark? Do you see anyone else hiding their mate's mark?"

"At least the mate mark is subtle. This is a gigantic purple bruise."

"The mating mark starts as a purple bruise too." She rolled her eyes. *"I thought you were excited about his mark. Do I need to remind you how turned on you got thinking about it? Or how turned on you were when he was physically marking you? You wanted this."*

"I did."

"Then why are you so anxious about showing the world you got what you wanted."

"If Nola sees it–"

"That bitch is beneath us." Circe rolled her eyes. *"She's going to smell it anyway. So, you may as well hold your head high and show it off. Don't let her or your anxiety win. Show her that even though she*

and her cronies attacked us, you'll still get the guy. Liam gave you back your advantage just like you asked him to. It's time to show your hand."

I looked in the mirror and smiled as I swept my hair up, braiding the top and swooping the remainder into a messy bun. Then I grabbed my bag and left the cottage, ready to walk to work. I sniffed the air and smelled my mate in the alpha's office inside the pack house.

Ever since the full moon, I was more attuned to where he was, and what he was thinking and feeling. That alone could be overwhelming, let alone our sexual desire for one another, which had amplified. It also became more intense every time we were intimate—the mate bond was working hard to solidify us. I now realized why most werewolves went radio silent, and I grumped that Liam was a ranked wolf. If I had my way, I would have abandoned work and given into my instincts. Repeatedly.

I felt the mate bond twinge, and I knew Liam had felt my unclothed desire. I felt his smile, and the promise of 'later' came down the bond. I could almost hear the gruffness of his tone, and I giggled excitedly. Circe paced, hating the idea that we both had responsibilities and couldn't just give into our instincts.

Lupus' came into view, and I smiled at Circe, who fluffed herself up and held her head high. She flicked her tail and then nodded at me, giving me a boost of confidence as I bounced up to the entrance. I entered, and Nola's reaction was instantaneous. I tried not to smirk. She went rigid before she spun around and looked at me coldly. Her blue eyes were an icy fire as they zoomed in on the mark displayed proudly on my neck.

"Good afternoon, Nola," I said as pleasantly as possible. I

went to walk past her when Circe had other ideas. "Too bad you didn't stick around earlier. You would have been in for a treat. I'm not usually one for public displays, but shit, when Alpha Liam wants me that badly, sometimes I just have to submit to him. Let's be honest here, he's the only wolf I would ever submit to."

Nola snarled, and her eyes flashed. Straw-coloured tufts of fur, the exact same shade as her hair, sprouted over her arms as she fought to get her wolf under control. Then Circe made me spin on my heel and show Nola my back. The waves of anger rippled off Nola, and I suddenly felt like Circe had made matters ten times worse.

"Fuck, Circe! You don't need to antagonize her. Need I remind you that I still don't know how to fight?"

"Tell everyone you're his mate, and they'll back off."

"Or they'll get fucking worse. I want to learn how to fight before I do that. Throwing a half-assed punch doesn't count as knowing how to fight."

"You shouldn't be scared of these fucking bitches. Once they know you're luna, they'll bow down. It's in their instincts. That's what Liam was telling you earlier: if you announce you're mated, they'll naturally fall in line."

"Can we stop arguing about this?" I snapped.

"Can you stop being so fucking human?" she snarled back.

I moved toward the office and put my bag down. Tina was sitting behind her desk and mind-linking judging by her vacant expression.

"Close the door," she snapped. I closed it, and she motioned to the seat in front of her desk. Her eyes seemed to focus on Liam's mark, and it was a minute or so before she spoke. She seemed to be choosing her words carefully.

"Nola had to go out and run. She was in no state to work."

"Okay," I said.

"Is that all you have to say?"

"What else would you like me to say?" I asked her, confused. "Nola is a loose cannon. If she can't control her wolf, that's on her. Not me." Circe smirked, and I realized that I had said that. Not Circe.

Fuck.

"I've lost a waitress because of this rivalry between you both."

I rolled my eyes. "She'll be back when she calms down."

"Clem, she's in love with Liam." Circe raised her hackles and snarled. "She has been for years. You're flaunting your relationship all over town, bringing it to my bar. She's going to react. I warned Liam of this months ago when Cassie threw wine on you. The she-wolves all want to be mated with him, yet here you are flaunting his mark." I ran my hands over the mark on my collarbone. Circe growled low in warning.

"She doesn't fucking love Liam," I snapped, feeling Circe's anger. "She's sleeping with Lincoln."

"You're new to these pack dynamics, but wolves often share at the beginning. She may be with Lincoln, but it's obvious she's waiting for Liam to pick her exclusively. She wants to be luna."

I snarled angrily, losing composure, and feeling a possessive instinct surge through me. "Over my dead body!"

"That's what I'm worried about, Clem," Tina growled back. "She's going to fucking kill you if this doesn't stop."

"She won't fucking touch me. I'm her luna," Circe voiced through me.

"No, you're not. Liam's picked you, but the pack has to accept you–"

"Liam has promised they will accept me," I said, pushing an irate Circe back.

"Stop being so ignorant, Clementine. There's still blood-hate in this pack. You'll never be luna. No one will accept that he's chosen you as his mate. You're best to split it off with him now. Trust me on this," Tina said, reconfirming my earlier apprehensions about this whole thing.

"You want me to reject Liam?" I whimpered.

"What?" She tilted her head at me, and her eyes softened slightly. "No, Clementine. The rejection only happens in two situations. If you've already mate bonded and you want to split up, or if you are true mates and you don't want to be. Both times, it's excruciating, but you haven't mated yet, so it'll just be as simple as telling him you don't want it. You'd be telling him to pick someone else to mate with."

"Wait," I said, screwing up my face and looking into her hazel eyes. "You think that Liam asked to be my mate?"

"Yes. That's what a bar full of people heard after your ex-boyfriend showed up in town and tried to claim you. Liam claimed that you had already agreed to be his mate." Tina gave me a small smile. "Nothing happens in my bar without me knowing about it, even when I have a day off."

"No, Tina." I shook my head. "Liam and I didn't choose this. It was chosen for us." I said super softly, and the mate bond hummed around my body.

Tina's eyebrows furrowed, then her eyes went wide with surprise. "You're true mates?"

"Yes. I can't reject him. It would destroy him. It would destroy this pack."

"Then you need to announce it."

"You just said that the she-wolves would never follow me."

"This is why you need to announce it. The she-wolves think this is Liam's choice. They don't know it's fated. There may still be a few that hate the idea, but no one can deny that a true-mate bond is sacred."

"I don't think I'm ready for people to know."

Tina looked at me sadly. "Being luna means that you no longer have that luxury. Being luna means you put the pack first, and in doing so, it might just save you from further animosity."

I WORKED BEHIND THE BAR, making cocktail after cocktail, and thought about what Tina had said. Whenever a she-wolf looked at me, there was tension in the air, but no one approached me. They'd seen Liam's mark on me before and probably thought we were just fucking, like I had told Liam. I frowned. That idea was starting to bother me.

Stacey bounded to the bar, breaking my train of thought as she leaned over to kiss Ryan.

"Can we go talk, Clementine?" she asked me softly.

"Stacey, now isn't the time," Ryan said, shaking his head. She gave him a frustrated look.

Now what? "Sure, Stacey. I'm due for a break anyway." I sighed, moving out from behind the bar and indicating for her to follow. Ryan made a low grumbling noise.

She followed me onto the patio, and I sat at one of the outside tables. "Can you ask Liam to lift the ban on my brother coming into Blackfern Valley?" she said, not wasting time.

"Why would I do that?" I asked wide-eyed.

"This whole thing has been a huge misunderstanding. He had no idea that you were mated. If Ryan takes the beta position, then I'll be moving to the pack house, and I would like my brother to be able to visit. I would ask Liam myself, but this ban is about you. You'll be the only one to convince him you're not in any danger from Brady."

"Your brother attacked Liam for staking his rightful claim on me."

"You know how wolf instincts work now, Clem. He got swept up in the moment."

"He didn't even sense Liam was an alpha," I muttered.

"Because he was so focused on you. It broke his heart that you're mated to Liam." Stacey smiled softly. "Brady broke down and told me that you were the love of his life, and you broke his heart back in Vancouver. He said it broke twice over when he discovered you were mated. He isn't a threat. I promise."

"Then why was he skulking around the pack border when he was told never to come back again?" I asked her.

"What?"

"Yeah. Liam and I were having an intimate moment, and I smelled your brother in the forest. He was spying on us. On me."

"Wait! You knowingly had sex with Liam when my brother was close?" She frowned. "Do you know how much that would have hurt him? I didn't think you were that vindictive." Her voice was hard. Circe bristled.

"What did you just say? Werewolves always get swept up in the moment," I replied without emotion.

She shook her head as if she didn't want to get into an argument. "Look, I think he just wants to apologize to you—to Liam. He isn't a bad person. You must remember that?"

Circe started to laugh hard. She tried to push forward to let Stacey know what her brother was really like. I didn't think her blunt and abrupt personality would help matters right now. This required a little more finesse. So, I pushed Circe back.

"Stacey. There's a reason the relationship between your brother and I didn't last–"

"Yeah, he told me you broke up when your mom was in hospice. He said you shut him out."

"Really? Is that what he said?" I bristled. Raw grief tried to push its way forward. Circe rumbled lowly and her hackles rose. She didn't like that he talked about my mom, nor did I.

"He doesn't blame you, Clem." She reached out and patted my hand. "He knows everyone grieves differently." My mouth fell open and fresh pain seared through me. I felt the tears prickle in my eyes and wiped them harshly. "Oh, Clem," Stacey mewled. She got out of her seat and gave me an awkward cuddle. "I'm sorry, but maybe this is why you should talk with Brady. It may help you heal. Brady is hurting too. It would be good for both of you to talk."

"What?" I said venomously.

"Well, I obviously brought up some painful memories for you. You both need closure, or you'll go on in life with regrets."

I closed off my emotions fast, then gently untangled her arms from around my shoulders. "Stacey. There's no way Liam will go for lifting this ban, even if I wanted to suggest it, which I don't."

She let herself drop down to her chair and glared at me. "Why are you being such a bitch, Clementine?"

"I'm not being a bitch, Stacey. I'm protecting myself, my alpha and this pack from your sadistic brother. I'm trying to be a luna. If you don't like it, you know where the exit is," I said through gritted teeth.

I stood up and stalked off, but not toward the bar. I needed space from everyone. It had been an exhausting three hours of work. I needed to go home.

I quickly mind-linked Tina and apologized before I reached out and instantly found Ryan's soft-brown and mossy aroma of his pattern scent.

"I'm out of here. Go comfort Stacey."

"What happened?"

"I told her that Brady's ban was staying, that I was protecting the pack from a sadistic asshole."

"I told her not to ask. She's blind when it comes to him, Clem."

"He has that effect on people."

"I'm sorry."

"Don't be. I feel like I made my first official ruling as a luna."

"Keeping Brady out shows me what a great luna you'll be."

CHAPTER 64

LIAM

THE PACK WAS abuzz with the news that I was taking over as alpha. Dad had sent out a pack announcement a few hours ago, and I already had an exhausting number of people congratulating me down the mind-link, making it very hard to concentrate on the alpha duties I had in front of me.

I understood being the alpha would come with distractions, and I honestly didn't mind them, especially if they came from my challenging but perfect mate. She had almost distracted me from my duties earlier when I felt her desire through our bond. But it had been silent ever since. I frowned. She hadn't contacted me when she heard the news. I wondered if Lupus' patrons were giving her a hard time.

I reached down the mate bond and was surprised to feel she was closer than the bar. I quickly finished my job and pushed myself out from behind my desk. I left the office and went straight to her house. I found her sitting on the window seat in her room, enjoying the afternoon sun.

"Everything okay?" I asked, crossing the room in three strides, and sitting behind her.

"Yeah, everything's fine." She sighed, leaning into me, and inhaling my scent.

Lucian rumbled happily as I wrapped my arms around her. "You're not at work?" I asked carefully.

"No, I wasn't up to it. I have more important things on my mind right now."

"Like what?" I asked.

"I have been thinking about our situation. Tina advised me that I need to tell people about our mate bond." Lucian's ears perked up. "Nola, in particular, took it hard that you marked me after her not-so-subtle warning to stay away. Tina also suggested that if people knew you didn't just choose me, but the moon did, they might be more accepting of a half-breed as their luna."

"Clem. I would have chosen you either way," I said earnestly. "And I was ready for the reprimand from the pack for choosing a human as a mate. Remember, I was ready to renounce my title and be with you."

"Yeah. I would have never allowed you to do that. You were made to lead this pack," she growled.

"And you were made to lead next to me," I growled back, tilting her chin up and capturing her lips softly.

She moaned into my mouth as the sparks flew between us. Her fingers ran into my hair, and she pressed her lips harder against mine, opening her mouth and offering me her tongue. My body buzzed under her affectionate touch.

She pulled away and gave me a small smile.

"I know. And although I'm not ready to be luna, I know it's inevitable, and I should just get over myself. I should allow you to tell people and just deal with whatever fallout happens as it happens. As long as you're by my side, I think it will be okay."

"I'm never leaving your side," I promised her.

"But I don't want our bond to take away from the fact you're going to be alpha. I thought maybe you could announce it after your ceremony."

"That sounds good to me," I said, beaming at her. I gave her another quick kiss. "Is this why you left work?"

"No, not entirely."

She pulled her plump lower lip between her teeth.

Fuck, I love it when she does that.

I was already sporting a semi from the moment I smelled her, from knowing how responsive she was; that just a few hours ago, I felt her desire down the mate bond. And only an hour before that, I had fucked and marked her, relishing in her marking me in return. I really wanted to bite onto her lip and coax those little moans out of her again. I sniffed my mark on her neck, and my semi turned to granite.

"Brady has been skulking around," she murmured.

That dampened my arousal.

Shit. "I know. I smelled him. But, Clemmy, I promise you he's not going to touch a hair on your head."

"Stacey tried to reason with me on getting his ban lifted."

"I hope you told her to fuck off!" Lucian's voice blended with mine as I tightened my protective hold around Clementine. Brady was never getting to her. Ever.

"Oh, Circe wanted to tell her a whole range of things. She's blinded by her brother, Liam. And as alpha, you need to be aware of her devotion toward him. Especially if she moves into the pack house."

"You think she'll defy my orders?"

"No, not at all. Stacey will be very loyal to her alpha. Her brother is just very manipulative and crafty. I just wanted you to be in the know. I could never live with myself if something happened to you. So please, be careful around Brady." Her voice came out sounding both concerned and protective, with subtleties of Circe flashing in her eyes.

"Don't worry, Luna. I will be." I cupped her chin and kissed her softly.

A warm feeling trickled down the mate bond, and I recognized it as the same emotion I felt the night of the full moon, the one I had committed to memory. It tasted of happiness, unyielding trust, warmth, respect, and comfort. It tasted of love.

Lucian yipped excitedly in my head. Was that what the feeling was? Did Clementine love me? My chest glowed, and I felt my eyes prickle as I basked in that notion.

Deepening our kiss, Clem had repositioned herself within seconds, placing her knees on either side of my hips, my already hardened cock hitting her heated core as she straddled me. She pulled her t-shirt up and over her head, and with the pure carnal look she gave me, the rest of the conversation was forgotten.

***

SUNDAY MORNING ROLLED AROUND, and I grinned as I snuck under the covers to wake my mate by kissing her stomach and moving toward her irresistible pussy. I couldn't get enough of her taste. She moaned and gasped as my tongue found her sweet spot.

"Liam," she chastised through moans of pleasure. "What are you doing?"

"Waking up, my beautiful luna."

"Well, Alpha, there are other ways to do that. Especially when you have a busy day ahead," she said, pulling my head up toward her mouth. I kissed her deeply, allowing her to taste herself on my tongue. She gave a sexy moan, and my body reacted.

"My favourite way to wake you up is with my mouth

between your legs. You're delicious." My voice was full of wild desire.

"Uh, yes, but if you start that, we will never get to your ceremony. You know how distracted we can get."

"I can be quick," I said, kissing my mark on her neck and thrusting my erection against her.

"No, you can't. But if you get up and get all your alpha stuff done, I swear you can tie me to this bed and fuck me until there's no feeling in your dick. Trust me, baby, I know how to serve my alpha, but he has to become alpha first." She nibbled at my earlobe. "And I'm talking hours of pleasurable reward."

Excitement flooded me at her suggestion, and I bit down excitedly on her mark. I knew it wouldn't give the same effect that the mate bond would, but she still gasped, and I smelled her instant arousal filling the air as her eyes ringed with her lustful wolf.

"I'll be thinking about that all day. Are you sure you don't want to help me with my erection right now? It might be embarrassing if I go to the ceremony flying high."

"Go take a cold shower. That'll help," she said, shivering as I kissed and grazed her neck with my teeth again.

"Join me?"

"Not a chance. We need to get you ready for your ceremony."

"We'll conserve water that way."

"No, we won't because you'll end up fucking me against the wall, taking your sweet ass time, making us use more water." She grinned playfully. "Then we'll dry off, and you'll bend me over and fuck me again. Of course, we would have to shower the smell of sex off, which will result in more shower sex and then you'll miss your coronation."

"There is no crown, sweetheart," I quipped as my erection got more painful at the idea of bending her over.

She smacked me playfully on the arm. "You know what I mean."

"Just a quick shower with me. I promise we won't be late."

"Later," she growled.

I groaned and rolled away from her. She reached out and swatted my ass with a decent slap.

"Do that again, and I'll retaliate," I warned. Lucian was begging for her to do it again. She smirked and gave me innocent doe eyes. "Little minx," I growled as I walked toward the massive ensuite of the alpha's bedroom. Cold shower it was going to be.

THE PARTY WAS in full swing by early evening, and the barbecues had all been lit. Festoon lights were streamed up along the amphitheatre, grandstand and training grounds, and music was blasting out of speakers as people chatted and waited for sunset.

Everyone was dressed up for the occasion. The men were in button-downs, and the women were all in summer dresses. Even the pups had outdone themselves with their attire. My mother, father and I made the rounds, chatting with pack members and taking the time to socialize. A few she-wolves tried to catch my attention as I walked through the crowd. Lucian scoffed at the absurdity that they thought they even stood a chance. There was only one she-wolf who would ever get my attention.

I spotted Clementine talking with Sophie, and I was tempted to take her away from the party and have a private party of our own. She sensed me watching her and gave me a shy smile before turning her attention back to her conversation.

She'd left her thick hair down around her shoulders and had

applied a small amount of makeup, not that she needed it. She wore a beautiful new blue dress that hugged her curves deliciously. She told me she had bought it mainly for the occasion. Then she also told me that she had bought sexy lingerie to go under it for after the ceremony, tempting me even further to abandon the party and steal her away from prying eyes.

I stood on the amphitheatre stage and looked at Clem, standing with her father and brother. I wanted her to take her rightful place next to me, but she reminded me repeatedly that she couldn't distract the pack from what was happening. She didn't want her being up there to cause discord. She would join me once I became alpha when we announced to the pack that she was my true mate.

People started to move at sunset. Thousands of people crammed into the amphitheatre. The pups were all at the front, sitting on the grass, and the adults were all squeezed in behind them, some sitting, some standing. The grandstand and training grounds were also full.

Holy shit!

My dad gave his speech, and my nerves ramped up. Lucian paced anxiously in my mind, so to calm myself down, I focused on Clementine's scent, our mate bond, her clear turquoise eyes swimming in adoration and pride. I turned back to my father but kept my focus on my mate, grounding myself in my love for her. And damn did I love her.

Lucian smiled at me before warm happiness infused my entire being, and I felt it go down the mate bond. She gave me a small smile as she felt the emotion. Did she recognize it?

Does she know I love her?

Before I could mind-link and tell her that's what it was, my father caught my attention and in his hand was the ceremonial dagger. I smiled at Dad as he cut my palm. My blood bubbled, but Lucian made no attempt to heal it. I took the knife and cut Dad's in turn.

"And with my final alpha command, I give my power to my first born and heir, Liam Henderson. May my power and leadership be passed unto him, and through him, for he is the pack and the pack is him. Liam, do you accept your duty as alpha of this pack?"

"I humbly accept my duty as alpha of the Blackfern Valley Pack," Lucian's voice merged with mine, rumbling loudly through the amphitheatre as Dad gripped my hand. A large jolt zapped through us, and I felt immense power wash over me.

A loud whooshing sound rang out, followed by silence and then cheering. My entire body felt hot, and Lucian let out a howl in my head which vibrated through my teeth.

I heard the call, *come back*, then my father shouted, "Your new alpha!" The cheers and howling continued, and I heard something that made my blood run cold.

"I challenge Alpha Liam to the position of alpha of the Blackfern Valley Pack."

CLEMENTINE

LIAM GRIPPED his father's hand, and both men erupted into a large orange glow. The air around them shimmered with power, and Liam started to grow larger as if it were possible. He was already a muscly, marbled god, but now, his shoulders seemed to become slightly broader with the power of an alpha. His arm muscles bulged out of the short sleeves of his button-down, and the buttons began to strain with his chest getting wider.

The alpha power whooshed throughout the amphitheatre, taking away my breath for a second. Liam's scent and power wafted over to me, and the mate bond vibrated, making me clench my legs together to hold back a moan of pleasure that rocketed through me. Circe wagged her tail and yipped excitedly as she witnessed her mate's metamorphosis.

Liam and Josiah had stopped glowing, and I knew it was finished. Liam confirmed that by sending out a mighty howl that connected everyone in the pack. I had no choice but to return it, as did the rest of the pack. I was bursting with insurmountable pride and warmth. I was so happy for him that I howled a second time.

"Brace yourself, Clementine. He's about to announce us as his

true mate. Then, let's take him back to the alpha quarters and give those new muscles a decent ride," Circe said in a lust-filled tone. I grinned back at her and couldn't help but agree. It had been a fun party, but I was more than ready to take it to a more private setting and show him the lacy lingerie I'd purchased for the occasion. And if he so desired, I would allow him to tie me to his bed as promised earlier. My body began to bubble with anticipation.

"I challenge Alpha Liam to the position of alpha of the Blackfern Valley Pack," a loud voice rang out.

My blood ran cold, and Circe immediately snarled, angry and insulted.

Silence washed over the amphitheatre. Tension covered the pack in a thick, unwanted blanket. The voice rang out again, clear, and strong, amplified across the area.

"I, Lincoln James, only living son of the late Alpha Jed Henderson, challenge Alpha Liam to the rightful position of alpha." I spun and looked at Lincoln as if he had lost his ever-loving mind, and then I felt an unexpected surge of alpha power roll off him.

Before now, he only had the power of a warrior. I hadn't sensed any alpha blood in him. And by the looks of it, no one else in the pack had either. But we were all feeling it now. Even in human form, it was overwhelming, and it tasted sour and tangy on my tongue.

My gaze snapped toward Liam, and I saw his eyes flash with pure hatred for his lifelong nemesis. I looked around the pack. Everyone had gone wide-eyed and instantly started to part as if the power from both alpha wolves were directing them to.

"Absolutely, Lincoln," Liam said with no emotion. "I accept your challenge. We can do it tomorrow at sunset."

"Tomorrow?" he roared, insulted. "I've waited ten years for this! Ever since that weak excuse you call a father got lucky and killed mine. You came to school so fucking proud of him. You turned into the golden boy that day. The heir that could do no wrong. But Alpha Jed already had an heir. Me. I couldn't wait to knock you down and make you suffer, and I'll be damned if I have to wait any longer."

"Alpha Jed fathered no pups. He killed them before they even got a chance to take a breath," Sean snarled, stepping forward angrily but remained behind his brother.

"Fuck, the ignorance really runs deep in your family. Glad I take mostly after my mother. Alpha Jed slept with his beta's mate. Repeatedly. Like most Henderson's, Jed was arrogant, and hiding me in plain sight has been the perfect disguise this entire time. Mama told me to hide my power, that it would get me killed. So that's what I've done. And I'm done hiding it. I've waited twenty-three years to be alpha, and I'm not waiting another second. Liam, I challenge you for the title of alpha. I challenge you to a fight to the death. Right now!"

Circe pressed forward and roared. I felt a hand around my wrist and saw my dad's fingers gripping it tight. I tried to pull out of his grip. I needed to get to Liam. I had to. My body thrummed with the need to protect my mate. I was going to kill Lincoln. I didn't know how, but I knew I would kill him. Circe was frothing at the mouth, and I felt my fingernails elongate into claws.

"You can't, Clemmy!" Dad's voice was firm in my mind.

"Dad! Let me go! I need–"

"You need to listen to me, Clem. You can't interfere with this! Liam needs to take the challenge. He needs to show his pack he's the rightful alpha. You can't get involved. It's Pack Law, Clemmy."

Circe snarled and paced my mind, her hackles raised. Dad wrapped his arms tightly around my shoulders and used his bodyweight to hold me back.

"Push Circe back, Clemmy. You can't shift right now. You can't

do anything to distract Liam. It could get him killed. He needs to focus on the fight, not his mate."

Circe whimpered and reluctantly relented. I could tell she would be ready to spring forward at a moment's notice, if needed. She might have backed off, but she continued to snarl and paced as we anxiously watched the challenge unfold.

Mocha eyes ringed in perfect gold found mine before they flicked back to Lincoln. I felt the bond tighten with the same warm and comforting feeling he sent me moments ago before it cut off abruptly, and I was left with a black abyss of nothing. I wasn't upset with this block. I instinctively knew that there was no malice behind it. He was putting me somewhere safe so that I wouldn't distract him, so he could focus on the task at hand. The best thing to do would be to leave, but I couldn't. There's no way in hell I was letting Liam do this alone.

"Fine, it's your funeral," Liam responded callously.

"You're so fucking arrogant, and that's what'll get you killed. I've had ten years to prepare for this day. While you were out there fucking around with she-wolves and unworthy half-breeds, I was training as a warrior and building my pack from inside yours."

He let out a sharp whistle, and suddenly, a hundred or so people pushed forward. There were a lot of faces I didn't recognize, but there were a few at the front, grinning from ear to ear that I did. Nola and Tammy were there, as was a young she-wolf with silver hair that I instantly recognized as the small grey wolf. There were a couple of male wolves I recognized from the bar, but everyone else wasn't familiar. I glanced at Vinny and noticed that he also could identify a few of the wolves. They weren't looking at Lincoln or Liam. They were watching Vinny and me as if they were awaiting orders.

Josiah and Sierra moved forward angrily, and Liam threw

out his hand to stop them. Dad growled, and he moved his position to stand in front of both of us.

"Dad?" Vinny asked, reading his body language.

"Fucking blood-haters," he spat as his body started to half-shift. Perseus had gone into protective mode, and my dad would get hurt if he fought.

"Dad–"

"No, we must get you and Vinny out of here."

"Stand the fuck down. I'm not leaving my mate," I growled. A small amount of power came through my words which shocked me. Dad shivered a little and looked at me, perplexed at my sudden power.

"Yes, Luna," he murmured, although he looked severely unhappy about it.

Wait, was that some kind of luna power? Did I just command him?

Lincoln's smooth voice resonated across the area. "Your old man thought we were just a small group of misfits to watch. He didn't realize I was their alpha. I'll order my pack to bring me the half-breeds once I have your head. But for now, it's time to take your pack from you."

THE FIGHT STARTED, and it wasn't like anything I had ever witnessed before. Liam came flying off the stage toward Lincoln. Both alphas were twisting and moving with such speed that it was hard to see what was going on. As Liam twisted, he half-shifted into his wolf. It was like his body was made of light, the way it bent and moved, giving him the strength and agility of his wolf while keeping him upright. Lincoln met each move with precision and grace but had hardly shifted himself. Years of warrior training had given him an advantage. Lincoln was just playing with him.

The crowd parted and gave them more room. Lincoln's pack members moved throughout the crowd, making it hard to watch everything all at once. I didn't care about them. I only cared about Liam. I observed as the two alphas forced themselves halfway between the stage and the training grounds, and the crowd moved in behind them. A large wall of people was suddenly between my mate and me. Circe's hackles rose, but we knew we couldn't distract them. We would stay put as long as we could still see what was going on.

Liam's eyes glowed, and his teeth were sharp. He lunged forward; his claws extended as he aimed for Lincoln's throat. Lincoln kicked him off and chuckled. Then Lincoln finally stopped taunting him and attacked.

It sounded like boulders colliding with each hit. A torrent of suffocating downward pressure was emitted from the two alphas with every blow. The pack members were too afraid to leave. Or maybe it was that they were compelled to stay.

Lincoln made a guttural noise as Liam got an advantage and managed to scrape his claws down his torso before running behind him, fully shifting, and sinking his teeth into Lincoln's calf. It only lasted a second before Lincoln entirely shifted too.

The wolves snarled and snapped. Black and brown fur flew as the fight progressed. Lincoln seemed to realize that they were equally matched in this form. He shifted back, and as Liam went to copy, Lincoln's fist collided with his nose halfway through the change, breaking it with a sickening crunch.

Liam stood back and spat out blood. Both men were naked, sweaty, bruised and covered in superficial scrapes. Neither alpha cared about their lack of clothing; both were too focused on killing the other. Lincoln was grinning with excitement and malice, and Liam barrelled forward again. Lincoln's eyes went vacant for a brief second before he feigned and avoided Liam's teeth by mere millimetres.

"Oh, good. My friend's just arrived. I hope you don't mind that I invited someone else to witness your demise." He gestured to the other side of the crowd as he dodged another deadly blow from Liam. I looked in the direction he pointed in and saw two crystal blue eyes staring straight at me. Lincoln was grinning as if he'd already won. Brady was here. "I told my friend Brady that he could have your half-breed whore after I finished with you, but now that I'm thinking about it, I may have to change our agreement." Liam growled, and Circe echoed it in my head. "I'm now thinking I may bring you to the brink of death but not kill you straight away. Instead, I'll make you watch as I fuck Clementine from behind and slit her throat slowly. What do you think about that?"

Brady's lip curled in defiance as he heard the counteroffer. He glared at the two alphas before his focus zoomed in on me again. His eyes were calculating, and Circe's hackles rose in response.

"I think you talk too much," Liam snarled. But I could tell he was momentarily distracted as his desire to protect me was sent down our reopened connection. I could taste his anger, panic, and desperation on my tongue. It sizzled and made me thirsty. I could feel his need for me, and I knew that the distraction of Brady had worked. Lincoln was playing dirty. The mind-link opened to at least four other members of the pack and me.

"Keep that fucker away from your luna. Keep her safe while I take this fucker out!" Then the mind-link went blank again, and the fighting continued.

I looked around and saw Ryan making his way toward me. Stacey's eyes were wide as she looked between her brother and me. Her panic was evident as she tried to keep an eye on the fight, an eye on me and one on Brady. I could see her loyalties were torn.

Both wolves snarled as they fought. Liam became more desperate in his moves. But being desperate didn't make him any more skilled. Lincoln had the advantage. Both were fluid as they fully shifted between human and wolf and back again in this world's deadliest dance.

My heart stopped beating. Human-Lincoln had caught my mate as he shifted back, and it looked like he was about to deliver a mortal blow. My face drained of colour. My blood froze.

This can't be happening!

Circe started to howl in my head.

"You said something about slitting my mate's throat? Good idea!" Liam quickly broke out of the hold and slashed his black claw along Lincoln's creamy neck. This happened at the exact moment Lincoln's claws pierced Liam's marbled stomach, sinking in deeply like it was made of butter.

I started pushing through the crowd, and it felt like I was pushing against quicksand. Ryan and Stacey were instantly next to me, urging the crowd to part. Vinny was tucked in safely behind me as Dad, Sophie, and a couple of other wolves I barely knew started protecting my blindside as I tried to make it to my mate in time.

Liam fell to the ground at the same time Lincoln did, almost embracing each other like brothers. Lincoln's claws retracted from Liam's stomach, and his fingers went straight to his neck to try and stop the bleeding, but it was no use. The tear was so deep that crimson blood oozed between his fingers immediately.

I wasn't focused on Lincoln's final moments which were unravelling in slow motion around us. I could only see the open wound, quickly losing blood onto the trampled ground from Liam, and then my mate went limp and closed his eyes.

"We need a doctor!" Josiah yelled out as he ran across the dirt-covered ground, followed by Sierra and Sean. He ripped his button-down shirt off and pressed it into Liam's wound. People started screaming, and panic weaved through the pack. The she-wolves began weeping, and everyone seemed to be useless. They were all in my way, and I needed to get to my mate. I needed to help stop the bleeding. My head was clear from panic, and my feet moved of their own accord as my instincts drove me forward. I growled and physically tried to push people out of the way, Circe offering her strength as I moved through the wall of people toward Liam.

"Move!" I shouted.

Sean looked up and saw Ryan trying to get me through the crowd. He tugged on his dad's arm and pointed.

"Move," shouted Sean and Josiah simultaneously, their joint alpha powers finally allowing people to stop screaming and dissipate. "Make way for your luna." Josiah snapped. It had the opposite effect of what he'd hoped for. The she-wolves snarled at me angrily and didn't want me near Liam. But every time one came to attack me, they were met by one of my entourage.

I finally made it to my mate. Josiah's blue shirt and fingers were now heavy with blood. I needed to stop the bleeding. Cool calmness ran over me even though I was petrified of losing Liam.

"Sean, shirt!" I commanded him. Sean ripped off his shirt, the buttons flying everywhere. I threw their father's blood-sodden shirt to the ground and quickly replaced it with Liam's brother's. Josiah backed up to give me some room and joined my entourage in protecting his heir.

The injury looked deadly, and he had already lost so much blood, but I had to try. The crowd parted, and I saw the doctor racing toward me with a field medic bag. The mate bond hummed low as I pressed into his wound, and I prayed that it would start to heal him, but I could tell it was weakened. It was as if every fibre of our bond was being snipped one by one. It felt like the moonlight that had joined our souls was dimming and falling into the darkness where shadows were invading. Circe tried to give me strength, anything to stop the flow of our mate's life source, as the doctor skidded to a halt beside us, and opened his bag.

"Liam, open your eyes. Please," I begged. He did, and his warm brown and gold orbs found mine.

"Luna," he breathed softly. He placed his bloodied hand on my face and ran his fingers lovingly over my cheek. He stared at me like I was the most beautiful thing in the world. Choking a little, he grimaced with the pain. "I...love...you," he whispered just before his hand fell limp, and his eyes closed again.

CHAPTER 66

LIAM

I HEARD SCREAMING. However, it sounded as though it was under bubbling, hot, steaming water. Intense vertigo spun in and out, making me feel much like Alice falling down the rabbit hole. It made me want to puke, but I was in too much pain to give into the urge.

I tried to grab onto Lucian as I tumbled headfirst into the abyss. I couldn't feel him. All I could sense was hot, burning pain searing through my stomach and over my body. My body wanted to shift, and I couldn't figure out why this shift was so painful, but worse than that, I didn't understand why I couldn't reach Lucian.

I tried to breathe through the pain, but red lava poured into my throat and closed off my airway. It filled my lungs until there wasn't any room. It spewed out of my lungs like a geyser and into my heart, which pumped it into the rest of my limbs before it solidified like concrete. Everything was heavy. I couldn't lift my arms. I couldn't even open my eyes.

Honeysuckle and pear. I could smell Clementine through the abyss. I tried to reach for her. I tried to push through the lava river and the blackened void's spinning vertigo. I tried to force my eyes open.

Turquoise and amber. Unyielding strength. A pure force of nature that was no longer hidden. I tried to reach up through the black hole and touch her cherub face to tell her I loved her. Before I could, I was sucked in once again, and the pain erupted around my body.

THERE WAS a gentle beeping as I slowly regained consciousness. I opened my heavy eyelids and looked up at the ceiling of the alpha's quarters in the pack house. My vision was blurry. I blinked a few times, clearing it, and I could make out the subtle patterns on the ceiling tiles.

I tried to figure out what had happened. I knew I was injured. I could feel cold air pronged up into my nostrils. I tried to move, but one hand was restricted by tubing, and the other had some sort of clip on my pointer finger. The bedsheet was pulled up and under my arms, and I could feel I wasn't just injured. I had been put through a meat grinder. I was in a very bad way.

Memories flashed across my mind. Lincoln. I let out a groan moments before pure cold panic permeated my soul.

Fuck. Clementine!

"Alpha Liam?" a voice asked. But it wasn't the voice I wanted to hear. A bright white light burned my eyes as the doctor flicked some sort of penlight into my eyes. "Welcome back to the land of the living, Alpha."

"Where's Clementine?" I croaked, trying to sit up. Pain seared through my stomach, and I grunted.

"Alpha, you shouldn't move."

"Where's my mate?" I demanded, and I coughed with the exertion.

"Asleep, Alpha," Doctor Todd pointed beside me.

I looked over, and sure enough, my mate was curled in an armchair beside the bed. I frowned. The bed was king-sized. She could have easily tucked up with me. She looked so uncomfortable on that chair, so pale, petite, and childlike in her slumber.

"How long have I been out?" I whispered to Doctor Todd.

"Five days."

"Five?"

"Yes, Alpha. You wouldn't have woken if it wasn't for your crazy-as-fuck mate."

"That's your luna you're talking about, Doctor," I growled weakly.

"Yes, Alpha, but she is crazy! She went above and beyond to save your life."

"W-what do you mean?"

"I've never seen anything like it. You lost far too much blood. You were dying, and she suddenly grabbed the rubber tourniquet and used her teeth to tighten it against her own arm. Then she grabbed a cannula, shoved it into her vein, connected an IV line directly into your arm, and transfused her blood into you, all while shouting commands at everyone else. Your brother. Your father. They all listened to her like she was the alpha. When I tried to stop her and tell her that your blood may not be compatible, that she could kill you, she looked me dead in the eye and told me that if a true mate's blood couldn't save you, nothing would." Doctor Todd moved his stethoscope around my chest. "That's when I realized she wasn't being the alpha. She was being our luna."

He smiled at me, moved the bedsheet further down, and gently peeled the bandage away from my stomach. He gave a slight nod and reaffixed it.

"After you became stable, I moved you here, and she hasn't left your bedside since. That girl is made to be a doctor. I told her as much, and she laughed me off." He smiled affectionately at Clementine, and I felt a rumble start low in my throat. He looked back at me, surprised, and his cheeks turned pink. He took out a clipboard and started writing some notes before he continued. "Your bond has been healing you. But honestly, Alpha, I don't believe the bond would have healed you without her drastic action. And you have had to have quite a few transfusions. So many that she'd become weak herself, but she just kept donating. She was giving her life for yours." He fiddled with a saline bag and gave me a warm smile.

"You're not healed yet, Alpha. You need to stay in this bed and rest up. But now that you're awake, I have every faith you'll be up in no time."

The doctor removed the clip from my fingertip and the prongs from my nose before he left the alpha's quarters. I felt for Lucian's presence. He was still out for the count, snoring softly. I reached back and gave him a gentle stroke, admiring his soft tawny fur.

"She saved us, Lucian," I murmured to him. He let off a wolfy snore, and I smiled. We were alive. Our mate had saved us.

Clementine furrowed her eyebrows in her sleep. She shifted slightly, making me stop checking in on Lucian and focus on her. I felt for the mate bond. It seemed weaker than normal, but it was still there. My heart swelled in my chest as I looked at my mate, my saviour, and the love of my life.

"My little force of nature," I said lovingly. I reached out and caressed her hand affectionately. The mate bond started to tickle lightly, and she began to stir.

"Doctor Todd," she mumbled sleepily, "does he need another transfusion?"

She wobbled slightly as she started to stand up, and I noticed that she still had a piece of plastic tubing sticking out of the inside of her elbow. The doctor said she had given multiple transfusions, and the fact that she could barely stand on her feet and had dark shadows under her eyes made me believe she had given me too much.

"No. But he definitely needs a kiss."

Her eyes snapped open the minute she heard my voice and went wide. Pink stained her cheeks and her eyes filled with tears, causing the turquoise colour to look more pool-like than ever.

"Come here," I said softly, opening my arms. She slowly moved toward me. I inhaled her scent as I pulled her in, and then I encased her lips with mine. She trembled under my kiss, and I felt the mate bond start to repair itself—growing stronger.

I smelled the salty scent of her tears and pulled away from her lips, kissing each tear as they travelled down her cheeks. The briny sweetness of her tears stirred Lucian, and I rumbled happily as the weakened mate bond started to glow with a little more strength.

"Why are you crying?" I asked her gruffly.

"You're okay," she whimpered.

"Thanks to you. The doctor said I wouldn't have made it without you."

"And I wouldn't have made it without you," she breathed.

She watched me with wide wet eyes. I recommitted her face to memory. It had been too long since I had seen it. She was so beautiful, even pale, and tired. She was my perfect little mate. Clem reached out and stroked my beard, her eyes twinkling with wetness. I rumbled happily into her fingers, loving the gentle zaps that tickled through my beard.

"I love you, Luna Clementine," I whispered. I heard her heart give a stutter, and I smiled. "And before you deny it and say it's just the mate bond, it's not. I realized I loved you when you came back from Vancouver. You were so beautiful even in your anger. And then you slapped me, and that was what cemented it. You literally smacked love into me, and at that moment, I knew I would do anything it took to keep you and love you for the rest of time." I brushed my lips against hers and smiled softly. "Now that I'm thinking about it, I think I loved you much earlier than that. I've loved you since I first laid eyes on you. The moment you walked into me. I mean, talk about trying to get a guy's attention."

"What? I spun around, and suddenly you were there. That really hurt my nose!"

I kissed her nose. "There, all better." I grinned mischievously, and she scowled. "I wanted to tell you the night I became alpha. I was about to just before the ceremonial dagger cut my hand. And then I planned to tell you as I announced our true mate status to the pack, but Lincoln came along and spoiled my plans. So, I just had to keep sending my love down the bond instead."

"And here I thought you planned to tell me as you're fucking dying on me." She glowered irritably.

"Sorry about that." I chuckled sheepishly, knowing I needed to address the elephant in the room. "Lincoln...is he...?"

"He died the moment you slashed his throat."

Relief washed over me.

"And his pack members?"

"They scampered. Beta Ryan and your dad are trying to hunt them down."

"Beta Ryan?"

"Yeah, almost losing his best friend made him finally decide on that. I'm sure he'll kick your ass about it now that you're okay."

"And Stacey?"

"She's here with him...waiting for the full moon to be initiated into the pack."

"Her brother?" I asked venomously. Lincoln was dead, but there still existed a threat to my happiness.

"Liam. You just woke up. Stop stressing over trivial crap."

"Darling, it's an alpha's job to stress. And your safety is not trivial to me."

"And neither is yours. You're hurt, and it's my job to take care of you."

"Not at the expense of your health," I grumped, then met her unyielding expression. "You really are stubborn, aren't you."

"I wasn't going to let you die, Liam," she whispered. "I'll always do what is best for you, even if you disagree with my methods. I'll always take care of you."

"Can you take care of me now?" I grinned cheekily, holding her tighter as she leaned against the bed awkwardly. I kissed her cheek, the taste of her tears echoing over my lips even though she had stopped crying.

"What do you mean?" she tilted her head.

"I believe I was promised hours of sexual reward. You were going to let me tie you to this bed."

"Liam! You're hurt."

"Not that part of me." She giggled as I pulled her on top of me, where she fit perfectly. I felt myself stir underneath her warm crotch. I looked up at her deep black hair, bright aquamarine eyes, pouty mouth, and soft pink tint staining her cheekbones.

"Stop it!" she chastised. "You'll get hurt."

"Nope. Never. This will heal me completely." I pulled her mouth toward mine and groaned in pain.

"See!" she scolded, getting off my erection.

"Where are you going?" I growled.

"You have no self-preservation, Alpha Liam, so I'm going to preserve it for you."

I gripped her hand and pulled her back down to me. I rolled over so she was on the other side of our massive bed, and I was lying on top of her. My stitches twinged again, but I knew that having Clementine this close would heal me. I just needed to give it some time.

I rubbed my nose down the length of hers, then over to where my mark had faded into a barely noticeable scratch with next to no scent.

"I see this has faded again."

"It has."

"You know, I can't wait for the full moon because, let me tell you, my delicious little luna, I'm going to enjoy making this mark permanent."

"Are you now?" she said playfully.

I nodded and hummed as I inhaled her scent. "But I do need something from you now."

"What do you need?"

"You to let me mark you," I begged.

"Liam. You don't have to ask permission to do that. You own my soul. I just don't think we can do it the way you want. You'll tear your stitches, and I'll have to give you my blood again. And as much as I love you, it's exhausting trying to keep you alive."

"You love me?"

"Well, duh!" she rolled her eyes and gave me a sassy smile.

"Say it."

"Well, if you make me say it. It doesn't count," she retorted with equal seriousness and sass. I started to tickle her ribs, and she giggled the most beautiful tinkling sound.

"Say it!" I commanded, releasing her ribs.

"I love you, Alpha Liam," she breathed, and my mouth descended on hers.

I felt another piece of the mate bond glow with strength, healing one of the stress fractures that my near death had caused.

CHAPTER 67

CLEMENTINE

As Liam lay in bed, pale and covered in a cold sweat, I had a horrible sense of déjà vu. There was no smell of chemo, no impending death, but the feeling was the same. The first time I watched someone I loved dying I couldn't do anything about it.

This time, I would do everything I could to save him. My arm still hurt from where I shoved the central venous cannula into my vein, almost piercing through the other side. That didn't matter, though. What mattered was that Liam needed blood, and I needed to give it to him. All of it if that's what it was going to take.

After he was stitched up, placed into our bed, and hooked up to monitors, my dad suggested that I have a shower. I had shaken my head vehemently in refusal. I couldn't leave him. What if I was showering and he–

Dad, unfortunately, didn't take no for an answer.

I stepped into the enormous ensuite but left the door open a crack so I could hear what was going on in the bedroom. Circe's possessive side had come through. People were abundant at his bedside, but after what had happened, I didn't trust the bulk of them. My instincts told me I needed to protect him, and only I could. It was difficult allowing more than Ryan, Liam's family, and mine.

I looked in the mirror and noticed how my eyes had ringed with a perfect amber, uncompromising and strong. Sometime during the rush to save my mate's life, I fully merged with Circe. I didn't have time to think or talk to her about it. It was unimportant in the grand scheme of things.

There was a large, bloodied smear over my cheekbone from where Liam had swiped my cheek and told me he loved me. My heart shattered when he lost consciousness. As it did, I found a newer, stronger determination that I didn't know was in me.

I stepped into the double-monsoon shower and turned on one showerhead, removing my blood-soiled clothes and dumping them at the shower door. The water ran in a murky brownish-red torrent down the drain, and for the first time since the drama unfolded, I let out a few tears.

I stepped into the bedroom and walked into the massive walk-in closet, where I dressed in one of Liam's t-shirts and a pair of my shorts. I brought his shirt up and gave it a deep sniff before I walked back into the bedroom and looked at my mate, taking up the left side of the bed.

Doctor Todd had mentioned that the closeness and warmth of my body would heal him faster. He told me to join him on the bed. I knew he was right deep down, but at the same time, I needed to distance myself from him in case he didn't wake up; to prepare myself for the possibility of losing him. And if I were cuddling him and he died, it would have broken me in a way that I would never have been able to come back from.

So instead, I dragged an armchair as close as possible to him and held Liam's large, calloused hand. Doctor Todd smiled warmly at me, his soft eyes crinkling at the corners as he set up a new IV line into my arm. He flushed saline through before taking another bag full of blood, just in case.

The next day, when Liam's stitches started bleeding through his bandages, and his heartrate dropped too low, I knew he must have had an internal bleed we had missed in the field. The doctor had to intubate him to perform an emergency surgery. Liam didn't just need one more bag. He needed two. Circe pushed all of her power through the second bag of blood before passing out, and she hadn't woken since.

Dark shadows were still under Liam's eyes, but the intubation tube had been removed from his mouth and replaced with nasal prongs. His pulse remained strong, oxygen saturations were high, and he looked as though he was improving. Finally. The second bag of blood seemed to do the trick, although now, he smelled sweet like honeysuckle and crisp like a pear. There was an undertone of canine and a slight, mostly hidden scent of human. Liam's cedar and spice scent had all but disappeared completely, what with so much of my blood flowing through his veins, but he was still my Liam.

I refused to sleep, keeping an eye on his machines, holding his hand, and rubbing soothing circles into the top. I would give the tops of his fingers gentle kisses as I silently begged for my mate to wake up.

Come on, Liam. Please.

Doctor Todd had hooked a bag of electrolytes up to my IV, muttering about how I should be eating and regaining my strength after donating so much blood. The electrolytes started to stir Circe, and eventually, she stretched and yawned, then frowned when she noticed that Liam was still unconscious. Then she began to pace my mind.

As Liam slept, his scent slowly started to morph and change back to his cedar and spice, but I still watched him closely, scared that it was a fluke, and he'd suffer another complication. I knew I wouldn't be okay until I saw his eyes' warm browns and golds. I wouldn't sleep until that happened.

Life outside of the bedroom went on. People were in and out every few hours. Sierra came into the alpha quarters daily and forced me to eat, even if it was just soup and bread. My dad and brother came to check on me, too. Stacey and Sophie tried to get me out into the sunshine, which I vehemently refused, and Beta Ryan kept me up-to-date on the running of the pack that he was co-sharing with Josiah and Beta Jerome. It sounds terrible, but I couldn't care less about Lincoln's pack going AWOL. It was an issue that could wait. The only thing I focused on was ensuring Liam got better—that he woke up.

And finally, he did.

***

LIAM WAS GETTING STRONGER. It had only been forty-eight hours since he woke, but already, he was up and walking around. It was only around the interior of the pack house, but it was better than the alternative—lying in bed—or dying.

I had a fresh bruise on my collarbone, which reinforced the fact that he was going to be okay. He was strong enough to bring forward Lucian and mark me. He probably was strong enough to be intimate, but after seeing his sutures bleed, I wasn't going to risk it.

I nipped him in return, although his scent had been dominated by mine for some time now. It was different. It was about me showing Liam how much I loved him. It was me ensuring the world knew I would fight for him.

I still couldn't stop clucking around him like a nervous mother hen, checking his pulse, pupil dilation and sutures for infection. I helped him shower, swatting his hands away as they pawed at me, lust evident in his eyes as I gently washed him with soap and water. His muscles were larger and bulging with rippled veins since he'd assumed the role of alpha. I washed over his arms, down his well-defined six-pack, and the smattering of hair that led to the treasure below. He growled when I got close to his manhood and pushed me against the granite wall of the shower, the monsoon showerhead providing a waterfall above us. His hands ran over my curves, and he gripped them desperately.

The mate bond buzzed, and our joint arousal infused the steam in the air, but I still refused, telling him that he needed to heal and get a doctor's clearance first. That didn't stop him from trying every time we were alone, though.

"What are you doing today?" he asked me over breakfast on the third morning after waking.

"I'm going to get some fresh air."

"Stay close to the pack house if you go for a run," he ordered. I gave him a pointed look, but he just shook his head. "Don't make me put a tail on you." His eyes flashed gold.

We had this conversation yesterday. In fact, we argued a lot yesterday. I soon realized that since his seduction and soft begging weren't working, he thought maybe having a hot and angry argument would. Despite his new ploy, there were genuine reasons behind his worrying. After all, threats still remained to the pack *and* me.

"Circe isn't up for a run. She's still exhausted from saving your ass," I smirked at him.

"She should be healed by now." He frowned slightly and cupped my cheek. His demeanour changed, and I felt his concern flow down our healing mate bond.

"We're okay," I promised him.

"You're more than okay," he said adoringly. "You've merged."

"Yeah. I guess saving your ass put us on the same page long enough for it to happen. She's just a little exhausted. She spent a lot of energy healing you," I said.

"Maybe I'm just going to have to heal you then," he whispered coquettishly. "Maybe I can join you for some fresh air, and we can rejuvenate each other." And we were back full circle.

I rolled my eyes. "Or maybe you can be good, Alpha, and wait for your body to heal before you try to seduce me," I countered, although the butterflies were already swarming.

"Trust me, Clemmy, when I get the okay from the doctor, I'm tying you to that bed."

"I look forward to it."

"Well, you are a doctor, so give me the okay, and you won't have to look forward to it."

"I'm not a doctor."

"Doctor Todd says otherwise. I think he's quite smitten with you after your field response," he growled.

I snorted. "You can't possibly be jealous of Doctor Todd."

"Yes, yes, I can. He's crushing on what's mine." His tone was a playful growl, but I felt a small amount of insecurity underneath.

"We're mated, Liam. He doesn't stand a chance. Besides, he's like thirty-five or something."

"You promise?" He pouted playfully. I pulled down the neck of my t-shirt and showed him his mark as an answer. He grinned when it came into view and shoved another mouthful of food down his throat. We were quiet for a few more minutes.

"That was going to be my field, you know," I said slowly.

"What was?"

"Emergency Medicine."

"I can see why. You're a natural in a crisis."

"What are your plans today?" I asked, redirecting the discussion. It was no use bringing up my old life.

"I need to sort out this rogue issue," his voice was gruff.

"Huh? What rogue issue?"

"Lincoln's so-called pack. They betrayed the Blackfern

Valley Pack and went AWOL. In my mind, they're now packless and without an alpha. That makes them rogues."

"How many?" I asked softly, chewing on a piece of fruit.

"One-hundred-and-eighty-three by Ryan's count."

"That many?"

"Yeah. He'd been plotting his coup for a while. He could have struck at any moment, but he was set on waiting for me to take the alpha position. It was never about Dad or his claim to the pack. It was always about beating me."

"I'm sorry, Liam."

"Don't be. He's dead. Now, I just have to deal with his rogues."

"Don't do anything physical. You have warriors for a reason," I ordered crossly.

"Yes, Luna." His eyes twinkled with humour.

"I'm serious, Liam."

"Oh, I know you are. And I promise, I won't put myself in danger." He then sealed his oath with a soft kiss. "I'm not going to do anything that will risk you holding out on me for even longer." He gave me a sexy smile, and his eyes roamed me lustfully. When I didn't take the bait, he continued, "Well, if I can't convince you to come to bed with me, I suppose I had better get to work."

I walked him to his office and smiled as he positioned himself behind his desk. I fussed around him for the first ten minutes, ensuring he wasn't straining his stitches. He then shooed me away with a twinkle of affection and started working.

I smiled as Josiah, Jerome and Ryan made their way into the pack house and down toward the office. A few minutes later, my dad entered, gave me a quick hug, and proceeded down to the office as well. Alpha Liam's first official meeting of the day had started.

THE FALL SUN was warm as I strolled around the town. In the hour I walked around, I had to admit that Blackfern Valley had grown on me. Besides the leaves starting to change colour, nothing else had physically changed. Even so, somehow, it seemed safer now that Lincoln was gone. Life was finally going to be peaceful.

I took a deep breath and closed my eyes for a moment, enjoying the golden rays of the sun warming my face. Circe growled as a musky scent hit my nose. Before I could do anything, a large hand suddenly gripped my chin and forced my mouth open. I felt something burn as I was forced to swallow whatever was placed into it.

I started to cough and choke. It burned so badly. Then I was shoved roughly and pushed into the open door of a car. He ran around the other side and stomped on the gas before closing his door.

I kept coughing, reaching out for Circe to give me strength, but I could no longer feel her for some reason.

"Don't bother calling out for help. That was wolfsbane. Your pack link," he sneered, "and any mate bond are useless."

"What the fuck do you want, Brady?" I coughed. "Let me go!"

"Lincoln promised me he would win your stupid pack, and in return, I would get you. Then he went and got himself killed. So I just had to take you for myself."

"I'm mated, you fucking lunatic."

"Ah, but you aren't, not officially. And Liam was mortally wounded. I watched as you attempted to fix him. You know it's all in vain, right? He's going to die anyway."

"It wasn't in vain. He lives."

"But he's unconscious. I've been walking around your pack

for days, getting all the necessary information. Oh, little wolf, you really shouldn't have left his bedside. With the distance between you, your mate bond will stop healing him. If he hasn't built enough strength himself, he'll be dead within the week. When that happens, I'll replace his heinous mark with mine on the full moon. And if he isn't already dead by then, the pain of our mating will surely kill him."

CHAPTER 68

LIAM

I SHIFTED in my seat and grimaced at the pain in my stomach. I knew this injury was going to take some time to heal. Even under the watchful eye of my fussing mate, it would take more than a week to get me back on my feet.

My first official pack meeting was going to shit, too. I listened as Dad and Patrick argued heatedly, letting them hash it out like an old married couple, but I didn't intervene. I needed to hear this as much as they needed to argue.

"I told you when you were alpha that those blood-haters were dangerous. Your gentle approach put my children at risk, Josiah. Again!" Patrick spat.

"And *I* told you that killing isn't the answer! That's how Jed ruled the pack. Do you not remember how many pack members he executed for small misdemeanours? Do you not remember how we lived in fear that he would get bored and start killing us for sport?"

"Of course, I fucking remember, Jos, but there's a difference between executing people for misdemeanors and crimes like attempted murder–"

"What fucking attempted murder, Pat? There was none! The intel was that there was a group of wolves that–"

"What attempted murder? Are you fucking kidding me? Clementine was targeted by these fuckers from the moment we set foot on your lands! I'm sure Vinny would have been, too, if he hadn't had a wolf. The most he got was slander and a few dust-ups, but you can't stand there and tell me there was no attempted murder. Clementine was poisoned, drugged, stalked, and some fucking lunatic tried to burn her alive!"

"We were keeping an eye on it," Dad snapped.

"That wasn't good enough, Jos! You needed to put down a firmer hand. You were so fucking afraid of people fearing you, but you never understood that people are meant to have a healthy level of fear when it comes to your position! That's what it means to be a fucking alpha!"

"I wasn't going to condemn anyone to death. That would have made me no better than Jed! It was live in peace or be exiled! I did my duty, Pat!" Dad argued.

"Yeah, and look what happened. You had a coup forming right under your nose!" Patrick's eyes flashed.

"It was one misguided werewolf! They all fled the moment Lincoln fell. Where's the proof that they're blood-haters?"

"You'll see this proof when they regroup and attack this pack again. And if you don't think they will, then you're foolish, and I'm glad you're no longer alpha!"

I growled at Patrick in warning, and he took a deep calming breath before turning back to my dad.

"Lincoln was just one fucking pawn in a larger game."

"This isn't a game–"

"No, it's not!" Patrick agreed with cold precision. "It's the life of my son and the life of our fucking luna!"

"Nothing will happen to Clementine," I vowed angrily,

Lucian's protective instinct rolling through my voice, "nor Vinny."

"And how are you going to protect them?" Patrick turned his attention toward me, then added, "Alpha," as a late sign of respect.

I stared at him for a few moments without saying anything. Then I flicked my eyes to my father. He gave me a slight nod of encouragement. I *was* alpha, and this *was* my decision.

"I agree with you, Patrick. They were given plenty of chances to toe the line. If they're a threat, they will be eliminated. However, if they can prove they aren't, they can petition to be reinstated into the pack. I will grant every one of them an audience and a chance to prove their truth, but I'm in no way going to let them threaten our pack and the lives within it—both current *or* future. This bigotry ends now!"

Patrick gave a single nod and lowered his head in respect. Where I thought Dad would be disappointed, he gave me a small smile showing his pride.

I turned my attention to Beta Jerome. His grey hair had started to thin, and there were deep lines on his face, but his fierce blue eyes and regimented demeanour told me he was just as deadly and authoritative as he's always been.

"One-hundred-and-eighty-three rogues may storm our borders at any moment and try to finish the job that Lincoln started. Have your warriors heard any whispers about what is going on out there?" I asked.

"No, Alpha. Everything has been quiet for a few days. Our intel tells us they're not in the immediate vicinity of our borders, and this includes Kempthorne. We're unsure where they've gone, but we're still searching."

"How many are out searching?"

"Five warriors with tracking expertise have been assigned to the job, Alpha," Jerome offered.

"Do we have any more warriors to help with the search?"

"Unfortunately not, Alpha," Jerome said, his tone stern and angry. "We had fifteen warriors who were apt in tracking, and we lost ten of them to Lincoln's defection. This is why we're having trouble locating them."

Well, fuck!

"We'll find them," Ryan promised.

I turned and looked at my Beta-elect. I sighed and rubbed my hand through my beard. If these men were going to be my counsel, they needed to know.

"There's another threat outside of the blood-hating rogues. What I'm about to tell you does not leave this room. Is that understood?"

"Yes, Alpha!" they chorused.

"The rogues aren't the only thing we have to worry about at the moment. There's also a direct threat to your luna's life."

"What do you mean?" asked Patrick slowly.

"When she was at UBC, she entered into a relationship unknowingly with a werewolf. He has recently come back into her life and is trying to claim her." Lucian snarled through me as he paced with agitation. "Lincoln met this asshole and made some sort of agreement before the alpha fight. Thankfully, Lincoln lost, but Brady's still out there. He's abusive and controlling. He's also crafty and manipulative. I don't believe for a single minute that he's given up. If anything, he's waiting for the perfect opportunity to strike. And I think he will, especially if the warriors are focused on the rogues."

"Intel tells us that he's retreated to his pack, Alpha," Ryan offered.

"What else did your mate say? Can I trust her?" I snapped.

"Your mate?" my dad asked Ryan, surprised.

"Unfortunately, the scumbag that Alpha Liam is referring to is my mate's brother," Ryan grumbled, then looked me directly in the eye. "Stacey is one hundred per cent trustworthy, Alpha. She was the one that told him to run home. She's disgusted he teamed up with Lincoln, and I think she finally got the wake-up call she needed to realize what her brother is actually like."

I nodded slowly as Patrick demanded more information on Brady.

An odd sensation floated down the mate bond and distracted me from Patrick's questions. It tasted of surprise, then anger, and then there was nothing. I stopped focusing on the meeting and searched for Clementine, wondering what the sensation had been about.

The bond was there, that much I could feel, but it felt dark, like a giant shadow had absorbed it. It was as if she had put a block on our bond.

Why would she do that? I reached out for the amber and honeysuckle pattern-scent to mind-link her. Lucian tilted his head and gave a low whine when it returned empty.

"What the hell, Lucian! Why has she turned off her mind-link?"

Wait! I was alpha. That meant she couldn't shut off her mind-link from me. That meant that something was blocking her mind-link, blocking Circe from her—from *me*. I took a deep breath and tried again. This time, I was met with a sharp burning taste on my tongue and the instant numbing sensation like I had been hit with a horse tranquilizer hit me.

Lucian whined. *"It has to be aconite. Someone's taken her!"*

I stood up fast and felt the stitches on my stomach protest. The pain didn't matter. All that mattered was finding my mate.

"Ryan, where is your mate?" I demanded.

Everyone looked at me in confusion at my sudden angry outburst. Alpha waves were rolling off me, and I was doing everything I could to stay calm.

"She's at the house. Why?"

"Bring her to me. Now!" I snapped. Ryan pulled out his phone immediately.

"What's going on, Liam?" Dad asked, trying to ease the tension in the room.

"My mind-link to Clem has gone dark, and so has my mate bond. That thing I was worried about, I believe it's just fucking happened."

A minute and a half later, Stacey knocked on the door, and Ryan got up to let her in. I stalked threateningly over to Stacey, and her hazel eyes went wide with fear.

"Where has he taken her?" I demanded.

"What?" Her confusion looked genuine. "Who?"

"Your brother. My connection has been severed. Where has he taken my mate?" I snarled.

She whimpered under the power that rolled off me. "I swear, Alpha, I have no idea. Brady went home. He told me he had left, and I told him to stay the fuck away!"

"You better be telling me the fucking truth, Stacey! Your brother is manipulative and evil. He wanted to own her and make her a submissive, weak human who would never question him. He abused her and manipulated her the entire time they dated. He broke her into a million pieces, and when Lacey was dying, he got incredibly territorial and tried to stop her from being with her mom. He's supposed to be a fucking doctor and forbade a grieving girl time with her mother! As if a dying woman was a threat to his proprietorship. You really can't get any more sadistic than that!"

Patrick's eye's flashed dangerously as the truth reached his ears. So much for easing the news of Brady and Clementine's past onto him.

"W-what?" Stacey stuttered.

"How can you honestly not know what your brother is like? He wants to own her still; not love her, but own her! He's been sniffing around this pack for two weeks. He even arranged to get her as a prize if Lincoln won. A fucking possession! So, tell me, where the fuck is my mate?!"

"I-I–"

"If you want a place in my pack, tell me where he has taken my mate."

"I honestly don't know, Alpha!" Her eyes went vacant before they came back to me. "He's blocked his mind-link."

"Of course, he has."

"I'll find him, Alpha," she whispered, then tried to look tough as she continued. "And if he has taken her, I'll go and get her myself, and I swear, I'll make sure he'll not bother you both again. He won't be a threat, I promise."

"Oh, no, Stacey. While he breathes, he's a fucking threat. I already told him I don't give second chances, and I meant it."

I looked at Ryan, who nodded in understanding and complete agreement.

No more.

This stopped here.

CHAPTER 69

CLEMENTINE

"He's my true mate, Brady. I'll never let you dishonour him by marking me. I'll kill you first." I coughed out as he continued to drive.

"Oh, honey. I would like to see you try and fight with the wolfsbane running through your system."

"He's going to wake up and figure it out," I glossed.

It didn't seem like a good idea to tell Brady that Liam was already awake and was strong enough to heal without my constant presence.

"That's fine too. Maybe I'll let you gain your wolf enough so he can feel you and track you. Or maybe I'll just torture you and let him feel that. He'll heroically and foolishly come to your aid. And I'm sure I can handle one weakened alpha. He'll be dead soon enough, regardless what I decide."

"He'll come with his warriors, Brady."

He chuckled deeply as he turned onto an old highway that travelled into the mountains. I tried to reach Liam. He would be freaking out the moment he realized I was gone. I had to keep trying. I even tried contacting other pack members like Ryan,

Dad, and Josiah. Anyone. Nothing was there. It was like I was human again.

"Oh, darling, let him come. I have an army of my own." Harsh reality slapped me right in the face, but Brady's arrogance remained unphased.

"You think they'll fight for you? They're blood-haters, Brady. I'm the one thing in the world they hate by definition. They won't. This is probably a ruse so they can kill me the moment you deliver me to wherever the fuck you're taking us."

"Not all of them are blood-haters, Clementine. A number of them simply hated their alpha-elect." He flashed his perfect white teeth. "And one girl in particular was never truly a member of Lincoln's pack. She saw the love of her life fall for you. She immediately opened up to me when she realized I was planning to take you away from Blackfern Valley. When I told her she could have Liam back, the luna title, and her pack, she jumped at the chance. However, she hasn't been told that you two are true mates. It's a pity she doesn't stand a chance because, by taking you, he'll be dead. By letting her think she was getting her way, she supplied me with all the information I needed."

"You're talking about Cassie, aren't you?" I asked. He gave me a look, then focused back on the road. "She's a crazy bitch who burned down my house."

"So I've heard." He chuckled. "As I said, I've heard a lot of stories. Did you know Lincoln's harem of she-wolves drugged you at some party? She watched as they slipped Rohypnol into your drink. Cassie was about to use the opportunity to win her loser back when she watched him seek you out and carry you away so heroically. She waxed poetic with jealousy when she described how he'd looked down at you with equal amounts of rage and love; how she knew then that he was angry enough to kill, and how he had never gotten protective or possessive over her like that. That's when she knew she'd lost him to a half-breed—worse—a human. Gag." He gave a dramatic shudder. "It was all very, Hallmark-chick-flick-pukefest if you ask me."

He stomped down on the gas as he drove further into the mountains. The road twisted and turned, and soon, the air got colder. I looked around my surroundings and tried to devise a plan to get out of this situation. I couldn't contact my pack or my family. I hadn't travelled too far, and if my bearings were correct, all I needed to do was run East, and I would hit Kempthorne. Then, he wouldn't be able to touch me, right? No werewolf could harm another werewolf in Kempthorne.

But my bearings had to be spot on. I had to be able to run in the right direction, and to do that, I had to make him stop this car and hurt him well enough in the process to get away. Could I do that without Circe? How long would it take for the aconite to wear off? Could I really risk being in the wilderness without a wolf?

Fuck!

I didn't know what to do.

I looked over at Brady one more time and shrugged. I was prepared to die to save Liam. Why wasn't I prepared to die to save myself? The pain of the aconite sliced through my system like tiny little shards of glass whipping around my blood, but I ignored it as best I could as I reached over and yanked at the steering wheel.

"What the fuck, Clem!" He pushed me away from the steering wheel, and the car swerved. "Do you have a fucking death wish?"

"Better than being with you," I spat, then tried it again. He slammed on the brakes this time, and my head smashed into the dashboard. Pulling my head off the dash by my hair, his fingers then encased my throat.

"I see that even if your wolf is asleep, you're still a bit feisty.

That's an unexpected turn-on, *Clemmy*." His mouth covered mine, and I bit down hard, tasting his blood. He pulled away and touched his lip, gave a slight cough, then grinned. "Now, now, Clementine, I've always been gentle with you, and I don't think you want me to start playing rough."

"Let me go, Brady," I said through blurry vision, and then I felt tears cascade down my cheeks.

"Sure, I'll let you go." He nodded. I looked at him, and he smiled sinisterly. "We're here."

Where the fuck was *here*? I looked around and saw that he had pulled off the side of the road in the middle of nowhere. He exited the car, and I looked at the ignition, hoping he was stupid enough to leave the keys behind. He hadn't.

As he opened the trunk, I got out and made a run for it. I got maybe ten metres down the road before he tackled me to the ground.

"You know, most wolves are knocked out with the amount of wolfsbane I shoved into your mouth. But you, you just keep on fighting."

He yanked me to my feet and wrapped a rope around my wrists tightly before he dragged me into the bush. We walked deep into the trees for about an hour before finally reaching a large cabin.

"You took your time getting back. I thought this was just a recon mission," a sweet voice tinkled over. "Oh, my God, you got her!" A tall redhead with piercing blue eyes looked straight at me. "What the hell did you do? Why is she bleeding?" I put my tied hands up to my forehead and winced in pain. My fingers came into my field of vision and were red with blood.

Ouch.

"Her head met the dashboard." He shrugged.

Cassie ran her fingers over her eyes exasperatedly. "Come on, Clementine, let's clean you up."

Brady growled low as Cassie reached for my roped hands. She stared him down.

"You fed her aconite so her wolf isn't going to heal her. You would think that you wouldn't want her hurt with how much you claim she's yours."

"She brought it on herself," he snarled.

"You're a fucking doctor; at least pretend to care about her welfare."

Cassie rolled her eyes and dragged me by the rope into the cabin. She opened a cupboard in the kitchen and pulled out a clean cloth before grabbing the first aid kit. Wiping my face with water first, she then dabbed at my forehead with antiseptic. It stung a little, and I glared at her.

"What the fuck are you doing, Cassandra?" I asked. "You think getting blood off my face will make Liam forgive you for all the shit you've done? You burned down my house, and now, you're an accessory to kidnapping–"

"I'm not the villain in this, Clem–"

"What, and I am because my father was mated with a human? Because I spent my first twenty years without a wolf?"

"I don't care about that. I'm not a bigot."

"No, you're a psycho obsessed with my mate."

"He's not your mate. He's mine. We've been in love with each other since kindergarten. I was waiting for him to get out of his playboy phase. I knew he needed to get it out of his system, and I was more than happy to wait."

I reached my tied hands up and started tugging at the neckline of my sweater to try and show her how wrong she was. Her eyes flashed purple before she took a deep breath.

"You don't need to show me, Clem. I know he marked you shortly before his alpha ceremony, but that doesn't mean you guys are mated. It just means he's temporarily infatuated with you, and once Brady marks you as his mate under the full moon, that infatuation will cease."

"It's not an infatuation!" I snarled. "And I will die before I let Brady mark me, you fucking psycho bitch!"

She shook her head angrily and threw the items back into the first aid case. "Believe it or not, Clem, I'm not psychotic. As a matter of fact, I've been trying to save your half-breed ass this whole time."

"Save my ass?" My laughter sounded unhinged as it echoed around the cabin.

"Yeah. I really did! When I noticed how much Liam cared for you, I wasn't going to jeopardize my relationship with him by acting like a jealous bitch. I did that once, and it backfired. I knew I had to think outside the box to win him back." She smiled softly as my brows furrowed. "After the wine incident, I couldn't exactly become your BFF, so I hung around in the background, keeping you safe from the actual blood-haters. I followed you through the trees every time you left your house, ensuring you weren't attacked. I even extended it to your brother, keeping an eye on him at school. Eventually, Liam would see that I was a good person. Eventually, he would remember I was luna material."

I frowned. This she-wolf was nuts! She returned the first aid kit under the kitchen sink and turned on the faucet. It whinnied from lack of use. She filled a glass with water before placing it in front of me, then sighed before continuing. "Lincoln and his friends kept targeting you. You were fine when you were in public, but when you foolishly went into the bush by yourself, you became free game. I tried to fight Lincoln off and protect you. I kept warning him that Liam was close. I kept warning him off you, and you got spooked and broke your ankle. Then we all felt Liam's alpha power coming through the trees and scattered. You were distraught and in pain. He would never have believed me, so I ran too. That's when Lincoln cornered me and forced me to join his pack. I suddenly felt his power, and I understood what was happening. I was desperate to tell Liam, but Lincoln's alpha command made it impossible."

I shook my head at her and looked at the water, refusing to touch it even though my throat still stung. "You fucking tried to burn me alive!"

"No. I didn't. I really didn't. We all thought you had moved back to Vancouver, but then you came back. Lincoln thought it was a good idea to order me to get rid of you for good, but he wasn't specific in his command. I overheard you talking with Sophie about getting some supplies for dinner, and when you were safely away, I set your house on fire. I lit it up like a tiki-torch to scare you away for good, but I never actually wanted to hurt you. Then it all turned to shit, and I got exiled. I wanted to explain. I was sworn to secrecy, but I had to try. Liam just wouldn't hear it. He had fallen in love with you. *You!* When I was exiled, Lincoln dropped me from his pack, saying I was no longer of any use to him. He didn't even try to kill me." She chuckled softly. "He thought I was terrified enough of him that he didn't need to kill me. He broke the pack alliance, and suddenly I was free to say whatever I liked."

"You tried to call Liam. You were trying to warn him about Lincoln?"

"And Ryan. A few times. But both of them blocked my number."

Brady burst into the room with a loud bang. His arms over-flowed with firewood as he went to the cast-iron stove in the middle of the cabin, whistling a show tune. I shuddered.

"You realize that he's a psychopath," I muttered, looking over at Brady as he started stoking the fire. I saw Brady smirk. He was listening.

"He loves you, Clem. And once you two are together, I can

go back to Liam and help him pick up the pieces. I know he's really sick right now, and I can help him get better. Thank you for saving him, by the way."

"You know how I saved him, right?"

"I wasn't there, but Brady told me you were always supposed to be an ER doctor. So I'm sure, however you managed, it was heroic."

"No, it wasn't. I gave him almost all of my blood, slowly killing myself, as I sat with him for five days, praying for him to heal."

"That sounds pretty heroic to me. You really are selfless." She smiled softly again.

"No, you don't understand! Cassie, I'm sorry to tell you that the only reason it worked–"

"Clementine!" Brady's tone was one of warning.

"Fuck you, Brady!" I snapped back. "Cassie. Liam is my–"

Brady smacked me. I tasted the metallic flavouring of my blood. His eyes were livid, and he started to drag me away. I spat, red saliva sprinkled over his face. I felt his fingers encircle my throat, pressing hard into my windpipe. The aconite was swirling razors around my bloodstream, my lungs were burning, and the pressure on my throat was vice-like. I started to see stars hovering on the periphery of my blurred vision.

"Liam is...my...true...mate," I managed to croak before the world went dark.

CHAPTER 70

LIAM

HALF AN HOUR later and the meeting had disbanded. Ryan and Stacey had taken off with a couple of trackers from the warrior squad. Patrick went to inform Vinny about what had happened, and Jerome and Dad helped me organize an urgent meet with the entire pack for this afternoon.

Even though it was the middle of the afternoon, it was getting cooler now in the fall air. The mountains and thick forest made it almost impossible for the sun to warm up the valley. The sun tried desperately to shine through the trees, but it was met with an invisible frosty wall that couldn't be penetrated. The chill in the air was almost foreboding, making me feel like I would never be warm again. Patio heaters and gas barbecues were lit up throughout the grounds. I smiled at the pack members as they filed in, wearing their summery clothes as if they were oblivious to the changes in the temperature.

I smiled at the five hundred odd people who had turned up. Five hundred wolves would be enough to start. The news would soon travel. I didn't demand the entire pack to be here; I didn't think that would be fair. Instead, I requested that if they could spare half an hour, I would answer some questions I'm sure they had since I assumed my role as alpha.

I walked across the amphitheatre stage and suppressed the sudden nervousness that enveloped me. The last time I was out here, I was challenged, and although I was confident it wouldn't happen again, a part of me was a little anxious because I knew I wasn't fully healed.

"I would like to thank you all for coming here on such short notice. The last time I was up here didn't end according to plan, but I thought it was important to show you that I'm still here, to rest any worries and rumours that may have been plaguing your minds," I said winging my speech. "It's true that a small army of pack members have left the Blackfern Valley Pack. These wolves were in line with Lincoln, and they've run off when he fell. Many of these members may be your friends and even family members. They may be scared to return." Some of the crowd looked angry; others looked pained. This was hard on everyone. "I'm going to ask this: reach out to them and ensure they're okay. Let them know I'm willing to hear petitions for those who wish to come home. Those who do not wish to return will not have to. But when you mention this to them, let them know that if any of them attack this pack or its members again, I will not be as lenient. They will not get out alive," I growled, an aura shimmered off me and across the grounds to solidify my intent.

The pack started rumbling and bowed respectfully under the weight of my power. A few howls sounded out, too. "The warriors have been working hard to find the remainder of Lincoln's pack. They have worked diligently to keep our land's perimeter safe. It would be foolish not to be prepared, so I implore you to keep up your training up for a small chance that the perimeter is breached. Keep your pups and elderly close.

Have an escape plan and a meeting point. Keep each other safe! I promise, as your alpha, I will protect this pack until my dying breath if it ever leads to that. I hope you'll trust me to do this for you."

A breeze blew through the air, and I swear I could smell honeysuckle notes within the cold wind. I braced against the pain that pierced my heart and smiled out at the crowd, nibling the inside of my cheek. I needed to know if anyone had seen Clementine. Someone must have seen something. Lucian nodded toward me in complete agreement with my sudden whim.

"Now, I'm sure you've heard countless rumours surrounding my love life. I'm going to clear the air once and for all. Clementine is indeed my mate." The soft and gentle noise of chatter began swarming, and I felt confusion and anger permeate the pack. "She's my true mate and will be the future luna of this pack," I roared, cutting off the confused and angry buzzing. "The only reason I'm here today is that your luna self-lessly transfused litres and litres of her blood to save me. She used the mate bond to keep me alive and rescue this pack from a potentially vile future. This couldn't have happened if she wasn't my true mate, nor if she wasn't destined to be your luna."

The swarming noise halted as the truth reached people's ears. One by one, people started whispering again, then cheered. There were a few scowls in the crowd, but no one voiced their disgust. I waited for it. I would welcome it as much as my dad taught me to. I would be as diplomatic as I could be, but I would not put up with blatant hate and disrespect against her because of who her mother was.

The pack members started looking around anxiously, trying to figure out why my mate wasn't up on stage with me or why she wasn't pushing through the crowd after the announcement. I reached for our mate bond and came up empty. Again.

Where are you, Clemmy?

"Where is our luna?" people started calling over each other.

"I'm not going to stand here and lie to you. Earlier today, I felt our bond weaken and go dark. I need to know if any of you have seen anything. I need information. Clementine, your luna, has been taken, and I promise you that I will get her back." My voice was sharp, and I felt Lucian rumbling within me as we waited.

The crowd was silent. How is it that no one saw a thing?

"Alpha," a female voice shouted in the crowd.

I saw Stacey and Ryan pushing toward me. I jumped off the stage and ran toward them. "What news do you have?"

"We found him," Stacey said. I turned to Ryan, who nodded enthusiastically.

"Jerome is assembling the warriors," he explained. "Brady is about two hours north from here, but we have to move. He's planning to move her today," he mumbled quietly, looking around the pack with reserved interest.

The buzzing had started amongst the pack again. The information would spread like wildfire, but at least the news was honest; at least five hundred pack members now knew the truth. Luna Clementine was my true mate, she was missing, and the warriors had a lead on her. They knew we would get her back.

When I brought my luna home, the entire pack would know she was my true mate. By the time I got my luna home, Brady would be fucking dead.

"How–"

"It sounds like your luna has at least one ally," Ryan commented.

"Alpha," Stacey murmured, smiling determinedly, "let's go get your luna."

THE SUN MADE its descent behind the mountains, turning everything dark. A green Ford sedan was parked on the side of the road. It was crisply clean, which made it stick out like a sore thumb. It appeared the driver had tried to park it as far off the road as he could, where he hoped it would blend into the trees. It didn't.

I discovered it was unlocked, and I opened the car door. Honeysuckle and pear infused the air within. I took a sniff, and like a drug addict getting his fix, Lucian growled angrily. The scent revved him up instead of calming him. I took another deep breath and turned back to Patrick and Ryan.

"She was here. She's somewhere in this forest."

"Alpha, we'll find her and bring her back to you, but you need to sit this one out. You're still injured," Patrick advised.

"That's my mate!"

"I know. Believe me, I know," Patrick said, closing his eyes. When he opened them again, they flashed with silver, and he started to strip his clothes off, shifting fluidly as soon as his boxer shorts hit his ankles.

"This fucker is going to wish he heeded your warning," Patrick's voice came across the mind-link. *"This fucker is going to wish he never crossed my family."*

A large black wolf with emerald eyes stood in front of me. The silver of those orbs seemed to glow in the waning daylight as his wolf eyes adjusted to their surroundings. I turned around and saw Ryan had also shifted into his sizeable brown wolf. Two other wolves stood on either side of him; one was cream in colour with green eyes, and the other with hazel ones and golden fur so pure it was almost white.

A communal growl echoed around them as Patrick sniffed the air before he sniffed at a tree. They all took off into the bush with a sudden yip of confirmation.

"Lucian, we need to shift."

"It's going to hurt like a mother fucker."

"I know."

I slowly started to strip my clothes and grimaced at the bandage on my stomach. I peeled it off and looked at the damage underneath. Among the claw marks were thin lines that were administered by a scalpel. A few tiny purple sutures were sticking out, but the majority had dissolved. Everything looked healed with delicate pink scar tissue, but I knew it wasn't. I could feel it wasn't.

"Well, if we tear something, our mate is just going to have to fix us up again," I said to Lucian as I pulled him forward and felt the low burning start.

"Yeah, after she punishes us for defying her orders."

"One problem at a time!"

"Who said it'll be a problem? I, for one, am looking forward to it," Lucian said, giving me a wolfy grin.

I felt my bones break and contort, and the fur started to explode in patches over my skin. Bubbling lava travelled through my bloodstream, and I grunted in pain. I panted and tried to breathe deep. The breaking of my bones was slow and torturous, and it felt like someone was gutting me with a dull knife. My throat felt like it was being sliced with burning-hot razor wire.

The soft scent of honeysuckle and pear from the green Ford calmed me slightly. I imagined turquoise eyes and a shy smile that made my heart flip. I focused on the image of Clementine in my head, and it helped to numb some of the pain. Twenty minutes later, I was looking at the world in wolf form, wobbling a little as I stood and sniffed the air before I scurried into the bush.

I'm coming, Clementine!

CHAPTER 71

CLEMENTINE

THE LOWER SIDE of my face was swollen. My throat felt like I'd swallowed razorblades, and my lip was split.

"Put some ice on your face," an unknown voice snarled. I opened my eyes and winced. I assumed I was still in the cabin, lying on a very uncomfortable cot in a small room.

I met the brown eyes of someone I had seen around town and flinched back from the ice in his hands.

"I'm not going to hurt you." He rolled his chocolate eyes and offered me the ice again. I gingerly took it, looked up at him again and took in his chiselled jaw and brown wavy hair.

"I don't understand. Why are you helping me?" My voice was rough and scratchy.

"Because you're injured."

"You were part of Lincoln's pack," I stated.

"I was." His eyes travelled down my torso as I sat myself up and placed the ice onto my jaw.

"And you know I'm a half-breed," I whispered timidly.

"I know. Are you hurt anywhere else?" he asked.

"No. I don't think so," I mumbled.

"Good. I just came in to give you some ice. Brady says he's moving you tonight."

"What do you mean moving me?" I squeaked.

"You didn't think he would keep you here, did you? This was just a pitstop. He never wanted to be a part of any war. He just wanted you."

"You can't possibly be thinking of attacking Blackfern Valley. It's your home!"

He looked away. "It's not my home anymore."

"It'll always be your home," I murmured sadly.

"The alpha won't forgive us for what we did. I accepted those consequences the moment I saw Lincoln fall," he said emotionlessly.

"You didn't want Lincoln to be alpha," I surmised, watching him curiously.

"No, but I didn't think Liam would be much better."

"Why?"

"Because he just didn't care."

"What do you mean?"

"He never cared about training, his duties, or his pack. He was ignorant and conceited, and it was always about what he wanted, not what was best for the pack." Chocolate eyes bore into mine, and the forest-green rings around his irises glowed. "You're a case-in-point. He chose you to be his mate. He chose you to be his luna without so much as batting an eyelash. He chose a half-breed to rule next to him, not caring that it would divide the pack. A pack divided is dangerous. A pack divided is a death sentence to the entire pack."

"Is that honestly what you think? He was going to give up his seat for me! I was human, and he was going to give it all up and follow me out of Blackfern Valley–"

"Yeah, like I said. Selfish."

"So let me get this straight, you're angry at him for picking me and bringing me into a titled position in the pack. And you're angry at him for choosing me and renouncing his title?"

"Yeah, because he still chose you over his pack."

I threw the icepack on the cot and glared at him. I was hurt and angry. He wasn't showing any obvious disgust toward me, but he still seemed to care that his luna would be a half-breed. It was amazing that even with the people who claimed they had no issue with my heritage, they still seemed to have a problem with me being with Liam—with me being in a position of power. It was the same level of bigotry, but they didn't seem to understand that. Well, I was happy to start educating.

"Alpha Liam is following his father's legacy by trying to bring the pack together, not split it apart! He's trying to reverse the damage Jed caused. The only way for the pack to live in harmony is to stop the fucking racism by keeping Blackfern Valley pure. Is that what you want? A pure Blackfern Valley? No half-breeds? No humans? Should we start rounding up all the humans and half-breeds in Canada and turn them into slaves? How about we just commit mass genocide?"

His chocolate eyes narrowed into slits, and he went to open his mouth, but I wouldn't let him speak. This was *my* teaching moment!

"How dare a filthy half-breed be luna," I shrieked in a sardonic tone. "A half-breed wolf will never be as good as a full-blooded wolf in your eyes, right? The hatred is ingrained so fucking deep in your culture that you don't even consider it racism anymore," I growled. He glared at me, but I raced on before he could say anything. "Oh, and by the way, although Liam did choose me, so did the fucking moon! The moon fated us to be together!"

"What?" he pushed a strand of hair out of his eyes, a confused expression on his face. "Why didn't he tell us?"

"He was planning on it. When he found out, he wanted to

throw a fucking party and tell everyone that the half-breed whore he had been dating was his fated mate, but I told him to wait. I was afraid of the reaction. I mean, look at the evidence! The slander, the abuse, the fact that no one wanted a half-breed to be with him. I've been getting blatant hate since my fat ass got out of the truck. I didn't trust the pack to accept me. So, if you want to blame anyone, blame me for making him wait. Actually, no, blame that fascist-wanker Jed for instilling such old-world views and fear so deep up your asses you'll need a colorectal surgeon to remove it." I shook my head angrily and released an indignant breath. "Liam was about to announce it, and then Lincoln challenged him. So, you know, we were a little preoccupied with the fight and saving Liam's fucking life. Sorry that our announcement got put on the back burner while I kept your alpha alive. Next time, I'll be sure to consult you first."

Rage flowed around me, and I knew that if Circe were awake, the need to shift would be pushing through, but the hollow part in my mind was still darkened. I still couldn't feel her. And even though she was annoyingly antagonizing and didn't have a filter, I missed her presence and strength. I felt like a part of me was missing.

"This changes everything," he said gruffly.

"It shouldn't. I'm still the same fucking half-breed whore. Being blessed by the moon hasn't changed me as a person. I haven't changed."

"No, your bloodline is the same," he agreed, "but the moon has made your bond sacred. That changes everything. Your birth status doesn't matter now. True mates are fucking rare—"

"It should never have mattered. You should have allowed him to make his choice without judgement."

He frowned. "No, you're right, it shouldn't matter, but it does. It's culture. I'm not saying it's right, but it's just how things are. I really wish you had made the announcement the day after the full moon. It would have changed everything."

"It makes no fucking sense. Blood-haters would still hate me," I snapped.

"Yeah, they still will, but the rest of us, who honestly don't care about your heritage, wouldn't. We thought Liam was dividing the pack, that's all. I promise you, Clementine, I was only doing what I thought was best for my pack."

I sat for a moment and stared into his brown eyes encircled in forest green. He crossed his arms, and his muscles bulged.

"What's your name?"

"Milo."

"Milo, you were right about one thing." I straightened my shoulders. "Alpha Liam isn't going to forgive you. You're an accessory to the kidnapping of your luna. And although I'm not educated formally on pack laws, I'm sure this is a pretty big no-no. So, tell me, what is the punishment for harming your luna?" I asked softly.

Colour drained from Milo's face as the realisation hit him. I heard a commotion somewhere outside the cabin.

"L-Luna—"

"You need to get a message back to the pack. Tell him I sent you with it. Tell him I've forgiven you and that Brady is taking me away," I whispered, looking anxiously toward the door.

"But Alpha Liam is too unwell to fight."

"No, Milo. The true-mate bond healed him. Alpha Liam has been awake for days. And right now, I promise you, Alpha Liam is gathering his warriors and is planning to take down Brady and anyone who threatens the safety of the Blackfern Valley Pack and its luna. That includes all of Lincoln's pack. All one-hundred-and-eighty-three rogues."

"He's going to kill us all."

"Only those who are a threat to his pack. If you aren't, tell him so. Give him proof. Tell him where I am or will be," I whispered.

He studied me for a moment, then nodded. "Yes, Luna," he whispered back.

The door swung open, and Cassie stood there with her hands on her hips. "I was wondering what was taking so long," she snapped, looking between us as Milo moved past her. "Brady is on his way back."

"Where did he go?" I asked.

"Scouting with some other wolves. He's making sure the coast is clear for your departure."

She led me to the table, and I sat down on the wooden chair. She stared at me and didn't say anything for another half an hour, but I happily filled the silence. "If he's out there scouting, now is the time to help me escape!" She scoffed as if what I suggested was ludicrous. "You know Brady lied to you to get information. He never planned on allowing Liam to live. He would have had to kill Liam while kidnapping me. It would have been the only way to sever the bond as neither Liam nor I will ever be willing to sever it."

Silence.

"I'm not saying any of this to hurt you. I really wish you all the happiness in finding someone who will love you, Cassie. It's just not going to be Liam."

"You're lying."

"Why would I lie?"

"Why would Brady lie?" I raised an eyebrow at her. *Seriously?* "Liam would have sung it from the rooftops if he'd found his true mate."

"He wanted to. Trust me; he did. I asked him not to, and then he got hurt before we had the chance to announce it. The only reason he's alive right now is that the true-mate bond saved him. No one else would have been able to save him. Talk to Doctor Todd. Lincoln's blow was fatal."

She scowled, and her purple rings glowed as she retreated into silence. A few minutes later, I tried again.

"I'm honestly telling you the truth, Cassie. You're just too stubborn to hear it. Liam is awake, and he's coming for me. You're putting yourself in danger by not helping me. He already hates you. Don't give him an excuse to kill you."

Brady stormed into the cabin and chuckled at what he had just overheard. He pulled me up and checked my ropes. He pulled, slid, and knotted an end to tighten them, ignoring my feeble attempts to stop him. He was pretty quick with his knots, and every time I struggled, the rope would tighten and bite into my skin viciously.

"You were always very good at staying by a dying person's side, even when I told you it was pointless. I should have wondered why you were wandering around Blackfern Valley and not by his deathbed. I really should have worked out he was awake, not that it matters now because we'll be making our way out of this shithole, and he's never going to find you. I'll have fun torturing him as I mate and mark you." He raised his fingers to his brow and saluted Cassie. "Cassie, it's been a pleasure. Some warriors have been surveying this land over the last couple of hours, so it's time for us to say adios. Good luck with the Blackfern Valley warriors should they find you." His voice was icy. "Come on, Clementine. Time to go."

IT WAS DARK, and I knew it would be hard to see without a wolf. I was at Brady's mercy as he dragged me through the forest, kicking and screaming. Twenty minutes later, my voice became even more hoarse as tears streamed down my face.

"Do I need to gag you?" he snarled.

"You need to let me go!" I cried.

"Keep moving, Clementine."

"You're a fucking psycho, Brady. Deranged. Has anyone ever sent you for a psych evaluation? Like seriously?"

He directed me through the trees without answering, and I could just make out the ground twisting toward a bluff's edge.

Can I push him over the side? Will that buy me some time to get help? He said that warriors were in the area a few hours ago. Will they still be around? Will I be able to find them? What if they aren't Blackfern Valley wolves? They could be anyone, but surely, anyone is better than this sociopath?

Fuck it!

I braced myself and tackled Brady to the ground. He landed with an 'oomph', and I tried to force him over the bluff's edge. He got the upper hand within seconds and lay on top of me, his erection evident as it pressed into my leg.

"Now, sweetheart, if you wanted me on the ground, you should have just asked."

His mouth covered mine before I could press my lips together, and his tongue invaded my mouth like a slippery snake, coating my lips and chin with his saliva. He looked slightly pained and definitely crazed when he pulled away.

"You just had to let a fucking alpha mark you." He coughed a little and grimaced in pain again. "As much as I want to fuck you raw, I physically can't while you have that disgrace on your collarbone." He pulled me to my feet and winked. "The ropes are a nice touch, though. I'll make sure I find a four-poster to tie you to, and the moment his mark fades, we can have some fun."

I was about to respond with disgust when I heard the thundering footsteps of wolves. My heart started pounding only to see Cassie's rust-coloured fur zipping through the trees. It wasn't my pack. Not my salvation.

Brady started dragging me away from the bluff's edge and

through the bush again. It was some time before I heard the low growl that made Brady stop in his tracks.

He smiled dangerously. "I think Daddy's come to play," he whispered. "Should I kill him? Maybe your little brother, too?"

I spun to look where his gaze was set. Sure enough, a large black wolf was stalking us. Next to him, a cream-coloured wolf flanked him, looking directly at me with piercing green eyes. Vinny!

Brady pushed me down and charged toward my saviours on all fours, his white-gold coat contrasting against Dad's ebony fur. Growling and snapping sounds rang out as Vinny ran to my side, whimpering and prodding me with his nose, trying to get me to move. I couldn't. I sat in horror as I watched more wolves emerge from the trees in droves.

And I couldn't tell if they were friend or foe.

CHAPTER 72

LIAM

THE SOUND of battle was emitted from deep within the forest. I was still a fair distance away, but the echoes and vibrations pushed my paws harder into the forest floor. The smell of Clem's scent caught on the wind, and Lucian barked, scaring a small frog off a rock and back into the nearby creek.

I followed the scent and the sounds of fighting in the distance, running past wolves in a combination of different fighting forms. Most of them were fully shifted, but those who had their level-three training swapped between wolf and human forms with the grace of deadly dancers.

Clementine was cornered against a dirt wall. Her hands were bound, and even though she looked calm, I could sense the fear rolling from her. There were four wolves with her, encasing her in a semi-circle—standing sentry. Her brother was closest, as if the others had pushed him back to protect him too.

Two large werewolves the colour of molten chocolate guarded the middle front from attack—Milo and his brother Luca. Sebastian, a warrior in training, guarded the left flank, and Cassie was on the right.

Wait, Cassie?

I looked back and scanned over her rusty-red fur and piercing blue eyes that were full of purpose as a grey wolf tried to get through the line.

Cassie's paw scraped the grey wolf's side as she bent and bit into her neck. There was the guttural sounds of a wolf yelping before silence ensued. The grey wolf's blood splattered over the ground as Cassie clamped her teeth and wrenched back, looking feral with her muzzle covered in the coppery-smelling lifeforce that now caked into her fur.

Cassie had killed Miley.

Holy fuck! Cassie's protecting Clementine—the woman she once tried to kill!

Before I got a chance to revel in this reality, Sebastian's golden fur darted forward. He barrelled into two wolves who were ganging up on a smaller one. I was unsure who this wolf was, but it was apparent Sebastian did with the amount of angry energy he exhibited to save her.

I ran into the opening he left and took Clementine in from head to toe.

Thank fuck!

The lower part of her face was bruised, and her turquoise eyes glistened with unshed tears. She was on alert. She looked like she was okay despite the superficial wounds.

She reached out with her tied hands and gently touched my fur, but there were no sparks. She awkwardly hooked her arms over my head and around my neck before she buried her face into the side of my head. I frowned and grumbled as Lucian tried in vain to reach for Circe.

"You're in big trouble," she managed to whisper. I tilted my head back and looked at her as she gave me a small shy smile. "But thanks for coming for me." I huffed and refocused on the battle. I knew I needed to get Clementine out of here, but first, I needed to assess whether it was safe to do so. I also needed to find Brady and kill him.

It was hard to navigate the battling wolves through the trees. This was no enormous open battlefield where I could see my pack fighting in their individual battles. There was no beautifully choreographed fight scene like in the movies. This was dirty, dark, and a lot of it I couldn't see. The thick brush obscured most of my vision.

I felt a sharp, piercing sensation ricochet through my body and knew I had just lost a pack member. I didn't know who was killed, but I could feel their last moment of pain. A few minutes later, I felt another. I knew I could switch it off, but I wouldn't. These wolves were dying for their pack. They were dying for me, and the best respect I could give them was to feel and mourn every one that fell.

Then another one fell. *Shit.* I needed to get Clementine out of there. I opened my mind-link to the three wolves in Clementine's protective circle.

"Milo."

"Yes, Alpha."

"When you get an opening, I want you to take this party toward Kempthorne, do you understand? Keep running until you get her there."

"She won't leave you, Alpha," Vinny said.

I huffed. *"She will. I'll shift and tell her myself if I have to."*

"Alpha, it will take you too long to shift back. You're still hurt. Let me shift and tell her the plan," Milo said.

I grumbled and nodded in agreement as I reached out and quickly searched the battle for my warriors. Someone had to be with Brady.

I refocused on my mate as Milo stood tall, naked, and proud in front of her and anxiously told her the plan I had mind-linked him. I tried to ignore that a male wolf stood naked in front of her and the jealous and possessive feelings it uncovered. Instead, I focused on him being my messenger. I concentrated on the fact that he was looking at her with anxiety, not lust. I absorbed the fact Clem's eyes remained on me and only occasionally flicked to Milo. And when they did, they never strayed from his face or fingers as they loosened the knotted ropes around her wrists.

Then she shook her head at me, her eyes full of tears. I rumbled softly. I needed her safe.

"You're injured," she snapped. "You need me close to heal. If I leave, you're coming with me!"

I shook my head as Milo relayed my message. I needed to stay with the pack. I needed her in an area where they couldn't hurt her. And I needed her to trust me when I told her I would come for her. More importantly, that I will always return to her.

Milo shifted back easily and stayed closer than I would have liked, especially when her fingers ran through his fur. I saw red and tasted the bitter rage on my tongue, but I bit down hard. Part of the plan required her to move quickly and with very little notice. She was going to climb on top of Milo's broad back and ride him out of here, with Luca and Vinny in tow. I didn't care what Cassie did. She could follow, or she could stay and die. Our mind-link was severed, and I had no idea why she was even here, but if she chose to follow and attacked any of them, Milo had my permission to brutally end her life.

In the few minutes it took me to instruct Clementine, another four of my pack had died. I couldn't feel who, but I had the primal need to get out there and join them. I looked back at Clementine and gave her one last look of pure love, wishing that she had Circe, or even the mate bond, to feel the size of my devotion to her before I bounced into the fight. I heard her scream my name, but I didn't look back. I knew that her guard would not let her follow. I knew that at any moment, her guard would take her to safety.

I focused all my energy on finding Patrick or Ryan, knowing they were the two most likely to be with Brady. A few moments later, I was travelling deeper into the trees, outrunning wolves that were stupid enough to try and take out an alpha.

I tumbled and rolled as an ex-pack-member snarled over top of me. His grey eyes bore into mine as his teeth aimed for my throat. I kicked him off, and Lucian gave me a boost as I raised my hackles in warning. My alpha-power lit up like a beacon, but instead of making the dirty mottled wolf bow down, he attacked.

My teeth sunk into his leg like it was made of butter, and he let out a howl of pain. I clamped down and ripped at the tendons that ran up the back of his leg. He instantly collapsed and started panting with pain. When he shifted back, I noticed he was only a pup. His dirty brown hair had sandy brown highlights, his eyes were large and grey, and he was pale and clammy with the pain I had just bestowed him.

Lucian attempted to reach his wolf. I was surprised when the mind-link connected us as I was sure that these rogues would no longer be able to connect to the pack. But then again, I could connect with Milo and Luca, who had abandoned my pack for Lincoln's.

"Are you okay, pup?"

"Fuck you," he spat angrily, his pride evidently hurt as much as his leg.

"You are far too young to be out here. Go home."

"I have no home now."

"Blackfern Valley is your home."

"Not anymore. Not since my parents joined Lincoln."

"Where are your parents now?"

"Dead."

Lucian whimpered. He said it with such animosity that I was unsure whether he was angry at me, his parents, or in general. I sent through a command to my pack for someone to take him to safety. This was no place for a sixteen-year-old. Sebastian came tumbling out of the trees and gave me a gentle nod before indicating to the pup to climb onto his golden back. The kid shook his head angrily, and I left Sebastian to deal with the tantrums of a sixteen-year-old pup.

I finally located Ryan and Patrick, running forward excitedly when I saw they had cornered Brady. Patrick was missing patches of fur. Superficial claw marks scraped through the bald patches, and he was hurt. But his determination seeped through as Ryan and he stalked forward. Brady's white-gold fur was matted with blood, one eye was shut, and he appeared to have an uneven gait as he braced himself for the attack.

A low growl sounded as Stacey landed lithely on her paws between Patrick, Ryan, and her brother. She lowered her head in warning as she went into protective mode. Patrick and Ryan stopped with equal looks of confusion as I came up to join them. Brady gave a glimpse of smugness as his eyes met mine. A look that told me he was expecting victory.

Anger burned through me at Stacey's betrayal. It sliced through my soul, and my jowls frothed with rage. I didn't care that this was Ryan's mate. I was ready to kill them both. I would make Stacey's death quick if only to ease my best friend's suffering, but Brady's death would be slow and torturous. I would enjoy killing him.

Brady stepped forward gingerly into Stacey's flank. I sent out a low alpha rumble that made Stacey's eyes meet mine. They weren't full of fear but full of unyielding tenacity. The stupid bitch was about to die, and she wasn't even cowering under my wrath or authority.

I stepped forward and let out a low snarl, letting my

displeasure shimmer, making Patrick move instantly. Ryan hesitated, his eyes darting desperately between his mate and myself. His eyes were in a world of panic, but Stacey refused to look at him as I approached. She denied acknowledging him, and that's how I knew she had turned off mate bond to him. She was ready to die for her brother. Brady's eyes were taunting me as he got closer to her protective zone.

Stacey observed me. She never changed her posture, and she never raised or lowered her hackles. Her eyes never darted back to her brother or her mate. She just stared at me, then closed her eyes as if she was saying a prayer. I took a step closer.

Without warning and with unforeseen speed, she pivoted and clamped her canines into Brady's jugular, blood spraying around as she shook her head like a rabid animal. There was a loud yelp as Brady fell to the ground, but Stacey refused to release her hold, even though his paws scraped at her fur help-lessly, or he made the most guttural and desperate noises. Then he went quiet. His blood pooled and watered the ground as the life left his eyes, and his heart stopped thumping in his chest.

Stacey let out a mournful howl as she shifted into her human skin. Her howl turned into a wail of despair, and she covered her blood-stained mouth with her hands as uncontrol-lable sobs trembled out of her.

CHAPTER 73

CLEMENTINE

I watched as Liam sprinted away and felt my heart fall into my stomach. My feet moved on their own, and Milo cut me off before I foolishly ran into the middle of a wolf fight. He growled, and I knew he was telling me we needed to get the fuck out of Dodge.

"Sorry, I'm not exactly light," I apologized as I clambered onto his back. He huffed and spun on his paws so fast I felt myself buckle. I grabbed fistfuls of fur and tugged. He grumbled.

Oops!

I tried to loosen my hold, but there was no good place to hold onto.

I had no experience riding a horse, let alone a wolf.

If I wrapped my arms around his neck, would I choke him? I felt awkward and clumsy on top of him.

"Milo, you need to stop and let me down." I got a grunt as a response, and, not surprisingly, he didn't slow as he whipped around the trees. "Milo, I'm going to fall." Another grunt.

Vinny grumbled at me too. His eyes darted around the forest and back to me, watching me fumble as I tried to balance on the back of a wolf. Not for the first time, I wished I had access to Circe. I didn't speak wolf grunts and grumbles.

"You aren't hurting him, Luna. He says to hold on tight and promises you won't fall." I turned to see Luca had shifted back.

He looked similar to his brother, with long chocolate brown hair and a chiselled jaw, but instead of matching eyes, his eyes were bright blue and seemed to see right through me. I only saw his human side for a second before he shifted into wolf form again and went to intercept a threat to our left.

I gripped onto Milo's fur as tightly as I could. My body was thrumming with adrenaline as more wolves started toward us. Our escape was not going as smoothly as we'd hoped. My brother turned to intercept another wolf.

"Vinny!" I shouted. He was going to get himself killed. I didn't know he had shifted until an hour ago, but I sure as hell knew that he was no match for the wolves in this battle. "Vincent!" I screamed again.

Cassie came out of nowhere and barrelled into the wolf my brother was fighting. We had left her in our dust as we escaped, and suddenly, she was back again. I didn't care what her motives were at this point. I just cared that my brother and I made it away safely.

We finally made it to a road, crossing it quickly into the woods on the other side. I suppose the image of four wolves running down the road with a human on one's back would look just as odd as four naked people running down that same road.

My entourage didn't show any sign of slowing down as they darted through this new section of forest. My butt was sore from riding Milo, and I felt like I was coming down from the worst hangover ever. I needed water. I needed food. I needed sleep and to know that my pack, my father *and* my mate were okay.

Milo suddenly slowed to a trot before giving a sigh of relief and stopping completely. He shrugged his shoulders, and I knew he was telling me it was safe to get down.

My crotch and legs ached as I climbed off. My legs felt like I had hiked up a mountain or done copious amounts of exercise. They wobbled like Jell-O as my feet hit the ground. I took a couple of wobbly steps and looked around. The forest seemed thinner here, and it looked as though it was frequented quite a bit. We must have finally passed the Kempthorne boundary which would mean hopefully we were out of immediate danger.

I frowned. *We* were, but my mate, Dad, and my pack were all still back there. I worried my lip between my teeth, hissing at the pain of my split lip. It started to bleed again. Without Circe, my ability to heal was gone. That's probably why I felt so rough.

Cassie and Vinny came thundering toward us. Well, at least my brother was safe. We walked through the trees until we found a beaten-down, dusty hiking trail and followed it out. I kept my hand on my brother's fur, letting him guide me. His wolf eyes were better than my human ones in the dark. My brother suddenly started making yipping noises as he ran forward.

"Vinny!" I called. He didn't reply, nor did he slow down.

Dammit, it was annoying not being able to communicate with my wolves. I reached out for Circe again and was met with the never-ending abyss. I hoped she would return soon and prayed that what Brady had done to me wasn't permanent.

Milo and Luca came forward to guide me in the dark. We turned a bend in the trail, and I quickly covered my eyes, horrified, as my very naked brother was throwing on some athletic shorts, his bony white ass in full display in the soft glow of a camping lantern.

Gross!

Sophie smiled at me as more wolves approached. There was

a kerosene lantern and a large hiker's backpack at her feet which seemed to overflow with shorts and t-shirts. Her arms wrapped around me as I approached.

"Thank God you're okay! When I heard that Brady had taken you, I was so worried. I wanted to come after you, but Alpha Liam said you would need a friendly face when you made it out, so he stationed a few of us around Kempthorne, watching out for pack members who may be coming this way. Where's Stacey? Where's my brother? Is everyone okay?"

"The fight is still going on," Luca said, fully human, fully naked and stalking toward Sophie's bag of clothes. "Our part was to rescue the princess and get her to safety."

I felt myself blush as he gave me a wink. "What is this, some kind of video game?" Milo sneered, pulling up a pair of shorts.

"Nah, if it were a video game, the princess would give me a kiss, and I would receive a handsome reward."

"If you'd like to keep your eyeballs in your head, I suggest you don't flirt with your luna."

"I was just fucking around," Luca grumbled playfully.

Vinny rolled his eyes and shook his head, giving me a look that said he'd had to endure their sibling antics for a while already. Suddenly, I was glad that Circe had gone to sleep.

"Yeah, I wouldn't use that term either," Sophie suggested good-naturedly before turning to me. "Luca is a shameless flirt. Infamous ladies-man."

He threw his hands over his heart in a dramatic fashion. "You wound me!"

"If you're done joking around, you realize there's still a battle going, and Liam isn't back," Cassie snarled, standing naked with her arms crossed. "Do any of you even care? I knew you were fucking lying, Clementine. I, for one, am going back for him." I stared at her with my mouth open like a fish.

What the hell?

"What the hell was that about?" Sophie asked, staring after Cassie, whose red tail disappeared back into the trees.

"Cassie doesn't believe that Alpha Liam and Luna Clementine are true mates," Milo said gruffly, rolling his eyes.

"Oh, this is going to be interesting," Sophie said with a twinkle in her eye as she observed my expression. I rolled my eyes and shrugged. A gleeful laugh escaped her lips. That girl lived for drama and gossip.

It was hours before I heard anything. We camped out on the hiking trail, and even though I felt like I could sleep for a million years, the cold mountainous air kept me awake and alert. I kept annoying my companions every thirty minutes, asking if they had heard anything through the mind-link. They would gently humour me with small smiles and tell me they hadn't before returning to their quiet conversations.

I looked at Vinny, knowing he was as anxious as I was. He kept rubbing his arm and breathing deeply. His eyes would flash now and again, and Luca kept telling him to breathe, kept him focused on anything but the eery silence of the unknown. His anxiety over my kidnapping had caused him to shift for the first time, and there was no way he could shift again. Not yet. I was safe now, and now his anxiety was for the only parent we had left.

I didn't talk to him about it. We still didn't have deep and meaningful conversations; it wasn't us. I simply tried to distract myself and prayed that my efforts didn't add to his stress.

I looked up at the crescent moon and counted stars, praying on every one that twinkled that this would end, that we would have some answers. Soon.

The crunching of footsteps coming through the trees made my head snap to the side. A black wolf limped toward us through them. Vinny's eyes met mine as Dad approached. Tears of relief glistened in Vinny's emerald gaze, and he looked away quickly, bracing himself and pushing his emotions away.

Dad went straight for the bag of clothes, shifted, and pulled on a pair of shorts. He gave me a small, relieved smile as soon as he was dressed. That's what broke me out of my trance. I raced forward, and his arms went around me. I couldn't smell his pine scent, but the hug comforted me as it always had before I'd discovered Circe.

Dad was okay.

"You're in serious trouble, young lady," he said with a grunt.

I looked up at him, confused. "Why? What did I do?" I croaked, but his eyes twinkled with humour.

"The one thing I missed out on was chasing boys away when you were a teenager. I thought, 'my girl is way too smart to date unworthy losers'. Only to find out you had a boyfriend. Not only a boyfriend, but one with sociopathic tendencies," he snapped, but his eyes didn't match his tone. "Do you know how much fun I would have had with him if I'd known? You denied me the chance to have some fun. I could have been very creative in getting him to stay away from you."

"TJ suggested a screwdriver to his orbital socket," I whispered.

"I was thinking more basement, chains, and torture. Perhaps some Celine Dion on repeat?"

"But, Dad, I told you that you weren't allowed to torture people anymore, remember?" He laughed and kissed the top of my head before hobbling over to talk to Vinny.

. . .

Fifteen minutes later, Ryan and Stacey came onto the hiking trail from the treeline. Sophie gasped and ran forward, wrapping her arms around them, even though they were very naked. I gave them a soft smile and saw Stacey almost catatonic with grief. One look, and I knew. Liam had done it. Brady was dead.

My heart ached for her. I wanted to wrap her in my arms and hold her, but I was sure I was the last person she wanted to see right now. Her brother was dead because of me.

More noise came from the treeline, and I turned and looked into the darkness. Instinctively, I knew who was coming toward us. His trajectory was determined, as was mine. I re-entered the treeline and sprinted toward him. Liam's mocha and gold eyes glowed and never wavered from mine. He held his arms wide and caught me, wrapping me in his embrace, inhaling my hair and peppering kisses all over my face before catching my mouth and giving me a long, deep kiss that made my toes curl.

Somewhere in the darkened recesses of my mind, a small fissure ignited with the glow of our mate bond.

"You're okay," I whispered before he captured my mouth again. I was amazed that kissing him didn't hurt, and when I pulled away, I licked my lips to find that the cut had healed.

"I told you I would be. I told you I would come back to you," he said against my mouth. His lips caressed mine, and I felt the low hum of the mate bond start against my mouth and travel down into my core. He pulled away, smiling, his eyes full of love and wonder.

"Never break that promise," I begged, my voice cracking with emotion.

"Never," he agreed solemnly.

"Can we go home now?"

He smiled softly and chuckled. "Yes, we can go home."

"Good." I leaned toward his ear and whispered. "Because I also keep my promises. And now that you're healed enough to shift, and because you broke your promise not to go after the rogues, I plan on punishing you. Then, and only then, we'll follow through with the promise I made you when you became alpha, but only if you think you can keep up."

He answered me with a throaty, lustful growl before capturing my mouth again.

CHAPTER 74
LIAM

THE FULL MOON WAS APPROACHING, and the entire pack could feel it. Everyone was on edge. There were several ex-pack members still missing. Everyone seemed convinced it would lead to another battle and more pack members would die.

Our pack had lost fourteen members in our quest to rescue my mate. Fourteen families had received visits where Clem and I delivered our heartfelt condolences to personally. I was unsure how many the rogue army had lost, but there were a lot of deceased wolves when we started to clean up and sort through the bodies.

I had left Clementine the next morning, tucked safe and sound in our bed. I knew she would be pissed about it, but I needed to go and help identify the bodies. Twenty of us marched out to the battle site and started to sift through the woods, pulling wolves out of debris and resting them together in a small area where their loved ones could collect them.

Usually, we would just burn the rogues, but as much as I kept saying it, these rogues weren't really rogues. These rogues still had families in my pack. These rogues were known and loved, and despite being disillusioned, they were still pack.

Fifty-seven wolves who had abandoned Blackfern Valley for Lincoln's coup returned the night Brady died. Another thirty-four trickled back over the next two weeks. There were at least another fifty-odd that remained unaccounted for. So, I understood the pack's nervous mentality, but I didn't expect them to attack, nor did I expect them to return.

Even so, Ryan and Jerome had taken it upon themselves to increase the training schedule for any pack member who wanted to get some extra defence practice. Other than that, life pretty much returned to normal.

Well, almost. It had been two weeks since Clementine was force-fed aconite, yet Circe still hadn't returned. We had gone to the doctor to get her checked over, and he simply shook his head as flummoxed as we were. With most wolves, it only took a day or two to clear their system of residual aconite, and once it was cleared, the wolf spirit would normally wake up.

Blood tests showed that she had no traces of aconite left in her system, yet Circe still hadn't come back. Clementine's eyes were still ringed with amber, and the mate bond was there, stronger than ever, but still no Circe.

Lucian said he couldn't feel Circe either, and when Clem heard that, she put on a brave face and pretended she wasn't worried. When her guard was down however, I could feel her distress over it. Her anguish.

It worried me, too, so much that I needed to put guards on her to ensure that she was protected. She argued that she should be safe in her pack, and I laughed with mild disbelief. I wasn't going to budge on this. My unyielding love and respect for her were challenged by the primal need to keep her safe, and until such a time when Circe made her appearance, she would remain in someone's sights.

The problem with negotiating with Clementine was that she usually ended up winning, and I would be left wondering how she spun the conversation in her favour. But this was non-negotiable.

"So stubborn. Need I remind you that you weren't safe in our pack? Need I remind you that you got kidnapped on the main road?" I snarled softly, running my fingers down her spine, and feeling her body quiver.

"Need I remind you that Brady is now tumbling around in the sheets with Satan himself?" She raised her eyebrow.

"Even so, it would ease my mind if you had someone with you when you're away from the pack house. A friend if you like, so you don't feel like it's protection." I kissed the spot which held my territorial mark, teasing and nibbling and feeling the warmth pool between her legs. Lucian grumbled happily. He liked this form of negotiation.

"It won't matter if it's a friend or not. I'll always know I have a bodyguard," she said through a small gasp at my ministrations.

"Most alphas and lunas have bodyguards, you know," I countered, holding her tighter and moving my mouth to her smooth neck and jaw.

"Sure, they do!" She rolled her eyes before letting a gentle moan escape.

I stopped my seductive kisses for a moment and gave her a serious look. "No, honestly, they do. It's usually for when they head out of town on diplomatic missions, etcetera. They name a small number of wolves to go with them. You'll notice that whenever other packs come to Blackfern Valley. It's never just the alpha and luna; it's the alpha and four or five other wolves. Depending on their party's size, they stay in one or two of the cottages."

"Well, guess what, I'm not heading on any diplomatic missions," she whispered with a small smile, one that told me she was most likely going to win this discussion.

I sighed against her and changed my tactic. "Clementine, you have no wolf. I can't be with you twenty-four seven. I almost lost you once. I can't lose you again. Please, just humour me." I kissed her gently and felt her mould into me, her resolve slowly crumbling. "Please, Clemmy. I need you to be safe." I kissed her again and felt her gentle moan against my tongue as her mouth opened to answer me.

"Fine, but only until Circe returns, and I get to pick who."

"Deal." And I sealed our agreement with a deep kiss.

I spoke too soon. I should have seen her eyes twinkling and realized she gave in far too easily. I would have sworn she'd have picked Sophie or Stacey to hang out with daily. I really should have known better. Stacey was still grieving and barely came out in public, and Sophie wasn't leaving Stacey's side. I knew Clem had done this on purpose. I knew she hated the idea of having a guard, so she picked a guard in the hope I would call off the idea of her having a protective detail.

Fat chance of that. I was just going to have to grin and bear it.

As much as I knew our bond was solid, and she had never really shown signs of jealousy around the she-wolves that still fought for my attention, *my* jealousy wasn't something to be trifled with.

Of course, she claimed innocence when I confronted her about it. She said she knew Luca was an outrageous flirt, but he was all talk, and at the end of the day, he protected her and her brother during the battle and took his job seriously. She was right, and I knew it, but my pride and possessive instincts made me claim her repeatedly anytime I knew she was about to meet with him. The mark on her neck would never be enough, not even when I made it permanent on the full moon.

Brady kissing her had imprinted that irrational and primal reaction when it came to other wolves. I had never heard of someone being stupid enough to make a physical move on someone who had a territorial mark. When she told me it physically hurt him, it did little to quell my rage. I wanted to bring him back from the dead so I could torture him and kill him all over.

Each day she met her protective detail, we would argue, have a hot make-out session, and argue some more. Even without Circe, she was still a force of nature, and she left me breathless. The mate bond sizzled and continued to grow between us, as it fed on our frustration as much as it thrived on our lust.

Clem had suggested that she could change her guard to Cassie if that made me feel more at ease, using the proverb of keeping your enemies closer to seal her argument. I scowled. There was no way I was letting Cassie anywhere near Clementine, nor would I trust her with my mate again.

Cassie was rejoining the pack on the full moon, much to my disgust, but I had promised that each pack member who had joined Lincoln's coup would be heard, and she allegedly had tried to save Clementine. My father convinced me to let her back in, and I grudgingly agreed. It's a decision I hoped I wouldn't regret.

The entire pack knew Clementine was my true mate, but Cassie refused to believe it. She would snarl and sulk anytime someone brought it to her attention. Clementine didn't react, though I could feel her emotions down the mate bond whenever Cassie was mentioned or hanging around on the off chance she could catch me. Sometimes Clem would grumble under her breath and roll her eyes, but mostly, all she felt was pity and the occasional stab of annoyance.

. . .

CLEMENTINE TIED her hair back and gave me a soft smile. I ran my eyes over her workout gear and felt my cock twitch as she bent over to tie her shoes. Even without a wolf, she needed to train, but I hated the idea that another wolf would feel her soft body. Even if there was nothing sexual about it, I hated the idea of anyone else's paws on her. She was mine.

She smiled impishly at me as we walked through the pack house to the kitchen to meet her guard, who was taking her to the training grounds. I swatted her ass as it bounced seductively in her yoga pants, taunting me, making me want to take her back to the alpha's quarters and bite it.

"Luca," I said, my eyes flashing with controlled anger.

"Alpha," Luca nodded before flicking his eyes toward my mate. He took a big chomp out of an apple and grinned at her. The juices ran down his chin as he tried to chew the fruit into smaller bits. "Luna," he nodded, his blue eyes twinkling mischievously, "you're looking as beautiful as always."

My fingers curled into fists.

She made a scoffing noise and smiled at him. I growled. She had to go and pick him. The one guy who rivalled me at school for being a player. He was a couple of years older than me and still the same guy he was back in school.

"Ready to get down and dirty on those mats?" he asked.

I tightened my fists and let out a low warning growl they both ignored.

"Sure." She nodded. There was no pink stain on her cheeks, no tickle of attraction coming from her. I reached out and tugged on the mate bond, and she turned back to smile at me, her eyes twinkling with knowledge.

"Tomorrow night," I promised with a note of seduction in my voice.

"What's happening tomorrow night?" she asked, feigning innocent ignorance.

I growled at her playful nature before giving her a chaste kiss on her lips and a smack on her ass. She grinned playfully, gave me a wink, then walked out the door.

She knew exactly what was going on tomorrow.

CHAPTER 75

CLEMENTINE

THE FULL MOON had come around again, but this time, it was different because I was a bundle of nerves. Okay, so I might have been a bundle of nerves the first time too, but at least I had Circe.

My wolf still hadn't shown up, and although I was wearing a brave face, the idea of being mated without a wolf made me nervous. Liam kept reassuring me that she would come back eventually, but as we got closer to the full moon, I became more agitated because I believed I couldn't be with Liam without a wolf. Not if he remained alpha.

I tried to convince him to hold off the mating ritual until we knew if she was coming back. I was trying to be pragmatic and develop a strategy in case I was left wolfless, as a human couldn't be luna. Liam had simply shaken his head, dropped a drugging kiss to my lips, and inhaled along my neck.

"Your scent is the same; that intoxicating honeysuckle and pear with the underlying scent of canine and human. Your eyes haven't changed back to the pure turquoise pools I fell in love with. You're not human. You're a half-breed, and your wolf will come back when she's ready."

"How can you be so sure? Even Lucian can't sense her. And there's no information on what aconite does to half-breeds–"

"You just have to trust me. We're going to be okay," he said with a small smile. Then he brushed his lips against mine once more and I shivered into his touch.

———

PACK MEMBERS STARTED FLOODING into the amphitheatre as the sun began to descend. The full moon was up against the blue sky and dusky pink clouds. It was a pale white orb, but it would glow brightly as the sky darkened. I frowned slightly as I felt no pull from the moon. I simply felt the empty chasm that Circe had left behind.

As the night drew nearer, Liam called the pack members to be initiated. Cassie was up first, and I had to suppress a growl of annoyance as she fluttered her eyelashes at him and spoke her vows very softly and with a hint of seduction. Her eyes never left his, full of lust and hope. He grimaced when he joined his hand with hers and caught my eye. I knew he wasn't happy about her coming back into the pack, but she had proven herself loyal, even if her reasonings were twisted.

Stacey was next. Her hazel eyes were sad as she took in her new alpha. He spent a little longer with her, whispering to her and receiving her reassurance that this was what she wanted. He was gentle and kind and told her how much he appreciated what she had done, that he could only imagine how hard it must have been. They spoke in hushed whispers for a few more minutes before she said her vows, and she became a full-fledged member of the pack.

He then announced the pack run as the full moon made its way higher into the heavens. The only light in the midnight-blue sky was the ambient glow from the bright sphere and twinkling stars above us. The pack members howled and began to strip, shifting instantly and running into the trees. The sounds of yips, barks and howls echoed as the wolves ran.

It was technically Liam's first run as alpha, and he probably should have run with them, but instead, he turned to me and whispered, "I have something special to show you."

"Oh?"

"Come with me." He took me by the hand and walked me through the trees, the moonlight glittering through, illuminating our way as we ended at a stream. We strolled alongside it and into a small meadow where he had laid out a picnic blanket with champagne, cheese, and crackers.

"I wanted to recreate our first date," his cheeks were coloured with a slight pink. "It's not too cheesy, is it?"

"No," I croaked, "not at all. But what about the pack run?"

"There'll be other runs," he smiled softly and popped the champagne bottle.

The wine fizzed over the top as he poured the champagne into two small flutes. I smiled and clinked our glasses before swallowing the dry-tasting bubbles.

As the full moon rose and got closer to its peak, I closed my eyes and tried to reach for Circe. Liam stroked my arms in loving circles as he held me close, watching the sky with interest. My back was against his large, hard chest, and I could feel his heart beating in sync with mine.

His fingers moved from my arms to the soft skin of my stomach, and I shivered as the mate bond tingled between us, unbreakable under the moonlight. I may not have had Circe, but I still had him.

I pulled away from Liam briefly before turning to face him. Kissing him tenderly, I straddled his hips. His crotch instantly found my sweet spot under the skirt of my dress. His tenting erection caused my core to throb with heat. He groaned into my mouth as his tongue found mine, and his fingers weaved into my ponytail. He gripped it and gave it a gentle tug, making me expose my neck, which he peppered with small kisses and grazes.

Grappling desperately at his t-shirt, I felt his hardened abs and chest against my fingers as I tugged it roughly over his head. I moaned against his kisses and felt his erection twitch against my throbbing, wet clit. The smell of my arousal was already thick in the air, and my folds were damp and throbbing with need. He grunted, and his eyes flashed with lustful gold when he pulled away.

Within seconds, my dress was pulled over my head, exposing the lacy boy shorts and bra I had worn underneath. His mouth descended, and he started sucking and biting on my nipples with hunger, making them peak through the lace in his desperation. Tingles were travelling all over my body, and I closed my eyes, enjoying the sensation—enjoying Liam.

I heard a ripping noise and opened my eyes as Liam lay me back gently onto the picnic blanket. My panties were left in a shredded mess to the side. His tongue started licking down the canyon of my breasts as he unclasped the hook at the front of my bra, and he let out a low possessive growl as both mounds spilled out.

"Mine!" he growled as he removed the bra entirely.

I felt my core bubble and clench at the purr of his possessive tone. His eyes roamed over my naked body lustfully. His hands ran in smooth circles down into my heat.

"Yours," I repeated. I felt his digits slide against my slick folds, and then I gasped as he pinched my clit. "Only yours."

I used my foot to hook into the waistband of his shorts, needing to remove them but not wanting his fingers to abandon playing in my folds. He grinned at me before giving me a gentle kiss as I fumbled some more.

"Need a hand?" he asked impishly.

I growled at him and used my fingers instead. His erection sprung free, thick, and solid in the cool fall air. He removed his fingers, and I whimpered longingly as he pulled his shorts off.

He hovered over top of me and grabbed his thickened cock, rubbing his head into the wetness but not entering me. He teased, made me gasp and groan, before pulling away for a moment, making me whimper for him. Then, he would do it again, teasing my clit with the head of his cock, sliding it up and down, finding my entrance and removing himself. Edging me. Repeatedly. My core clenched in anticipation only to feel the cool air instead of his perfect, hot cock.

"Liam!" I groaned as he pulled away for the third time, chuckling softly.

"Yes, Clementine?" his voice was full of lust.

"Don't tease me! Fuck me!" I reached for him, and he grinned seductively, pulling away, stroking his perfect thick rod between his fingers, making me watch the precum bead at the tip.

"Is this what you want?" he asked, his voice velvety, making me desperate. His hands stroked his cock instead of me, making me writhe. I bit my lip and nodded. His eyes instantly went to my mouth, and he growled softly. "Your wish is my command, Luna."

He aimed his head at my slick entrance and slowly slid himself into my channel with a primal groan. His cock stretched and filled me, and I moaned at the sensation as he pulled out and slammed into me again with a grunt. Then he slid out ever so slowly and did it again, hard and fast. Slamming himself right up into my cervix with primal repetition, it hurt so good. Each time I would gasp and moan. Each time he would give a satisfied grunt.

We moved together in the throes of passion, grunting and

moaning as the sounds and scents of our coupling filled the air. His breathing was laboured as he pumped into me and whispered sweet words in my ear.

"The moon," he arched backward suddenly, bringing me with him. I gasped at the sudden jolt of pleasure. "It's at its peak, baby." He kissed my mouth hard and started pumping upwards into me at a strange but sensual angle. I didn't know how long I would last like this; the rubbing against my clit and the pressure inside me was an addictive overly intense duo. I felt the thundering pleasure consume me, and I tightened myself, trying to cling to it.

"Baby!" his voice was gravelly with need.

I saw his eyes flash gold and his teeth elongate.

The instant I stretched my neck out for him, he slammed himself upwards into me and his teeth tore downward through the top of my skin. I yelped in pain, but it was soon taken over by the most intense orgasm I have ever had in my entire life. Wave upon wave shuddered through me as I sought out his marking spot and bit down hard. Almond and honey infused my tongue, and I swirled my tongue over it to taste every last drop.

He grunted and groaned beneath me and suddenly stopped thrusting. He was spent. He was satiated. He was glowing, but he didn't remove himself from me. He smiled softly and kissed me as I felt the bond solidify with intense, unbreakable pressure. My entire body buzzed. My heart was filled with so much love that I knew it couldn't only be mine.

I smiled softly at Liam before looking up at the moon. My canines had come through, and I had managed to mark him, but I still couldn't sense Circe.

We didn't say anything for the next hour; we just basked in the sensations of the newly completed mate bond, admiring, loving, and needing each other. The kissing sent tingles throughout my body, and the emotions I felt were all-consuming and perfect. Every kiss moulded itself deeper into my essence. Every stroke sent vibrations into my soul.

The mate bond sang between us as Liam rolled me over and placed himself between my legs, kissing me intensely, his tongue sweet against mine. I felt his erection twitch against my wetness, and I knew we would be up all night, absorbing and loving each other in the most unbreakable and sacred ways.

I knew that this was the start of the rest of my life. I didn't know if Circe would return, but with the strength of our love and the mate bond, I knew nothing could stop me from committing myself to Liam in every way possible. The pack had accepted me as Liam's mate, so maybe, they would accept me as their luna even though I had no wolf.

"Tell me about the luna ceremony," I murmured between kisses.

The gold rings of Liam's eyes flickered as he studied my face. "It's a pretty formal event. We get dressed up, and you walk down an aisle toward me. A ceremonial dagger is used to cut your palm." He raised my hand and brushed his lips against the soft skin of my palm. "Then I cut mine, and our hands are bound together with a red ribbon. We say some vows, and you, my beautiful mate, become luna of the Blackfern Valley Pack."

"So it's like a wedding?" I asked, trying to ignore the thundering in my chest.

"Yeah, sort of, I guess. But you're marrying the pack *and* me. Your mind opens up to everyone. Your aura physically changes to that of a luna." He smiled. Solid, unbreakable love danced in the golds and browns of his eyes. "Why? Are you ready to marry me? Are you ready to be my luna?"

"I'm more than ready. Circe may be gone forever, and we may receive backlash from the werewolf community, but I couldn't imagine my life without you. I cannot take you from this pack. This is your birthright and your destiny." My voice cracked with emotion. "I want to bind myself to you and this pack in every way possible. You're my all-consuming love, my happily-ever-after and I'm confident our love will conquer anything."

He grinned and kissed me deeply. The kiss tickled into the depths of our bond, and within seconds, I felt his hardness tickling the entrance of my heat. He slid deep inside, stretching, making me moan in ecstasy.

Then I felt a spark in the hollow of my mind.

"What did I miss?" Circe asked in a sleepy voice, yawning as she stretched.

ABOUT THE AUTHOR

Anna Elle is an up-and-coming romance author.

She grew up in New Zealand and was encouraged from a young age to write. She's always had a passion for reading and writing and could spend hours entrapped in a book (whether it was a story she was writing, or one she was reading).

Follow her writing journey on social media and be sure to check out her stories.

facebook.com/61553201715235

instagram.com/annaelle.writes

tiktok.com/@annaelle.writes